PRAISE FOR CORINNA TURNER'S BOOKS

PRAISE FOR *I AM MARGARET*

*Great style—very good characters and pace.
Definitely a book worth reading, like* The Hunger Games.
EOIN COLFER, author of the *Artemis Fowl* books

*An intelligent, well-written and enjoyable debut from
a young writer with a bright future.*
STEWART ROSS, author of *The Soterion Mission*

*Margaret, Bane, Jon and the Major have stayed with me
long since I finished reading about them.*
RACHEL FRASER

PRAISE FOR *ELFLING*

*"Her story is extremely imaginative and unique, her characters
so colorful and satisfying, and you just don't want to put the
book down."*
T.M. GAOUETTE, author of the *Faith and Kung Fu* series

*"This book was very different from a lot of fairy tales
in a good way."*
WILLIAM SL

D1484542

The I AM MARGARET Series

Brothers *(A Short Prequel Novella)**
1: I Am Margaret*
2: The Three Most Wanted*
3: Liberation*
4: Bane's Eyes*
5: Margo's Diary*
6: The Siege of Reginald Hill*
7: A Saint in the Family *(Coming Soon)*

The YESTERDAY & TOMORROW Series

Someday: A Novella*
1: Tomorrow's Dead *(Coming Soon)*

The UNSPARKED Series

BREACH! (A Prequel)*
1: DRIVE!*
2: A Truly Raptor-ous Welcome*
3: PANIC!
4: Farmgirls Die in Cages
Book 5*(Coming Soon)*
A Mom with Blue Feathers *(A Prequel) (Coming Soon)*

STANDALONE WORKS

Elfling*
Mandy Lamb & The Full Moon*
Secrets: Visible & Invisible *(I Am Margaret story in anthology)**
Gifts: Visible & Invisible *(unSPARKed story in anthology)**
Three Last Things *or* The Hounding of Carl Jarrold, Soulless Assassin* *(Coming Soon)*
The Raven & The Yew *(Coming Soon)*

*Awarded the Catholic Writers Guild *Seal of Approval*

Elfling

CORINNA TURNER

unSeen

Cover Artwork by Katy Jones
www.KatyJones.co.uk

Cover design by Corinna Turner

ISBN: 978-1-910806-40-1 (paperback)
Also available as an eBook

This is a work of fiction. All names, characters, places, incidents and
dialogues in this publication are products of the author's imagination
or are used fictitiously. Any resemblance to actual locales, events or
people, living or dead, is entirely coincidental.

* An imprint of Zephyr Publishing, UK—Corinna Turner, T/A

Contents

CHAPTER 1

Raven

I was hungry. So hungry that most twelve-year-old girls of my rank would have been crying, throwing a tantrum, or fainting. Perhaps all three. Not me. I was thinking what to do about my hunger. I began each day with the same all-consuming thought.

I sat on a thin blanket under the overhang of an old, crooked stone house near Smart's Quay. I had to bend my head to sit up, but I scarcely registered the minor discomfort. Rain splashed from the eaves to the cobbles of the street only a few feet in front of my nose, but under here it was fairly dry; a good sleeping place. I contemplated the various possible solutions to this particular morning's hunger, until a tiny scuffling noise preceded a whiskered nose from a narrow crack in the wall. When I remained motionless, the rat scurried almost soundlessly to the side of the blanket, attracted by a few crumbs so tiny even I hadn't noticed them.

My hands shot out and seized the rat, wrapping around its plump body. Ignoring the squealing and the snapping teeth, I gripped the head and twisted, feeling the sudden give as the vertebrae in its neck parted company. Laying the twitching rodent beside me, a rare smile snuck onto my face.

So early in the morning and I had already acquired my day's meal! I would take the rat along to the Water Lane cookhouse, where I would skin it, cook it, and eat it. The bones would go to Old Joe the gluemaker as payment; the skin to the skin man in return for a precious half copper. In the new language I had learned since my mother's death, a half copper equaled a piece of bread. If I was extravagant, I would eat it for supper. Otherwise it would go some way towards staving off the hunger on the morrow.

The smile fading, I shuffled to one side, picked up the blanket and knotted it around my shoulders like a cloak. The rat I tucked out of sight in my jerkin. I wriggled out into the street, straightened and froze.

Two urchins stood waiting. Unlike me, who merely dressed as a boy, these were actual boys, bigger than I. Born in the gutter and never slept on a feather bed in their lives. They would cut my throat for the rat.

"We heard a squeaking," said one boy, holding out a hand, his eyes cold.

"Do you see anything?" I said—running even before I had finished speaking.

The boys followed close on my heels. So close that when my bare foot slipped from under me on a slimy cobblestone the first was on me immediately. As I fell I caught sight of a mangy dog lurking by the side of the street. I struck the ground painfully, one hand already inside my jerkin. The boy landed on top of me, a knife appearing in his hand like magic. Dragging the rat free I flung it towards the dog, which moved in a brown streak. The urchin had a choice of cutting my throat or getting the rat. It was no choice at all; he was already in mid-air after the meal. Back on my feet even as the rat struck the ground, I bolted.

I stopped in the comparative shelter of a lopsided building off Lowe Lane, wet, tired and sore. I didn't bother contemplating the downturn in the day's fortunes, too busy checking over my clothing. My knees and elbow were badly bruised, but nothing was torn, so I headed for a disreputable inn I knew where the landlord did not keep a porter on and usually allowed me to earn a few pence carrying the luggage.

When I arrived outside the Fylpot Arms, the cheap coach was throwing out a passenger at the door. It was nothing personal; that was just how the cheap coaches went about things. The passenger, having gained the cobbles, ducked as his two cases were thrown down beside him. The coachman flogged his broken-down horses for a good few seconds before they were convinced to move and the coach swayed unsteadily away through the wet streets of London town.

I was already in motion. Stopping beside the passenger I put on my stolid, dependable expression and, with a tug of my forelock, took hold of the cases.

"I'll get those, sir," I said, in my feigned gutter accent. Was it really feigned? When had I last spoken as myself?

The traveler did not want to spend money on a bag boy, I could tell. He had planned to carry them quickly into the inn himself. Recoiling from appearing miserly when actually put to it, with a poor attempt at grace he gave me a curt nod and entered the inn, looking back only three times to check the luggage was following.

I dragged the heavy cases up the stairs, appreciating why the man had ducked their descent from the coach top. But my scrawny frame was up to it, and I set them down carefully in the room and waited. I only ever stuck my hand out as a last resort, it frequently seemed to do more harm than good. The traveler noticed my continued presence with a flash of irritation, dug a coin from his purse and threw it in my general direction.

I caught it and left quickly. It was a good-sized copper, and I was hungry enough that I went straight down to the inn kitchen and swapped it for a half copper and a chunk of bread. Retreating to the inn courtyard to eat my meal and watch for the next traveler, I eyed another urchin lingering there. Did he also have the landlord's permission to carry bags?

The bread was finished all too quickly, as always, and I sat wishing another traveler would arrive. More at that moment for the distraction from my own thoughts, than for the coin I could earn. Only when I had some amount of food in my belly was I troubled by thoughts of the future. It was the only time I could afford to be.

I had lasted three years on the streets, three long, painful years since my mother died and my uncle threw me from the place that had always been my home.

"Be gone, witch child," he'd snarled at me, "or I'll duck you in the pond till you're clean and cold."

Even at nine years old I'd recognized a death threat when I heard one and I hadn't tried to go back. Of course, I had always known my uncle hated me, but to be thrown from my own home to what should've been almost certain death? It had been utterly unexpected. The house in which my uncle now lived was mine, was it not? My rank came to me from my mother and there was nothing legal to take the property away from me.

Legally, though, my uncle was my guardian. No doubt he assumed me dead long since and it was a fair assumption. *Serapion* the urchin had no more chance of reclaiming what belonged to Lady Serapia Ravena than the morning's rat had of breathing again.

In fact, Serapion the urchin had only one chance in the world and it was tied around my waist, carefully concealed under my clothing...

I looked up as the kitchen staff burst from the doorway, chattering excitedly to one another and followed by the cook, who swept something ahead of her with an expression of grim courage. They were calling for the landlord and I darted over to see what the to-do was about, slipping to the front. I'd have seized any distraction.

The heap of ash was tipped over the doorstep onto the cobbles of the yard. The landlord came striding out of the building even as I crouched to peer more closely at the tiny creature floundering weakly in the midst of the soot. As grey as ash, it resembled a bird, for it had a curved, beaky upper lip and a pair of little things that were clearly undeveloped wings on its back. But it was entirely featherless and had two tiny front paws, just now making feeble movements in the ash. Fragments of broken, blackened eggshell lay around

4

it, showing it to be newborn. Or rather, new-hatched. I had never seen anything so intriguing.

"A demon-creature, sir, a demon-creature in the fire..."

"I was sweeping out the grate, sir, and I sees it..."

"It ain't nat'ral, sir, ain't right..."

"Shall we have a priest, sir? Don't like the thought of it otherwise..."

A priest? Whatever for? I'd sensed evil often enough, and there was nothing of it here. But I'd learned long ago that other people just didn't seem able to sense things as I could. Even my mother couldn't. I had stopped mentioning my strange sensitivity only a short time after learning how to talk about it at all.

The landlord leant over to scrutinize the 'demon-creature'. "Evilest looking blighter I ever did see," he pronounced, "but soon sorted." He raised his foot. His intent was obvious.

The baby animal raised its head and peered around with a pair of huge golden eyes. It gave a little cough and a cloud of ash came from its beak. It must be half choked. Without even considering it, I reached out and snatched it from the path of the landlord's foot.

The assembled group turned a look of astonishment on me and the landlord swelled with rage. "You impudent little..." He took a step towards me.

For the second time that day, I ran for my life. Or in this case, the life of the creature I held pressed to my chest. I would survive a beating, it would not.

The landlord did not pursue me beyond his inn gates, but his furious shout followed, ringing in my ears. "If you *ever* come back..."

An inn without a porter was rare. One where I was trusted to carry bags was rarer still. I had lost the closest thing to a real job I had ever achieved, and for what? A deformed chick? I must be mad. Panting and heart pounding, I slipped into an alley off Lyme Street and sank down on the cobbles to take a closer look at just what I had saved.

My hands were filthy with soot and the chick, or whatever it was, still grey, so that must be its natural color. It could not be a chick, I realized, as I looked more closely. Apart from its four legs it also had a tail, a very lizard-like tail. Its little, clawed front feet scrabbled gently at my thumb in a way that reminded me of a mouse. It could hold things in them, I suspected.

It was, I concluded with a sense of shock, some rare exotic creature from across the seas. How its egg had come to end up in the inn fireplace was a question I did not even bother pondering. But if it was rare and from far away, then it was worth an enormous amount of money.

I looked at the tiny thing again. It fitted snugly in my palm, leathery hide soft against my skin. I'd never get close enough to the nobility to sell it for a pet. I'd have to sell to a middleman and it would go to an apothecary to be dried and powdered for potions. And much as I usually ignored the fact, I was terribly, achingly lonely. The creature raised its head again and gave another little cough, and I knew I could not sell it. It was mine and I would keep it. It would not eat much.

Talking of food... I looked again at my new companion in distress. It would need milk, or something. I tucked it securely inside my jerkin for warmth and set off once more along the streets, giving Fylpot Lane a wide berth. Reaching Puddinge Lane I climbed up some abandoned scaffolding to the rooftops and entered the attic of a deserted house through a hole in the roof. The rotten floor groaned under my weight, but I moved lightly to a pile of old rugs in a dry area of the room. There, curled in a little nest, lay a cat and her five kittens. The mother cat regarded me warily with yellow eyes, but did not run or move to attack. The cat and I had shared the loft on many a night.

Now I put my handful down carefully at the edge of the nest and crouched there, watching, ready to snatch it back out if the cat tried to harm it. This was a very longshot, and I knew it. The creature was unlikely to know how to get to the food on its own, for one thing, and the mother cat might try to savage it if it got close. I'd probably have to catch the cat and hold her down while carefully guiding the lizard-chick to the teat. But I wouldn't do it immediately when there was just the feeblest chance I wouldn't have to shatter the trust that existed between us.

The lizard-chick peered around, coughing again. Its babyish gaze travelled from me to the mother cat and it swayed forward unsteadily, opening its beaky mouth again to let out a soft, quavering cry not unlike those of the kittens. The mother cat went on watching me, seeming scarcely aware of the intruder now easing its way slowly, but persistently, in among her brood. Finally the lizard-chick's mouth closed around a teat and it began to swallow. Every so often it released its mouthful to give the kittenish cry again. The cat still did not react.

I watched in something close to wonderment. The mother cat hadn't noticed the interloper, of that I felt sure, and the back of my neck prickled in the way I associated with my odd senses. My new pet intrigued me more and more.

Although I usually avoided staying in the same sleeping place for more than one night at a time, I remained in the loft for over a week. By then, desperate to sleep elsewhere, I began to consider coming to the loft in the daytime to let my pet feed. But my problem was solved when my casual offering of a crumb of bread was eagerly swallowed by the lizard-chick.

"You don't need milk any more, huh?" I said, stroking under the soft leathery chin. "Well, time for a name, I suppose."

I turned my pet around in my hands. I had already established as well as I could that the lizard-chick was female, something most young noblewomen could not have done. Now I considered the question of a name. The baby was still a uniform grey all over, apart from her beautiful golden eyes.

"You are quite like a bird," I mused softly. "And you're mine. I'm a Ravena, in name, at least. Ravens are black not grey, but you're close, and there are girl ravens as well as boy ravens. I'll call you Raven. Then you're part of me."

CHAPTER 2

Winter's Tail

I huddled into my cloak and blanket, shivering, and pressed closer to the chimney wall at my back. That blessed spring weather had been swept away by a very nasty sting in winter's tail. I needed more food. Food was money, though. Raven fared better than I did in cold weather, of course, tucked away inside my clothes, not only for warmth but also kept from prying eyes.

I touched the ring tied so carefully around my waist. I hadn't been out to the palace this week, but I knew I could not go. Not until this weather broke. I could spare neither the time nor the energy. It wasn't as though I had ever heard so much as a *word* about the Duke of Albany. A man I had never seen, nor knew anything of, but whom I believed to be my father.

Not that it was conclusive in the slightest. In my entire life, no one, not my mother, nor my own maid, nor any of the other servants, had ever mentioned my father to me or even in my hearing. There was an obvious conclusion to be drawn from this, even by a well-brought up girl, and I had eventually reached it. Astonishing as it might seem, considering my pious and impeccably behaved mother, I must be illegitimate.

Which might have explained my uncle's dislike for me, had it not been for the fact that he liked my mother. Though I'd sometimes wondered how genuine that liking really was, when all his visits seemed to end with my mother giving him money. But only after he had paid his deathbed visit had I, for the first and last time, heard of the Duke of Albany. My mother had been almost gone by then but had insisted upon seeing me again, probably, I now suspected darkly,

9

because my uncle had divulged his intentions, leaving her in desperate straits regarding my future.

Only then, in such dire necessity, had my mother spoken of this man. And only a few words. A few words—and a ring—pressed into my shaking hand.

"Go to the Duke of Albany," my mother had whispered, and with her last breath, "he will look after you..."

Of course, going anywhere as an urchin was far from easy, let alone going to find a man one did not know and had not the slightest idea how to find. Initially, I had naively believed I could seek help from one of my mother's few friends, sure they would have a carriage harnessed for my conveyance to this Duke's residence. My already disheveled state and the common belief I was with my uncle on his country estates had denied me access even to the upper servants and brought threats of what would happen if I persisted in my 'lies'. Before long, survival left me with no time to worry about the Duke of Albany.

Thanks to Siridean, and later kind old Father Mahoney, I had slowly mastered my new life and eventually managed to take up my weekly pilgrimage to the one place where I thought I might hear of, or even find, this elusive Duke. The old gossips that hung around the Courte Gate could be guaranteed to know all who had attended court in the past week, and all the scandals of my old world. But it had been over three years, and I had learned nothing...

Another urchin, slightly bigger than me, but thinner, was coming along the backstreet, shoulders hunched and shaking with cold. As he came level, his eyes darted to me. His desperate eyes.

I rose to flee just as he lunged. I raised my arm before my face and swung it sideways, feeling the jar as my wrist struck his, but his other hand reached my throat, or more specifically, the fastening of my precious cloak. I felt it come loose and hurled myself forward, knocking him to the ground.

10

We struggled in a breathless silence. He landed several blows to my head and took advantage of my disorientation to break free and flee. With my cloak. I sat up, willing my head to stop spinning, and wound my fingers into my blanket. I'd tied it over my shoulder, like an ancient Roman's toga, and it had not come free as easily as the cloak.

Raven chattered a warning and I looked up quickly. A much older boy walked rapidly towards me, staring intently at something that lay in the mud. I struggled to focus on that tiny circle of gold.

My ring!

Raven shot forward, and the boy and I dived after her. My hand closed around the ring and I twisted halfway to my feet, turning to grab Raven and flee. But... *Oh no!*

The boy held Raven. He had his hand wrapped around her long neck, and her body dangled. Her head twisted helplessly against the circle of his fingers, but she could not bite.

"This'll fetch a tidy penny," said the boy. "I'd rather 'ave the trinket, though."

I looked at the ring in my hand, anguished. It was my only hope.

"The 'pothecary won't care if it's alive, 'long as it's fresh," the boy sneered. He took hold of Raven's body and began to pull. Raven's head tilted up and her legs flailed. He would break her neck!

"Stop!" I gasped. "Stop, you can have the ring!"

I held it out carefully, my other hand extended for Raven. With the utmost caution and mutual mistrust, we carried out the swap. I stumbled backwards several paces, out of immediate reach, Raven clutched to me.

"You jus' gotta be a girl," sniggered the boy.

"Am not!" I retorted, with suitably boyish indignation.

The boy shrugged. "Ain't short of coin now," he said, grinning at me and twiddling the ring between finger and thumb. "I can do better than you, anyway. Master Simmons don't bother with the likes of you."

11

He won't bother with you for long, if you boast like that, I thought to myself. The boy had lifted one foot and turned the heel of his boot to reveal a secret compartment. He placed the ring inside, closed it, smirked at me and left. I sniffed in disgust. If I had a compartment like that I certainly wouldn't show it off, even to a helpless urchin. I'd need boots first, of course. Now that I thought about it, he probably had the compartment to keep things from his Master Simmons. Lunatic. Even I had heard of Master Simmons. And stayed well away from him.

Shivering twice as hard, I made my way to Fenchurch, to a small area of greenery tucked behind a triangle of houses. I sat down with my back to the high, encircling wall and stared despondently at the grass in front of me, with its great stone cross towering in the centre. The pauper's graveyard was too recent to have been built over. On Sundays there might be poor folk there, placing some single flower on the communal grave. Some urchins would take these and sell them to the next person, and so on, until they wilted.

Today it was quiet and I could sit there alone, shaking with the shock of my loss. *What do I do now?* A comforting warmth stirred in my nape in response to this desolate question, although no answer presented itself. Raven pressed her face to my neck, making soft cheeps of apology. I stroked her gently. It wasn't Raven's fault.

Sometimes I came to this particular graveyard to escape the bustle. After Siridean had died they'd tossed him in there, with everyone else who couldn't pay for better.

I drew my dagger and held it in my hands, my thumb rubbing around the pommel, cleaning away the protective layer of mud. Hematite gleamed underneath. The shiny silver stone passed well enough for plain steel when strategically daubed with muck. I stared down into it. For a long time, until I found Raven, the dagger had been my only friend. The eyes were there today, looking up at me out of the stone. They looked like Siridean's eyes. I hugged it close, remembering the last time I'd felt as bereft as I did now.

Selling the dagger had been the rational thing to do. I couldn't eat the stone, and a plain dagger would surely do just as well. So I'd reasoned. I'd felt miserable about it, though. Misery turned to pure panic the first time I tried to hunt something. I'd never missed so badly before!

I fled to the quiet cemetery and threw the new dagger at a sapling over and over again. I hardly hit it once. What was the matter with me? I'd chosen a dagger that felt almost identical in my hand: the shape, the length, the balance.

It didn't make the back of my neck prickle, though, the way Siridean's dagger did when I held it and concentrated on my target. The harder I'd concentrated, the better my success. Siridean had taught me the importance of concentration. But I concentrated until I thought my head would explode, and still the new dagger would not fly true. It was then I accepted that the eyes I'd often seen looking back at me probably weren't just a trick of the light. Siridean's dagger had been a very special gift. It had kept me alive this long, and now I had sold it. I felt near despair.

I went back to the shop with the coins, though the shopkeeper would not have bought if he didn't think he could sell it for more, so I held out little hope of being able to buy it back.

But the man answered the door with dark-shadowed eyes and wild words. "Such a night! Such a night I have never had!" He thrust the dagger at me and snatched the coins. "Take the cursed thing and be gone with you!"

I had appreciated the dagger much more after that. It had forgiven my ignorance and come back to me. I doubted I would get the ring back so easily. Common sense whispered that I would never get the ring back at all, but I couldn't accept that. To accept that would be to accept that I was an urchin and would never be anything else, other than an inhabitant of the latest pauper's graveyard.

If *only* he'd put the ring into a *pocket*, I might have been able to get it back. It was just barely possible, anyway: but only just. He'd surely know better than to let me get too close. But a *boot compartment?* How was I supposed to get into that without him noticing?

A movement opposite drew me from my thoughts. I tensed, peering, my hand shifting its grip on the dagger. A dog was slinking from the undergrowth—a big dog, but thin-sided—and limping, which was probably why. One look at its hunting stance was enough to bring me to my feet in a crouch of my own. It sniffed my scent and showed its teeth in a silent snarl. I eyed it back, just as intently.

If I let that thing get to me I'd be in trouble. I touched the hematite and my resolve strengthened. The dog still advanced, head low and teeth bared. There was definitely nothing wrong with its teeth.

Wait, I cautioned myself as it came closer, wait... Its muscles bunched to rush me, and I threw the dagger with all the force and concentration I could muster.

Staying safely where I crouched until it had stopped its demonic howling and thrashing, I then advanced carefully to reclaim my dagger. It was my stomach's turn to growl, and I looked the animal over with rather more interest. Thin, but large, which meant there was still plenty of meat. It might keep me alive until the weather broke. But even this could not raise my spirits by much. I'd lost my mother's ring. Why would the Duke of Albany listen to me now?

I shifted the dog slightly with the point of my toe, considering how best to proceed. The entire dog would be quite heavy to carry, but I would keep the skin and bones and not lose a ha'penny of its value. It wasn't like I wanted to leave any of it behind; even the offal was valuable sustenance. I would just have to carry it. Reluctantly, I reached for the knot on my blanket, to undo it and use it as a makeshift bag.

Again a movement drew my eye. I looked over to the streets and saw the boy who'd stolen my ring. I stiffened,

14

ready to leave the dog and run, assuming he'd followed me to try and get Raven after all. Then I realized he was turning and walking away. I hesitated, torn. A dead dog would go nowhere towards the price of the ring, but if I could ever hope to get it back, I needed to know where the boy was to be found.

I dragged the dog quickly into the bushes and concealed it as well as I could, hesitating one last time. All that meat! Another stray dog might well find it in my absence, but I left it and hurried after the boy.

He walked purposefully, and the streets through which he passed were familiar to me, making concealment easy. Trying to follow someone without it being obvious to everyone else around was rather less easy, but I'd had cause once or twice before and managed well enough.

Eventually, I peeped around a corner to find that he'd stopped in a little back square behind Seethinge Lane and was speaking to a man. I eyed the man suspiciously. He had rather yellow hair and a youth with feral eyes much like the dog's prowled nearby, watching everything. The square was deserted.

"...Y'know Ralph Fletcher were taken for cutt'in that purse? 'An the throat with it?" the boy was saying.

"I know Ralph Fletcher's got himself in jail to hang just after I paid him to do an extremely important task, aye," the yellow haired man replied malevolently.

"Aye, your honor, well, I know'd what Fletcher were good at," the boy continued, "and if you were needing a one for such jobs I thought you might..." he dropped his voice and spoke rapidly for a few moments.

He wasn't just boasting. That was Master Simmons. Time to go.

I made to ease back out of sight, but even as I did the boy turned and pointed directly at me. So much for my unobserved stalking.

Master Simmons' head rose. "Wait." He hooked a finger at me.

15

I bit my lip but did not dare to disobey. I advanced warily. The boy accepted something from Master Simmons, writhed fawningly and left. The feral youth was still there, out of earshot but close enough. Still...slightly better odds. Numerically, at least.

"Well, boy," said Master Simmons, when I stood before him. "How does this take your fancy?" He held out a fat gold piece.

I stared at it, more enthralled by the sight of gold than I had ever been in my life. That tiny thing would buy back my ring.

"Thomas tells me," Master Simmons went on, when he saw he had my attention, "that you are uncommonly accurate with a dagger over a long range."

My insides began to curdle and I shrugged as non-communicatively as I could. I had a feeling that precious coin might as well have been on the moon.

"Do you know a man," asked Master Simmons, "called Sir Allen Malster?"

I swallowed. Everyone knew Sir Allen Malster. He was one of the Queen's special agents, and he'd seen an awful lot of men like Master Simmons tried and executed. I shrugged again.

"I would be very happy...*this* happy, in fact," Master Simmons twitched the gold coin, "if Sir Allen were to suffer a very accurate sort of accident from a very discreet sort of range."

I swallowed again. "I jus' killed a dog, s'true, sir," I replied. "But the dog were terrible fierce, I'd never even ha' tried, else. I'm glad I hit it 'cus I'm terrible hungry, but it were a surprise, sir." I shrugged as though the implication of my words were obvious.

Master Simmons' hand closed around the gold piece. He might suspect the true reason for my modesty, but he would not risk a bumbled attempt.

"What a shame," he said, with one of the most insincere smiles I'd ever seen. "You'd best go eat your dog." He turned away in brusque dismissal.

I was only too happy to get back to my dog and away from him. I hurried off, resolutely trying to turn my mind to the matter of the dog's preparation and consumption. But before I'd gone very far, my niggling conscience spawned an idea that was not easily ignored. An idea about how to acquire at least part of the ring's value. An idea that made my mouth dry with fear.

My conscience told me that I ought to warn Sir Allen Malster. And my head told me that he might be grateful enough to pay for details. I tried to shake the thoughts away. It was absurd. People were probably trying to kill the man all the time. And money would do me no good if Master Simmons found out.

If I could manage it without being seen... What did I really have to lose? If I couldn't find the Duke soon, I probably wouldn't be alive to do it at all. And finding the Duke would be of doubtful use without the ring. I swallowed very hard.

The dog would have to wait a little longer.

CHAPTER 3

The Price of a Ring

I lay on the roof of Sir Allen Malster's modest Fleete Street town house, gutter sludge soaking through my breeches. Raven sat at the back of my neck, under my hair, still and quiet. I prayed the guttering was well attached as I leant out and pitched the first stone at the balcony window. It was pitch black, and the town house nestled in the midst of a terrace. This was the most secret method of contacting the man I'd been able to think of.

I'd waited until it was good and late and a candle had been lit in the room, and I thought there now a very strong chance that it would be Sir Allen Malster in there, alone. I threw three more stones before I saw the window open silently on well-oiled hinges. My breath caught in my throat as a fully-cocked crossbow came first through the opening. But I held my tongue. I needed to be sure it was Sir Allen Malster, not a servant.

I could just make out a pale-haired head in the window. "Who's there?" asked a harsh voice.

I thought it was him. I hoped it was him. "Friend," I whispered.

The crossbow rose to cover me as he stepped halfway onto the balcony. "Put your hands on the guttering."

I shifted carefully until I could do so without falling. My open hands were dimly visible in the light coming from the window, and to my relief the crossbow was lowered slightly.

"Sir Allen Malster, sir?" I checked.

"Yes. What do you want?"

"Someone seeks your life. But I suppose you already knew that." I could not keep a trace of bitterness from my voice. I'd taken this terrible risk for nothing.

The man glanced at the crossbow. "A normal precaution when answering mysterious taps on the window at this hour," he said coldly. "Who is it?"

Hope flared again. He had not known. "I forget," I muttered.

"What?" he snapped.

"Too hungry," I persisted. "I've forgotten."

With the light behind him I couldn't see his face. Sir Allen Malster got results, but his methods could be rough. I prepared myself for being dragged from the roof, dangled off the balcony and threatened with dropping. The moment's silence seemed very long. I could hear street noise coming faintly over the roof from the front of the house, but my heartbeat was the only other sound.

He reached into his pocket and drew out something that gleamed silver. He held it up to me and I took it quickly.

"Are you less hungry now?" There was a hard edge to his voice that warned me not to try my luck. Still, Master Simmons would probably have gutted me already. Not a reassuring thought.

My voice shook as I said very quietly indeed, "Master Simmons."

The pale head jerked up. "You're *very* hungry."

I swallowed and said nothing.

Sir Allen Malster's hand went to his pocket once more, this time coming out with a fat gold coin much like the one Master Simmons had offered me. "Would you care to say that again, under oath, before a select group of people?"

I eyed the coin. There it was again, the price of my ring. "Have you heard of a Duke of Albany, sir?" I asked in a low voice.

Sir Allen Malster appeared to think for a moment. He was a self-made man, his title a reward from the Queen for his hard work. He spent his time on his job and rarely rubbed shoulders with his supposed peers. So I was disappointed but unsurprised when he shook his head. "No."

He still proffered the coin. But no group would be select enough; everyone would know it was me. I was no closer to finding the Duke, and if I took that coin I might get my ring back, but I wouldn't keep my life long enough to use it.

"No," I said.

Sir Allen Malster returned the coin to his pocket. "Hungry, but not insane," he said sarcastically.

I swallowed nervously. That gold coin was so tantalizing. "Sir," I ventured, "you've got a man in jail, a Ralph Fletcher."

"What if I have?" replied Sir Allen blandly.

"Well, sir, he knows about what I warned you of. In fact, he took money to do it, 'least, I'm almost certain of it. Seems to me, a man already set to hang hasn't got much to lose, if you see what I mean..."

Sir Allen stared up at my barely visible form. "Indeed he has not." His hand went to his pocket again and held up another gleam of silver. I took it quickly, disappointed but unsurprised. Sir Allen couldn't know if anything I was saying was worth so much as the breath it took him to reply.

Sir Allen made to turn away, then paused. Another silver piece appeared in his hand, twinkling in the candlelight from his window. "What can you tell me about... sorcerers?"

"Sorcerers?" I was startled. "You mean, information about actual ones?" For surely he wasn't simply asking if I knew what a sorcerer *was*.

"Yes, information about actual ones." He twitched the coin.

I couldn't help gazing at it with longing, but try as I might, my mind was blank. Except...something he probably knew already... "Well, it is *rumored* that Master Simmons has recourse to them. But such rumors always swirl around such men," I added reluctantly.

He jerked his head dismissively. Yes, he'd already known that. "Anything more substantial?" He made to return the coin to his pocket.

I pummeled my brain but could dredge up nothing that might interest him. I avoided all rumored sorcery too assiduously to know the sort of details he clearly sought.

"No, sir," I said glumly, and sure enough, the silver went back into his pocket.

"No matter. All the better for you, in fact. Well, off with you then," added Sir Allen curtly, but I could *feel* his satisfaction. "Let's hope you live to spend those coins." He ducked back inside.

Free from the menacing crossbow, I began to edge back along the roof. Simmons was done for. That man had just been waiting for a chance like this. If he could persuade Fletcher to confess, and Fletcher would scarcely refuse if Sir Allen offered him his life...

I licked my lips nervously and forced myself to concentrate on the job at hand, which was to get back to that drainpipe and down it without breaking Raven's or my neck.

The yellow-haired man on the Smithfield gallows seemed tight-lipped with rage as much as fear. He stared hard at two people in the crowd. Safely hidden in the shadows of an alley, I took note of the men's faces. One was the feral youth from the back square, the other a rather older man with cruel eyes.

They both nodded respectfully to the condemned man and I shrank back further, afraid Simmons might see me and point me out to them. How many people had known whom Simmons' target was? Fool that I was, for giving Sir Allen more than the information he needed simply to keep himself alive. Unless I was very lucky, I probably might as well have taken that gold piece.

Simmons had used his last words on a flowery speech about his love and care for his poor neighbors, to which I had listened with an open mouth. No one had quite dared respond to this, with men such as those two in the crowd, but if thoughts were rotten vegetables, Simmons would have been covered in them. Simmons' gaze became fixed as they pushed him towards the noose, but he maintained his strained look of composure until he was turned off. His neck did not break and his face underwent the usual contortions of strangulation before finally sagging in death.

I crept away, trembling. *I know he deserved it, but...* The words wouldn't come, but undoubtedly the Almighty knew how I felt.

Hiding down an alley near Newgate Market, I cupped those so carefully retained silver pieces in my hand. The dog had saved me from having to spend any of them. I couldn't imagine how I would gain the rest of the ring's value, and if someone found those incriminating coins on me... But I had no boots, let alone a secret compartment, they were too big to swallow, and a pouch anywhere about my person could be found.

Raven stuck her head out and chattered an inquiry, as if sensing my fear. I went still as something occurred to me. Raven was virtually undetectable. She had exposed herself to Thomas in a misguided but conscious attempt to be helpful. But in the scuffle for my cloak, and several such struggles, Raven's quicksilver body had always escaped harm or discovery.

I handed the silvers to Raven. "Raven, I know this will be a nuisance, but it's terribly important. You've got to hang onto these, no one must see them any more than they must see you, do you understand?"

Raven hefted the silver pieces doubtfully between her two forepaws.

"Wait, I have a better idea," I added. I ripped some strips from my shirt and swaddled the coins until they were held securely, then fastened them around Raven so that they hung under her belly. Raven made a few experimental runs from shoulder to shoulder, then nodded her little head. She could bear it.

Well, that was the evidence hidden, anyway.

~+~

I moved about the city even more than usual for the next few days, choosing my sleeping places with the utmost care. They found me anyway, as I'd known they would. I looked up from where I sat in a sheltered alleyway in Chepesyde and they were there, just like that. The youth grabbed me and slammed me into the wall. I yelped, then regaining some control, peered at him and affected relief. "Thought you were Thomas," I said, saying the first name that came into my head.

"What does Thomas want with you?" asked the older man, eyeing me very narrowly indeed.

"N'thing," I replied, evading his eyes. I had no plan, I couldn't think further than simply covering up that terrified yelp, so open to ill interpretation. I felt Raven run down the inside of my breeches and squeeze out at the knee, and knew she would be safely hidden in the nearest crack.

"Well then," said the man, leaning around my captor to put his face close to mine. "What did Master Simmons want with you in that back square four days before he died?" He gave a tiny nod and the youth pressed a knife to my throat.

I hardly dared to breathe. I struggled to think. They knew I'd met Master Simmons. Did they know exactly what he'd told me? Had he had time to tell them all the details, or had he been arrested too suddenly?

I continued to evade the man's gaze. "He wanted to know 'bout Thomas too," I gasped, saying the first thing that came into my head.

"What about Thomas?"

"That...that he had a fine gold ring," I blurted, improvising frantically. "He seemed to find that quite interesting." I'd wager he would have done, too, if Thomas had kept it from him. But... My face went cold with shock and dismay... *Oh no, no, no, I shouldn't have said that.* Too late.

The older man did not move back. "We find that quite interesting as well," he said silkily. "And where did he *get* this fine gold ring?"

23

The knife pressed still more closely, a hot line of pain. I could feel blood trickling down my neck as I frantically sought some way to undo what my words had just done, but my mind was blank.

"I dunno," I whispered, no need to feign fear and desperation. "I dunno, I just saw 'im selling it, that's all. Just saw 'im sell it. That's all I know, sir, I swear it, 'an I told it all to Master Simmons, sir..."

The older man proceeded to search me thoroughly. He even checked behind my ears and in my mouth. He found my dagger, of course, and my femininity, but the dagger's hilt was well daubed, and men such as these had no need to pilfer plain steal from urchins, nor sell urchin girls, either.

"Let the brat go," he ordered, when he'd finished. "It was the boy. Always too big for his boots."

The feral youth eyed his companion doubtfully. "Fletcher could'a just *told*."

The older man rolled his eyes impatiently. "And just why would Fletcher confess to an intended assassination when 'e were already in jail for murder? Sir Allen already knew everything when he went to Fletcher, must'a done. S'why he gave 'im a real good reason to confess. But *someone* told Sir Allen first. An it weren't this little alley cat so it were the boy. Now let's go..."

I sank down on the ground when they'd gone, shaking, one hand pressed to my bleeding neck. *I'm sorry...I'm so sorry...* Once the unthinking words had come out I simply hadn't been able to call them back, but I really *hadn't* meant to incriminate Thomas with my impromptu cover story, thief though he might be. I mean, I'd done enough thieving myself, before Father Mahoney had broken it to me that what Siridean had told me, at age nine, (whilst correct as far as it went) was not in fact the blanket permission to pick pockets I had taken it as.

It was lucky I was so young. They didn't really believe Master Simmons would hire someone my age. Or female.

And he wouldn't have tried to, either, if Thomas hadn't seen what I could do with my dagger...

Raven crept back up my sleeve and started licking the cut gently with her tiny tongue. I snuck her a quick kiss. If they'd found those two whole silver pieces, they might have reached rather different conclusions.

I waited a few minutes until the shakes died away, then I set off, looking for Thomas. He'd stolen my ring, and he'd been running with Master Simmons, but still... I didn't want him to die because of my lie. If I didn't tell him why they were after him, with a bit of luck he'd just skip town, and there'd be nothing to incriminate me.

Not knowing where to find him, I had to ask after him. I told each person that two of Master Simmons' men wanted him. They'd pass it on if they saw him, and if the men heard, I could pretend I was trying to help them find him out of self-interest. After my pretended fear of Thomas, they'd believe it.

"Been sleeping in a hovel down there," said a bootblack, indicating a nearby alley off Towre Street. "Back before dark, most times."

Like everyone else who couldn't afford lanterns, I thought, but I thanked him and slipped down the alley. I found a concealed spot to wait.

Before long footsteps turned down the alley. Two pairs. My breath caught and I remained motionless, not daring even to breathe. The footsteps stopped. There were a few shuffles, as of two people arranging themselves one on each side of the alley, and then silence.

It wasn't really silent. The main street was still busy with the last few people hastening home, the last hawkers trying to make a few last sales, and the last slops of the day being tipped from upper windows. It seemed silent, though, as I huddled there. It seemed like a long time, too, but it probably wasn't. I'd moved my hand just enough to encircle Raven's muzzle with a gentle finger.

25

Footsteps approached. They halted abruptly with a faint, choked sort of gasp. Something heavy struck the floor. Two sets of footsteps left the alley.

It was almost full dark. I remained still for several more endless minutes before finally creeping out, releasing Raven. I made my way towards the still figure just visible on the ground. Crouching beside it, I remained there for several long moments, shaking, a few tears of shame escaping down my cheeks.

I'd refused gold, rather than kill. And now, in a few moments of terror-stricken babbling...but the greater quiet of true night was settling over the city and every instinct screamed at me to be gone. Gone from this incriminating scene and into a place of comparative night-time safety.

Drawing one last shuddering breath, I forced myself into action. My hand found one of the booted feet that lay before me on the cobbles and I fumbled with the laces, yanking it off. Feeling the shape and realizing that it was the wrong boot, I shoved my rag-swathed foot into it and reached for the other without stopping to tie it.

I tore the second boot off in a near frenzy and gripped the heel, twisting. The hinge was so stiff I knew there was probably a hidden catch somewhere, but I didn't have time to search for it. I pushed until my fingers felt ready to bleed and gradually inched it open. I shook it over the filthy cobbles and after the longest moment of my life, I heard something ring on the ground. Letting the heel spring back, I felt carefully until my hand closed around the cold ring.

I knelt there, the ring clasped in my hand, and despite what lay beside me, my chest felt so tight with joy it brought tears to my eyes and my nape prickled in response to my whole-hearted, *Thank you!*

I had hope again.

Eventually, though, my fingers began to inch almost of their own volition towards the warm coat that swaddled the cooling form beside me. But a footstep sounded loudly in the silence, far too close, and I shoved the second boot blindly onto my foot and bolted into the night.

CHAPTER 4

The Duke of Albany

I trudged along the wet road, blanket held close against the creeping nip of approaching winter. Rain fell on my face and hair. It seemed like it was always raining. It had been raining that day in the spring, when I found Raven, and it rained still. Perhaps the heavens shed tears at my hopelessness, but I doubted it.

Raven fared better than I did in wet weather. In any weather, really. She hadn't grown much, yet, but her tiny frame had filled out. She still coughed soot, but I had long given up worrying about that.

Lowering my head for protection from the driving rain as far as I safely could in the throng of horses, carriages, and persons that choked Temple Barre, I found myself regretting—and not for the first time—the recent hungry patch that had driven me to sell Thomas' boots. I was already missing them so much, and winter wasn't even here yet.

Trying to forget how cold and vulnerable my bare feet felt after several long, lovely months encased in leather, I returned to consideration of my current problem. Not hunger today, for I had already eaten. I was engaged upon my weekly trek to Westminster to learn what I could from the gossips at the Courte Gate.

I frowned because I questioned my judgment in going that day. Winter was almost on me and somehow I had to find a way to buy, or failing that, acquire, another cloak or blanket. I really didn't like stealing things, not any more. It had always made the hair stand up on the back of my neck, as it did during prayer, or in the presence of certain...things. But stealing was worse because of the feeling of disapproval that often came with it—most especially if I resorted to it too easily.

I'd never put my finger on *why* the feeling was sometimes so much worse than others until Father Mahoney had explained that stealing was only actually permissible in a case of truly dire need—and even that permissibility was apparently a subject of some debate among scholars.

The revelation had stunned me at the time, like a cloud had just shifted to let a ray of light illuminate my grubby, desperate existence. All the confusing feelings I'd suffered for almost two years had suddenly made perfect sense. After that, I must've been one of the few urchins who'd turned up for Father Mahoney's daily catechesis sessions for something other than—or at least *as well as*—the slice of bread and glass of milk the holy old priest dished out to each attendee, at his own expense.

When, after only three months of this wonderful triple nourishment—food, fluid, and facts!—I'd arrived one day to find the priest's tiny house cold and dark, and a neighbor informed me of his death, I'd been devastated for more reason than that he'd just started to talk about trying to find me a bit of scribe's work, despite my tender years.

Scribe's work. It would have been my route out of the gutter, no Duke of Albany needed! But without a trustworthy reference, without a respectable contact to arrange the job...

I shook the thoughts away. Father Mahoney was dead—in heaven, surely, and probably praying for me—but that tantalizing possibility had died with him. Along with all those fascinating details about God and the Saints and Heaven and Hell... I'd delighted in it...

I shook my head again, dragging my thoughts back to the grim present as I trekked along the seemingly unending Strande. It *was* a nice walk, for all it was tiring. When the wind came from the north—as it did now—you could actually smell the fields, the open countryside, hidden just behind the single row of good houses that lined the long road. I couldn't help drawing in deep breaths. It was good when it came from the south, too—then you could smell the river, equally hidden behind the even finer mansions lining the river bank. The river didn't smell quite so sweet, but was an improvement on the aroma of the teeming city to the east.

But I couldn't eat nice smells and they wouldn't keep me warm. Surely my time would be better-employed seeking money towards a cloak, or indeed, if I was prepared to stoop to it so soon, seeking a cloak more directly?

Yet, to abandon my search for the Duke, I could not help but feel, would be to resign myself to the short, painful life of an urchin. To live hand to mouth for however many more days, months or years I could scrape by, to die forgotten and unloved in a handy gutter. Or, sooner or later, failing to conceal my sex, I would be forced into a brothel to live an equally short but infinitely more degrading life. I dreaded that fate more than death itself.

I touched the ring at my waist. I could not give up. I *would* not. Whether the Duke of Albany was my father or not, my mother had said he would take care of me. So long as I had that precious ring as proof of my blood, I would keep trying.

Raven's tiny forepaw touched my hand gently, as though in support of my decision, and I smiled slightly. I did not think my strange pet relished the thought of lifelong urchinhood any more than I did.

Anyway, I had reached the Charing Crosse, and the Courte Gate was visible ahead. I darted under the shelter of a nearby stall. The gossips I sought were closeted under there, drinking wine with the off-duty palace servants. I slipped into a seat beside a graying man who sat alone.

He peered at me short-sightedly. "Is that young Serapion? I'll wager so. It's been a quiet week, you know. But I do like a boy who takes interest in important matters."

Actually, he liked anyone who would sit and listen to him, and I had often restrained myself from observing out loud that most of the things he recounted were not remotely 'important'.

But my source was already continuing willingly, "Rumors of the Marquise de la Salde's fat belly are continuing, more substantiated now. But that's the Frenchy's problem. Ah, yes, Duke Collingwood's horse, what was its name...?"

I partially tuned out as the flow continued. Trivial, and to my mind, deadly boring, incidents slipped through my mind unimpeded. Old Roberto, or Robert, as I had no doubt he had been christened, fancied himself as something of an orator and always kept the juiciest things till last. Or perhaps he had learned it was the only way to keep his audience.

Finally, knowing he was drawing to a close, my mind drifted back to the cloak problem.

"...No, the only real event of any note this week is the return of the Duke of Albany from the continent..."

What! Did he just say...?

"...Been away for years, travelling," Old Roberto went on, obliviously. "Not that he *is* the Duke of *Albany*, apparently, they just call him that, seeing as he's a Duke, and his name's Alban. Witty, like. I don't know what he's actually Duke of. No, but he came to court just today; it's only politeness to greet Her Majesty when you're a Duke and all, and gone so long. A minor to-do, though. He's not what you'd call a prominent player at court..."

My head spun. After so long, I realized I'd actually stopped believing I would ever find the man. My weekly visit was more a refusal to succumb to my fate than a real hope. How I swallowed down my pounding heart enough to speak casually I did not know. "Is he away again already, or still at court?"

Old Roberto looked startled, unused to questions from this particular audience. "Nay, to be sure, he is still within. His coach bears his coat of arms; I have not seen it pass."

31

"Oh, what is it?" I asked, all innocence. "Coats of arms are fascinating, I think. I never know how they don't run out of designs."

Old Roberto blinked at this interest, but I knew he loved nothing so well as to memorize coats of arms, and he was always more than willing to keep his audience a little longer. "'Tis a black bird, wings all a'spread, an eagle, I'd say, most coats of arms carry that bird. It holds crossed sticks in its claws, and sits thus upon a background of gold."

I wondered how one reminded one's heart to beat. I thanked Roberto in my usual manner and left, but I did not go far. I took up a station under the eaves, in an alley off the street with a clear view of the Courte Gate, the main entrance to the Palace of Whitehall. I glanced around, and when as certain as I could be that I was unobserved, I lifted my shirt a little to peep at the ring. There it was, as clear as in my memory, that little black bird, wings outspread, and the two straight sticks in its claws, crossed.

Raven poked her head from under the shirt, tilted up her face and cried out softly. This was her true voice, I had learned. It was rich and mellow, and not at all kittenish, but somehow equally appealing. I pushed her back out of sight with a gentle hand, hiding the ring away again. My eyes went back to the gates. Within those towering walls was the man who might be my father. Never mind *father*, who might look after me! Sooner or later, he would come out. I wrapped the blanket more closely around myself and leant against the wall to wait.

CHAPTER 5

Lovers' Rings

The rain carried on, driving sideways with frequent fickle changes of direction, so that whichever side of the alley I stood, I found little protection under the eaves. Eventually I gave up and stood, blanket gathered around me, rain dripping from ears and nose. Soon the icy bite of the water against my skin had me stirring uneasily. Even though it was early in the season, to get wet through could be terribly dangerous.

Almost, I abandoned my post to seek somewhere drier, but the wine stall was too conspicuous—people would grow suspicious of my watch—and to go elsewhere was to abandon my last hope. I gritted my teeth with rather savage abandon. What did it matter? I could stand here worrying about a fatal chill on the morrow, only to be knifed or run down on my way back this very night.

My fingers clenched as I realized I was assuming this would come to nothing. After so long, real hope was hard to muster. I probably would not even get to speak to the Duke, safe as he was behind his urchin-proof wall of servants. Still, if I did not at least give it my best attempt, I might just die of despair.

It was late afternoon by the time the gates rumbled open for what must have been the fiftieth time. I did no more than raise my head; the long day had left me drained from disappointment as well as cold. My back straightened with a jerk almost of its own volition when I saw the black bird of the crest on each of the lead horses' breastplates. I looked again. Breastplates? And face guards and mail, too, while the coachman's seat was shielded on both sides.

Strong shutters, just now wide open, could close the glass-less windows of the coach to narrow defensive slits.

I paused, numb with astonishment. Not primarily because of the coach's heavy defenses, but more for it being, finally, the right coach. Then Old Roberto's comments about the Duke being just returned from the continent filtered into my mind. Travel on the continent was chancy at best, I knew, and clearly he was so newly returned that the coach had not yet been de-rigged of its defensive fitments. At least the shutters were open.

All the same, I hesitated, my heart lurching around in my throat in an appallingly uncomfortable manner. Now, at the very moment, I quailed. What if I could not speak to him? What if he sent me packing? Then I would have no hope at all, and I wasn't sure I could bear it. It didn't have to be now, I could come back tomorrow, wait again...

And if he never comes again? I asked myself scornfully. *How will you survive that?* Common sense, and will, overcame fear before the coach passed me. It was going slow, the horses at a mere trot, but the lead pair had just been put into a canter, and I saw the second pair's muscles bunch to follow. I ran forward in a desperate burst of speed, I gripped the doorframe, hand passing easily through the glassless window, and I leapt, feet landing safe on the step.

I heard the footman's oath, and the next moment the coachman peered back at me, yelling, probably for me to get off, but I scarcely heard. The whip snapped through the air beside me, and I felt a momentary flicker of hope. Most coachmen would have laid it across my back... I crushed this ridiculous notion immediately. An unusually kind-hearted servant was no reflection on the master.

Tightening my grip on the doorframe, I pulled myself up and looked into the coach, thrusting the curtain aside.

A pair of piercing green eyes arrested me, gleaming back from the dimness of the coach's interior. The Duke was lowering his arms. He held a clip in one hand and his hair, black as the bird on his crest, fell around his face. Clearly he

34

had clipped it back in the current fashion out of respect for the Queen. I was already summing up what I saw. My uncanny knack for accurate readings of people on first sight had largely contributed to my early survival on the street, albeit with some near misses.

I saw a man dressed in dark green velvet trimmed with black. He looked close to forty, but might've been a little younger, and he was lean and powerful in build. His nose was rather large and very sharp, and he had a firm chin. His only jewelry was a small gold cross and a ring that looked the twin of my own. He was clearly a powerful man, and also a wealthy man, but he did not flaunt it. Despite the velvet, the cut of his clothes was more practical than fashionable, his ruff on the small side, which fitted with the sword that lay beside him.

I sensed he would make a bad enemy, but I did not fear him on sight. I was still staring at him when he spoke. He seemed unalarmed by my sudden appearance and did not hasten to call down curses on his servants for allowing me to get so far. Instead, he said firmly, "If you want alms, apply at the back door of my house."

I did not move. I was having difficulty unsticking my tongue and felt equally unsure what to say with it.

The hard eyes softened by a degree. "If I give you so much as a penny, you know, I shall never be able to drive the length of the city again." There was a definite flicker of humor in that. "I should be mobbed," he added, for clearly my expression showed no trace of understanding and he thought I did not comprehend what he meant. On the contrary, I knew that for a noble to give alms from their carriage was to curtail all future speed through the city, hence why most coachmen would whip beggars away ruthlessly.

When I still didn't move to let go, the humor in the Duke's eyes faded and fear unlocked my tongue. "Please, my lord, I must speak with you."

For a moment I thought he would still dismiss me, but then his eyes ran over my face with a look of sudden intentness. "Very well, lass." His hand closed on the collar of my jerkin, and in a few seconds I found myself on the seat opposite him.

I gaped at him. He had actually deposited my dripping, reeking self on his upholstery! Then the true import of his words hit me. He knew I was a girl. His depth of perception was frightening. *I* always knew if a fellow urchin was male or female, but since others clearly did not, I'd always assumed it was...one of those unique talents of mine best not discussed. Maybe...maybe this really *was* my father.

The Duke sat back on his own seat, tucking his clip safely in a pocket and eyeing my evident terror with amused benevolence. "I'm not going to hurt you," he remarked. "And may I remind you that it was *you* who jumped aboard wanting to speak to *me*."

Aboard, yes, but not quite this aboard. I tore my eyes from the man long enough to take in the coach interior. A longbow and a crossbow hung on one wall, and a heavy shield on the other. Arrows and crossbow bolts stuck from an open-ended box. Just returned from Europe indeed. I looked back at the Duke.

At my continued silence his expression became very firm. His patience had been far beyond what I could possibly have expected but apparently there were limits to his forbearance. "I don't eat urchins, and I am as much flesh and blood as you are. Now what do you want?"

I had to speak, and I knew it. I had to speak now, or he would put me from his carriage and it would be over. My chance gone, perhaps forever. But after so many years of solitude and silence, I could not frame what I wanted to say.

Groping at my waist, I felt a second of pure panic as the string came loose, then tiny sharp claws pressed cool gold into my hand. I took the ring from Raven, willing my heart back down into my chest and giving Raven a little push to remind her to stay out of sight. I tried once more to find words, but they would not come, so finally I simply held the ring out towards the Duke, crest forwards.

The Duke opened his mouth as if to make some tolerant enquiry, but in the same moment his eyes narrowed and he reached out slowly towards the ring, his face suddenly expressionless. Uncertain and racked with suspense, I allowed him to take it from my numb fingers. He turned it slowly in his hands, finally tilting it towards the window so he could read the inscription inside the band.

It was, I knew, a romantic inscription in Latin. Or half of one. A commonly known metaphor on courting birds. 'You shall build my nest, and I shall fill it,' it ran, but my mother's ring had only the part about filling it. I eyed the Duke's ring in speculation. It seemed a curiously domestic inscription for lovers' rings, but all this romantic stuff left me rather cold anyway.

"Where did you get this?" the Duke managed at last, his voice changed to a whisper. The eyes that stared back at me were haunted now.

I swallowed hard and had to try twice to find my voice. "My mother gave it to me," I said haltingly, but gaining confidence, continued, "when she was dying. She said...she said to take it to the Duke of Albany and that...that he would...look after me."

He went on looking at me, his mouth curved in a hard line, while hope, pain and confusion mingled in his narrowed eyes. "And...who was your mother?"

"Lady Isabel Ravena," I said promptly and proudly, my chin rising in defiance of my ragged state.

The Duke closed his eyes for a second with a tiny sigh. Then his eyes fixed me to the spot again. "She sent you to *me*?" he murmured, but I felt sure he was not expecting an answer to that and remained silent. "You're her daughter?"

"Yes, as I said," I replied, my chin untroubled by his gaze.

"How old are you?"

I could tell from his tone that this was a subject of vital importance and I could understand why. I had to stop and think, though. "Thirteen. My birthday's in February, and that's definitely past for this year."

"Indeed it is," he replied, still watching me with disturbing intensity. "Why, may I ask, is a young lady like yourself living like...this?" He gestured to my urchin's attire with a strong hand.

I swallowed, but with anger this time, anger for my thieving uncle. "My uncle threw me from my mother's house...from *my* house," I added with a spurt of anger, "before Mother was even cold! I've tried to find you ever since, but..." My anger trailed off, I was too exhausted to sustain it. "It's so *hard*. Has been so hard," I corrected and trailed off entirely.

"Your uncle? That crawling snake Baron Hendfield?"

"Him," I confirmed, shaking with cold and suspense.

"And *your* name?"

"Serapion," I replied automatically, then embarrassed, lowered my eyes for a second before looking back into his. "Serapia."

I almost *felt* that touch some nerve inside him, and his face softened. "You don't know how happy that makes me."

He leant forward to take my chin, which had sunk again. I flinched back, but his grip tightened slightly as he gazed intently at my face. I forced myself to remain still. His fingers traced my nose, which my nursemaid had always called strong, but which I knew was sharp and pointed. He touched my matted hair gently. It was as black as his, which hung in glossy waves, bar a single streak of white at the front. Mine wasn't doing anything but dripping limply. It was a long time since I'd been embarrassed about my appearance; I'd had much more important things to think about.

The Duke ran his fingers over the unusually bumpy vertebrae at the back of my neck and concluded his scrutiny with a searching look into my green eyes. Which, I noted, shivering with hopeful pleasure, could have been reflections of his own.

"Serapia," he said at last, sitting back in his seat, "without any doubt, I am your father."

I closed my eyes and a long sigh of relief escaped me. *Oh, thank you! Thank you!* He was my father. Surely he would look after me?

"That does not surprise you?"

I opened my eyes again to find him still watching me.

"Well, no. It seemed fairly likely."

"She did not tell you?"

"I have never heard one word about my father...about you...in my entire life, until today."

"Likewise. I hadn't the slightest idea that you existed." He closed his eyes for a moment and smiled, and it transformed his face with joy. "I have a daughter," he murmured, "a child of my blood."

I breathed even more freely. He was happy! But if he was so happy... "Why didn't you know about me?" I challenged.

A tiny frown etched itself between his brows. "I've been travelling for a long time, and your mother never contacted me," he said shortly, and patted the seat beside him. "Come, sit here."

When I hesitated, he held out a hand to me. Since he was my father I gave him the benefit of the doubt and took his hand, but I made sure I sat far enough away that I did not get my filth on his fine clothes. And it gave me room to maneuver. I touched the hematite under my jerkin for reassurance. The slight soothing warmth I sometimes felt from the stone was there now.

I was shivering violently by this time, for I had been drenched to the skin for some hours, and with the excitement as well, I thought I might just shake to pieces. Indeed, it was now impossible for me to hide and after a sharp look at me, he wrung out my hair with careful twists of each matted lock. I let him do so, reminding myself sternly that this was my father who was going to look after me, and he was not to be upset in any way.

Taking a blanket from inside the opposite seat, he wrapped it around me, engulfing me in its thick, warm folds. *Oh, to have had a blanket like that last winter*, I thought, so lost in my sudden ecstasy of warmth that only after a moment did I realize he had put an arm around me, tucking me to him. He reached up and banged on the roof, making me jump, and shouted to the coachman, "Straight home, Richard, straight home!"

He fussed with my blankets for a while, dropping a second over my bare feet, by now mottled blue with cold, before seeming satisfied that I was well wrapped. I felt snug beyond belief; the shivering had nearly stopped.

"I have a very nice house here, Serapia," he was telling me. "Or *I* think so. I think you will find it comfortable, at any rate. And you shall be its mistress. It has not had a mistress for a long time. Will you like that?"

I was too busy thinking about what he was saying to answer that question immediately. I would live with him, in his home? I could scarcely believe it. I had judged him a man who scorned fashion and had no interest in the politics of the court, but surely he would not be prepared to scorn all propriety?

"Are you not going to send me to live quietly with some...lesser relative, in the country?" I asked rather timorously.

"Why ever would I do that?" He seemed genuinely surprised, but then he stopped and his lips pursed, and I could see he understood me.

To my surprise, he smiled, and his eyes almost danced. "I see I should tell you my name. And that is Alban Serapion Ravena. I was your mother's husband, and you are my legitimate daughter. No 'lesser relatives' will be necessary."

CHAPTER 6

A House of Stone

My mind raced as I sought to digest the Duke's words. I was not illegitimate? Not a bastard? All this time I had thought...why had no one told me? Illegitimate, even to a Duke, hush it up, but *legitimate* to a *Duke!*

My thoughts paused. My uncle...how? I backed up a bit and carefully sorted my memories. Had I ever *actually* heard my uncle called by his name? His full name? I knew his first name was Eliot, while Baron Hendfield was his title and he usually used it, for he was vain about it. But I had never seen that much of him and had been too young to go anywhere where he might have been announced in full. I had always assumed him a Ravena, assumed to the degree that I had not even known it was assumed. I had thought I had known. But it could not be so.

"What is my uncle's name?" I asked my father, half-embarrassed.

Alban Serapion Ravena cocked an eyebrow at this odd question, perhaps not so odd to him now, knowing the delusion I had lived my life under. "Eliot Jacob Pellenporth. Does that clear a few things up?"

I nodded silently and tried to let myself relax. I had not been so near another person for longer than I could re-member, and he was a man. I felt hideously guilty at being so suspicious, but I just couldn't help it. Looking up suddenly, I caught him looking down at me with what I suspected was an unusually soft smile on his lips and I suddenly felt much more comfortable with him. He was not a bad man. I felt sure of it.

~+~

41

I was never quite sure afterwards how it happened; no doubt a combination of the wonderful warmth of the blankets, the gentle swaying of the coach, and the sheer physical and emotional exhaustion of the day, but I fell asleep, tucked in the circle of my new father's arm. Father, yet complete stranger, and I fell asleep! I stirred as the coach turned sharply. We had left the city—were we on the road to Islington?—and I glimpsed great gates rearing up in the dusk. I sunk back into a doze.

By the time the coach drew to a halt, I was almost completely asleep again, and I struggled to muster the energy to open my eyes.

Fingers touched my shoulder gently. "Serapia..."

I dragged my eyes open and sat up as memory flooded back. Licking my lips nervously, I glanced at this man, my father. He'd gotten out of the coach and now offered me his hand to dismount. I stood up rather carefully, for my head felt hot and heavy and spun when I moved. Normally I could have jumped down in one leap, but I knew ladies descended calmly with the aid of a man's hand, and anyway, I didn't want either the blanket or my aching head to fall off.

When I had alighted, I stood for a moment, swaying slightly. Concentration was very difficult, but after a few moments I blinked in puzzlement. It was raining still, I could hear it pouring on the ground, but it was not falling on me. Peering up in the painful light of a guttering torch, I saw that a roof stretched from above the door outwards, to be supported by two stone pillars. It was so large that the whole carriage stood beneath it. How odd. How *useful*.

"Oh, the carriage-porch," said the Duke, noticing my distraction. "My father thought of it and had it built. There's one over the back door as well. The tradesmen and beggars bless him. Everyone else says it's ugly as sin and they wouldn't dream of having one on their own home. Which is fine by me, they can be as fashionable and wet as they like."

He laughed, and I understood better his comment about how *he* thought his house was nice.

42

Unable to summon any reply, I silently followed him inside. I had a dim impression of antique weapons and old flags hung from the rafters of the entrance hall as a memorial to past military victories, but it smelt very musty, as if long disused, and there was no fire lit in the grate. My nape prickled with the *emptiness* of it.

My father led on towards the next room, gesturing around him. "The place is miserable as anything right now, but it hasn't been lived in for many years; it will soon wake up again."

The room we approached was better, I was glad to feel. Someone, either the Duke or servants, had already spent much more time in there and the stone walls were warming in a way that had nothing to do with heat. But I had to catch the end of the banister as I passed the stairs and stand for a moment. The pain in my head I could almost ignore, but the dizziness threatened to overwhelm me.

My father was turning back towards me, so hastily I stepped forward. But something caught my eye and I jerked around to stare up the stairs. "*Mother?*"

The movement was too much; that indistinct figure spun into a grey haze along with everything else and I was falling. I was dimly aware of strong arms catching me, then everything dissolved into blackness.

CHAPTER 7

Siridean

I bit my lip to keep from moaning; surely I was in hell, I was so hot...so very hot. Raven crouched on my chest, chattering fiercely at the shadowed figures around us. Knowing Raven was frightened from the occasional wails she shot in my direction, I tried to speak to comfort her, but I just couldn't manage it. There were voices, but I was unable to make out what they said.

A hand came down towards me. I saw the speck of scarlet blood as Raven sprang and bit, and it was gone again. A face appeared instead, on our level...my father's face. He spoke sternly to Raven, and reached out once more. Raven watched warily, tail lashing, but did not attack again. Something wonderfully cold touched my forehead and with this slight relief, I sank into fever-sharpened memory.

I huddled against the wall, arms wrapping around my ragged silk dress. It had been such a fine, pretty dress barely... I could not quite remember when. The last few nights and days bled into one another, a long nightmare of terror and confusion.

I pressed closer to the wall, but the cold stone sucked heat from my back and I shrank away again. It was only October, but no sun shone that day and I was so desperately hungry and so very tired. I'd barely slept for days.

Two men staggered from the tavern opposite and I eyed them warily, trying to make myself small and still. I hadn't forgotten the man who'd tried to throw me over his shoulder, or the man with the apples and the wandering hands.

The bright pink silk defeated my efforts, not yet wholly darkened with grime. I saw the one man nudge his companion and nod in my direction, caught snatches of their thick speech. A fine little sow, the one said. Nay, a fine filly, said the other, the pale skin on her. Worth a penny, despite her age, the other replied. It went something like that, as far as I could tell.

Decision taken, they headed towards me at a lumbering run, and I snatched up my tattered hem in one hand and fled. They were faster than their initial lack of grace would have implied. I had a rather imperfect idea of the fate I fled but still I ran until my lungs strained desperately for breath.

I took the corner as fast as the slippery cobbles permitted and ran headlong into a tall man coming the other way.

"Watch where you're going, brat," he snapped, his irritated tone such that my meager experience already made me to cower from the anticipated blow.

Something much worse happened. The upraised hand darted like a striking snake and closed around my wrist. I twisted, tugging, but for one of such a slender build, the man was uncannily strong. And something about him frightened me far more than my pursuers did. He had oddly pointed ears, but was nondescript in dress and must have been either respectably well off or extremely poor sighted, for he wore spectacles. But there was a choking feeling around him that I could not ignore. The nape of my neck prickled fiercely as that sense which I could not but heed, flamed into life.

The man drew me to him as if reeling in a fish and seized my chin with his other hand to get a proper look at me. Ignoring my futile struggles, he slid his hand from my chin to the nape of my neck and ran a forefinger down those three bumpy vertebrae that my maid pretended not to notice and my mother sniffed at if mentioned. I shivered, my fear momentarily soothed. I stared up at my captor as he put a straggle of hair back from my face and took a second look at me.

His eyes behind the spectacles were brown and a myriad of things lurked in their depths, tumbling together in a way that made me want to flee. But I could not flee, and besides, dominant in those brown eyes just then was something wonderful, something I had not seen for far too long.

That thing was kindness.

"What are you doing alone here, elfling?" the man asked, his voice still harsh but no longer angry.

I cringed inside, appalled that this man had taken one look at me and seen that strangeness even my uncle had only guessed at. Though lack of certainty had never protected me from that most hated name, 'witch child', nor saved me from the terrible result of my uncle's hatred. But there was no condemnation in this man's voice, despite his more imaginative choice of aspersion.

"My...my uncle..." I croaked, but his hand slipped back to the nape of my neck and I fell silent, too out of breath to go on.

Only when his head jerked up an inch and his eyes darted behind me did I remember my pursuers. I spun around, backing towards my captor until the renewed impression of darkness from his proximity reminded me that he was not necessarily the lesser of the two evils.

The two men stopped and eyed the individual who had beaten them to their prize. Edging sideways, I distanced myself from my disturbing captor/rescuer until I could look from one to the other. The brown-eyed man calmly transferred my wrist to his left hand and with the same absolute matter-of-factness pushed his cloak back to give the men a clear view of the dagger at his belt.

There were two of them, and they probably had knives as well. I was trembling but steeled myself to run again if necessary. Two big men like that would surely not be so cowardly as to fear a willowy man like this.

The two men looked their adversary in the eye for a few moments. Then they glanced at each other with an eloquent shift of body language that popped the seldom-heard phrase 'like hell' into my mind. And they turned and hastened away.

"Good riddance," retorted the brown-eyed man, in a tone that hovered halfway between a snarl and a hiss. He looked at me again, and I searched hastily for the kindness in his eyes.

"I am Siridean," he said distractedly, then unaccountably looked around at the surrounding rooftops, speaking to himself as though he'd forgotten I was actually there. "Let's get the elfling fed before sunset; I've time for that much..."

46

Hand still clamped like a vice around my wrist, he turned and towed me away.

A cup was being pressed to my lips. The liquid tasted bitter, but I was so very thirsty. I sipped weakly and it was held patiently to my mouth until I slipped away again.

The sun was low in the sky when we reached Siridean's lodgings. My legs had soon given out trying to keep up with my companion's long strides, and he bore me in his arms without apparent effort. I licked my dirty fingers in a way that would have appalled my mother, scavenging the last shreds of grease from the bread and meat Siridean had bought me.

The stairway was narrow and something scuttled away into the darkness as we ascended. Safe in my new friend's arms, I turned a fearless gaze in its direction. It was a garret room we entered, about the size of Cook's pantry at home. I was quite impressed to see a bed, table and chair fitted into such a space. And a chest, I saw, as Siridean set me down on one end of the bed and lit several candles before drawing it from underneath.

I watched in silence as Siridean took out some garments, then drew the dagger and chopped off sections of breech leg and shirt sleeve. He stopped only once to look at the window and talk to himself; he'd done this several times by now and I was getting used to it.

Eventually he shut the chest with a thud and slid it away, gesturing to the pile of garments on the bed. "Put those on. So when... Just in case. You're safer as a boy."

I blinked at him, confused. Just in case of what? But I got up and started to pull the breeches up under my skirts, struggling with the unfamiliar garment. Siridean turned away and stood by the window, looking out into the twilit street, so I rid myself of the dress entirely and got the breeches held up with the belt, pulling the shirt on over the top. Last I slipped on the coat, welcome warmth despite the hot meal in my stomach. The coat was baggy but fitted surprisingly well, considering. He's like a sword blade, I thought, remembering Cook's phrase for someone who needed more of her fine cooking.

When I was still again, Siridean turned from the window and sat in the chair beside it, running an appraising eye over me. "Come here." He held out a lean hand.

I obeyed, and he took my shoulders and turned me so my back was to him. I heard the whisper of a blade being drawn and before I could react there was a firm pressure on my hair and an unmistakable 'sniiiick' sound. Spinning around, I reached behind me and my hands closed on thin air, even as I saw that he held what I sought. Finally locating what was left of my hair, I found that he had cut it off along the line of my shoulders. I must look like...like...like a boy, I realized abruptly, remembering his earlier words. So I looked sadly at the mass of long locks in his hand, but the words of furious protest died in my throat.

He seemed blind to my pain at my loss, simply coiling the hair and handing it to me. "Put it safe, it's worth coin."

Hair? Worth coin? But the past few days had impressed upon me the previously unknown necessity of coin, so I tucked it carefully into the inside pocket of my new coat.

"There's the dagger," he said, placing a hand on it, eyes straying back towards the setting sun. "And my coins here, if... you've a need." He took my small hand and laid it on his doublet; I felt the hard lump of the purse from which he'd paid for my meal and nodded obligingly to show that I understood. I couldn't imagine why he thought it important I know, though, when he would be doing the paying.

"That won't last you long, though," Siridean went on. "And you're too young to be employed for anything but the wickedest kind of work—no, trust me, you don't want to know what that means, and still less do you want to be driven to it. You can beg, but that'll lead you to a whorehouse fast enough—or the grave, like as not—or, you can pickpocket. So I'll teach you. Just... just in case you need it."

I felt I'd understood less than half of that. "What's...pick... pocket...ing?"

His eyes widened, then he bent his head and pressed his hands to his forehead. "Ah...innocence..." he murmured. "I had almost forgotten...beautiful..." But after a moment he dropped his hands and his head came up again. "Pickpocketing is when you take someone's purse out of their pocket and use their money to buy what you need."

I frowned. That sounded rather like...stealing. "Isn't that... wrong?"

"Yes," he said frankly. "But it is more wrong to have enough and ignore a starving youngling. Saint Thomas Aquinas—a very wise human—would have been quite happy for you to pick pockets, desperate little elfling that you are. Now, pay attention." He rose to his feet, all the great length of him, turned his back, his arms moving as though rearranging something under his doublet, then faced me again.

"So, elfling. You only need to do two things. First, concentrate on what you want. Imagine the purse and the coin—copper, silver or gold, as you think it most likely to contain. When you have concentrated hard enough, you will know where the purse is. Then concentrate—hard—on the idea of 'unseen'. Invisible. Unremarked. Unnoticed. Concentrate hard, really hard. Get that wrong and you will merely swap starving to death in the gutter for starving to death in jail. So, go on... Take my purse from me."

I stared at him, growing more and more confused. No one had ever given me such a strange set of instructions before, yet he spoke as though doing what he said was obvious and easy.

"Come on," he gave an impatient jerk of his head. "Try and take it. Think...concentrate..."

Concentrate... That was both his instructions, actually. What did he say the first thing was?

Where is the purse?

How could concentrating tell me that? I was loathe to disappoint him, though, when he'd helped me so much, and still a little nervous of him. I had to try. I thought about the purse I'd seen earlier. It was green, made of cloth. Full of coppers and silvers. He'd taken it from under the left side of his doublet. I stared at him...where was it?

It? The image of the purse had dropped from my mind.

"Concentrate," purred Siridean, as I struggled to fix image and question in my mind alongside one another.

This was ridiculous. How was this going to tell me where the purse was? I knew where it had been, but he could have moved it...anywhere.

But...as I stood there looking at him, I found I had an unaccountable certainty that the purse in question was now under the right-hand side of his doublet. How could I feel so sure? But I did. The nape of my neck prickled, almost tingled.

So...number two was...unseen. Siridean, I noticed, had closed his eyes.

Unseen. I tried to think of nothing else as I stepped the short distance between us and reached up to slide my hand through the right-hand pocket slit of his doublet. He didn't react. My fingers touched the purse, closed around it, drawing the strings free of his belt; I began to lift it out...

Yes! I'd done...

His hand darted up with that frightening speed and snagged my wrist. His brown eyes—open again—studied me curiously, as though he had perhaps not been so positive I could do what he asked after all. Almost do what he asked...

"Very good," he said. "You found it all right. And you got hold of it. Then you rejoiced too soon, did you? A mental pat on the back? Save that until you are completely out of sight, or you will reap a very different reward. Say rather, you will be the one reaped." He spun away from me to stow the purse away somewhere, then with his back still to me, said, "Again."

I bit my lip. He was right. I'd let my concentration waver. Concentrate, he'd said. That was clearly the secret. Again I built the image of the purse. Again, that subtle certainty slipped into my mind. Tucked inside his doublet, this time, on the top right hand side. Unseen. I held the thought in my mind like a protective barrier, held it tight as I slipped forward, as I eased three small buttons undone, as I slid my hand into his doublet, as I drew the purse all the way out, as I slipped back again. Only then did I let it go.

"Does here count as out of sight?" I asked.

He turned, a faint, almost-smile skittering across his face in a way that made me suspect he'd already known I had the purse. But someone else...wouldn't have known?

The sun was almost gone.

Siridean stared at the orange sky as though he'd forgotten my presence again. Finally, he shot an unquiet glance at me. "I'm free," he muttered rapidly to himself. "I'm free and I'll stay free. Only one way to be free; there's no such thing as staying free after getting free, but I am free and I shall be free. I think the price cheap..."

He fell silent and stared at that fast-diminishing orange for some time before finally turning back to where I stood, waiting in anxious silence, still clutching the purse. I might already be growing accustomed to it, but I was not too young to perceive that my protector didn't behave...entirely like normal people did.

"Don't worry, elfling," he said, his eyes calm again, "first thing tomorrow we'll see about finding this Duke."

I blinked up at him, all previous confusion forgotten in the face of this. I hadn't told him about the Duke I needed so desperately to find. He seemed to have gleaned an awful lot from that croaked, 'my uncle'.

"We'll find him," he repeated, and I had the strangest feeling that whilst he meant what he said, he didn't believe it in the slightest and I could not understand that at all.

Silently, I offered him his purse. He looked at it with utter disinterest, as though he could hardly be bothered to take it back from me, but after a moment accepted it and refastened the strings to his belt.

Settling himself in the chair again, he held out a hand and drew me towards him, and I perched on his bony knees, staring up at his face as he again watched the sunset slipping from the sky. He looked afraid. Just a little. But mostly tired. So tired. Even in my current state of exhaustion, I could tell I'd never felt as he felt. It was no bodily tiredness in his eyes but something worse, something deeper, something inside. When he finally turned back to me, I gazed up at him, seeking the reassurance that his eyes gave and his presence most emphatically did not.

He ran a strand of my jet black hair through his fingers, returning my scrutiny. "You're not much of an elfling, are you?" he murmured. "Still, elfling enough..."

I curled in on myself, wishing he could not see it. "I don't mean to feel those things."

And then, because he was the very first person I'd ever actually dared to ask, I added, "Am I evil?" I didn't really believe that; my mother had never acted as though the things I felt were bad like that...

Siridean snorted. "These things you feel are not evil. Evil is what you do."

"I don't do anything," I replied, baffled.

He looked down at me, and for the first time a real smile played on his lips. "Then you're not evil, are you?" he retorted rather sharply, but his hand ran gently over the back of my head.

I wrapped my arms around his narrow chest and cuddled close, my wariness overwhelmed by the acceptance even my mother had failed to provide.

Hand running again over my hair, he added ever so softly, "Nay, for you clearly would not know evil even were it right before your eyes."

His arms settled around me, thin and sinewy and strong as an oak tree's roots, and for the first time since my mother's death I felt safe. I snuggled my cheek to him and twisted my head so I could see his face. His distant expression made me think of lost things.

Lost things...my mother...

And finally the tears came, the numbness broken and washed away by the knowledge that the worst of my ordeal was over. I wept and wept until my throat felt raw and his coat was soaked. Not blind to this much greater distress, Siridean rubbed my back in silent comfort, pausing only once to address some muttered thoughts to the darkened window.

"Weep and survive," he murmured in my ear when his attention returned to me. "Weep, but survive. Don't ever let anyone take your life away from you. Yield it to no one. No one!"

He continued in the same vein until his quiet voice lulled me to sleep, but I stirred as he settled me in the bed and drew the blanket over me.

"Where will you sleep?" I mumbled drowsily, shyness and fear largely gone now. Everyone at home had their own bed, even the scullery maid.

"I will just sit here and look at the stars," he replied, reseating himself as he did so, and then to himself, he growled with soft malevolence, "How I hate the stars. I hate the night. The stars are cruel and the night crueler still. How I hate the night..."

I closed my eyes again, sleep sucking at me until I realized that I'd forgotten my prayers. Too tired to drag myself from the warm bed and kneel down, I simply formulated some sleep-garbled thanks for my deliverance. The familiar prickling at the nape of my neck reassured me that my informality was not taken amiss. Sleep would have claimed me then if three words had not reached me from my protector, so soft I might have thought they came only to my mind: "Pray for me."

"Of course," I whispered, and holding Siridean's name in my mind, I finally slipped into that velvet blackness.

I twisted, moaning, and gentle hands soothed me, replacing the damp cloth on my brow. A soft voice comforted me, and I braved the light to find my father's face still hovering over me. Quieting, I felt Raven's cool little body curled against my burning neck. There were voices, and I could understand them now.

"My lord," that was a woman's voice, "my lord, you must get some rest yourself. It's been two days...you haven't even *eaten.*"

"Make more tea for the child, Anna, and leave me be." That was my father's voice, inflexible as granite. "I will *not* allow some chill to snatch her through my fingers just when I've found her!"

He spoke with such determination that I pictured him locked in combat with the grim reaper. The grim reaper was just a story, though. Death was an angel with black wings. I wasn't sure how I knew about the black wings, but I was sure it was an angel. I'd felt it brush me from time to time.

I woke with a start to find the room lit with the grey light that signaled dawn's arrival perhaps an hour hence. Looking for the cause of my awakening, I saw Siridean on his feet, his whole body rigid as he stared at the window. Something was wrong. My nape all but burned and the air seemed suffocating-thick.

"Siridean?" I quavered.

For a moment his head twitched from side to side as though he did not wish to look at me, then it snapped around. As his eyes fixed upon me I jerked back with a little cry. Every foreboding of darkness his presence had evoked had come to fruition in his eyes. My mind struggled to name it, but some more primal part of me knew that I was in the presence of pure evil. He moved towards me with stiff steps, drawing the dagger from his belt. The horrors his eyes promised me—promised to enjoy doing to me—locked my muscles with terror and confusion. Where had my kind protector gone?

Siridean was almost at the bed now, the dagger tip moving slowly from side to side as though its first use was under consideration. I flinched back against the wall. Siridean paused. The dagger wavered. Was raised to strike. Another hesitation and it drove forward...and slammed through the palm of his opposite hand with a crunch of breaking bone. His lips drew back in a silent scream of pain and fury and something strangely akin to defiance.

"I am free of you!" he screamed. Tearing the blade from his mangled hand, he spun around and lunged with all his strength at the place in front of the window at which he had originally been staring.

The next moment he stumbled backwards as though under the force of a heavy blow, his dagger flying from his hand. My eyes widened in shock as I saw the gashes appear across his chest. I could only watch helplessly as he jerked again, most of his face disappearing in bloody ruin, and once more, scarlet spraying across wall and window as another slash ripped open his throat.

He fell slowly to the ground, arms out flung; a pool of crimson collected quickly around his shoulders and then he lay still.

A gentle presence brushed past me, and by the time nature forced me to breathe again, I realized that the evil feeling was also gone, leaving only emptiness behind. For some time I could only sit and shake. Finally, I tried to move forward and stopped to disentangle myself from the blanket. And the cloak. The cloak that Siridean had laid over me at some point in the night. Breathing in shocked gasps, I lowered myself onto the damp-specked floorboards and approached hesitantly on hands and knees.

I'd seen that utter stillness too recently to hold out any hope; had already learned that all the tears and shaking and pleading, however heartfelt, would achieve nothing. But I had never seen a human body that resembled the meat that day Cook really lost her temper and laid to it with her cleaver.

I fought it, but my insides tried to escape me until finally I crouched, feeling strained and empty. Eventually I edged the rest of the way and surveyed what was left. One eye still stared out, undamaged, though his spectacles had been torn from his face and lay nearby. I picked them up, ignoring the shattered lens, and reached out to set them back in place, only to hesitate, leaning closer as I peered in the pre-dawn gloom.

The blank eye that stared up at me was no longer that lovely brown I remembered. In fact, it was like no eye I had ever seen. It was gold around the iris, actually gold in color, radiating to green around the edges. I stared for a while before finally sliding the lid down over it with a trembling finger and slipping the spectacles back into place as best I could.

Sitting back on my heels again, I closed my eyes. I could feel myself going numb again, but I took a moment to try and fix Siridean's face in my mind, alongside the image of my mother. It wasn't too difficult; his thin sharp face had been very distinctive, until this bewildering, unknown thing had happened. At last I opened my eyes again, stuffing the ball of screaming panic-stricken grief to the bottom of my hollow stomach and squashing it down as hard as I could.

'Just in case', I remembered. He made a point about two things...

Tentatively, I reached out and peeled what was left of the coat away from the still chest. The purse was still tied to his belt, damaged, but holding together. I transferred it to my own belt and looked around for the dagger. Pausing to disentangle the sheath, I settled the reunited weapon at my own waist, tucked awkwardly inside my breeches for concealment. For a young lady to carry a blade... I felt ashamed.

But I left it on my belt and took the cloak from the bed, drawing the blade for the first time to hack off the excess length before throwing it around me. Rolling the blanket as well, I fastened it with Siridean's belt, then pulled off the sheet and spread it carefully over him, ignoring the way its clean whiteness was instantly marred.

A small voice inside demanded that I break down, that I wait for someone to come and look after me; that I was little and helpless and there was surely nothing else I could do. But I didn't believe anyone was coming to look after me. And an older, clearer voice whispered that it was not a good idea to be found in that room with a knife when I myself would swear on the Bible no one else had entered.

There is someone who'll look after me, I reminded myself. My mother told me so. But I have to find him. She didn't say he would come to me. She told me to find him. And...God's still looking after me...

Isn't he?

So I bundled up the bright pink silk dress, in case that too was worth coin, and I headed out, down the dark stairwell and into the street.

CHAPTER 8

The Portrait

I woke slowly at first, then all in one go, as a towering mountain of strangeness crashed down on my senses. The soft bed, the warm covers, the smooth sheets, the glowing coals in the fireplace, the bed curtains, velvet and drawn back, the bed itself with its tall posts...

I sat up with a jerk that made the blood rush dizzily to my head, and by the time I had stopped blinking, I'd remembered the carriage, and the Duke. This was my father's house. For the first time in far too long, I had a home, and this was it. My head was cool now, though spinning slightly from the violence of my awakening. I rested my weight on my arms and looked around more slowly as Raven scrambled up to my shoulder, alternately chattering and wailing her displeasure at being woken so abruptly.

The sun's rays streamed into the room from the windows. Judging from the quality of the light, it was afternoon. Of what day, I was unsure. I started as my eyes fell upon the Duke, asleep in an armchair beside the bed. A book lay open on his knee and in great danger of falling. I shifted shakily to the edge of the bed and reached out to rescue it. It was a beautifully illustrated Bible, in Latin, and I flicked through it, my mind straining as I read. Before long I bit my lip. I was quite rusty.

"You must be better."

I looked up to see my father's eyes were open and guessed that he had been watching me for a moment or two.

"Well, yes." I blushed and offered him his book.

"You can read it all you like," the Duke said, stretching as if stiff.

I continued to hold it out. "No, it's giving me a headache right now. And this is your book."

The Duke took it back and smoothed a hand over the battered, but still beautiful, leather cover. "Yes, this is my book. You may have one of your own, if you wish. Or would you like it in English?"

"Well, both," I said rather absently, thinking of my childhood Bible, with which I had learned my Latin in the first place. Then I realized what I had said and felt embarrassed. "I mean, either will do. I'm not greedy."

My father laughed at that, and pulled a cord on the wall.

"Is that a servant's bell?" I asked, distracted from my discomfort. A lot of the better families were having these fitted now, at great expense, but my mother had always used a hand bell.

"My father put them in when he built the house," the Duke explained, as a maidservant entered. "At the time they were thought as odd as the rest of the stuff, so perhaps some of that will be common one day." He turned his attention to the waiting maid. "Bring food for my daughter; keep it simple, nothing fancy. Also prepare a hot bath and send up whichever of you is best with lady's hair."

The maid bobbed a curtsey and left, looking faintly aghast at the last order. I touched my hair in sudden dismay. However many days and nights of fevered tossing had been the final straw. I hoped it could be untangled. I didn't want it cut; it was still shorter than it had been when Siridean chopped it off.

My head still swam slightly, so I lay down again and my father tucked the blankets over me. I wondered just how ill I'd been, then frowned as a confused memory crept back into my head. "My mother! I saw my mother!"

The Duke sighed. "Yes, I expect you did. I'll show you." He pulled the cord again and gave more orders, this time to a footman. A few short minutes later, two rather more solid men arrived, both in the Duke's livery, which was black and gold like his crest. They carried a large, full-size portrait, which they set down in front of the bed with suppressed puffs.

I stared at the picture, captivated. There sat my mother, younger than I had ever seen her, wearing a beautiful lacy dress in pale green. Younger, but perfect in every detail. My vague memory snapped into sudden clarity as I stared at those beautiful locks of straight blond, that delicate face, the tiny nose, the big brown eyes, the dainty chin. My mother. Young and beautiful. Not tired and...withdrawn.

Eventually I dragged my eyes away enough to look at the other person in the portrait. My father stood behind my mother, one hand on her shoulder, the other resting on his sword. My mother's hand was raised to his. He was dressed elegantly in a slightly darker green, and he too was younger. His face was unlined, his hair still the same glossy black as now, only lacking the single streak of white that I had previously noticed. A hound lay at my mother's feet, gazing up at her, while another stood beside the Duke, face also upturned. A horse stood behind, a magnificent black beast partially armored. Its reins hung on the ground as it waited patiently for its master. A familiar ring graced each of the joined hands.

I finally looked at the living Duke, realizing he was dressed as usual in very dark colors, black today, trimmed with dark green. His face was rather closed. Glancing back at the portrait, I noticed that one corner of the frame and a small part of the canvas was blackened and burned. "What happened to it?"

The Duke gave a pained smile in which there was no humor at all. "Your mother put a torch to it as she was leaving. Fortunately we managed to save it."

I gave him my full attention, as an assumption I had been making ever since learning of my legitimacy crumbled. "*She* left you?"

The Duke nodded, his eyes distant. "She left me. I would not have left her for the world." The last sentence was so soft that I barely heard.

"Why did she leave?" I demanded.

"It wasn't her fault," said my father quickly. "She couldn't have done anything else."

"Then what happened? What did you *do*?"

The Duke turned his head to say a few words to the footmen, who hefted the painting again and made their way from the room. A maid came in before they could close the door, carrying a tray of food.

"You'd better eat," said the Duke.

I ate a thick slice of bread. It was a lot bigger than what I would have paid a half copper for, but this was soft, white bread, made from flour into which no sand or grit had been mixed. Then I had a piece of cheese, but I could only eat half of it, it was so rich. I ate a little slice of lamb, and then couldn't eat anything more. I hadn't been so full in years.

"Are you sure you don't want anything else?" my father asked, as I settled back in the bed, smiling in satisfaction at this feast.

"No, really, I couldn't eat another bite," I told him. Raven moved in eagerly on the remains of my meal. The rest of the piece of cheese disappeared, and a slice of lamb, then she curled up in sleepy satisfaction.

"You are my daughter for sure," murmured the Duke, but before I could ask what he meant by this cryptic comment, he asked, "Where did you come by a dragonet?"

"A what?" I glanced at Raven, startled. "Is that what she is?"

"Certainly."

"Are dragonets even real? I thought she was an exotic foreign creature."

"Well, she is exotic. Not foreign, though, she could easily be a British species. And they are real. They are a sort of natural, ah...supernatural creature, if you see what I mean."

I nodded, looking Raven over again. Raven was still so small that her body fitted in my palm, although her tail trailed and her neck stuck out. She stretched her neck out now and chirruped at the Duke, blinking her large golden eyes at him until he rubbed her under the chin.

"That explains...quite a lot," I remarked.

"I've told the servants she's an exotic foreign creature from the Americas," the Duke added. "Best if she's not seen outside the grounds, though."

I nodded, yawning, happy with the precaution. Satisfied with the attention, Raven curled up again and the Duke smiled at us both.

"Get some sleep. You're certainly not allowed up today," he added, as he left the room.

Just before my eyes closed, I realized that he'd never answered my question.

CHAPTER 9

Warrior

I woke with dawn's light filtering through the curtains. I'd had the postponed bath the previous day and the maids had successfully untangled my hair. I'd slept for most of the rest of the day, but now I jumped out of bed, pleased at how much better I felt.

My father had not been idle whilst I was recuperating. In addition to the servant's bell cord, a little hand bell now sat on the bedside table. I racked my mind back to my old life and tried giving it a little ring. In came my brand new lady's maid to dress me. Susie was only a few years older than myself, but highly accomplished. She had already found some old dresses in the attics in something like my size and having put me into one of these, she proceeded to do something incredible with my newly reclaimed hair.

I submitted to all this in a slight daze and hastened downstairs to escape the bewildering efficiency. Passing the disturbingly charred portrait at the head of the stairs, I met my father halfway across the hall. He was dressed for riding, had a crop in his hand and smelt slightly of horse.

"Are you going riding? Can I come?" I asked, recent illness, inexplicable hairstyle and unaccustomed skirts all forgotten.

"Fortunately," declared the Duke, "I am not going, I am coming back from. Perhaps you can come with me tomorrow, but we shall have to see." He spoiled the sternness of this latter declaration with a smile.

"Oh," I said, rather disappointed, then brightening, I asked, "Breakfast isn't finished yet, is it?"

"Breakfast is in fact my destination. And for that, you are most welcome."

He continued towards the dining room and I fell in beside him, almost literally, for I kept treading on the hem of my skirt, which was too long and would have been so even for a girl who had not been wearing breeches for the past four years.

He caught my final headlong plunge and laughed as he steadied me. "You'll be glad to hear," he said, as we helped ourselves to sausages and toast and several other tasty things that made my stomach rumble just to look at them, "that the seamstress is due sometime today. She's bringing a few of her needle girls too, so by the end of the day you ought to have clothes that fit properly."

I managed to control my madly chewing jaws long enough to say, "That will be nice."

Alban Ravena glanced at me again and covered a smile. "What's her name, by the way?" he asked, nodding to Raven, who had launched an assault on a sausage with similar fervor.

"Oh, she's called Raven," I said, taking the sausage away from the 'Raven' in question. "You can't eat all that," I said firmly, "your stomach simply isn't large enough."

Raven screeched angrily but didn't try to reclaim the sausage and soon curled up on my shoulder in a way that suggested she might just have stomach-ache. Whatever her uncanny intelligence, she *was* still a baby.

"What do you want to do until the seamstress arrives?" the Duke asked me. "This morning, I am at your disposal."

"Can I see the stables? And the kennels?"

"Certainly, but we'll have to wrap you up well."

I heard this with some trepidation and sure enough, I went out to the stables swathed in a ridiculous number of warm things, from hats and scarves to coats and cloaks. Mostly the maid's fault, although I felt pretty sure that if I hadn't looked like a woolly ball on legs the Duke wouldn't have let me out.

We were met part-way to the stables by what turned out to be the head groom, an elderly man, who limped slightly from one fall too many. "Ah, my Lord, I was coming to find you. I keep putting it off but it's no good. It's about Warrior."

My father's face fell. "How is he?"

The groom looked very uncomfortable. "We've given him special care for years, my lord, knowing how you feel about him, but he won't eat at all now, not even his special mash. Perhaps you could...look at him, my lord."

The Duke sighed and most of the happiness seemed to have leached out of him. "Yes, I'll come."

Warrior must have been an immense animal when he was younger, I thought, looking at the massive frame, now all but bare of flesh and horribly gaunt. He stood in a warm stall, head hanging. A blanket covered him and an un-touched bran mash still steamed faintly in a bucket.

I looked closer at the mixture and by dipping a finger and licking it, established that it was an oatmeal mash laced with syrup. If the old horse couldn't eat that, then it couldn't eat anything. I couldn't help dipping my finger a couple more times, for I had rarely eaten anything so tasty and nutritious since leaving my mother's house. Then I noticed the groom eyeing me covertly and desisted. I'd just eaten a good breakfast, after all.

Alban Ravena stroked the great, bony head and was rewarded with a faint, but undeniably affectionate, nudge. "This horse carried me into battle when I was younger," he told me quietly. "Kept me safe...fought better than I did," he added, with a shadow of a smile.

Now was not the time to ask eager questions about when and where he had fought in battle, so I kept my mouth shut.

"Let's try you with some grass, old fellow," the Duke said after a moment, but it was only with a great deal of effort that the old horse was persuaded to walk as far as the nearest pasture. Warrior lipped at a few blades of grass, but they fell from his mouth untasted, and he went back to standing with his head hanging listlessly.

One arm around the great muzzle, Alban ran his fingers through the thin forelock. "Very well," he murmured to the big horse, "you make yourself quite clear, old friend."

He swallowed and his jaw tightened. He glanced at one of the grooms standing by. "John, my crossbow," he ordered curtly. He glanced at me, "Go inside, child."

I failed to suppress a snort at that. If I'd met this old nag wandering owner-less down a street, I'd have cut its throat and had a feast.

The Duke clearly realized his concern for me was misplaced, for he did not repeat the order. He slid his arms around the horse's neck and ran his fingers through the patchy coat. "When I returned, I feared he might not remember me, after so long. I was very happy that he did. Ah well," he finished softly.

John had reappeared and wordlessly held out a crossbow and a pair of bolts. The Duke drew away from the horse to take them. He stuck one bolt in the ground, set the other in place and cranked the handle rapidly. Then, expression set, he placed the tip to the back of the horse's head and pulled the trigger.

The crossbow went off with a vicious *thwack* and Alban stepped back as the horse lurched, went to its knees and then rolled over to sprawl on its side. For a while the great hooves jerked, then they lay still.

Alban handed the crossbow and the second quarrel back to John. "Bury him between the oak trees on Gallant's Rise," he ordered, and strode off back to the stables.

I hurried after him, trying to think not of all that meat, tough as it might be, going to waste, but of my father's pain at losing an old friend, even an equine one.

CHAPTER 10

Mistress of the House

The first batch of clothes arrived from the seamstress, and my wardrobe began to look much less bare. More to the point, a riding habit now hung there. I had managed no more than two small meals a day to start with, but I had just managed three, and that had clearly pleased my father. In fact, I was feeling so much stronger that the Duke had said that I might go riding with him the next morning.

I could hardly wait and strove to remind myself that the fact that I would be put up on the oldest, calmest nag in the stables was really a good thing, considering my lack of recent practice. To be honest, even the thought of the gentle ambler on which I would sit in the morning could not dull my excitement. I hadn't really noticed, during my long fight for survival, but I had missed my horses.

I changed a few more things around in my wardrobe and shut the door. Springing across my bedchamber, I headed downstairs, already at home again in my skirts, now that they were at least the correct length.

After knocking on the study door, I paused a moment before entering, collecting myself. It hadn't taken me long to realize that I must do what I was about to do, but still, I couldn't help feeling ill at ease about the whole thing.

My father sat at his desk and smiled at my approach. He seemed to be taking Warrior's loss stoically enough, as far as I could see. If he'd been a little distracted now and then over the last few days, that was only to be expected. I'd heard all about the mighty, or once-mighty, Warrior from Anna, the housekeeper. The horse had been given to my father when just a boy, by *his* father, as a newborn colt.

I realized that I was eyeing my father rather scrutinizingly and quickly looked away, reminding myself that he was not my mother. I didn't even like to think about my mother having such a dear old horse shot, let alone doing it herself. There would have been gloom in the house for weeks. My father's attitude was clearly that his old friend had had a long, good life, which was now over, and what more could anyone ask for, human or equine?

I perched on the edge of the desk, for the study was not really designed for conversation, and drew in a breath. My expression must have been solemn, because my father raised an inquiring brow.

"I need to speak with you," I said in a bit of a rush. "I've been thinking, and I think it would be best if I...made a sort of confession."

The eyebrow went up a little further. "I am not a priest," he said neutrally.

"No, not for that reason, exactly. Just so that you know...the worst things that I've done. Just so that I don't have to guard myself night and day for...*forever*, in case something slips out that you didn't know about, and makes you angry...once you're...*used* to me..."

He returned my gaze seriously. "Perhaps you are right that it would be better for me to know all now. I will endeavor to be understanding."

I didn't find that last bit entirely comforting, but I supposed it was better than a rash promise of forgiveness; it showed he took me seriously.

"Well," I began hesitantly, "there's the lying. I've been lying for years. I've been telling everyone I'm a boy and my name's Serapion."

"I noticed," remarked my father. "Lying is certainly a sin, but so is stupidity, even if it is not generally listed in church. In this case, I think you were very sensible to lie. I am very glad you did. Of course, I speak as a parent not a priest. Go on."

I breathed a little easier. I hadn't expected him to be cross about that, of course, and in truth, it didn't worry me much, it was just habit to begin a confession with the small things. And I was feeling more comfortable, having begun.

"There's the stealing," I pressed on, "I've done some of that. When I was younger—when I was first on the street—I picked pockets most of the time, to survive. Siri...Someone taught me how." Even to my father, I didn't want to discuss Siridean. I didn't even understand what had happened in that garret room, and anyone who heard that tale would think me either mad or a murderer. How could they think anything else?

"It saved my life," I went on. "But eventually I figured out—with a little help from Father Mahoney—that I shouldn't really be doing it, not as an everyday thing. It helped that I was old enough by then to start getting the odd bit of work here and there. So the last year or two, I only resorted to it when it was a question of my life, when I couldn't go any longer without food, or I had to have a warm garment. Only then."

"I can see that," said the Duke seriously, eyeing my gaunt bones. "But I won't say I'm sorry for that. Theologically, there's never any excuse for sin—well, there are different opinions on when stealing is sinning, I suppose. But I shan't beat you for doing it to stay alive. I'd probably do the same. It would take a saint to resist in such extremity."

I swallowed slightly. It hadn't occurred to me that he might decide to punish me. I hoped that he was joking.

"One day I was carrying a man's bags at the inn," I went on. "I took them to his room and waited for him to pay me, but he just shut the door and grabbed me. Maybe he'd realized I was a girl, I don't know. He was a man, so you know what he wanted." I shot a look at my father. His expression was dangerous.

"I fought very hard," I continued, "but he was very strong and I couldn't get away. So I took out...a knife that I

68

had, and I struck him with it. I stabbed him in the chest because I was afraid if I cut him somewhere else he'd just be enraged. He fell down and moaned a bit and then he...stopped moaning. I didn't mean to kill him," I declared firmly, "but he was dead, so I did. I took my knife back and..." I hesitated, wrestling with myself, "and I took his purse," I admitted at last, "and I left. It wasn't the sort of inn where they'd be bothered about a body, and no one ever asked me anything about it. I was able to buy a cloak for winter, though," I added, then wished I hadn't, in case it gave him the wrong impression.

I shot another glance at him. His face was still grim.

He glanced at me when he felt my gaze. "I cannot scold you for this," he said quietly, "when I myself have killed, and at less provocation and with much more intent. It is lucky you did kill him though, or I would do so," he added under his breath. He hesitated, then went on, "as for the rest, stealing from the dead is considered in a very bad light, but it's really just stealing, and the man wasn't going to miss it. Not that it was right," he added quickly, "but considering what he tried to do..." He shook his head. "If you want an estimation of how much you sinned, go to a priest. I am not angry with you."

I breathed slightly easier. "I've confessed all this already and been absolved. Anyway," I said, opening my mouth to continue, and I saw a faint shade of horror flick through my father's eyes.

"There's more?" he interrupted.

I nodded, aware that as I was progressing from bad to worse he must be wondering what was worse than killing, even in self-defense. I told him about Master Simmons.

"He said there was this man who he needed dead, and if I'd do it for him there'd be some gold." Seeing my father's horrified look, I added quickly and somewhat angrily, "I said no! And I went and told the man that someone wanted him dead, and he asked who, and I...I pretended I'd forgotten. So he gave me money and I...remembered and told him. I saw

69

Master Simmons hanged a few days later. So I suppose I killed him too," I finished softly.

Alban Ravena closed his eyes for a moment. "You did not kill this Master Simmons. He killed himself by his own actions," he said firmly. "I hope you've finished?"

"Not...quite," I said. There was still the matter of Thomas.

"...And I just stayed ever so still and didn't make a sound to warn him. I knew they'd kill me if they found me," I concluded, feeling very small.

"Hmmm," said the Duke. "You feel you were a coward? Personally, I've always thought rash, mindless courage ought to count as a form of suicide. Suicide is one of the worst sins of all, Serapia, so you were right to avoid it. Please tell me that that is now all?"

I breathed entirely freely at last. He did not seem angry, and I had finished. "Yes, that's all," I said quietly, feeling drained. Well, it wasn't *quite*, but words about Siridean still stuck in my throat. Anyway, often as I might have wished that I'd been able to do something to help my ill-fated protector, I'd never blamed myself for his death. It wasn't something I'd *done* and therefore had no place in my confession.

"Good," my father said with obvious relief. "I'm not going to reproach you for any of what you've just told me, but your circumstances are very different now, you understand? No lying and stealing. Least, not unless it's terribly, terribly important," he added as a rather pragmatic afterthought. "Now, I've got something for you."

He opened a desk drawer and handed me a large bunch of keys. "These are for you to keep."

I gasped. The house keys! The housekeeper would have the second set, the everyday set, which she wore at her belt, but it was for the mistress of the house to keep the master set safe. I accepted them eagerly. They were heavy and there were a lot of them. My cheeks burned with delight, and I held the keys tightly with both hands. I was mistress of the house. Despite what I'd just told him... "Thank you," I said, trying not to let my voice wobble. "I'll take good care of them."

"I'm sure you will," he said, sitting back down behind the desk. Raven had woken from a post-dinner nap and climbed out at my collar, going to inspect the keys. Raven turned them around on their ring, one after another and I counted them. What a lot of locks. Certainly my father was a very rich man. But what else was he? I wondered abruptly.

"Surely," I said, "you should tell me your bad things, since I've told you all mine?"

My father gave a faint snort as if trying to pass it off as a joke, but he didn't look up to meet my eyes. "Really, child, I've accumulated nigh on three decades more misdemeanors than yourself, it would take far too long." He picked up a large ledger and opened it. He regarded it for some moments before abruptly turning it the right way up.

I was not to be put off that easily. "Then you could just tell me the very worst thing you've done. Then we'd be even."

A pained laugh escaped from the Duke. "Suffice to say, child, that I am not a good man, and leave it at that."

I eyed him for a moment. "You're not a bad man," I said, and it was more statement than question. I was sure that he was not.

He looked up at me, his eyes a tiny bit too bright. "I hope," he said quietly, "that I am not quite a bad man, but I am very much not a good one.

"Enough," he added more firmly. "Go to bed."

I felt indignant at that, for he had not seemed inclined to order me around like a child, but just then there was something in his eyes that made me, at any rate, leave him to himself in his study.

71

CHAPTER 11

Elfindale

My father's reticence on the subject of his own misdeeds niggled at my mind for the entire of the following day. Well, I didn't remember while I was out riding with him in the morning, being too happy to be astride a horse. By the end of the ride, I was trying to ignore my aching thighs.

Afterwards, I gave the ancient pony a carrot I'd tucked up my sleeve and concentrated on not hobbling as we walked back to the house for breakfast. The Duke watched me out of the corner of his eye with a faint smile that suggested he saw right through my pretence. But he didn't say anything. I was coming to the conclusion that it would be very easy to love this father of mine!

The Duke went into London after breakfast, to make some calls. I spent some time wandering around the house, although nowhere that would require too strenuous a use of my legs. I'd already explored the enormous library and now I found myself in the picture gallery. This was a long, narrow room with windows all along the outer wall. On the inner wall hung the family portraits. I walked along, staring up at my ancestors with interest. I even found a painting of the old fashioned (and much smaller) manor house which, judging by the landscape behind it, my Grandfather had replaced.

Eventually I came to an older portrait of my father as a young man, with an equally young Warrior looking over his shoulder. The horse had clearly not finished filling out yet, and both sets of eyes were bright and almost excessively lively. Were my young eyes supposed to look that bright? I knew that they didn't. They were dark and wary and showed little of my feelings.

There was also another individual portrait of my mother. I spent longest of all looking at this. It was perhaps not that surprising I'd found it so hard to remember my mother's face. Most of my glances at my mother had been stolen, swift glances when she was not looking at me. It gave me a pain inside remembering how it had always been.

When I was very young, I would be playing in the room where my mother sat and I would look up to surprise my mother watching my play with a loving smile. Only, the moment I raised my face and met my mother's eyes, the expression slid from Lady Ravena's face and she would look away quickly, sometimes leave the room entirely. It happened *over* and *over* again. Before long, I learned never to look at my mother directly, to keep my head down when speaking to her, and to only ever look upon my mother's face when there was no risk of my mother glancing around and looking on mine.

After luncheon my father spent most of the afternoon closeted in his study with the steward of his northern estates, those of which he was Duke. The steward had arrived that morning and by questioning Anna, I learned that he made the long journey once every six months when the Duke was in England and that many messengers went to and fro the rest of the time.

"So what are you *actually* Duke of?" I asked my father at dinner, after some gentle hinting about how much I'd like to hear his own confession, even in part.

Alban cocked an eyebrow at me, perhaps relieved by the subject change. "Ah, so you know that Duke of Albany is just some courtier's idea of a highly amusing joke? First inflicted on my father, actually, who bore it with a good grace. When I became Duke, I renamed this house. My father called it Ravena House, but it was one of the few things about which we never agreed. Seeing my name carved in stone every time I came through the gates always depressed me. So I renamed it Albany House, whereby you could say I have the last laugh with regard to the nickname!"

I laughed at that. I had not yet been through the gates while awake, and I had not known what the house was called.

My father seemed to realize that he had not yet actually answered my question. "Well, I'm the Duke of Elfindale," he said, in a tone of some amusement. "Which does not sound anywhere near so grand, does it?"

"How's that spelt?" I asked curiously.

"Why, as in The Elfin and dale, the geographical feature. One word. It's the name of my estate in the north, of course."

"Hmm," I said, eyes narrowed in thought, "so...are things like the Elfin real too? I mean, if dragonets are real?"

My father smiled a decidedly inscrutable smile. "Yes, child, the Elfin are as real as Raven, an ancient race, and generally one very uninterested in humankind."

"But where do they live? That is, there are forts on some farmers' land, those mysterious mounds that they leave strictly alone, but those are so small. They're not small creatures like faeries, are they? So where do the majority of them live?"

Alban smiled at me. "You are astute. Indeed, I believe the forts found on more isolated farms are no more than cottages or manor houses are for us, isolated dwellings only. Most of the Elfin are believed to live in much larger forts, far away from humans."

"Like towns!" I said. He nodded. "But where?"

"Why, in the wild places."

I mulled this information over for a while. The older I got, the more a certain suspicion had been forming in my mind. I had not paid Siridean's pointed ears much attention at the time, but his truly bizarre eyes had ensured that I had not forgotten either.

When the Duke began to direct an inquiring look at me, I pushed the thoughts away and shifted my attention rather

74

strategically back to the previous subject. "Why won't you tell me?" I demanded. "It can't be that bad. The stuff I told you was awful."

He glanced at me sharply. Raven retreated from his wineglass and started robbing mine instead. "No, it was not awful. It was awful that it happened to you, but you bore yourself throughout it in a way that was *far* from awful. The devil is certainly in no danger of finding himself with you on his hands!"

His dismissal of my own bad deeds stung. They had hurt enough when I was forced into them. "I still can't see why you won't say," I snapped. "I told you *all* of mine, and you won't even tell me your one worst. It's not fair!"

He jerked to his feet, his hand smashing down on the wineglass and sending it flying in broken fragments into the nearest wall. "Since when is *anything* in this life *fair?*"

The door slammed behind him with a crash that shook the crockery on the table.

CHAPTER 12

The Mirror

I sat for a moment in a frozen stillness, shocked by my father's sudden fury. Eventually I started to get indignant, but I pushed it down again. A crimson splatter marred the tablecloth, mingled with fragments of broken glass and a wider, pinker wine stain. It had been quite clear last night that this whole subject touched some very tender nerve in my sole surviving parent, so why had I pursued it so relentlessly? Simple curiosity, of course.

Or would that be selfish curiosity? Now that I thought about it, there was nothing unfair about my father's refusal to answer. I had chosen of my own free will to make my 'confession' to him, but nothing had been mentioned about a reciprocation. I was beginning to feel rather ashamed of myself.

I had no appetite to finish the meal, so I went in search of clean linen strips, a bowl of water and some ointment. Then I made my way to the study door and tapped gingerly. There was no answer, although I could sense quite clearly that my father was inside. I knocked again, harder, then opened the door anyway. Looking around it, I saw the Duke standing by the hearth, one hand on the mantelpiece as he stared down into the flames. He raised his head to look at me but didn't say anything, leaving it to me to speak. Did he think I would continue to pester him?

"I brought these for your hand." I held up the linen strips.

My father still did not reply, just watched me as I came in, shut the door, and went over to him. As I got closer I saw that his hand was leaving a little pool of scarlet on the stone of the mantelpiece. Blood dripped slowly into the flames below. I firmly took the hand from its high roost, set down the bowl on a nearby table and poured water into it. I wiped the blood from his hand as well as I could and led him over to the lamp so I could check for glass. I drew out one slender shard as carefully as possible, and when he still made no sound, I said abruptly, "I'm sorry I was so stupid. I think I must just be a little girl after all."

I positioned his hand back over the bowl and tipped a measure of brandy over it.

He drew in his breath sharply, almost pulling his hand away. "Is that *brandy*?" he queried incredulously, sniffing.

I nodded firmly. "Drunkards' wounds never fester, you know," I told him. "The ones who get the drink all over themselves. Everyone else's festers, but not theirs."

He pursed his lips thoughtfully and didn't tell me that I was a silly girl who had just wasted some very expensive liquor.

I dried the cuts with a piece of clean cloth, then bound his hand firmly with the linen strips and tied it off neatly. "Are you still angry with me?" I asked carefully, as I returned his hand to him.

He let out a long breath in something close to a sigh. "No. Of course not."

He set his hands gently on my shoulders to look down at me. After a moment his hand moved to lift my chin, and he smiled. "Your cheeks are filling out already. You look more and more like me. In fact," he said after studying my face for another moment, "you look *just* like me. She can't have liked that," he added softly to himself.

My heart seemed to freeze. "What?" I whispered.

He glanced at me quickly. "Nothing, child. Nothing."

But it wasn't nothing, and I knew it. I twisted away and ran.

"Serapia, I didn't mean anything," he called, coming after me. "You're very beautiful. I'm sure your mother thought so. I'm sure she loved you very much."

I stopped in the drawing room, in front of the fine wall mirror. I looked into its silvery depths and my father appeared behind me. It was true, I realized. Even gaunt as my face still was, I did look so like my father. A little feminized and a lot younger, but...

And that was it. That was why my mother could not look at me. *Why*, when *she* left *him*? How could it hurt that much?

My breaths came jerkily, quivering. "Why could she not look at me?" I whispered. "I was there for nine years, why could she see anything but me? God gave me this face, so it must be the right one! Why could she not see that?"

Tears were squeezing down my cheeks. A pair of strong arms encircled me and I buried my face against my father's chest and wept, while he stroked my hair and back and told me he was sorry.

When I finally felt better, and my eyes were dry, I found that he had sat down in his armchair and I was curled on his lap, face still pressed against him. I uncurled slowly and raised my chin to meet his eyes.

"Better?" he asked. I nodded. He hesitated, then said, "I think I have been alone too long. Things slip out. I'm sorry."

"Why?" I said rather harshly. "It was true. You didn't know that when you said it, though, so it's not your fault. She *hated* my face."

"No, child, she hated *my* face," said the Duke softly. "You, she loved."

I contented myself with a snort.

"Shall I see if Anna has some cake for us?" he asked after a moment.

I nodded, still feeling shaky and rather delicate inside. He rang the bell and spoke to the maid, and smiled at me again. I rested my head on his shoulder, absently fingering the back of his neck. Such bumpy vertebrae weren't as unusual as my mother's behavior had always led me to believe, for his were just like my own.

CHAPTER 13

Confession

When we arrived at church the following morning, the priest was waiting patiently beside the confessional, dozing on the bench that ran around most of the wall. I'd been pleased to hear that the Duke always confessed on Sundays before Mass, since it was high time I went.

"Father Francis," said Alban, "I'd like to introduce my daughter, Serapia."

The priest showed no surprise; apparently rumor, on its swift wings, had already reached him. He smiled and greeted me graciously. Though stooped with age, he was taller and less gaunt than Father Mahoney, but his kind smile and aura of holiness reminded me of him rather a lot.

"Shall I go first, child?" the Duke asked me.

I understood the meaning behind his question and nodded unhesitatingly. My father could explain the peculiar circumstances of my appearance and so save me trouble and awkwardness. Alban followed the priest into the confessional, and I crossed the nave's open expanse of flagstones, worn smooth by the standing feet of—centuries?—of prayerful (or restive!) Mass-goers but just now empty of people, and went into a side chapel to pray. I soon found myself distracted by the lovely, unfamiliar old church, and thoughts about my new life, and even the attention of that wonderful presence at the back of my neck could not entirely keep my attention from wandering.

When I went in, I suggested that I should give the priest the same confession I had given my father. "Though I've been absolved of it all," I hastened to add. "But I thought it might be useful for you."

"I have to admit, it would make it easier to look after your soul," the old man agreed.

So I went through it again. It was much easier this time round, to a priest, not my father. Then I made my latest confession. I hadn't got to confession very often as an urchin, so there was a backlog of little things, but it didn't take too long.

All the same, when I came out, I found the church almost full for Mass, and I joined my father immediately in his place near the front. I just had time to say my penance before Mass began, but I would have to do my thanksgiving later.

When the Mass ended, I followed my father to the rear doors, distributing coins carefully but liberally to the crowd of hopeful poor at the back. It felt rather surreal to be doing the bestowing, when so recently I would have been amongst the ragged press myself.

The better off of the parish stood around outside the porch, exchanging a word or two before going home for their Sunday dinner. I allowed the Duke to steer me to and fro with a hand on my shoulder, introducing me to those he received. It did not entirely seem to have any relation to their wealth or social standing, I noticed with pleasure, as he shepherded me from an Earl to a country gentlemen who really had 'farmer' written all over him.

Eventually I became aware of eyes on me and looked about for the watcher. He was a plain sort of man, but he was staring at me as I stood beside my father. I didn't remember seeing him in church. When I met his gaze and refused to look away he turned to speak to someone, but I felt sure they were talking about me.

"Who is that man?" I asked the Duke, as he finished his latest conversation.

Alban directed a hard look at the man indicated, then gave a negating jerk of his head. "No idea," he said, and hustled me off to meet the next acquaintance.

I looked around again for the man, but he was gone. I tried to push it from my mind. It was the most natural thing in the world. He'd seen me with my father and thought he knew that the Duke had no children so had stopped to ask someone about it. It was that simple. I just really hadn't liked that man, with his cold, staring eyes. He made the back of my neck feel odd.

When everyone had dispersed I explained that I needed to go back into church for a while, but my father seemed wholly unconcerned by the delay. In fact, when I got chatting with Father Francis again, he went on ahead, retreating to the side chapel to pray. He seemed rather better at it than me, in that he didn't seem to notice when I peeped in.

Rather than disturb him, I knelt at the main altar rail, and spoke briefly to God about my now relieved sense of guilt over my various misdeeds. The last few years had not exactly developed my eloquence, so it didn't take all that long, and I went to sit on the wall bench and wait for my father to finish.

The priest came out of the sacristy, back in his normal robes. He glanced at me, then went to the side chapel and looked in. "Oh dear.' He came back over to me. "He looks well settled into it. He could be hours, and I mean that quite literally. Did any of the servants come to church?"

"Most of them, but they've all gone back to the house."

"Oh. Do you think you'd feel happy walking back on your own?"

I laughed outright at that, before realizing that I was laughing at a venerable old priest and choking it off quickly.

Before I could frame an apology, the priest, with a wry expression, said, "Ah. Yes, I don't suppose it does bother you. Well, you may as well go, I think."

I ate luncheon in the Day Room with the Housekeeper and the Butler. It wasn't very proper; the Day Room was for those two upper servants' use only, and eating with the servants...well, definitely not proper. But my father wasn't back yet, and I couldn't see the point sitting alone in the big dining room. I spent an enjoyable afternoon playing with Raven for some hours, marbles and naughts and crosses and so on, and then wandering around the stables, looking at the horses and wondering which ones I could persuade my father to let me get astride.

By the time I'd dreamed around the kennels for a while, Raven began to get bored, so I went back to the house and enjoyed exploring the lower levels—at least until I came to a door near the kitchens. My nape prickled, and the closer I got, the stranger I felt. I stopped short of it, afraid I would vomit if I drew any nearer. Raven hunched on my shoulder, turned restlessly then hunched herself up again, looking as confused and uneasy as I felt.

I would normally have associated my reaction with the presence of evil, but what could possibly be down here that would warrant that? Here in the basement of Albany House? It was ridiculous. So after galloping up to my room to retrieve the house keys, I advanced determinedly on the doorway. I'd soon find out what was upsetting me...

I tried the keys just as fast as I could, for despite my intention to brook no nonsense I was very afraid I was going to lose my luncheon—or pass out. But none of the keys fitted.

"Oh, that door don't go nowhere any more, my lady," said a passing scullery maid, as I finally backed up a bit and stared from keys to door in frustration. "'Least, the key's lost and it's such a small cupboard now, Cook says it don't matter anyhow. Though I suppose," she added reflectively, "You could have a locksmith along, if you wanted."

"Where did it used to go?"

"Some sort of larger storage chamber, I think," said the maid vaguely. "One of his previous lordships ina'vations. But it didn't work out so well as most of them. I think it

82

collapsed, some years ago. Around the time... Well, it was bricked off, after that."

I groped for an explanation in all this. Hang on... "Was anyone hurt when it collapsed?"

"Don't think so, my lady. A workman died when it was being built, though. Cursed, that place was." She shivered, then looked slightly embarrassed. "'Least, that's what everyone says, my lady. Probably just foolish talk."

A man had died in there, no doubt untimely...and just how unpleasantly? No wonder it was giving Raven and me the creeps. At least it was all bricked off and locked up, so I'd never have to visit the chamber itself for any reason.

We retreated upstairs for a much pleasanter exploration of the great hall, and when, by dinnertime, my father had still not appeared, I put on my cloak and made my way back to the church. I was most of the way down the aisle when Father Francis came out of one of the side chambers and started. "Serapia! You made me jump! Are you after your father? He's still at it."

I went to the side chapel and looked in. As far as I could tell, my father had not moved an inch. I felt rather overawed. I liked to pray, but there was no way I could *sustain* it like that. Of course, perhaps he couldn't when he was my age.

"It's dinnertime," I said to the priest, "I thought perhaps I should... Well, I don't know. I don't want to disturb him."

However, something, perhaps the priest's sharp exclamation in the silence, had clearly broken the Duke's trance-like concentration, for stirring, he crossed himself, and stood up, stretching stiffly. He saw me, and his eyes flew to the dark windows. "Oh... Has it been *that* long? You haven't been waiting all this time, have you, child?"

His calling me child did not bother me, I had realized, because he didn't *treat* me as a child.

"No, I've been up at the house all afternoon," I reassured him. "I just came back because it's dinner time now."

He hastened out of the chapel to me. "I'm sorry, Serapia. When I get like this I completely lose track of time."

I was still very impressed. "What do you say? Or don't you? Do you just open your heart and let Him look around?"

Alban smiled a little at my method of expression, then his lips tightened as he answered dryly and almost under his breath, "Mostly I just weep for forgiveness."

Then as if he had not given this strange answer, he went on briskly, "Let us go to dinner. Goodnight, Father," this last to the priest, who blessed us and started to put out candles.

Dinner was a tasty leg of lamb and I took advantage of my expanding stomach and ate ravenously. Raven did likewise and then spent the rest of the meal draped over my shoulder, fast asleep. The Duke sat silently, his eyes glittering as he gazed along the length of the table. I could not help remembering my first judgment that he would make a bad enemy.

"I'm going to court tomorrow," he told me when we'd eaten our fill. "I trust you'll be able to amuse yourself?" His would-be casual tone caught my attention.

"Court?" My mind shook itself awake from the heavy meal. "Oh. I don't suppose you'll run into my uncle, will you?" I asked in a gently mocking imitation of his would-be casualness.

The Duke made a very gallant attempt at taking my words at face value. "It's possible, I suppose." He eyed the fruitcake as though trying to decide if he wanted a slice.

I gave up the pretence. "I don't suppose you're likely to *run* a few feet of your sword *into* his belly?" I challenged, watching him closely.

"Now why would I do that?" Alban said blandly, sliding the knife into the fruitcake.

"Can't imagine," I replied, "but if that's not what you're thinking of, then I can come too."

"Certainly not," he said rather too quickly. "You don't want to be bothered with court. *I* wouldn't be going if..." He broke off and transferred the cake to his plate.

"If you weren't going to challenge my uncle?" I asked sweetly.

"Don't be ridiculous," he said sharply. "If I hadn't been away so long, is what I meant."

"Well, I may as well come and be presented to the Queen and all that. I don't expect I *shall* want to go *very* often."

"I really don't think it's necessary," said Alban, then paused and crumbled cake between his forefinger and thumb for a moment. "Still," he went on at last, "you can come if you like, of course. I dare say I shall be leaving at about ten."

I pretended pleased triumph, and took a slice of cake myself.

When the Duke of Elfindale climbed into his coach at five to nine the following morning, he found me, correctly attired for a royal audience, already within. He sighed heavily and bade the coachman to drive on.

We were silent for some time, the Duke rather grim faced and absent-mindedly stroking his sword hilt, and me touching the beautifully set diamond and emerald pair that hung around my neck with something close to awe. It seemed my mother had taken only those jewels that had come to her from her own family, leaving all the rest behind. My father had now given these to me. It redoubled my curiosity about my parents' separation, for my mother must have truly hated my father to leave these behind. She could have been a very wealthy woman. I was certainly now a very wealthy thirteen-year-old.

Eventually the tiny ball of fear that sat stubbornly under my rib cage compelled me to speak. "You'd better not get yourself killed. If you die I shan't forgive you."

My father turned a look on me that I found myself entirely unable to interpret, but after a moment his face relaxed into a smile and he sounded genuinely amused, "I assure you, child, that is not my intention."

"Never mind intention," I muttered, "just don't let it happen."

He smiled again at my rejection of his reassurance. "Right is on my side, in this," he said, and went back to looking out of the window.

I turned my eyes to my own window but paid little attention to the passing scenes. Really, I ought to hate my uncle at least as much as my father did, if not more, but I wasn't sure that I did. I had just been too tired for the feeling to really develop properly, and now...now it didn't matter. I had won. I was alive and I'd found my father. I lived in a magnificent house with a constant supply of food and a warm, dry bed and although I hadn't really thought about it yet, one day my father's wealth would all be mine. My uncle suddenly seemed a small, greedy and grasping man.

A cruel, bad man, certainly, to try and kill his own niece, even in so indirect a way, but a small man all the same. Even the house didn't really bother me. I would never want to live in it again, for few of my strongest memories of the place were happy ones. I *certainly* didn't think that getting it back was worth putting my father's life at risk. Revenge was a bad motive, anyway, I knew that.

"Do you really have to do this?" I demanded.

My father turned his head to look at me and gave a fierce smile in which there was nonetheless more than a touch of sadness. "Yes, I do, Serapia. Justice demands it."

I wasn't quite sure what to say. The silence had become decidedly solemn. Seeking to break it, I picked Raven up and addressed her. "We're going to see the Queen, Raven, so you have to stay out of sight. Pocket or bodice, take your pick."

Raven disappeared head first down the front of my dress and I could feel her cool little body curled up between my breasts. After a few moments' silence, I couldn't help asking something that I had been wondering about. *"Do you have a mistress tucked away somewhere?"*

Alban Serapion Ravena looked excessively taken aback. *"What?"*

"Well..." I said meaningfully.

He stared at me for a few moments, apparently near speechless. Finally he said rather tersely, "It perhaps escapes your notice that until four years ago I was still a married man, and that I have since been travelling on the continent. I most certainly do not keep a mistress. A mistress is just a whore paid in jewels!"

I blinked at him for a moment. "Oh."

"You have a *really* low opinion of my sex, don't you?"

"Yes," I said bluntly.

"God above, I cannot believe I am discussing this with my thirteen-year-old daughter!" exclaimed the Duke and fixed his attention back on his window. Concluding that I had only succeeded in shocking and offending him, I decided to consider the conversation over, though I was more bemused than ever. What could his secret sin be, then?

Raven appeared to have gone to sleep, which was what I had hoped for. She was so small, she was easy to hide, but that brought to my mind another question I'd been meaning to ask. "Raven's a dragonet, so that's a baby dragon, right?" I asked. "So how big is she going to get?"

The Duke took his attention away from the grey streets and gave it to me again. "No, a dragonet is not, thank heaven, a baby dragon." His smile was very welcome. Perhaps I had not offended him too deeply. "A dragonet is a member of the dragon *family*, just as a lap dog and a wolfhound are both members of the dog family. A dragonet is a natural miniature dragon. A real dragon, well, it couldn't easily be hidden, they're too big."

I felt rather relieved. I'd been having an unpleasant image of Raven, grown to the size of a horse or even a carriage, and me having to sit on *her* shoulder. "And Raven?" I prompted.

"Oh, she may get to be about the size of a large cat. No more."

"How fast will she grow?" I questioned.

The Duke pulled a perplexed expression. "How can I know, child? I am not an expert. I have one or two books on supernatural creatures, one of which seems better than the others. Still, I think she may not even attain her full growth in your lifetime, so I wouldn't worry about it overly. They're very long-lived."

That was a relief. A cat-sized dragonet could still pass as an exotic foreign creature, whereas anything much larger and the truth would begin to be a bit obvious.

"She doesn't breathe fire," I remarked. "Is that just a myth, then?"

"No, of course not," Alban said with a laugh. "She's just too young. I'm pretty sure she will, in time. Fortunately not very much of it, though," he finished wryly.

"When?"

My father laughed at my eagerness. "I am not an expert, child," he repeated. "However, I believe they become physically mature long before they attain their full growth. Still, I should think it will be a number of years at the *very* least."

Finally satisfied that I had picked his brains on the subject as much as possible, I leant back to await our arrival at Westminster.

CHAPTER 14

Baron Hendfield

I was excited to pass through the palace gates, let alone step through those marvelously carved double doors into the royal presence. Pride filled me when I saw that my father entered the royal presence with his sword at his hip. Only those noblemen that had not only been called upon by the crown to provide levies, but had also led those levies into battle, could wear arms in the presence of the monarch.

I walked demurely beside my father as we approached the throne, the herald's voice still ringing in our ears: "The Duke of Elfindale; Lady Serapia Ravena."

Hmm, so I *was* a Lady. I'd wondered, since learning of my legitimacy. Then again, I'd always known that the title came straight to me from my mother. Although...maybe I would have been referred to as 'Lady' anyway, since my father was a duke.

I saw from the way the courtiers drew aside to let us pass, that my father was a powerful man, whether or not he chose to involve himself in the affairs of the court. I couldn't help feeling slightly relieved. I had been a little worried that my uncle, with his constant dabbling at court, might actually have more influence, but clearly it was not so.

Speaking of the devil, or in this case, his minion, there stood my uncle, near to the dais, but at the back of the throng, staring thunderstruck. Then I was past him and concentrating on making the most graceful curtsey of my life.

"Ah, Elfindale," a regal voice declared, "always pleased when you deign to grace us with your presence."

My father responded to this double-edged greeting with another bow, so I kept my eyes on the floor. Whatever his position and wealth, I knew my father held his power only at the sufferance of this woman.

"This your daughter? Look at me, girl."

I straightened my backbone and lifted my chin to meet the sovereign's eyes. They were blue and clear, and the woman herself, although heavily made up against a few encroaching wrinkles, was not old.

"Yes, little need of an introduction to know who she is. Come up here, dear Alban, and explain this ordeal she is rumored to have been through. You too, dear."

My father and I approached much nearer to the dais, and, still standing, of course, my father gave the Queen a succinct and unemotional account of how I had come to be in the gutter, and how I had come to get out of it again.

Glancing at the two of them, I saw that the Duke was calm and at ease in this highest of company, though very respectful, and that the Queen listened as attentively as any woman hearing a juicy tale. It was easy enough to read. The two were on good terms, and any small pique on the Queen's part at the Duke's infrequent visits to court was tempered by an awareness that he would not be so interesting if he were yet another groveling face among the courtiers. I breathed a little easier as that first comment from the monarch shrank into its correct place as an habitual grumble and nothing more.

"She is rather young to be at court," the Queen commented, when the tale was told.

"She wished to be presented to Your Majesty, nothing more," the Duke said calmly. Only then did it occur to me that most of the girls at court were after husbands. Certainly I was much too young for that!

"Well," the Queen was saying, "I shall not detain you a moment longer, since I see your brother-in-law is making for the doors and I'm sure you'll want a word with him."

Alban's head lifted like that of a hound that has caught a scent and with a low bow, he headed for the Baron, who had become cornered by the Queen's Lord Chancellor, rumored to be an extremely astute man.

"Hendfield," snapped my father, as, rudeness or not, the Baron attempted to break away from the Lord Chancellor in the direction of the door. My father caught up with him quickly and the Lord Chancellor walked away, smiling to himself.

Trapped, the Baron attempted to smile at the Duke, his eyes darting wildly over me.

"I'm sure you'll be glad to see that Serapia is safe and well," remarked the Duke in a dangerously pleasant tone.

"Oh yes." The Baron simpered in a sickening manner. "So pleased to see you found her. She just ran away, distraught, you know, because of my sister. So tragic. Can't tell you how hard I've been looking for her."

"I wager you can't," said the Duke, much less pleasantly, "because you didn't look at all."

"Didn't look? Of course I looked. My dearest, dearest niece. I am overjoyed. Come here, my dear." He made a determined effort to kiss my cheek, clearly considering it a cheap price to pay to get away from the Duke's anger. I dodged, partly in disgust and partly to avoid having Raven pop out and bite my uncle on the nose.

My uncle hesitated in his attempts, then caught the Duke's eye and stumbled forward again, as though convinced that getting his lips on my cheek would protect him. I dodged once more and Alban gripped the Baron's shoulder tightly, stopping him from following. "I'm afraid that my daughter gives a rather different version of the story."

"I tell you," exclaimed the Baron, "she was mad with grief. Couldn't reason with her. She ran right out of the house the day her mother died, and I've not turned up hide nor hair of her since."

"Your lies are not making me feel any better disposed towards you," remarked the Duke in a dispassionate voice, his eyes hard with anger.

"I tell you," said the Baron more stridently, clearly desperate to convince his brother-in-law, "the little witch child has been nowhere to be found!" Seeming to lose his head completely at the look in the Duke's eyes, he blathered on, "I even searched the *whorehouses*..."

My father's hand dropped gracefully to the hilt of his dagger. Smoothly, the dagger slid a full inch from its sheath, then I clamped my hand around my father's wrist, arresting its progress. His face was like stone and his eyes were drowned with rage. Fortunately, he did not try to break my grip on his wrist, and I stood on tiptoe to hiss in his ear, "*He did not kill my mother!*"

Alban drew in a breath as though I had struck him and swung around, his back to the Baron, jaw rigid and eyes momentarily aghast before he closed them for a long moment. Finally he looked down at me.

"How did you get so wise?" he asked, then with no more ado, he spun around and his fist connected solidly with the jaw of the Baron, who was in the process of sidling away. The Baron flew a remarkable distance, but his landing was cushioned by an ample matron, in whose skirts he became entangled. As the matron strove to eject the unwanted encumbrance from about her person, the Duke touched my head gently.

"Thank you, child," he murmured. "It is better to observe the formalities."

He made light of it, but his cheeks were a shade too pale.

The Baron was not a brave man, but he was even more afraid of being known throughout the entire court for a craven than he was of the Duke's sword. I watched him warming up, my expression sour. According to every story I had ever read, a bad character such as my uncle ought to be either short, fat and helpless, or gaunt, emaciated and weak. He was neither. He was a little on the short side but not particularly podgy or particularly slow with a sword. Not especially fast, either, but I had seen too much of the world to assume that my father's superior skill would definitely win. In a duel, anything could happen.

The duel was to take place right there in the throne room. The Queen wished to watch and had no inclination to go and sit in a cold practice court. Servants had swiftly rolled back the rugs from the floors, and a sword and dagger had been fetched for the Baron, who had never led anyone anywhere. Both noblemen had stripped off their outer tunics and ruffs, and began stretching. A few courtiers had firmly sent their wives home, sure there would be blood on the ground, but most were grouped eagerly around the open area, packed together to achieve the best view. I was honored with a place near the dais, where I was not jostled, which was something.

As my father crossed swords with the Baron and they waited for the Lord Chancellor to bid them begin, I feared that the thunderous pounding of my heart would wake Raven. Then in a sudden burst of motion, the duel began. My father had snatched out his dagger as well, so that he held bare steel in each hand. My uncle looked wrong-footed by this, for he was no soldier and had learned to deal with only one blade at a time. Thus he was on the defensive from the start, parrying constantly, no sooner blocking a stroke of the Duke's sword, than that gleaming dagger would dart in towards his stomach, necessitating another frantic block or a retreat.

It was quite clear from the start that quarter formed no part of the Duke's intentions. It must have been clear to the Baron too, as he stumbled backwards to narrowly avoid another flashing sword stroke that would have slit him from rib to hip, only to be nearly impaled upon his enemy's dagger.

Soon the Baron was sweating heavily, like a man who had not practiced as much as he ought and who was sinking in fear. My father was light on his feet and barely perspiring. He practiced every day.

I suspected that with the immediacy of the threat posed by the Duke's sword, the Baron was beginning to revise his idea of what he feared most. Blood ran down his left arm from a nasty gash, and even as I watched, the Duke's sword glanced across his thigh in a stroke that would have all but taken off the leg if it had struck squarely. Hendfield's breathing became ragged, more than a hint of a sob audible. I watched his constant backward flight and his trail of blood emotionlessly.

Perhaps I don't hate him as I have a right to, I thought rather distantly, *and that's good. But I feel no pity for him either. Pa can kill him, and I shan't care.* I stopped and only just swallowed a smile. *Pa. I have a Pa.*

I hope my Pa is doing this for justice, though. Not just for revenge.

I turned my attention firmly back to the matter of life and death in front of me. The end came suddenly. With a flurry and a gasp, courtiers dodged as the Baron's sword came shriiinging across the flagstones into their midst. The Baron remained frozen for a second as the Duke raised his sword for a final blow.

You'd better yield, you fool, if you want your life, I thought.

Completely unmanned with terror, the Baron went even further than that. He *flung* himself to his knees and actually seized the Duke's legs, sobbing something incoherent and shaking with terror. I very nearly looked away in disgust and didn't bother trying to imagine my father acting in such a manner. What was wrong with a graceful knee (one knee only, of course) and a dignified, 'I yield'?

The Duke looked near revolted and freed himself from his opponent's grasp with a none-too-gentle kick. His sword tip darted down to touch the Baron's throat as the Baron scrabbled backwards, slipping in his own blood and ending flat on his back. I wanted to cover my eyes. Enemy or not, the man was, most embarrassingly, related to me.

"Do you yield?" demanded the Duke of Albany in a decidedly pitiless voice. Apparently that had not been what the Baron had said, either that, or the Duke hadn't been able to interpret the words either.

"Yes, yes, I yield," gasped the Baron.

"And do you freely acknowledge before all these witnesses that you tried to bring about my daughter's death?"

The Baron turned slightly purple; apparently his fear of public humiliation wasn't entirely gone. But a poke of the sharp metal at his throat reminded him that his choices were limited. "Yes, I acknowledge it," he growled, face paling again.

"Tell them what you did," demanded the Duke.

The Baron tried to speak, choked, coughed and finally said, "I, I put her out of my house..." He flinched as a trickle of blood appeared on his neck. "That is, her house," he amended hastily.

"On what day?" prompted my father mercilessly.

"On...on the day her mother died," the Baron whispered, but the shocked murmur made it clear that he had been heard.

For several more, long moments, the Duke went on looking down at him, then, finally, after what must have been an age for the Baron, he turned away with a sound of eloquent disgust, beckoning a pageboy for a cloth to wipe his sword.

The Baron, left alive, which he probably had not expected, might reasonably have been grateful, at least to divine providence if not to my father. But humiliation was a very powerful spur. The thought leapt into my mind as the back of my neck prickled and my hand flew instinctively to my dagger. The hilt seemed warm and eager for my touch.

The Baron whipped out his own dagger and, launching himself from the ground with a powerful thrust of hands and feet, flung himself towards his adversary's unwary back...

Only to jerk to a halt and stand motionless for a long moment, staring in stunned disbelief at the plain, unadorned dagger that had sprouted through the palm of his hand.

I folded my hands together demurely and hoped that no one had seen where the dagger had come from. Small hope of that, any eyes that were not on the Baron were on me.

The Duke had been spinning around even as the dagger sailed through the air, though he would have been too slow to save himself, and he raised his sword towards the Baron, who finally seemed to drag enough attention from his impaled hand to see his danger. He stumbled blindly backwards, hand still clutched in front of him, and for the second time in minutes slipped on his own blood and landed flat on his back. The Duke stepped up and set his sword far less gently to the Baron's throat.

"You have my full permission, dear Alban. I have never seen such a shocking display of cowardice. And after you showed him mercy, as well!" The Queen's collected tones broke the silence, and the Baron's gasps of pain turned to gasps of terror as the Duke's knuckles whitened on the hilt of his sword. Dampness spread over the Baron's breeches.

Perhaps my father also saw this, for after a moment, with a noise of utmost contempt, he bent down, yanked the dagger from the Baron's hand, wiped it clean on the Baron's expensive velvet coat and walked away. The Baron promptly fainted.

The Duke walked over to me and handed me the dagger. "Thank you," he said softly. "My reflexes these days..." He broke off, his mouth twisting, and turned away.

I flushed at his thanks and tucked the blade away, glad to have Siridean's dagger back and gratified that he did not mind me displaying my unladylike skill in public. I took his slighting of his own reflexes with a fond pinch of salt. They seemed pretty good to me.

"I believe we are expected to forgive even the worst wrongs done to us," the Duke said grimly to the court at large, clearly in explanation for the Baron's still-breathing condition. "Besides, I believe I have rarely been so revulsed in my entire life. Even were our Lord's commandment not so clear, I could hardly bear to shame my sword with his blood." The Baron was stirring weakly and flinched at the court's unrestrained laughter.

"Baron Hendfield," said the Queen sharply, her voice cutting off all other conversation, "you will return Lady Ravena's house and belongings. Anything that you have sold, you will replace with another of like value. Do I make myself clear?"

"P...p...perfectly, Your Majesty," whispered the Baron, still clutching his bloody hand, but when the Queen had looked away, I sensed his hate-filled gaze on me.

CHAPTER 15

Witch Child

I rested my head against my father's shoulder on the way home, rather shaken by how close we had come to disaster. My uncle's deranged attack could all too easily have succeeded. I myself could have missed, even with Siridean's dagger.

Still, they were all might-have-beens and what *had* been was on the whole, rather satisfactory. As for the Baron...

"I probably should have killed him," said the Duke abruptly after a while. "It would, no doubt at all, have been perfectly *just*. Yet...*unforgiving*. I can't make up my mind."

"You seemed fairly decided at the time," I replied, "but I was wondering the same. He's a live enemy."

"You think I should have killed him, then?"

"No, not necessarily. I mean, we *are* supposed to forgive..."

"Well," said the Duke, "it's not of much matter. With the orders from the Queen herself, he will scarcely dare do other than obey."

The Duke tucked his arm around me and we sat in silence for a while, watching Raven scurrying and leaping around the coach in great high spirits.

"You know, this seems familiar," said my father after a while, looking down at me with a smile of gentle amusement.

"Yes, doesn't it, Pa," I replied, watching to see how he would take his new title.

He smiled. "You didn't call me that last time. In fact, if I'd put a foot wrong I think you'd have stabbed me."

"Oh! Then, the dagger; you knew?"

"I knew you had it fairly early on."

My cheeks heated. "I haven't been carrying it because of *you*. Not since...not since I was ill. I'm just used to having it." I hadn't had any idea he knew about my dagger, or I would have made this reassurance sooner.

"For which I am very grateful," said the Duke in a humorously devout tone.

We sat in silence for a while, but eventually I could no longer hold the question back. "Pa? My uncle...why did he always call me witch child?" Watching my father's face closely, I felt emboldened to add, "And devil spawn, he sometimes called me that, too."

The Duke sighed dismissively. "Oh, that. Don't worry about it, child. It's an old slander directed at our line by the ill-meaning, dating from long before you or I were born. And what truth there is in it has nothing to do with the devil. As most acknowledge. No, child, it is a very old slander and no one pays it any heed."

I nodded, "Umm, everyone was listening and no one seemed worried."

"Quite. Because there's nothing in it."

I sat in silence, reassured, but still wondering. I'd always assumed my uncle called me that because of the strange things I felt. But it was just an old slander and nothing to do with me.

"Why does he hate me so much?" I asked eventually, in a rather small voice. "He's *always* hated me."

The Duke's face hardened in a way that suggested he was regretting his merciful urge more and more. "He always hated *me*," he replied curtly. "Called me devil spawn behind my back, trying to stir up trouble. You, I fear, have inherited a double, even triple measure of his ill feeling, for you are my daughter, your very existence takes his sister's property from him, and in time my own fortune will make even that look a pittance.

"In short, old hate, greed, and envy, an unwholesome mix that he seeks to conceal from himself and the world behind the empty words of a tired slander." The Duke spat the final words with such disdain that I did not venture to ask anything more. What he'd said matched with my own memories of my uncle, anyway.

After a moment, with a clear determination to lighten the subject the Duke remarked, "It's Christmas soon."

"Christmas?" I said wonderingly. "I can hardly remember. S'been six years since I had a Christmas."

He gave me an inquiring look. "*Six* years?"

I tried not to look crestfallen. "The year before, Ma was ill at Christmas. She had a wasting disease, you know. I mean, she could get about and all, but...I tried to get the servants to decorate the house a bit, but she wouldn't have any of it." I could not express my childish disappointment, my confusion at the unexplained change to the order of my world, nor the creeping fear at my mother's hopeless dejection, her complete loss of heart and lack of effort.

My father looked so pale I felt sorry I'd mentioned my mother, but as he met my eyes I couldn't help feeling that he did, in some measure, understand.

"Well, I promise," he said gently, "that if I am ever struck by a wasting disease, Christmas and everything else will go on as much as normal—as is humanly possible—until they're nailing down my coffin."

First my mother and then Siridean, and Father Mahoney too...the very idea of losing my father... I gave him a quick, fierce hug. "You're *not* going to get a wasting disease," I whispered with savage determination.

He turned his attention to his window, perhaps regretting his poor joke, but as we passed along Paternoster Row, his eyes lit on something. "Ah, toffee apples." He banged on the ceiling. The coach drew to a halt, and he pushed back his curtain to purchase two of the sticky treats from the stallholder.

My mood improved as I felt the toffee on my tongue, still sticky and warm beneath its cooled crust, and bit into the sweet, juicy apple. Due to the science of a toffee apple's anatomy, I also had the added bonus of seeing, long before we reached home, my father as sticky as a schoolboy.

I trimmed my candles against the night's dark and tried to attend to the book in my hand. A servant had arrived earlier from Baron Hendfield to start arranging the hand-over of the property, and my attention was rather lacking. Raven was amusing herself dipping her paws in the ink well and walking back and forth over an old sheet of paper. She started to get quite artistic, and distracted or not, I spared the occasional appreciative murmur and finally suggested that Raven show her work to my father; then hastily seized the dragonet and cleaned her feet before she could bound across the rug and up the armchair with inky paws.

Raven ran onto the Duke's shoulder and inserted her piece of parchment in-between his eyes and his book. The interruption was taken with good humor.

"Very nice, Raven," Alban said. "I'm not going to try guessing what it is, although it does look rather like an artistic rendering of a particularly fine game of 'round and round the Mulberry Bush'."

Raven sat there, head on one side, tail twitching, and seemed quite at a loss to decide whether she'd just received a compliment or not.

"I'm sorry she's using so much ink," I said after a while, rather absent-mindedly.

The Duke laughed. "No matter. What's on your mind, anyway?"

"Oh, it's just the house, you know," I replied. I opened my mouth to continue, then stopped as a really rather embarrassing realization struck me. "Oh."

"Oh?"

"Yes. Oh. I've just realized that I've been rather a silly fool. You're Ma's husband so...it's not my house, is it? It's yours."

"Ah," said the Duke, the slight lines of strain appearing around his eyes as they always did when we spoke of my mother. "Well, you're right that's the usual thing. But she left the house to you, along with everything else. She wouldn't have wanted me to get my hands on so much as a tea spoon. Of course, if I wanted, I could hire a good law clerk and they could no doubt eventually untangle everything in my favor. But your mother's wishes are quite clear. The house is yours."

I felt somewhat relieved. I didn't *need* a house, but...

"I was wondering," I said, "were you going to give me some sort of allowance?"

He gave me a mildly intrigued look. "I imagine so. I hadn't noticed you needing money just yet, that's all. Why the sudden curiosity?"

"Well, nothing urgent," I said. "It just occurred to me that I could turn the house into a home for urchins, but I'd need to employ a certain number of people for that."

"And you want to pay the wages from your allowance?" inquired the Duke, with a slight smile.

I couldn't help blushing. I might be a Duke's daughter, but I still knew I was talking about a very respectable allowance, especially if I was to have *any* money for myself.

"I'd make it as self-sustaining as possible," I said slightly defensively, my mind already teeming with ideas. "But that wouldn't cover everything, and not to start with."

The Duke smiled again, a rather secretive, knowing smile this time, and stood up. "Come into the study and let me show you something."

I followed dutifully. From his desk he picked up a sheaf of parchment and began flicking through it.

"The house was your mother's main possession," he told me, "but there were one or two little things, the most significant being a small area of land from which she received most of her income." He drew out a document. "This also belongs to you. I think it would supply you with ample funds to start and maintain your home. I'll still give you an allowance, but that will be for you."

I took the parchment and held it near the hearth in an attempt to make out the heavy, legal English. The figures were easier to read, and they delighted me.

I really would be able to turn it into a home!

CHAPTER 16

Grace

The following morning I took advantage of my father's post-breakfast retreat to his study and made my way down to the church. The purse containing the first installment of my new allowance nestled in my pocket. I was pleased and slightly relieved to find Father Francis on his own.

"How can I help you, my child?" the old priest asked, when I sat beside him on the wall bench.

I rubbed the fat little purse. "I was hoping to have some Masses said."

"Of course," the old man replied. "Naturally. How many were you thinking of?"

Determinedly, I set the entire purse in his hand. "As many as this will cover."

Father Francis hefted the heavy purse, looking startled. "It is Masses for the *dead* that you want, child?" he exclaim-ed rather incautiously. "Surely you do not feel that your mother..." He stopped abruptly as my face froze.

I bit my lip, struck by a wave of guilt. I hadn't even *thought* of Masses for my mother! "It...wasn't my mother I was thinking of," I admitted in a low voice. "But of course, I would like..."

The priest held up a hand to pause my stumbling words. "A Mass is said for your mother in this church every week and has been for the past four years," he informed me.

I nodded my satisfaction with this, feeling much better. Of course my father would not have overlooked such things.

"And what is the name of the person you would like Masses said for?" the old man asked gently.

"Siridean."

"Siridean," echoed the priest. "That's an unusual name. Are you, ah, in some doubt about his state of grace?" He glanced meaningfully at the full purse.

I bit my lip again. "He helped me," I said rather haltingly. "I think...I think he saved my life. I don't think I'd have survived without him. But then he...died. And..." I frowned fiercely as I wrestled with the memories of something that had never quite made sense.

"Well, I don't think he was very well," I said at last. "I think he'd done bad things, *really* bad...but, I don't know how much was his fault."

The priest gave me a narrow look. "Not his fault?"

I took a breath. "I think he was possessed."

There, I'd said it. I'd thought about it over and over again; the memory of the look he'd turned on me and the feeling of pure evil that had filled the room had never left me... It didn't explain how he'd died, but I'd long since concluded that it was surely the only explanation for the rest.

I feared Father Francis would laugh at me, but after looking at me for a moment, he just asked softly, "Did he hurt you?"

"*No!* No, he took care of me. He was kind! He wasn't *bad*, I'm sure he wasn't, but..." I hesitated, as confused as ever, thinking about it. "I just want him to be *all right*," I whispered at last.

Father Francis laid a soothing hand on my head. "Now, child," he murmured. "Our Father in heaven knows the true worth of each one of us. You may let your Siridean rest safely in his hands."

I nodded jerkily. "But you will say the Masses?"

The old priest smiled. "Of course, child."

I sank back against the cool stone wall for a moment. It felt as though an old weight had been lifted from my shoulders. *Pray for me*, Siridean had requested, the *only* thing he had asked in return for his care and teaching and worldly wealth, and I had, over the years, diligently. I'd always longed to have Masses said too, but you had to provide an offering for the priest, who could not, after all, live on air, and I'd never had any spare money. But now I finally did.

After a moment, I rose to go but stopped abruptly. "Father, *you* must know why my mother left?"

The priest lifted his hands in gentle protest. "Now, my child, anything I might or might not have had in confession I cannot pass on, you know that."

But something about his expression made me think that he did not truly know. Had my father's explanations to him on that subject never been what you might call complete?

I did not miss the concern that mingled with the perplexity on his face. "Did he do something?" I asked softly.

Father Francis shook his head at me. "I do not know, child, I do not know."

CHAPTER 17

A Horse of my Own

On the whole I could not decide whether to be aghast or relieved. Every room of my childhood home had been re-decorated in some overdone approximation of the latest fad. If someone had led me in blindfolded, I would scarcely have realized that this was the house in which I had grown up.

And it was for the best. I felt a bit treacherous somehow, to think that, but think it I did. I could look at these rooms without pain, without memory sharpening in my mind. What I had on my hands was merely a useful building on Aldersgate Street, not a place with which I had any emotional connection.

I was halfway down the stairs when another thought struck me and sent me running for the stables.

Tulip!

I reined in my run as I approached the stables, admonishing myself sternly. *She won't be here*, I told myself. *She was too valuable.*

Still, my heart was in my mouth as I circled the stable courtyard, looking into one stall after another. But no little dapple-grey mare stood prancing eagerly within. I sat on the mounting block for a moment to recover my equilibrium. So, Tulip was gone and had long been carrying some other keen youngster on her back. That was that. Tulip, too, had long since been mourned and forgotten.

Wait a minute... I stood up and brushed down my skirts, before moving back to the last stall and looking in again. *I say!* A giant stood within, giant and black, like a Warrior in his younger days. Or perhaps not quite, for this animal's mane was extremely long, and the gaze that was turned on me was steadier. 'Velvet,' said the name plaque on the stall door.

This one, I would give to my father.

My urchin home came into being with surprising speed and lack of hassle. My father helped me interview people for the various positions, and after only a brief tussle with my uncle over the last four years of rents from my mother's land, I was able to fit out the house as necessary. My father sent the ancient ambler he had originally inflicted on me down to serve as a first horse for the would-be grooms to learn on, claiming that the animal would like to be doing something. Soon, with all the staff and furniture installed, I set about filling the place.

Urchins were suspicious, if not outright paranoid, and usually with good reason, but it was still easily done. I went into rough areas with a carriage full of bread and soup (and an army of hefty footmen, my father's doing), playing the empty-headed, naive, well-meaning rich girl, my silk dress all the disguise I could possibly need. No one recognized me. I babbled amiably as I distributed the food, and when I came back day after day, the urchins were soon waiting for me.

I told the girls all about how this great new home was firstly for girls, and how if they knew any they should tell them where it was, since all they had to do was turn up at the front door. Feeling superior to me, feeling they had triumphed over me by concealing their true gender, and so extracting the precious address, the first few girls quickly arrived at the door of the home.

When all the girls were gathered in, I filled it up with boys, although a boy would always be demoted to a day attender if another girl were to come to the door. Soon the place was heaving, especially during the day, and I hastily took on more servants to teach (and control!) them all.

~+~

108

I looked with keen attention at the passing streets. My father had been very mysterious about the purpose of our outing today. When the carriage turned into Smithfield I held my breath, hardly daring to hope—it was the day of the horse market. The carriage drew to a halt.

"A horse! Is it a horse for me?"

"Indeed," he said, with a touch of amusement for my enthusiasm.

I could barely keep myself in the carriage until my father had dismounted, and I scarcely touched his hand in descending. A horse! A horse of my own again!

I took my father's arm demurely, giving him a shining smile that brought a gleam of pleasure to his eyes.

"You're having a gelding, by the way," he informed me.

"I am already quite decided on that."

"I had a mare before," I pointed out, but I wasn't concerned.

"Yes, and from what you tell me I can scarce believe Isa...your mother was so foolish as to let you have such an animal."

"Well," I said, unable to entirely suppress smugness, "Ma wasn't exactly a judge of horse flesh. If it stood still while she was looking at it, she assumed it was quiet."

To my surprise, my father laughed at this confession. "I won't," he told me, making me laugh as well, and we started to walk along the lines of horses.

I knew better than to choose a horse by color. All the same, I had to admit that after seeing my father's new horse, that gentle giant with a flowing mane and tail, as dark as Warrior, my imagined horse did seem to have a black coat.

"We'll look at the blacks," said my father, when I admitted my preference to him.

Pleased, I walked with him along the line until we found a black, but we both looked at it and pronounced it no good. The next was far too big, the one after that, would you believe, too small. Sway-backed, fat and lazy and ancient followed, until finally we saw a very fine animal, which even

109

early in the day as it was, ought to have been attracting attention already. It was jet black all over with one single white sock.

I went eagerly to look at it but saw the way its eyes followed the hand I reached out towards its nose. I glanced at the horse trader and saw that he looked anxious, chewing his lip. No doubt he wanted to sell the animal very badly but feared trouble if a young lady should be bitten. I withdrew my hand and seized its head collar instead. With a firm grip on that, I stroked its nose. It eyed me in distrustful anger, but I sensed its fear. Surely ill-treatment, not natural ill-temper, was responsible for its bad habits?

"That one's no good," my father said firmly, and tried to shepherd me on.

"We can look at it," I urged him. "It's not the worst we've seen."

Indeed, its conformation was the finest yet.

"You'll have the lazy one before this one," Alban replied, but he obligingly ran his hands over the strong back and fine legs. "Too big," he said dismissively after a moment.

"Not by much," I pointed out, "and I'm going to grow."

"Not this one," said the Duke more firmly, and taking my elbow, led me on.

I couldn't help glancing back as we looked over another mediocre black. I saw a rough looking man stop to examine the horse; he had livery stable written all over him. The horse snapped at his hand and he struck it hard across the nose with his crop, making it toss its head and scream in pain and defiance. I could see its fate all too clearly. One of these livery yard owners would buy it for less than its worth and it would be hired out to all and sundry, whipped more and more until it was too vicious to keep, or until its spirit was broken.

I realized that my father was waiting for my opinion of the current black. "This one's useless," I snapped. "I don't know why we're even looking at it." Most of my pleasure at choosing a horse seemed to have evaporated.

110

The Duke looked at me rather closely but walked on with me without saying anything.

It took us until gone midday to finish the market, and we didn't find anything that satisfied either of us.

"Oh well," said the Duke. "We'll try again another day."

I hesitated. "Couldn't we walk round once more?"

"Again? Any of the reasonable ones will be gone by now..."

"...just a row or two?" I pleaded.

"All right," sighed the Duke with more than a suggestion of resignation.

The biter was still there, being restrained from trampling the latest livery yard owner under its fine hooves. The horse trader beat it into submission with his own whip, while the prospective buyer dusted off his cap.

"See, man, who's going to buy a nag like that," he told the trader. "I'll give you three guineas, and that's generous." His eyes said clearly that once he had finished with the horse it would carry anyone on its back and he would have got himself a bargain.

The trader looked all too tempted, but his eyes fell suddenly on me and my father, strolling along the lines in his direction.

"I'm holding out for at least four," he prevaricated.

"Blue murder, for a vicious beast like that," claimed the yard owner.

I went to take the horse's head collar again and the yard owner caught my shoulder. "Hey, watch it, miss, that's not a little girl's horse."

I shook him off angrily and seized the head collar. "I'll give you five guineas for him," I told the trader, whose mouth fell open.

The Duke sighed softly. "You really want this one?"

I bit my lip and nodded.

"Fine," said the Duke and turned to the trader. "You wanted four guineas, here they are." He dropped the coins into the trader's hand. "Sort out a bill of sale and we can be off."

The yard owner elected not to try and compete with a Duke, and took himself off. The trader gave the Duke a guardedly sour look for dropping my price but made no demur. He would've ended up selling for three to the yard owner.

I stroked the horse's nose, a firm grip on the head collar. "What's his name?" I asked the trader.

"Hellion," said the trader reluctantly, "I thinks, anyway. Chap also called 'im Hellfire, so you can takes your pick."

"Hmm," I said, and would have taken charge of the horse myself, only one of the footmen, beckoned by the Duke, appeared beside me and took control of Hellion, if that was his real name. I followed eagerly as the footman led the horse away; my father stayed to sort out the practicalities of the transaction.

By the time I'd seen Hellion securely tied to the back of the coach and the footmen were nursing their bruises and glowering from a prudent distance, the Duke had not arrived. I headed off to look for him, unperturbed at navigating the bustling market alone. I spotted him halfway to the coach with...my step paused and I slipped casually behind a nearby pony and peeped over its back.

My father was speaking emphatically to the staring man from the churchyard, the one he'd denied knowing. The man had a markedly disrespectful expression of supercilious disbelief on his face, and the Duke looked angry. My father finished the conversation with what looked like several very hard words indeed and an eloquent hand movement that I wouldn't particularly have liked directed at me, and strode off. The man looked sullenly after him before stalking away in turn.

I slipped between two cart horses into the next alley and walked as fast as I could back to the coach, slowing to an amble as soon as I came in sight.

My father was already there. "Not having second thoughts already?" he teased.

I smiled a rebuttal and let him hand me into the carriage.

"Dear me," said the Duke, as we drove home. "I have never made a worse purchase in all my days. We haven't seen its paces, haven't backed it, and we know it bites and kicks and it's called Hellfire! I unreservedly apologize to the shade of your mother; I have just lost any right to call myself a judge of horseflesh."

I let him grumble, looking out the window to check that Hellion wasn't savaging the footmen—and trying to put my father's deception from my mind. *Perhaps it's just some slightly disreputable associate he'd rather you weren't exposed to,* I reasoned to myself. Though if the man were, I didn't think the association was proving very amiable...

Satisfied that the coach was moving fast enough for my new horse's attention to be sufficiently engaged on the task of keeping up, I sat back in my seat and gave my father's hand a consolatory pat. "It was me who wanted it," I reminded him.

He smiled at my comforting tone, but his expression became firm. "You're not to get astride that beast until I say you can, do you understand? The animal may be completely unrideable. Five guineas, indeed! The yard owner was right; it *was* worth only three. Next time perhaps I *will* make it a surprise."

I patted his hand again and smiled. "If you'd surprised me with a horse, I'm sure it would've been a lot finer than anything we saw today."

The Duke sighed, perhaps somewhat mollified, at least until we drew to a halt at Albany House, and a sharp, "*Zounds*, watch it!" came from the back of the coach.

"The grooms," he said to me, *sotto voce,* "are *never* going to forgive you."

I winced.

113

CHAPTER 18

Of Bolts and Brandy

I had accompanied my father on a call to Bride Well that day because the people he was visiting had several daughters near my own age, and he had clearly hoped that I would be able to strike up a friendship with them. In truth, I had gone to please him more than from any real hope in that direction. I had long since called on my childhood friends, those that were in London, and been called on in return, but such calls had already petered to nothing.

I had nothing to say to butterflies like these, I thought glumly, struggling to maintain an expression of polite interest as the oldest of our host's daughters described in exhaustive detail the love note she had received at a ball the previous week, before finally producing it from her bodice with affected sighs.

My attention was wandering, and the back of my neck prickled slightly, uncomfortably. I ascribed it to boredom and blinked, trying to put the sensation from my mind. Despite my best efforts, my ears gravitated to the adults' conversation, helped by the mention of a familiar name.

"...And that Baron Hendfield, you know him, of course, Alban," said the lady of the house, with a little titter. "Well," she became more serious, "it's looking like there's little doubt about it. The rumors are true. He's vastly overspent—that'll be through living off what was not his own—and now he can't pay his debts. Nothing's out in the open, yet, but unless he can get an informal loan from someone to pay off the moneylenders, he's for the debtor's jail a'fore too long."

My brows drew together. That again. I could go nowhere without hearing the rumors of my uncle's troubles. It was getting on my nerves. It was like seeing a vicious stray lying in a gutter with broken legs. It might have bitten you, but you still wanted to either help it or put it out of its misery.

Would my father give my uncle the money to pay off his debts, strictly as a loan, of course, but an informal one that could be paid back gradually? If anyone could sort out my uncle and set him fair on the path of his unexpected second chance, it was my father. I had to admit that my motives were not the best. I just felt sick of hearing my uncle's name all the time. My father would have to be pretty sick of it, too, to give him any money. But he might be.

He didn't look greatly enthralled by the turn of the conversation, rubbing the back of his neck absent-mindedly, and as the speculation continued, he excused himself to leave. Delighted at this unexpectedly early escape, I politely withdrew from my own circle and joined my father at the room door, my mind still on that human dog of the gutter, my uncle.

"It's very good for one's soul to help an enemy, is it not?" I asked my father a trifle musingly, as we walked towards our carriage, which was waiting opposite the house in the square outside St Bride's church.

He glanced down at me and half-smiled. He looked away again, as if to hide it, and I saw the sharp jerk of his head as something caught his eye. The next moment he cannoned into me, throwing me violently forward. Even as my reeling mind tried to identify the 'thwack' sound that still echoed around the square, he was pushing me onwards, and I hastily threw myself behind the nearest carriage. He was beside me in a moment, leaning against the coach, his breathing heavy and catching slightly.

My mind went near blank with shock as I saw the crossbow bolt that protruded from his upper left arm.

He reached up swiftly and snapped the shaft off, throwing it away and catching my shoulder again with his right hand. "Run to our carriage," he ordered, "*run*, now..."

I had already sprung forward, hearing him following me, and not needing his breathless, "weave, weave," to do so. Despite the precautionary weaving, I ran as fast as I possibly could, skirts raised clear of my flying feet, not blind to the fact that by running immediately behind me, he was effectively using his body as a shield. I made to spring up the steps and through the nearest carriage door, but my nape positively *seared* and I pulled up short with a convulsive, wholly instinctive jerk, gasping as another bolt smacked into the door just in front of me.

Without further hesitation, I turned and dived between the horses' legs, reaching the far side safely. To my huge relief, my father was right behind me.

"Into the carriage, stay on the floor, that's right..."

He crawled in after me, staying low, and reached up his uninjured arm to lift down his crossbow. The horses were no longer armored, but the rest of the coach hadn't been touched. I quickly chose a slender bolt from the box and offered it to him. He took it with a grim smile of thanks and got on with the awkward business of loading and cocking a crossbow with one wounded arm while lying on the floor. He managed surprisingly well and carefully poked aside the curtain with the quarrel tip and peeped out.

"*Where are you...?*" he whispered, then said to me, "prod that curtain above you with a bolt."

I did as bidden, keeping my head down, and jumped as another bolt thrummed through the window and clean out the other side.

"Got you." The Duke set the crossbow butt to his shoulder. He sighted along the weapon with eyes utterly hard, and his hand closed on the trigger.

A terrible choked off cry came from across the square, but the Duke simply held out his hand for the bolt I held and reloaded the weapon.

"Swap places with me," he told me quietly. "Keep your head down."

I obediently switched with him and again prodded the curtain now above me. A bolt cracked into the wood of the coach wall and the Duke's weapon thwacked in almost the same moment. This time the scream was drawn-out and long, but it finally ceased.

"Stay down," cautioned the Duke, then banged on the wall of the coach. "Richard, are you all right?"

The coachman's reply came swiftly. "Aye, m'lord."

"Home, then. Fast as you can."

Only once we were well away from the square did the Duke allow me to sit up, and even then he reloaded the crossbow, applying the safety latch and putting it beside him on the seat. There was no color left in his face, and his entire left sleeve glistened wetly. I hastened to look at it.

The head of the bolt was still lodged in my father's arm. "Shall I try and get it out?"

He shook his head, bracing himself with his other hand against the swaying of the coach. "No, we'll do it when we get home."

"It ought to come out as soon as possible," I persisted.

"Yes, hence..." He cocked his head forward, where Richard's whip was most unusually audible.

I yielded and lifted my skirts to reach my petticoats, from which I cut strips with my dagger. "If you read stories, this is the only apparent reason why the women wear these things."

He smiled a little tautly at this, and I bound his arm to try and stop the bleeding. When satisfied I'd done all I could for the time being, I sat back in the seat.

He did not look happy. "I'm a cursed fool," he said, more to himself, but at my inquiring look he gritted his teeth and expanded, "I assumed there was just one and that he wouldn't have had time to reload. It's only by God's good grace that the second was a bad shot, or one of us would not be here."

I snorted, "I think you managed everything perfectly. How did you even know?"

"I saw the first one standing by the corner of an alley. I wouldn't have noticed, but he held his arms up to fire and that's not a normal position for anything else I know of."

I stared at the makeshift bandage, quickly turning crimson. "He was aiming at me, wasn't he?"

My father nodded. "Yes, I think so. But they were after both of us, hence why there were two. We came out sooner than they expected; they weren't ready. I'd guess the second one wasn't cocked. The first was, unfortunately, but at least the bolt missed the bone..." He trailed off with a grimace. He would have lost the arm, I knew, and probably his life with it.

"Do you have any enemies?" I asked him quietly.

He shook his head. "I've been out of the country three years, and out of London for most of a decade before that and never inclined to enemies even before *that* thanks to my disinterest in politics. I'm afraid that this enemy I have inherited—backwards, so to speak—from you."

"My uncle," I said.

Alban nodded. "Your dear uncle."

My dear dead uncle, I thought grimly. I could see that my father was kicking himself for leaving the man alive, and I too had underestimated him. Or overestimated him, depending on how one looked at it. My father would not make that mistake again, of that I was certain.

"So he wants us both dead, so he can have Ma's property back?" I queried my father, sure I was right but wanting confirmation from an older, wiser head.

My father nodded. "Aye. And it makes me wonder... I have no near relations, you understand, with the single exception of yourself. Could he have somehow hoped to lay his hands on the rest of my estate through his relationship to you? It's possible. But in truth, from the sounds of things, his difficulties are extreme enough that he might have thought only of your mother's things. He should have paid more on

118

the assassins, though I doubt he would have even if he had the money."

"Well, I'm *glad* he didn't have the money," I said.

"Oh, so am I," replied my father with feeling, then added rather wryly, "I would wish that he'd had even less."

When we got home we immediately turned our attentions to the removal of what was left of the crossbow bolt from the Duke's arm. Anna dithered so much at this evidence of violence that I delegated the acquisition of bandages and ointment to her and took over. Eventually I had to use a pair of pliers to get a grip while my father held the back of a chair, white-knuckled.

"It's not barbed," he told me through gritted teeth, "so it can come out the way it went in. Now stop being so gentle with me and pull it out or give me the cursed pliers and I'll do it!"

Nettled, for all I knew that his anger stemmed merely from discomfort, I set my teeth, got a good grip, and yanked with all my might. It came out with a nasty sucking sound that almost masked my father's long drawn-in hiss of pain. For a moment, he said nothing, as if he did not trust himself to speak, then, finally, he remarked, "There, that wasn't so hard, was it?" His voice only shook a little.

"It's all very well for you," I grumbled as I went after the brandy bottle across the room, "you've been in battle and so forth. I didn't want to make it worse." I bore the brandy back to where the housekeeper was dabbing frantically with a piece of clean linen, trying to stem the fresh flow of blood.

Relenting, the Duke told me, "You did a very good job. I'm sorry if I was a bit harsh. It was fine to give it a good yank, you see, for it was nowhere near the vein, but you could not know." He noticed what I was carrying and winced slightly, "Oh Lord, protect me," he said with near seriousness.

I gave him a pleading look.

"Oh, all right then," he said resignedly and wrapped his fingers back around the chair.

I tipped a good measure of the brandy into and over the wound, making him flinch and take deep strained breaths. His pain was so obvious that I found myself casting my mind back, seeking greater certainty that this torment did actually help. But it *did* seem to. Somehow, it was better than water for keeping wounds free of infection. I took the bottle back across the room to give him a chance to suppress his gasps.

"That must be very good for my soul," my father sighed, as soon as he was able to un-grit his teeth.

"I'm sure your soul is fine," I retorted, but my father did not reply.

I helped the housekeeper bandage his arm in an uncomfortable silence, but it was not uncomfortable enough to quiet my anxious thoughts. A wound like my father's, if it became infected, as it all too easily could, would kill even the strongest of men. My stomach knotted at the thought and something must have shown on my face, for my father said, "If it will make you feel better, you can tip that cursed stuff in every time the bandage is changed, all right?"

I was touched that he would volunteer for such torture just to alleviate my worry, but I wasn't going to spurn the offer. "Then I will," I declared, and laughed at the glum look he shot to Anna.

"That's better," he said when he heard the laugh. "I've had worse than this before now, you know."

CHAPTER 19

Acorns and Willow

"It's very good for one's soul to help an enemy, is it not?" I asked my father a trifle musingly, as we walked towards our carriage, which was waiting out in the square with several others.

He glanced down at me and half-smiled. He looked away again, as if to hide it, and I saw the sharp jerk of his head as something caught his eye. The next moment, he cannoned into me, throwing me violently forward. My reeling mind tried to identify the 'thwack' sound that still echoed around the square, even as I clutched him, trying to support him as he slumped to the ground. I flung myself down beside him, trying not to see that bolt, that deadly bolt protruding from his chest. His head had fallen sideways and I brushed aside a tangle of black hair, calling his name desperately. His eyes were open and glassy, and they stared lifelessly through me.

I awoke screaming soundlessly, my hands batting at the enveloping blankets as though they were what might have been. I emerged at last into the faintly moonlit darkness of my bedchamber, breathing raggedly and trying to quell the sobs that rose in my throat. Raven ran to my shoulder and rubbed her face against my cheek, crooning softly in comfort. I raised a hand to stroke her cool aliveness, struggling to get my breathing under control. A dream. Just a dream.

That could so easily have been.

I swallowed hard, struggling to push it away. But the memory of that glassy stare was not going to leave me quickly and foolish as it was, the dream had left every nerve screaming that my father was in danger. After some minutes, it became too much, and I got out of bed and put on my chamber gown. I wasn't sure I wanted to risk going back to sleep just yet, even if I could. And I just wanted to check.

I stopped and bit my lip. My father was fine. A dream was just a dream and the danger it spoke of was past. But still, his arm must be hurting him; he might not be asleep. Perhaps I could get him something.

It was a good enough excuse, anyway, and I hurried out into the corridor without any further ado. Raven wound herself in a fold of my gown and lay down, for the night was cold.

I reached my father's room and knelt briefly to check for light under the door. Nothing. I would not knock and wake him, then. I turned the door handle as quietly as I could and peered in. It was dark, but enough light from the cloudless full moon outside seeped around the curtains to illuminate the room dimly. I could make out my father's form in the bed, his breathing deep and steady. I could smell willow tea in the air. Willow tea was the best thing for pain, I knew. Releasing a breath I had not even known I was holding, I backed out of the room and closed the door silently.

Burrowing under my own covers, Raven cupped to my chest, I felt increasingly furious with myself. Reason and the evidence of my eyes had shown me that there was nothing whatsoever the matter, yet the feeling of dread continued wholly unabated.

"I'm just going for a stroll this morning, stretch my legs," my father told me. "You can ride Hellion, but the head groom must ride with you."

"I'll take Hellion out later," I replied, "and walk with you now."

So we strolled gently around the gardens, a groundsman sauntering some distance behind with his yew bow over his shoulder, thus removing the need for the Duke to carry the heavy crossbow.

"He'll probably know by now that he's failed, and he'll know that we'll know it was him," my father told me gravely. "He'll be truly desperate and he may try again. We must both be very careful."

"For how long?" I inquired meaningfully.

"Until my arm is better," replied the Duke, significantly.

We walked along the top of a steep, long rise. An oak tree stood at each end, and the Duke stopped under one of them and crouched down. Staring rather absent-mindedly at the house, his fingers picked up one acorn after another, quickly discarding most of them.

"What are you doing?" I asked, after watching him for a moment.

He started and looked quickly at the acorns. "I'm just finding one that will grow strong." He picked up one from the small pile he'd been keeping. "See how healthy this one looks?"

I pursed my lips as he took his acorn and continued along the rise. Certainly it looked healthy, but so did all the others and he hadn't been *looking*. I crouched down and picked up an acorn, turning it in my fingers. This one seemed all right—I put it aside. This one looked a bit rotten. That one looked very good; a perfect specimen...but as soon as my fingers touched it I somehow *knew* that it was rotten, rotten inside, in the core, and it would never grow. My fingers recoiled from it. Did the back of my neck prick slightly? So. That must be it.

I rose and walked on after my father, my heart pounding with sudden excitement. It was not just me then, in the whole of anywhere, who felt these things. My father must feel them too. But I didn't say anything. Even if my own experiences hadn't impressed it so firmly on me that such things should never ever be mentioned, my father's evasion made it clear that he also did not want to speak of it.

My father had paused to bury his acorn carefully in a little rockery that stood in the middle of the rise. It looked quite new, so I guessed that we stood on Gallant's Rise. But we walked on in an easy silence, without any mention of Warrior.

I pondered as I walked, though. My father spoke with certainty of the existence of elfin and dragons, and I rather thought he shared my strange senses. Perhaps I *could* tell him about Siridean. Might he even be able to explain what had happened, how Siridean had died?

But no sooner had the impulse formed, than it withered again, as long-held caution reasserted itself. What had happened with Siridean was so very, very...strange...and ultimately very, very incriminating. The two logical conclusions were surely that I'd imagined it all—that I was insane—or that I'd killed him myself—and simply sought to cover it up with an outlandish tale.

Surely my father would not think either—I'd told him all the worst things I'd done, after all...

And yet.

And yet quite apart from my life-long conditioning to *never, ever, ever* mention anything at all uncanny, the thought of planting even a seed of doubt, a seed of distrust, in my father's mind was too horrible.

I wasn't risking my new-found relationship with my father for something that was past and gone. I'd lived with the not-knowing all these years. I could go right on not-knowing.

CHAPTER 20

Sacrifice

Christmas Day dawned clear, crisp and fine. We rode out together before breakfast, as usual, and the horses' hooves crunched in the frost. We didn't talk much as we rode, for my attention was wholly absorbed by Hellion. Only the other day he'd seen a swishing branch from the corner of his eye and clearly thought it a whip, for it had been a mile and a half before I'd been able to pull him up. He was fast though; it had been quite a ride. I didn't want to let him get going like that today; it was too slippery underfoot.

His last owner must have been some young idiot who thought brandishing a whip and having a horse that sweated and plunged looked good. I quelled my anger for this unknown individual, who named his horse Hellion. All the same, by and large, I was able to keep him under control, and when we got back to the stables, my father commented, "You've not had him long, and he *is* improving."

I was still glowing when we went to church—confession before Mass, for Christmas had fallen on a Sunday—and afterwards I was a trifle relieved, when I finished my post-Communion prayers, to find my father sitting on the bench waiting for me. More often than not, he spent at least half of Sunday lost in prayer, and he gave me a slightly wry smile for my surprise.

We had a fine goose for Christmas dinner, and I actually caught the Butler licking his lips as he served the meal. The Duke ran a traditional household, and the servants would feast on what was left, unlike some households, which were starting to cook separate—and vastly inferior—meals for the servants. I did not approve of that.

When we were both full of goose and Christmas pudding, and Raven was actually giving tiny snores from my shoulder, we sat in the living room and exchanged a few little presents. Before long there was a knock on the door and the servants, their own Christmas dinner finished, filed in to receive their gifts. I gave my maid Susie a pair of silk handkerchiefs, for she was an excellent maid, despite my having had to ask her to do my hair rather more practically, since it kept falling out mid-gallop.

Later in the day, I drove down to the urchin home to oversee the distribution of several crates full of oranges, one per urchin, including day attenders, which caused great joy. My father accompanied me, bringing a sack which turned out to contain raisins! Profligate indeed, there being minor gentry who could not afford such delicacies.

I'd been supervising the home closely but from a distance, and I was very pleased that already the first, least immoral boys and girls had been placed as stable boys, apprentices, scullery maids, and sewing girls, and managed not to disgrace themselves, and more importantly, the home.

In the evening, we sat by the fire and took it in turns to read favorite passages from books, eating a few raisins ourselves. That was, until, after being enrapt in a particularly gripping extract, we looked back up to find that Raven had emptied the dish.

My father, I thought a few days later, after catching sight of some papers on his desk, was a true subscriber to the idea of not letting the left hand know what the right hand was doing. He being the right hand, and I the left.

I'd known he was involved in charity, but not the extent. Already I had seen papers listing the impressive sums of money with which he endowed various charitable institutes each year. And I knew that he was the sort of benefactor who was as much a curse as a blessing to any less moral institutions, for he visited one each week to check where the money was going. But now I saw the details of a very reasonable acreage on the far east of the city, beyond the Tower, which he was, and clearly had been for some time, engaged in covering with almshouses. I looked at the designs and approved.

"Have you got your nose in my papers *again*," inquired my father from the armchair beside the fire in a rather long-suffering tone, without raising his head from his book.

I flushed slightly and moved away, but remarked a trifle slyly, "Nice little houses."

He made a dismissive noise and continued to ignore me. I smiled to myself. He was so delightfully modest about his charitable works. I couldn't help poking him a bit.

I took my set of keys from my belt pouch and shot him a look.

The clank drew a glance from him. "What are you carrying those around with you for?"

"I was afraid there might be one missing."

"One missing?" he echoed. "Why ever would you think that?"

"Well, I was giving Raven things to count; it's a sort of game," I explained, "and I suppose it's good for her learning. And I had her counting the keys. She likes doing it because she gets to turn them on the ring, one at a time, and I saw the rusty marks on the ring, where the keys had been lying for a long time before you gave them to me, so I had her count them.

"I wasn't really paying attention, but she began to make a fuss, so I counted them myself, and I saw what was bothering her. There's the mark of one key on the ring that's not *on* the ring, if you see what I mean. It looks far too recent to be the one for that spooky old storeroom that was lost years ago. So I'm afraid *I've* lost one, but I can't think where."

A rather long silence greeted this account, then after a moment my father blinked and raised his head. "Sorry," he apologized for his inattention, before saying succinctly, "Safe key, child, it's the safe key."

"Oooh," I said, understanding. "Of course. Good. *What my mother would have said if I'd lost a house key...!*"

The Duke laughed at my relief, and I laughed with him. But Raven glowered so sullenly at Alban that I almost began to fear she might, rather belatedly, be getting jealous.

I glanced again at my father. The fire and the candelabra beside him threw him into sharp relief and he looked thinner than he had been. No doubt his wound accounted for it, that and the winter's cold. My dream niggled still, but that was ridiculous and I refused to dwell on it.

Perhaps I'll have a word with the cook, I thought, smiling to myself.

I stroked Raven's little crest as Susie brushed my hair. The three little pointy ridges were growing sharper. I might have to start being careful not to cut myself.

My mind drifted. It was a Sunday, and we had been to church earlier, as normal, and chatted with our local acquaintances afterwards. I could not help remembering the staring man. He had been there again, looking at me. I didn't think my father had seen him; he had been in a rather technical conversation with a learned gentleman that had been quite beyond my comprehension, hence my wandering attention. But the staring man, he had not been in church, I was sure of it this time. It was silly to let it bother me, but...I really didn't like that man.

Susie had laid down the brush, so I shook myself and bade her good night. The maid left, and I knelt by the bed for a while—*my mother...my father...Siridean...the poor*—before climbing in and blowing out the candle.

I woke with a start. It was pitch black inside the curtains of my bed and I stayed still, listening, wondering what had woken me. I heard a slight scuffing sound, like a shoe on a rug. There was someone in the room. Was it Susie, having forgotten some small task and hoping to complete it before morning? My father, looking in on me with paternal fondness? Surely not, the quality of the silence told me how late it was, or rather, how early. Then I realized Raven was pressed against my neck, shaking. It was a stranger. An assassin?

I reached out to my bedside table for my dagger, just as arms thrust aside the curtains and seized me. I drew in the breath for a scream, cursing inwardly. There were nearly two score other people in the house, my very first action should have been to scream, not reach for a weapon. Now a hand wrapped around my mouth, choking off any sound. I tried to bite it, struggling, but when the hand slid away to evade my teeth, a rough piece of cloth was slipped in instead, like a bit into a horse's mouth and knotted tightly behind my head, pulling my hair painfully. Now the only sounds I could make were ineffectual indeed.

I still had one hand free, and I used it to grab Raven and stuff her down the front of my nightgown. Raven would certainly attack this man without some alternative instruction, and one blow of a man's fist could smash her fragile little body. Then that hand was also seized and as I was dragged free of the clinging curtains, I realized in horror that there was more than one of them. When I kept up my struggles, my arms were twisted painfully behind me and I was dragged stumbling across the room. A hooded lantern was opened slightly, allowing some light, and I recoiled violently as I recognized the staring man from the churchyard.

I flailed about, desperate to somehow make noise. Kicking out with my legs, I struggled to send a table or chair crashing to the ground. The staring man, lantern in hand, calmly kicked me in the knee with painful precision and my leg buckled under me. Forced to hop on one leg or be dragged, I knew that all hope of making noise was gone. I would have freely admitted that I was terrified. But puzzled as well. If my uncle had sent these men to kill me, why were they bothering to gag me? That suggested they were kidnapping me.

Of course. My father was an extremely wealthy man, and my uncle must know perfectly well that he doted on me. This *was* a kidnapping. My uncle might give me back if my father paid the ransom, but more likely he meant to keep me as a permanent source of revenue. He was a fool to try it, for my father would surely destroy him the moment I was either recovered or beyond recovery, but that didn't change what was happening.

We had reached the bottom of the stairs by then and I had a sudden thought. Raven! Raven could fetch my father. But how to tell her? I felt Raven run down the inside of my nightgown and drop from the bottom, to streak away into the darkness, her grey form invisible, and to my relief, unnoticed. It was not the first time I had suspected my pet of being a bit of a mind reader, but I had no thought for it then. I was too busy wondering where they were taking me.

I'd expected them to hurry me out of the nearest exit, but they were taking me down, down to the basement. We went past the kitchens and I felt a flash of hope. My leg was recovering and if we went in there, I might be able to kick over a stack of pans large enough that someone might still hear.

But we did not go in, we continued along the subterranean passages, past storerooms and the servant's dining hall, until finally we stopped outside a door. I frowned, my nape crawling. It was *that* door, the one with the lost key, the one where the workman had died...

But the staring, lantern-carrying man produced a key and put it into the lock. It turned stiffly, but it turned. I almost stopped struggling as a terrible thought hit me.

The safe key! There was no *way* my father would have kept the *safe* key on a ring of keys that rust proved had lain in a drawer for years and years, a location no doubt known by every house maid who had ever dusted or cleaned in that room. When he'd opened the safe to give me my mother's jewels he had taken the key from about his person and I'd wager that was where he'd always kept it. There *was* still a key to this storeroom and *he* had it.

But how had my uncle gained a copy? My thoughts grew increasingly desperate as I was dragged through the door. Well, it had lain in that easily accessible drawer for years, I reminded myself, that was no mystery. But why had my father lied to me?

This rather plaintive question died in my mind as I saw that we had entered not a small storeroom, or even a larger storage chamber, but a passage. No doubt it ran to outside of the grounds, perhaps to London. What father of a young (or not so young) daughter would put such a key in her hands, or even wish her to be aware of such a passage's existence?

I breathed more freely with regard to my father, whom I prayed would soon be racing to my rescue. I found myself calculating in my head how far Raven might have gone. She was fast as a mouse, but it would take even the fastest mouse some time to reach my father's bedchamber from the hall. Now she might be racing along the upstairs corridor, I thought, as we continued our swift journey along the passage. Now she might have reached his door, but how could she open it?

Did she know of, or could she find, any mouse hole through which she could fit and so reach the inside of the bedchamber? How long would it take her to find such a hole? How long would it take her to wake my father and make him understand he must follow her? Then I felt a sudden pang of fear for my father. There were three men here and would he even pick up a weapon, or would he assume some sudden illness or accident had struck me and rush out after Raven unarmed?

And where was this passage *going*? I'd assumed it would lead to somewhere beyond the park walls, but if it did, it would have to start going upwards soon. We must be deep down below the grounds by now, yet the passage showed no sign of rising. Finally we reached another solid wooden door and passed through it. We were on a balcony, along which I was swiftly led to where a flight of steps descended a short way to a large, circular, dome-ceilinged stone room. Maybe it really was some sort of innovative storeroom, or had been once. There were two more men there, but I recognized this with only a flicker of dismay, for I was too busy taking in the room itself, a room that struck horror to the core of my being and made my stomach churn. My nape felt like it was being crushed in a vice.

Blood red tapestries adorned the walls, depicting unearthly beasts doing depraved, unthinkably violent things to people. A wooden table...no, an altar, stood in the centre of the room, wood dark with horrible stains, and age-yellowed animal skulls and bones lay discarded on the floor around it. Torches flickered in brackets between those loathsome tapestries and I did not need to see the pentagram painted on the floor, one point at the altar, to know what I had entered. This was a temple, a temple for devil worshippers, for Satanists, for sorcerers, those most damned of the damned.

I had been stumbling down the steps between my captors, too numb with shock to struggle, but now I yanked away and tried to run. I almost got free, then my nightgown was seized again, and I was dragged roughly down the steps backwards and pushed into the middle of the circle. I faced them warily, feeling like the beast that has nowhere to run to.

What was this place *doing* here? How could this evil place be here, below my *father's* house? He knew that man; did he know this was here? If he had the key, could he *not* know it was here? He *would* come and save me, wouldn't he? This couldn't have anything to do with him, I just *couldn't* believe it, I just couldn't!

The three men who had brought me there had thrown on red robes over their normal clothes and now looked the same as the other two. They closed in around me, reaching

132

for me. I flung myself out of the circle, heading for the steps, but one of them tripped me and I fell, my face smashing into the stone floor. They seized me and picked me up. Blood streamed from my nose, staining the white of my nightgown, and I fought like a mad cat, twisting and scratching...but there were five of them in all and I didn't stand a chance.

"This isn't any simpering maiden," remarked one man, "this is an urchin, right enough."

The other men laughed nastily and shoved me down on the altar. They slipped nooses around my wrists and ankles, ropes that seemed badly positioned, as if they normally held less human victims. The staring man waved the others to their own points of the pentagram and drew an ornate dagger. I twisted, terrified, blood running down my wrists as I fought against the ropes. The devil couldn't get my soul, could he, if I died like this?

But I didn't want to die at all! I yanked wildly at the cords that held me. The sorcerers were chanting now, and the weight of evil in the air scorched the back of my neck. The chanting went on and on, rising and rising. I struggled and struggled with hopeless tenacity, watching as the man raised the ceremonial dagger into the air, leaning forward to line it up over my heart. But he could not hold it up forever... I refused to allow the burning tears to escape my eyes. After surviving my long urchinhood, my serious illness, after everything...I was to die like this?

It was not fair, I thought, and immediately thought of my father, who was right. Life was not fair and it seemed that my death was not to be fair either. *They* may be damned, I thought furiously, but I shall not be damned! *I believe*, I whispered in my mind, slipping into the creed. My neck prickled in a much more comforting way and that painful fear in my chest eased a little. I waited for the stroke, seeing the man's arm muscles begin to bunch in preparation...

"*Stop!*" snapped a dry voice, harsh with fury.

My head jerked around, along with those of my captors. Alban Serapion Ravena stood halfway down the steps, Raven coiled on his shoulder. He did not look surprised by the place in which he found himself and my heart twisted painfully within me.

"My lord," said the staring man in almost petulant irritation, "you have interrupted the ritual. We will have to begin all over again."

"You shall *not* begin again," declared the Duke furiously. "*What* do you think you are doing in the first place? Did I not make myself *absolutely* clear?"

He *did* know them. My mind was almost blank with shock.

The staring man gave the Duke an almost...dismissive... look. "We work for pay, my Lord, as you well know. Besides, I hardly thought you were serious. You should be pleased that your salvation should come at someone else's expense. We are completing the sorcery very much in the nick of time, are we not?"

The Duke stared at them for a moment, then abruptly laughed, harshly and scornfully. "You fools," he said. "This child is not of my blood. She is just an urchin taken from the streets for her useful resemblance to me."

The sorcerers stared at the Duke. "Would you explain further, my Lord?" said the staring one.

"Explain myself to you?" inquired the Duke scathingly. "If you cannot understand a simple statement, I suppose I will have to. I'll try and make it as simple as possible. I have been alone a long time. I wished for an heir. I was lazy and did not wish to be troubled with legal adoption. This urchin girl—who has very much my looks, I think you will agree—approached me for aid. I took her home as my daughter and everyone takes her as such. Including you fools, I see."

"And her...uncle?" said the staring one. I could see he was not convinced.

"Your paymaster in this, I presume? Another fool," said the Duke coldly. "Turns out this one," he indicated me, "is

134

his illegitimate child. He gave her to my wife to raise as a consolation, but he hates her himself, fearing her true lineage will be discovered. Obviously I wanted to reclaim my wife's property anyway, so I challenged him over his treatment of my supposed daughter. He could not reveal the truth without revealing his own little secret.

"No, in short, *gentlemen*," that word came very sarcastically, "all you will achieve by killing this girl is my displeasure. I will have to find a new heir, and quite how I will explain the tragic death of one long lost daughter and the immediate acquisition of another, I don't quite know. So release her."

The staring one regarded him for several long moments. But he lowered the knife fully. "My lord," he said more urgently. "You must realize that the sorcery is still operational. There is nothing that can stop it. Unless you can provide us with a child of your blood..."

The Duke cut him off. "I think it ought to be quite clear by now that I cannot do so. For obvious reasons I hardly wish to discuss it further. You think I would not have tried everything? Now release the girl."

The staring sorcerer gestured to one of the others, and he came forward and eased the nooses from my bloody wrists and ankles. I scrambled from the altar and stumbled towards the steps. Reaching my father, I stared at him in silence, still too numb with shock to really think.

"Go back to bed," he told me coolly. "I'll speak to you later."

Seeing the anxious stirring of the sorcerers, I hastened up the stairs.

"Do not concern yourselves over her silence," I heard the Duke remark. "She is a bastard urchin at heart and would sell her soul for my money."

I didn't know why it was so important they believe I was not my father's daughter, but I certainly wasn't going to say anything to the contrary. Nor was I going to leave. I went to the door, opened it and slammed it hard, but without going through it. Creeping back to the edge of the balcony, I hid in the shadows, peeping around the corner. I was afraid for my father, alone with these men, for whatever his connection with them, he was my father. And he had saved me yet again. *And* I was afire with curiosity.

"I do believe," my father was going on icily, "that I said you were never to come here again."

Some of the sorcerers shifted uneasily, but the staring one, who seemed their leader, remained unconcerned. "We thought that in the circumstances..."

"You thought that in the circumstances..." mimicked the Duke scornfully. "You think I would refuse your services should I find myself in possession of a child of my blood at long last? Blundering idiots. You are not welcome here. Now *get out.*"

Most of the sorcerers moved towards another door I now noticed on the far side of the temple. Perhaps the passage did eventually come out in London.

The leader stood his ground. "The sorcery..." he began.

"Out," snarled the Duke, stabbing a finger towards the door. "Out or I'll see you all burn."

The other sorcerers hurried out at this, but the leader stayed long enough to give the Duke one long, sardonic look. "And you with us, my lord?" he asked softly, "and you with us?"

Then he too, slipped through the door, and was gone.

CHAPTER 21

Truth

My father remained frozen for a long, long moment as the sound of the key turning in the lock echoed to nothing. Then he strode down the last few steps and in a burst of savage, furious energy, he tore down each of the wall hangings in turn, flinging them onto that wooden altar. He added those old bones and finally flung the wall torches one after another onto the pile, which flared up into a violent blaze.

He stood by the pile, too close, for so long that I was ready to run down and pull him away. But he finally stepped back from it and flung himself down at the base of the stairs, his face buried against his arms. His shoulders shook, and I realized that he was weeping as I'd never seen a grown man weep.

I crouched there for a long time while he sobbed, my mind in utter turmoil and my stomach sick with what I had just seen and learned. How could he explain it? How? But I would listen to him, I knew that. I would listen to what he had to say.

Finally the blaze sunk down to a red glow and my father's tears ceased. He pushed himself up to a sitting position on the lowest step and turned his face towards me. There was a painful dignity in his refusal to wipe the tears away, and his face was composed, even while drawn with pain and grief. And shame.

"I know you're there, child," he said quietly, his voice tired and a little hoarse. "Come out."

Unsurprised, I stood up and went down the steps, taking with me the lantern he must have abandoned there upon entering. I stopped and sat on a step a couple up from him, beginning to shake violently with cold and relief. He slipped off his chamber gown, which he had clearly not even stopped to tie, and held it out to me wordlessly. Pulling the gown around me gratefully, I noted that as I had feared, unnecessarily as it turned out, he was unarmed.

He wrapped his arms around his chest and looked at me in silence. I could tell he didn't quite know what to say and for the first time since I'd met him, he looked very vulnerable. Raven coiled on my shoulder, and I stroked her in rather absent-minded gratitude. He might know them, but he could not be one of them. He *couldn't*.

Finally, I said "Well?"

He drew in a long breath, as if he had been forgetting to breathe. "Will you hear me then? You who would never sell your soul for my gold?"

"I will hear you," I returned just as softly.

"Very well," he said quietly. "Then I will have to tell you everything."

It hit me then, in a flash of dawning understanding. "This is about my mother, isn't it?"

He closed his eyes for a moment. "Oh yes. This is all about your mother." He remained silent for a while, as if collecting his thoughts.

"After I was married... No, that's no good, I shall have to go much further back to start this tale. My great, great grandfather lived on the family estate at Elfindale, which seems to be a place aptly named, for he married an elfin woman. Elfin female, I should probably say. It was true love, apparently, and neither regretted it, for they lived happily until finally life intervened with its usual lack of pity, and they were killed in a carriage accident.

"Leaving, though, my great grandfather to carry on our line. And he, of course, was half elfin himself." He paused for a moment, looking at me thoughtfully. "Have you ever...felt things? Things that no one else seems to feel?"

I nodded eagerly. "*Yes*, I always have. And *you* do too, *don't* you?"

The Duke nodded, a very faint smile flickering across his drawn face. "Alas, the acorns. I was careless. Yes, child, I feel these things too. My father did not, although his father did, but he taught me that I should never speak of it or let it be observed, by anyone. Although most scholars and clerics accept that creatures such as the Elfin are of nature, not of the devil, there are some who are less understanding.

"That, child, is the old slander I told you of. Our family's elfin blood raised a lot of eyebrows at the time, for all they never admitted publicly that she was elfin; enough eyebrows that it has never quite been forgotten.

"This may not seem relevant, but it is. As well as this extra sense of ours, I was at one time visited by another elfin skill. I believe it was the sheer degree, the sheer power of my love for your mother that woke it, but I do not know so. We had been married for some years, and no child forthcoming, not that I minded, for your mother was young, and I am not a fool who will assume that a young woman who takes more than two years to conceive is barren. Far from it. I was happy to be patient.

"But the," he broke off to laugh bitterly, "the *gift*, as they call it, of Foresight came to me. It began in dreams, but it got stronger, until I could see it all around her whenever I looked at her. That through some untimely accident or event, your mother was going to die. It drove me to distraction.

"I came to London—we lived at Elfindale, your mother and I," he added, "did you know that? She liked the country. But I came to London to search for a cure to this doom. It seemed to me that if I could Foresee it, surely I could also prevent it." He was silent again for a while. "It is possible to love too much, did you know that?" he asked at last.

"I suppose you can do anything too much," I replied collectedly, though the talk of dreams sent a cold prickle down my spine, "although loving certainly isn't what comes to mind as an evil."

Alban sighed and hung his head. "It can work as much ill as any evil. The only hope I could find for your mother was sorcery." He glanced at me. "That does not seem to surprise you."

I snorted. "Strangely, it doesn't." I threw a sharp look in the direction of the smoldering heap.

"No, I suppose not," went on the Duke, heavily. "I was half mad with love of your mother and fear of losing her. I say this to explain, not to excuse, for though I would not have been driven to it otherwise, there is no possible excuse. I learned from the sorcerers I finally managed to contact that it was indeed possible to avert such a doom; that there was a sorcery that could do this.

"Once I decided to take such a course, and in my madness the decision was quickly made, I followed their instructions. I prepared this horrible place for them, let them consecrate it with their animal sacrifices. It was an ice house, before, you know, one of the first in London. And when all was ready, I performed the sorcery. Which I suppose I must explain to you.

"The initial ritual cast the sorcery, which would prevent any accident befalling your mother for nine years and, if the sorcery was completed within those nine years, for the natural span of her life. If it was not completed by the end of the nine years, then she would die.

"But as one never gets anything from the evil one without paying at least double for it, there was to be a security as well, so that even if the sorcery was not completed in time and your mother died, the evil one was to get a price of sorts, this price being the security. Five years were allowed after the time of your mother's death, for the sorcery's completion, before this security would also be taken."

He hesitated, and I knew he was coming to the crux of it, not that I expected it to be much of a surprise after what had just happened. "I pledged myself for the security," he said quietly, "and I pledged a child of my blood as the payment that would complete the sorcery. However, your mother joined me suddenly in London, having grown weary of my absence. She found out enough that I had to confess all to her."

His face twisted in pain. "She left; she would not stay another moment. I think perhaps I now know why she was in such a hurry," he said, looking at me. "She did not betray me to the authorities, but that was all the mercy she had for me. And that, really, was no mercy at all. For when I understood that I had truly lost her it was only then that I really realized fully what I had done. The two combined...

"I was hard put to keep from doing myself harm," he confessed very quietly. "I left to travel around England, to seek distraction enough to keep me sane and in one piece. Your mother sent me a letter after a time. She said that if she found herself living beyond the nine years, she would know that I had made the sacrifice and she would no longer hold her tongue. But the threat was unnecessary by then. I knew what I had done. The scales had, metaphorically, fallen from my eyes. I could never have finished the sorcery.

"If I could actually ever have gone through with it," he added, his mouth twisting, "There is a great difference between the idea of a babe, even one's own, and the squalling reality. But it never came to it, so I will never know, which is a blessing and a curse at once.

"The problem was, while your mother lived, there was this tiny glimmer of hope. It wasn't a real hope, not by then. There was no child, or so I thought, and even so, it was irrelevant. My connection with sorcery was completely at an end. But your mother lived, and I still loved. When she died, however terrible this may sound, it was in a way a relief. Sometimes it is easier to have no hope at all.

"All the same, the British Isles were not large enough to contain my grief, so I went to the continent, again seeking vital distraction.

"Eventually I was emptied out and weary with the travel, and I wished to return to my childhood home and live quietly and with what peace I could for what time was left. And when I got here, a grimy urchin girl leapt aboard my carriage, which shows that God is indeed merciful, to send such comfort to even a damned soul. Although in truth, He was probably thinking of your need for my money. Which *will* all be yours," he added, and was silent.

I regarded him narrowly. Money? I was hardly interested in his money at a time like this. But I caught the faint glimmer of fear in his eyes as he watched me, and suddenly understood. He was waiting for me to draw away from him, to revile him, to hate him. To leave him. So afraid of it that he could not help offering his worldly wealth to tempt me to stay.

How could he expect me to stay just for his wealth? He was my father! He was human, he had sinned very badly and he had been repenting of it ever since, I could see that quite clearly. It was not as if he was a sorcerer or had ever actually been a *sorcerer* as such, and saw no harm in it. He saw the harm all right. How could he think that I would leave him?

My mother left him, I realized. That's why. He loved her enough to give his soul to save her, foolish as it might be, and she didn't love him enough to try and save him from himself. Oh, it was clear why she left so quickly, she was already pregnant and dared not let him know. But she could still have tried to save him once her baby was safe. But she didn't. She just left him.

My mother was pregnant with *me*. I looked at my father, who still watched me with the guarded eyes of a dog that has been beaten so badly it no longer hopes for love, or perhaps, feels that it deserves it.

"Me," I said at last. "You were going to sacrifice *me*."

He bowed his head, covering his eyes with his hand. "Yes," he whispered, "it would have been you. But consider, child, while the wrong is the same, the doing is a little easier with a tiny babe that has no personality or name. As I said, I might not have been able to do it, even then. I pray not. But what is certain, Serapia, is that since you appeared in my carriage, I have not once thought of sacrificing you, not even in the darkest corner of my soul. That was all over long ago, though I dare say the punishment keeps still.

"I will say, though," he added, "that since I met you I have ceased to regret that your mother did not hand me over for my rightful punishment. You make every long year worthwhile."

I was touched by this quiet, sincere confession, but I recoiled from the idea that he could have wished for punishment. "They would have *burned* you!"

"They still could," he said calmly, then went on, without a trace of self-pity, "it would have been a few minutes of physical agony, which might have gone some way to mitigate my future punishment. Instead, I have suffered anguish like hell fire licking at my soul for years, and who knows if that even counts?"

I gave a dismissive snort. "Of *course* it counts. Pain is pain, isn't it? I may have said it dismissively before, without any idea of what I was talking about, for which I apologize, but I say it again now, in much fuller knowledge; I'd wager quite heavily that your soul will be fine."

He shook his head quietly and made no reply.

"*What?*" I said in frustration. "True repentance equals forgiveness, and if you don't truly repent then no one does."

He just shook his head again. "There is no forgiveness for me," he said softly. "You see, when I first engaged upon the sorcery, in my half-mad state I committed a much worse sin: I thought to myself that it didn't matter if what I did was wrong, I could always repent later. How do I escape that?"

"By repenting it, which you clearly do!" I cried furiously. And then, because I obviously wasn't getting through to him, I shuffled down two steps and put my arms around him. He remained still in my tight grasp for a long moment, as if even now disbelieving that I could forgive him and love him still. Then, finally, he wrapped his arms around me and held me close. *He is getting rather bony*, I thought to myself, *I must see he eats more.* That was when it really hit me. I jerked backwards so I could see his face.

"Pa," I said in something of a gasp, "what did you mean? What did you mean about the security?" My voice cracked in sudden fear.

He turned his face away, as if unable to look me in the eyes. "I'm sorry, child," he whispered.

"No! I must have it wrong, *tell* me!"

He sighed heavily. "I was the security for the sorcery," he said, almost under his breath. "If the sorcery is not completed five years after your mother's death—and rest assured, it shall not be—then, I too, will die."

"No," I whispered numbly, my mind racing. "*No!*" I cried more vehemently, "that's March *this* year. *No!*"

"Peace, child." He gathered me in his arms again. "I have known the outside limit of my days for many years. It does not trouble me, though I do regret that I must leave you. But you will want for nothing."

"Nothing save a father," I sobbed, "who I would rather have without a penny than not have with all the money in the world!"

He seemed hard pressed to answer that and simply held me tightly for some time, before finally rising and lifting me in his arms to carry me back to my bedroom.

I sat on the bed while he cleaned the wounds on my wrists and ankles. He also gave me a piece of raw meat from the larder and I pressed this gratefully to my swollen nose. I knew he was feeling bad, because as he dabbed my wounds with brandy, he didn't even make any comment about getting his own back. When he had bandaged everything carefully with strips of clean linen, he left me to sleep.

But sleep was impossible. Everything that had happened, everything that I had learned in the last few short hours, churned through my head, and while I knew that I would never be able to settle it all into sense in my mind without sleeping on it, sleep evaded me. But I had not been twisting and turning for long when I heard a soft tap on my door, and at my 'enter', my father came back in.

He held a teapot and a pair of cups, which he set on my bedside table, where my dagger would have been if I had not slipped it under my pillow. "I made you a cup of tea," he said quietly. He still evaded my eyes, and I very much hoped that that would wear off by morning. "It will help you sleep. I fully intend to drink whatever you leave. It beats getting falling down drunk, come morning," he added under his breath and rather to himself.

"What's in it," I asked, sniffing.

"Hops, cloves, chamomile, valerian and ginger."

"I'll have some," I said, so he poured two cups and sat by the bed companionably as we drank, albeit a very silent, bow-headed, floor-studying companion.

When I had finished and refused another cup, he departed, looking a rather forlorn shadow as he went, teapot in hand. I lay down again and eventually I slept, for the next I knew, it was morning.

CHAPTER 22

In Search of Hope

When I first woke, I didn't remember anything, but then it began to creep back like a bad dream. A *very* bad dream. When I sat up in bed, I received incontrovertible proof that it was no dream. I still wore my father's chamber gown, and the sharp pain from my bandaged wrists and ankles as I moved could scarcely be imaginary.

I glanced at the window, alarmed, but it was only just dawn, no one would disturb me yet. Quickly I stripped off both garments, which were bloody at cuffs and hem, and pulled on a clean nightgown.

My father's chamber gown was a dark color and the blood didn't show, so I threw it over a chair. I could return it to him and let him worry about how to get it washed. The nightgown was a different matter. I wasn't sure how I was going to explain my injuries, but I doubted the explanation would involve my having been in my nightgown at the time.

I got scissors and quickly cut off cuffs and hem, then, more carefully, cut the rest of the gown into handkerchief sized pieces. I threw these into a basket of similar, waiting to go down to the urchin home for embroidery and sale.

The bloody scraps I tucked into the pocket of my own chamber gown. Once the fire was lit, I would dispose of them. And if any of the maids actually missed the nightgown, I could say quite truthfully that I had been so careless as to stain it badly and had therefore cut it up for handkerchiefs. I was not in the habit of needing waiting on hand and foot; there would be no surprise that I had done it myself.

As to the injuries themselves, I was at a loss. Injuries to my wrists alone, or my ankles alone, well, I could always claim I had been tangled in Hellion's reins and dragged, but no one would believe I had got hands and feet tangled at the same time. I'd probably better consult with my father before I gave out anything about that.

My father. I sank down in a chair and my mind seethed, as I considered my father. To be involved in sorcery was indeed damnation and the particular sorcery he had unfolded to me was certainly an evil thing. But he was not an evil man. Nor a fool, generally, but one need be foolish only once to fall very badly indeed. He had been foolish, and fallen. And picked himself up and struggled on as well as he could, unwaveringly repentant despite the fact that he could see no salvation ahead.

I gave a faintly irritated sniff. I was no believer in irredeemable sins. The God I felt when I prayed was as loving as a parent. I was not greatly worried about my father's soul. I was worried about his life.

It was so clear now. His increasing thinness. His tiredness. Just like with my mother. He would waste away before my eyes and then I would be alone again. I had not noticed before because my father was very different from my mother. My mother had always been sunk in gloom, alternating between bursts of visiting and gossip, and drawn-out days of moping. Wallowing in self-pity, she had wasted the years she had mourning for the years she would not have. The years she had which she would never have had in the first place without her husband's rash actions.

I shook my head, hands pressed to my forehead, trying to drive the traitorous thoughts away, but it was no good. Everything I had never understood seemed to have come into clear focus. I had never been able to understand my mother's despondence, but finally I did.

My mother had used up all her courage and strength in leaving her husband, securing my safety and the safety of any other potential children of the Duke's blood with that letter. Then, finding herself with a child that reminded her

147

of nothing but the husband she had abandoned, she spent the rest of her life pitying herself.

That's not fair, cried part of me. *No one can be* expected *to stay with their spouse after they've had recourse to* sorcery! *That sort of thing breaks all bonds.* But I wasn't sure that it did. After all, had my mother hated him or not? I wasn't sure. Certainly, if she hadn't, she had been too proud to go back to him and make up. *In which case she had no reason for self-pity,* I thought angrily. *She took the time he bought her and left him, then squandered it!*

I rubbed the heels of my hands into my eyes. I was getting a headache. I pushed consideration of my mother away. Just then, that was not the point.

The point was that my father was made of sterner stuff. He'd ploughed on through the years with an utter determination to live out his allotted time as fully as possible, and by doing so keep from doing violence against himself and further damage to his soul. *He* was not moping already. Mourning still, maybe, but not moping. He was physically stronger, hence the wasting disease, if it could be called a disease in this case, had taken longer to show itself.

But now that I knew it was there, I could see it all too clearly. And I knew that it would kill him. That thought drove a spear of icy terror to the pit of my belly, and I wrapped my arms around myself and shivered.

I would be alone again. Alone, and rich, and wanting nothing, which would be ten times worse. I wasn't sure if I could survive it. Surviving before, at least in regard to my mother's death, had been very easy. Staying alive was extremely distracting.

But this time there would be no distraction and no ring at my waist. No hope of another person who would love me and take care of me. Except a future husband, and the thought of having to pick one out from among the throng of fortune hunters, unguided, made me feel sick. I'd rather be an old maid than get *that* wrong.

But I'd be *alone* again! Raven pawed at my cheek comfortingly and I fought against tears. I loved Raven very much, but it was not the same. My father was going to die...

No, I thought desperately.

No, I thought fiercely.

No! I thought with utter determination. *I will not let him die. There must be some way to save him and I'll find it. I've got to find it. There is nothing in this world that cannot be undone. I won't let there be.*

With this new resolution thrumming through my veins and holding that icy fear at bay, I jumped up and hurried to my father's bedchamber, blind to the pain walking caused in my ankles. I tapped and heard a soft 'enter'.

The Duke stood by the window, gazing out. He did not turn to look at me, so I suspected the eye-evasion had not yet worn off. I put the chamber gown on the bed.

"I'm afraid I've got blood on that," I told him. "It will need washing discreetly."

"I'll arrange it," he said, still ostensibly looking out of the window. "Don't worry about it. Your nightgown..."

"Already dealt with." A maid must have just lit his fire, so I crossed the room to cast the blood-stained strips of cloth into the blaze.

He turned around at last but went to sit by the fire without looking at me. I threw myself on his lap and hugged him tightly, determined to break through his shame. It seemed to work, because he finally met my eyes with his own, which were very sad. "Try not to fret too much about all this."

I couldn't help snorting at that but replied eagerly, "We'll find something, it's just a question of looking. There'll be something..."

He shook his head at me firmly. "No, child, do not distress yourself further. It is not an illness exactly and cannot be cured, and even if I would stoop to it again, there is no way of removing it through sorcery. Please do not cling to a false hope. It will only cause you more pain."

I squared my lips and returned his gaze firmly. "Nothing's impossible."

"For *God!*" he said, with a breath of exasperation. "Just think about it sensibly, child, I could fall from my horse and break my neck tomorrow or be struck by a real wasting disease next week. There's no difference, we just know, that's all."

"There *is* a difference! You *could* break your neck, certainly! You *could* get sick, of course! But it's not the most likely. The most likely is that you wouldn't do either, and you'd live to be an old old man and die in your bed. And *there* there is quite a difference. Is there not?"

"There's no cure, Serapia." He looked me squarely in the eyes. "I want to be very clear about that now. I will not have you hurting yourself with a foolish hope. Do you understand me?"

I nodded. *I understand you,* I thought, *for you are speaking plain English, but I do not believe it. I cannot believe it. Anyway, have you looked? I do not believe that you have. And if this is what those sorcerers have told you...well, they're the very last people I intend to believe.*

CHAPTER 23

The Fate of the Dog

"What are the chances we'll even find my uncle at court?" I asked my father as the coach pulled up outside the palace.

"Where else can he get the informal loan he so desperately needs?" the Duke replied, alighting as the footman opened the door.

My father had already spoken to the City Watch about the two dead bodies at Bride Well, although naming no names, having no proof. Once inside, he advanced to the Queen, made his bow, and was requested to tell Her Majesty about the affair. He did so, presenting the facts with careful neutrality and again naming no names. He didn't need to. I watched the monarch's face from under demurely lowered lids. Anyone who had heard about that business would have a pretty good idea. Needless to say, he didn't mention the sorcerers.

The Queen released my father far more quickly this time, for Baron Hendfield was heading for the doors like a runaway carriage, offering nothing but the most superficial excuses to even the most powerful in his path. Alban caught up with him rapidly—people moved out of *his* way. He grabbed my uncle by the scruff of his over-sized ruff and dragged him behind the nearest curtains into the window embrasure. I slipped in as well, to hear what was said. No doubt a lot of ears were applied to the curtain.

"Hendfield," said my father curtly by way of a greeting. The Baron did not reply. His face had gone milk white and apparently he could not speak.

"Right, you miserable little rat," the Duke informed him, "I'm feeling generous, so I'm going to give you two choices. We can duel again and I'll kill you this time, you can count on that. Or you can go before Her Majesty and confess what you've been up to. Which is it to be?"

The Baron stared into the Duke's pitiless eyes for a long, frozen moment. It was clear he saw death on the point of that ducal sword as being a lot closer than anything else.

"Well?" snapped the Duke.

"I..." gasped the Baron, and cleared his throat with effort, "I'll...I'll go before Her Majesty..."

Fool, I thought, but did not speak. All the safer for Pa if he were a fool.

"Very well," said the Duke icily. "I will not put words into your mouth, so you go out there and confess what you've done. I'll know if you tell the truth." The last was uttered so darkly that it was clearly a threat, and the Baron paled a little more and went sideways into the curtain, flailing his way through it and heading for the dais.

The Duke followed, with something of the stalking tiger in his stride. Or perhaps that would be the stalking tigress, when she moves to protect her young.

Scurrying out into the space before the dais, the Baron bowed low. "Your Majesty, please hear me," he cried.

You should have knelt, I thought, *if you wanted even to hope for your life.*

The Queen fixed him with a frosty look. "Speak," she said curtly.

"Your Majesty," said the Baron, his voice wavering, "I am your most loyal servant and it is with the most abject despair that I throw myself upon your mercy. I have been a very weak, fallible man, and tried to commit a most terrible crime, which God, in His great mercy, has seen fit to prevent. For which I most earnestly thank Him."

That would have come across better if you didn't sound so sour, I reflected.

The Baron stumbled on, "Accepting this clear chance granted from above to mend my ways, I hereby do throw myself on your mercy..."

"You've already said that," said the Queen, sounding rather bored, "come to the point."

The Baron paused and swallowed, taken aback, and shot one last look at the implacable face of the Duke.

"Have mercy on your fallible servant," he went on after a long, pregnant pause. "I...I am in terrible want of money, due to an...an...unexpected reversal. I...I hired two men to...to...do to death my...my...brother-in-law and my niece." Shaking, he fell silent.

The fool had actually done it. In a duel, anything could happen, but royal justice was likely to be swift and sure.

"All here are witness to this confession," said the Queen coolly. "Guards."

With my uncle safely behind lock and key, I was free to throw myself into my search for a cure. I did not go to any particular trouble to hide what I was doing from my father, whom I wanted more than anything to decide to help me, but I didn't flaunt it under his nose either. I took the carriage all over the city, Susie in attendance, visiting learned doctors, physicians, libraries and institutions, finding out all I could of wasting diseases.

What I found was not encouraging. They generally concurred that if the disease wasn't caused by fretting, grief, or some mental oppression that could be relieved, and that if the patient did not respond to careful diet and cosseting, then it was almost sure to be one of the incurable wasting diseases. These were caused by many things, ranging from tumors somewhere in the body to incurable coughs to unknown causes. I already knew something about the latter category and since this was clearly one of those I had to admit that my findings were not such as to make me feel very optimistic.

How do you cure the sorcerous incurable? I wondered, as I sat in the library turning the pages of an old Latin text on anatomy. *Without* going to the Church, that was. No doubt the Bishop's exorcist *could* deal with the sorcery—the gates of hell could not withstand the Church, after all—but why would an exorcist bother saving a man whom it was his duty to turn over to the civil authorities for punishment? And even if he *did*, my father would then be burnt at the stake. No. Because of the self-inflicted nature of the sorcery, the one place I was sure could help was also the one place I absolutely, totally and utterly could not turn to.

Unfortunately, the only other answer that came to mind was a miracle and so far my prayers did not seem to have produced one. In truth, I had not expected it. I was quite aware that such things were granted even less often than in former times, when they had hardly been common, and my father was scarcely going to be the most likely candidate, having, after all, brought it on himself.

I stared at the pages of the book without seeing the crude diagram of the heart that adorned the page. As far as I could see it, I had three options. Find a cure, check that there was indeed no sorcery to remove the sorcery causing the problem, or pray for a miracle. I was trying to do the first, but I doubted I would succeed. The second, I was not touching with the longest barge pole in history, and the third I was doing, but again, without hope of success. Could I be asking the wrong question? I wasn't sure how; the question seemed simple enough, but...

"*Serapia.*"

I jumped as the Duke leant over my shoulder, his tone faintly accusatory.

"I shall have to lock up all these books," he went on with a sigh, gathering the few that lay on the desk in front of me. "Must you be so determined to hurt yourself?" he added, leaning to place a kiss on the top of my head before bearing the books off to his study.

Undaunted, I scowled at the library shelves. Now where hadn't I looked?

The Baron's trial had proceeded as swiftly as I anticipated and the verdict was as sure. Since the Baron had confessed, there was scarcely, in fact, any trial needed. All the same, Her Majesty prided herself on the fairness of English law courts and several witnesses had been called. The Duke, primarily, to narrate the attack in the square, and several witnesses of the same event. The Baron's confession was enough to place the affair at his door. And as my father remarked to me, the Queen was very angry about it. Attempted assassination reflected badly on the entire country, and thus on Her Majesty. The Baron was sentenced to death and the date of the execution appointed.

There would be no reprieve. Reprieves in such cases did not make good examples.

I dressed soberly and for all my strenuous argument to my father that I had seen plenty of executions, even of men I knew, my stomach felt slightly unsettled. With one last, delaying look around the room, I let Susie slip my cloak over my shoulders and I headed for the door, fastening the clasp as I went.

My father stood waiting in the hall, stroking the head of Arthur, his favorite deerhound. He made no mention of my tardiness. "I'd rather you stayed here," he said quietly, without looking at me.

"I'm coming."

He sighed and headed for the door. "I'm expected to be there, you are not."

I'd heard that plenty of times. "I'm coming," I repeated, and more quietly, "I'm going to see this to the end."

"Very well," he said, and handed me up into the coach.

Noble blood or not, the Queen had decreed that the Baron be hanged like a common murderer at Smithfield. A brand new scaffold *had* been erected for the occasion— though in the circumstances even my vain uncle would probably take little consolation from this small concession to his rank—along with a stand of tiered seating for the nobility, where my father and I took our places. The sweet smell of sap from the freshly sawn timber was still just about distinguishable above the smell of all the humanity packing eagerly into the area and it seemed incongruous.

In the circumstances I didn't find it too difficult to pray for the condemned man as we waited, but the prison cart soon appeared. A drummer walked ahead, beating out a steady step. The Baron was led up the sweet-smelling steps. Prayers were said, and he was invited to speak his last words. He seemed to have no address ready, for he looked around wildly, until he caught sight of me and my father.

"*You!*" he cried, "you *witch child!* Witch child and your hell spawn father! You've no right to do this to me! A normal man like me! I'm just a normal man. What are you? Devil spawn!"

I flinched slightly from the vehemence of his attack and looked about me. But I could see that no one took the Baron seriously; a few were laughing. My father's face remained smooth and unconcerned, but his eyes told another story. The references to hell and the devil clearly cut deep. I pressed his hand silently.

The executioner seemed to decide that this was not what last words were for and pushed the Baron towards the ladder. He stumbled, his abuse trailing off and his lip trembling as he saw the noose before him. He swung round again, looking back at the Duke. *Now he realizes*, I thought grimly, *that in only one choice was there any hope, and it was not this one.*

"I'll fight you, Ravena!" the Baron cried, "I'll fight you! Get me down from here!" His voice broke, and he wept and struggled as they pushed him up the ladder.

I almost couldn't watch; it was too painful. A matter of moments. A matter of a few more moments to keep his composure and he could have died with dignity. But he sobbed, and he went fighting. They dragged him up the ladder, forced the noose over his head and turned him off, as efficient and disdainful as if he had been an animal for butchery. He kicked, and then he was still. People dispersed, grumbling, dissatisfied with the spectacle. They had expected a grand, penitent speech, and a dignified, admirable end. Or the commonalty had. The nobility had perhaps known better.

I turned to my father, and he turned to me. He looked a little sick. "Well, that's that," he said quietly. "Let's go home."

"Let's go home," I echoed and took his arm.

In the carriage, the Duke settled back in his seat as if he were more than emotionally tired.

I rested my head on his shoulder. "So that is that," I murmured to myself.

"Aye. That is that. You are safe now."

I glanced at him. "And you too." I would not let him die.

"Ah, yes," he said, with a slightly lop-sided smile, "and me too. As far as your uncle is concerned," he added under his breath.

We drove on in silence.

CHAPTER 24

The Angel in the Graveyard

My birthday passed almost unnoticed—at least by me—as I kept a hawk-like eye on my father's condition. The deterioration was not rapid, but it was steady, and perceptible. Whichever way I turned in my search, I met a brick wall. I fought to hold onto hope when everything seemed to point otherwise.

I sought my father in the church one evening, directed thither by his chamberlain, and expecting to find him lost in prayer. Instead, I found him in one of the wings of the little church, among the fine marble tombs of the parish's wealthy deceased.

His cheeks were damp, but when he caught sight of me he made a valiant attempt to speak as if all was normal. "I don't know why people like these cold, hard things," he told me, would-be-lightly. "Lay me in the churchyard under grass and sky with a simple stone seeking the prayers of those who pass by, and I shall be happy."

"Pa..." I said, my own voice tight with pain, for I could not bear to hear him talk like that.

But he turned away from me, fingers gripping the ornate edging of a tomb and head bowed. "Leave me, child," he whispered, "I shall be well soon."

I wanted to stay and try to comfort him, but his tears frightened me more than anything else had done and I ran from the church. I didn't stop until I reached a secluded corner of the graveyard, where I threw myself down in a tumble of skirts, arms folded on the top of an old tomb and face pressed to them to muffle my sobs. The possibility that there really was no cure loomed over me, filling me with terror. I wasn't sure when I had last felt so small and helpless.

"*Please,*" I whispered desperately as I wept, "please, please, there must be a way, *please let there be a way...*"

There was a strange silence in the churchyard, total, not eerie but peaceful. I raised my head. It was midday. The sky was cloudless and blue, the sun warm on my back. And there was something behind me. I remained motionless, waiting in awe rather than fear. Though I'd only ever felt such a being before if it actually brushed me, I knew what was there.

It stepped up to me; leant close to my ear. I had a dizzying impression of hands resting on my shoulders, soft feathers curving around me.

"*You carry the answer with you always.*"

My head slipped from my arms and banged against hard stone. I sat up with a jolt, looking around in confusion. It was twilight and the sky was clouded. I rubbed my forehead and sat back on my heels.

That was such a strange dream. So strange I wasn't sure I wanted to dismiss it out of hand. It sounded as though I ought to know the answer. No, not exactly. 'You carry the answer with you always.'

I held out my palm to Raven, who had climbed out at my neck in response to my sudden movement, and lifted her to eye level. "Can *you* save my father?"

Raven's tiny ears pricked in surprise, then drooped. She shook her head. I sighed. I hadn't thought so. But what else did I carry with me enough to warrant an 'always'? My ring was in a box in my room. I didn't want to wear it; it was, after all, my mother's wedding ring.

There *was* one more thing. I reached through the pocket slit of my dress and drew out my dagger. Siridean's dagger. I clasped the hilt in my hands, running my thumb around the hematite from habit more than need. No mud daubed its shining surface now. I gazed into its comforting depths and the eyes looked back at me.

Siridean would have helped me, I thought sadly, and not without a flash of anger for my father, who would not even try. Then my breath caught in my throat, for I *knew*.

When in trouble, to whom do you turn, if not to your kin?

CHAPTER 25

The Cure

"But Pa," I objected, "why can't we at least go and ask? They *can* do it, I'm sure of it, or this wouldn't have been my answer! We can at least ask! The worst that can happen is that they say no!"

The Duke looked at least as exasperated as I felt, though for rather different reasons. "Child, you have no idea what you are speaking of! First, the elfin that are kin to us are somewhere around Elfindale, which is in the shire of York, hundreds of miles to the north. And secondly, the Elfin hate sorcerers above anything else. There is no way on God's green earth they are going to cure a man of self-inflicted sorcery, distant relation or no. They'd probably execute me themselves and save a lot of time and bother!"

"Pa!" I cried, "don't talk like that! Don't you *see*, this is the only hope for you; I'm convinced of that now! We *must* go and find them."

"We are going nowhere," declared the Duke with grim determination. "My days of charging up and down the roads of this country are over. At least previously I've always sought something that can be found! *Find* the Elfin! *Child*! As well try and catch smoke in your bare fingers!" He saw me open my mouth again. "*Enough*. Let's go to dinner, and no more of this foolishness."

Slowly I closed my mouth, my jaw set in a mutinous line. I knew better than to push him too far all at once, but he had *not* heard the end of it.

I had just tallied up the days and realized with horror that it was over a *week* since I had received that unexpected answer to my prayer. I'd been as tenacious as a terrier with a rat, but with much less effect. We were still there, at Albany House, not a step closer to Elfindale and my father's only hope. Now there was a cure within sight, I fretted almost more than before. This *was* my answer.

Everyone knew that the Elfin had powers. The ignorant termed it magic, but from what my father said it was something less sinister. A heightened influence over nature? An ability to touch the spiritual? A bit of both? But whatever the details, everyone knew that farmers with elfin forts on their land had livestock that never died of sickness and families where virtually every child born would live to adulthood. The healing powers of the Elfin were legendary. And my father and I were the Elfin's direct kin. I was sure that was why Siridean had helped me.

But it might well take some *time* to persuade the Elfin to help, I thought, anguished, as I ran my father to earth in his study.

I was starting to get the impression that he was avoiding me. Perhaps not surprisingly. But he showed no signs of budging. I was in a particular panic today, because he hadn't even ridden out with me for the last few mornings and although he claimed he was busy with his own affairs, I had a horrible suspicion that he was simply finding it too tiring. I just *had* to persuade him.

With that thought, I squared my shoulders, gritted my teeth like a knight sallying into battle and strode into the room. His book lay on his knee when I entered and he was staring rather bleakly into the fire, but he raised it quickly and fixed his attention on it. Frustrated before I had even said a word, I sat on the arm of the chair and took the book from him, ostensibly to look at the title. I shot a sidelong glance at him and put the book out of reach on a nearby table. He looked *so* thin, now.

"Pa..." I started, but he cut me off, an irritation approaching real anger warring with sadness in his eyes.

"Child, you seem dissatisfied with the speed at which the sorcery is dispatching me. You clearly intend to nag me to death."

This unusually harsh remark told me I had already pushed him too far today, but what could I do, but push further? I wasn't getting anywhere.

It wasn't hard to pretend to be upset. "*Pa*," I objected, "why can you not at least try? Can't you think of *me*? Do you *want* to die?"

He looked at me sharply, at that. "I wish to be saved," he said softly, "which is not the same thing. I have made my bed, child, and now I must die on it. It is only proper." He touched my cheek with a rather bony finger. I drew breath, but he moved the finger to my lips. "Quiet, Serapia. One more word from you tonight and I shall probably say something I do not mean and hurt both of us. Would that you could understand that when I say nay, I mean it."

I bit my lip and after a long moment, I withdrew quietly, leaving him again staring into the flames. I was getting desperate, but I had no wish to really draw his wrath. He did not get angry very easily, but when he did...

I went up to my bedroom and sat gazing into my own hearth. I just couldn't understand *why* my father wasn't prepared to at least try. He professed himself certain that the Elfin would not help, that at best they would turn him away with anger and contempt, and at worst, do him harm themselves. But I was not convinced. I doubted the Elfin would do more than turn us away, in which case we had absolutely nothing to lose by asking. In *either* case, we had nothing to lose! So why wouldn't he go?

And I realized that he had finally told me why, though I had not noticed at the time. *He wished to be saved.* He did not expect it, but he still wished it. And he felt, reasonably enough, that to accept without demur the consequences of his sin, as an earthly penance, might mitigate his eternal punishment. That was why he was not prepared to stir so much as a foot in search of bodily salvation, not even for me. The Duke had learned by now that one did not put one's soul on the line for another's worldly happiness or longevity.

I could not blame him for it. He was terribly afraid that he was damned, a fear I had not been able to talk him out of and perhaps that was only proper as well. But it still meant that my hopes of talking him around had just plummeted. *When I say nay, I mean it,* he had said, and I rather believed that he did.

Hearing the stairs creak a little later, I peeped out to watch him making his way to his own bedchamber. He walked as if weary, and his hand rested on banister and side tables as he went. He was growing weaker by the day, though he tried to hide it. I bit my lip. Very well. I would have one last try.

I waited a while, then went to his bedchamber and tapped on the door. I couldn't tell if there was more wariness or weariness in his 'Enter' but I did so. He still had one candle lit, and I went over and sat on the bed. I looked at him, and he regarded me with cautious serenity. *I am being selfish*, I thought to myself. *He thinks of his soul, but you think only of his body, trying to force him to what he knows he must not. He has the right of it. What he must do, and what you must do, they are not the same.*

So I leant over and kissed him on the cheek. "I just came to say goodnight," I said. "I'm sorry I've been such a nag."

He gave me a thoughtful look. "And I am sorry I have to say no. But I must, and I hope perhaps you understand...?"

I nodded and hugged him tightly for a long moment before returning to my own bedchamber.

He could not go in search of an elfin cure without harming his soul, but that did not mean that *I* could not do it for him.

CHAPTER 26

Serapion the Groom

I waited several hours into the night, fearing that my father might take a while to sleep. Finally, I got off the bed and, moving as quietly as possible, quickly made up a bundle of necessaries, including money. I also included several very fine pieces of my mother's jewelry, for a two-fold purpose. If the Elfin were reluctant to help me, it was always possible that a 'gift' would ease things along. And although I did not *intend* to let bandits get me, I was too worldly-wise to overlook the possibility, and if I was taken by bandits on the road, it was vital I could provide proof that I was a Duke's daughter, not a horse-thieving urchin girl. The first was worth a ransom, the second was...definitely not.

I tied everything up in a large handkerchief, for I did not keep saddlebags in my bedroom. Then I slipped silently into the hall, gently shushing Raven's inquisitive chatter. My first port of call was the attics, where I quickly dug out a groom's uniform from among the old clothes and shook it out to check the size. I swapped my nightgown for this livery and checked my reflection in an old mirror, by the light of a single candle. What I saw horrified me. This was not Serapion the groom, this was a Serapia. It was my chest, confound it!

It would not do at all. The tunic strained across my breasts and no one with halfway reasonable eyesight was going to take me for a boy. I dug around in the old clothes feverishly, finally emerging with an antiquated corset. Quickly I cut the cups off, removed my tunic, laced the corset on backwards, and slipped the tunic on again. I inspected my reflection in the mirror. Much better. Not very comfortable, mind...

Next I folded some of my hair double and put it into a tight plait so that I had something the correct length for a groom's braid. I pulled the cap on and checked once again in the mirror. Serapion the groom stood before me.

Grinning, I headed downstairs, for despite the serious nature of the venture, excitement was beginning to infect me. I went first to my father's study and searched until I found an old passport in the Duke's hand, of the kind he would bestow on servants travelling to his Northern estates on business. It basically certified the person bearing it to be upon the Duke's business and that they were to be aided on their way rather than hindered.

Then I took parchment and pen and wrote a short note of explanation for my father. I stressed that I would be back as soon as possible, for I couldn't bear the thought of him giving up and dying in my absence. I sealed this and gave it to Raven to look after.

To the library, next, where I took the map of England on which Elfindale had been marked by some Ravena forebear. It only showed largish towns, but that would be enough for me to find my way. I finished up in the kitchens, where I appropriated enough food for several days. My father would surely send men after me, so I did not want to stop at inns until I had to.

Now that everything was ready, I wanted very badly to tiptoe upstairs and steal a goodbye glance at my father, but common sense won out, and I did not risk it. My note was far from lacking in affection. I crept to the stables and loaded some saddlebags before making my way to Hellion's stall. This was the bit that worried me, for Hellion was still not entirely amenable to being saddled.

With this in mind, I had brought a handful of carrots and an apple from the kitchen. Distracting him with the first while I got the saddle on, I used slices of the latter to get the bit into his mouth. I fastened the saddlebags on firmly and took Raven onto the palm of my hand. I'd been thinking about this a lot, and though it hurt...

"Raven," I said softly, "I'm sorry I have to ask this of you, and I really wish I didn't, but I think I must. Please will you stay here with Pa? Keep him company. Look after him? I think he's going to feel very lonely with me gone. And he'll be worried, too. Will you take care of him?"

Raven looked up at me with rather vulnerable golden eyes. Her tiny wings drooped and she pawed my thumb in silent appeal.

My heart melted. "I won't *make* you," I reassured the dragonet. "And I'll miss you *so* much, but I can't bear to just leave him all alone. If you stay with him, he'll know I'm coming back. Otherwise, for all I know, in a few weeks he'll have convinced himself that I thought he was so evil I couldn't bear to be near him anymore, or something like that. I can just see it! You'll give him hope if you're with him."

Raven's minute ears drooped with her wings, but she nodded her little head, her eyes becoming more resolved. She waved the letter, which she still clutched in both paws.

"Yes," I told her, "that's for him. Will you be all right curled up in Velvet's mane tonight? Will you be warm enough?" When the dragonet nodded again, I added, "Don't give him the letter until it's clear he knows I'm gone and is getting worried. The moment he opens it he'll send people after me, so I want as much of a head start as possible. He won't be suspicious at first, if you stay out of the way. With Hellion gone, he'll assume I'm taking a long ride. Which I am," I finished dryly.

"Let me tuck you up with Velvet, and I'll be off," I said, carrying the dragonet into the next stall and planting a kiss on her tiny muzzle. My father's horse raised his great head sleepily and made a faint whuffing sound, but I simply placed the dragonet on his mighty neck, covered her well with mane and fed Velvet the last piece of apple. The gentle giant was wholly unconcerned by his new companion and was asleep again before I had even left the stable.

167

I lit a hooded lantern and fastened it to the saddle, then led Hellion out of the stable yard. Walking to the nearest park gate on the Islington side of the grounds, I let myself out quietly, my heart leaping to my mouth when the hinges squeaked. But the groundsman who lived in the gatehouse with his wife did not stir, so I mounted, opened the lantern a bit further to shed more light on the country road and urged Hellion into the darkness.

CHAPTER 27

The Wild Places

A week later, Hellion was going along the road at a brisk trot. I had been careful not to choose the main north road, for along this Ravena servants, probably on post horses, would already have been flying, bearing news of a missing daughter to Elfindale before me. This road, while no minor route, was much quieter and I felt safe enough stopping at inns, for there was clearly no knowledge of the Duke's missing heir.

What description my father would have sent out, I was not sure. If he'd stopped to think, he'd probably have realized that I would never be so foolish as to take to the road as a young lady, obvious and appetizing prey for every rascal and bandit encountered. Whether he would guess my exact disguise, I couldn't know for certain.

I had ridden for many days and many tens of leagues undisturbed, keeping up a good pace, but not pushing Hellion too hard. I'd rather keep him at a pace he could sustain than have to stop for any long period of time to rest him. Thus far my disguise had passed without any question at every inn, supported by my Ducal passport, but I felt to stay very long would be to push my good fortune.

I jerked from my thoughts as my ears caught the sound of hoofbeats. A large party of horsemen was coming up fast with me and I quickly looked back at them. I caught the gleam of sunlight on weapons and reacted without thinking, driving my heels into Hellion's sides.

He exploded out from under me, eyes bulging, and if I had not managed to seize the pommel I would have been unhorsed. I pulled myself back into a secure position, letting him run and lying along his neck, my back pricking with

169

excruciating sensitivity, as it anticipated the result of the 'thwack' that would be the last thing I ever heard. But it did not come, and the increased tempo of the other hoofbeats told me that they were giving chase.

They were also catching me! Of course they were! Hellion was fast for his size, but he was a very small horse. Large enough that he seemed too big for me, supporting my pose as a groom delivering a horse to my master's northern estate, but smaller than other animals, all the same.

I kicked him harder, fighting rising panic. I might escape from bandits with my life, if they ransomed me, but I would lose all hope of saving my father, who would probably lock me up until there was no more time for rash journeys. And they might not bother ransoming a young girl...

Struck with a sudden idea, I gathered the reins together in my hand, and then, with a silent apology, lashed the ends hard against Hellion's flank. This time I made sure I was holding on very tightly indeed with my free hand, fortunately, for he half-reared in mid-gallop and went off like a creature possessed. He kept up this insane burst of speed for so long that when he finally dwindled to a trot and then a walk, head hanging with exhaustion, there was no sign of our pursuers, for all we were in open country.

I let him walk for as long as I dared, then urged him to a gentle trot. A canny leader of a group of brigands might well perceive that no horse could keep up such speed forever and have followed at a brisk pace. But no riders appeared on the road behind me, and I soon came to a small town, which was probably why. I took a room for the night, to allow Hellion the rest of the day to rest, and made sure to let the mayor know he had a brigand problem.

I pulled Hellion up at the cliff edge and looked down into the valley. There stood Elfindale Manor. *I was conceived there*, I thought, and remembering the bustling town of York that stood only an hour's drive away, I had to admit that my mother would have liked it here. On the one hand, this wonderful scenery, and on the other, the society of York, at a feasible distance.

The manor house was an ancient building, very beautiful, and stood within a park fenced in with walls and a gate. But I would not be going up to that gate. I had left the road a mile back from it and started to ascend this hill. At Elfindale Manor, I would find a reception committee that would see me loaded aboard a coach and taken straight back to London. But I had no need to go there. My search lay elsewhere.

I remembered the conversation I'd had with my father before the whole matter of the sorcery had ever reared its ugly head and turned Hellion away from the cliff edge. On the other side the hill dropped down again, more gently. There lay a stunning vista of high moorland, hills and further in the distance, a mountain peak rising above them. I could see no human dwellings, although, town bred as I was, I assumed I'd simply overlooked them.

What was a large elfin fort, after all, but a hill or a mountain? This was the wild place of Elfindale, and this was where I believed I would find the Elfin. Behind me lay farmland as far as York.

I let Hellion walk on towards that distant peak.

By mid-afternoon I was looking anxiously at the darkening clouds above me. I had hoped to find a croft or somewhere to spend the night, but since setting off from within sight of Elfindale Manor early that morning I had seen nothing, not so much as distant smoke from a chimney. It was worrying. It felt as though there wasn't a human creature for leagues around me. Which was in a way encouraging. I was looking for a wild place, after all.

But I was already shivering. It had been near spring in London. Here it was still the tail end of winter and although I'd packed a warm woolen cloak, I'd had this wrapped around me since morning, and I was still very cold. Hellion had made his steady way deep in among the hills by now, and the wind came racing off the snow-tipped mountain now towering before me and cut me to the bone with its icy kiss. All it would need was for it to start raining and I would quickly be in a bad way.

Again I scanned the surrounding slopes for any sign of human habitation. I could see none. And I could see no obvious sign of an elfin fort either, although that would have been a bit much to ask. But there was one around here somewhere, or there had been little more than a hundred years ago.

There was no way I could go back the way I had come, so I let Hellion walk onward, hoping I would find some sort of shelter before those clouds made good their threat.

It was a forlorn hope. The light was fading into evening when the clouds, now purple black, opened and I looked about the desolate mountain slope in vain for a place of shelter. There were no trees and even as I established this, the distant rumble of thunder removed such a non-existent shelter from my extremely small list of options. Already drenched to the skin and shivering with both cold and fear, I considered riding Hellion to the side of the nearest rock slab and sheltering under him.

Then the world split open. Blue light sheered across my vision, illuminating all around me in an unearthly flash. A crack louder than any gunpowder hit me in a solid wave of sound. My heart seemed to stop within me; shock held me paralyzed.

Hellion recovered first. Silent in his terror, he bolted, going from stationary to full gallop in one bound. I managed one desperate swipe for the pommel...and missed. Then I was falling, tumbling through an inky blackness. I hit the ground painfully, still too stunned as I fell to curl into a protective ball.

I lay there for long moments, swimming in pain and panic at the darkness; I was blind! The sound of hooves clattering on rock died away into the distance and the rain still fell in sheets, soaking every inch of me.

Eventually I began to be able to distinguish the sky, which was slightly lighter than the skyline, and I knew that I was not blind. I dragged my aching body into a sitting position and tried to push myself to my feet, but my arm crumpled under me, drawing a small cry of pain. Broken, I was pretty sure. I used my other arm to get to my feet, only to stumble and fall again, disorientated by my still imperfect vision and frighteningly weak.

Why am I so weak? I thought in panic, then remembered how I had ridden all day blue with cold, and cursed inwardly. But I knew I had to find shelter, so I pushed myself up again and staggering, stumbling, falling, and finally crawling when my strength gave out entirely, I made my way up the mountainside.

Finally, finally, when I was at the limit of my endurance, I almost fell into a crack in the rock. It was very small and only by squeezing myself up could I get mostly inside it and out of the rain, but it was all I had found and I could go no further.

I lay there shivering, until finally I began to feel a bit better. Everything seemed soft and much more comfortable, and the exhausting, racking shivering had stopped. I was drifting snugly into darkness when some wild part of me that still retained reason tore me awake again.

Fool, it told me, *have you not seen this before? The cold-sapped urchin, shaking and shaking, and when the shaking stops? Then they sleep. Forever.* I drove my nails into my palms in a desperate attempt to wake up more fully. I could not sleep. I could not. To sleep now was death, yet the shivering had stopped and staying awake consumed all my attention.

I can't die like this, I thought desperately. *I'll disappear, and my father will never hear of me again, and he'll be worried, so worried, and he'll die without ever seeing me again! And if he thinks I'm dead somewhere, he'll blame himself for it. And Raven will have no one to take care of her!* But such thoughts, while agonizing, were not enough. Still my head nodded, and time and again I jerked back from sleep at the very last moment.

Please help me, I thought, making my neck prickle in prayer, *Please help me. Don't let me die like this! I must save him! Please help me, please help me. Please help me, please help me!* I repeated it over and over again with all the force I could muster, clinging to the prayer as if it were the last thing in the world that could keep me awake, and it probably was. But still the darkness drew in closer and closer and the prayer faded to a feeble murmur in my mind.

I was barely conscious when there was a patter of hooves on the rock outside. I was dimly aware of two strong arms reaching into the crack and drawing me out. The arms lifted me onto the back of a magnificent stag that stood patiently by, mighty antlers rearing through the rain.

My rescuer got up behind me and whipped his cloak around me, enfolding me on the inside against his warm self. He tucked a fold of the cloak over my head as the stag moved off through the storm. As blackness tore at me, I managed to raise a hand and brush a tangled lock back from my rescuer's ear.

Then I let the darkness take me with a smile of triumphal satisfaction, for that ear rose to a graceful, tapered point.

CHAPTER 28

Memory

I swam slowly up towards wakefulness, feeling as though I fought my way through a mass of fluffy clouds. Eventually, my father's face wavered into view.

"Serapia?" He spoke urgently, his voice hoarse. "*Serapia?*"

"Umm..." I managed, focusing on him with rapidly increasing anxiety. He looked terrible. The skin was drawn over the bones of his face, cheeks and eyes sunken, fingers skeletal. He looked desperately ill. I could scarce believe that such a change could have been wrought in so short a time. "Are you alright?"

He looked startled. "As well as can be expected," he said with an extremely dismissive gesture. "Are *you* alright? What happened?"

"What...happened?" I echoed. What *had* happened to me? I looked around at the familiar curtains and walls of my bedchamber and tried to think. "I must have fallen from Hellion," I groaned in frustration rather than any discomfort. "And just after setting off!"

My father was giving me a very odd look indeed. "Just after setting off?" he echoed. "Whatever do you mean? If you just set off to Elfindale *yesterday* where in perdition have you been for the last six weeks?" His fury spoke of deep and long held concern.

I stared at him, a cold prickle running down my spine. Raven nuzzled my cheek lovingly but I scarcely noticed. "What...what do you mean, the last *six weeks*?" I asked haltingly, bewildered by his words. "I...I set off yesterday, didn't I?"

My father's rising eyebrow was all the answer I needed. That and the appalling change in his condition. The more I looked at his gaunt body, the more I realized that the change could not have been wrought overnight.

"What happened?" I demanded.

"Well, a gentleman carried you to the house unconscious a few hours ago. He brought Hellion as well. He said he'd found you on the verge nearby."

Raven pushed her face against my cheek and trilled excitedly, as though the stranger fascinated her.

I frowned. "Who was he?"

Alban shrugged with scant apology. "A nobleman. Foreign, I think. I only saw him from the window. By the time I'd got to the hall he'd gone on his way."

I bit my lip. "I've really been gone for over a month?"

My father nodded. Raven nodded too, blinking her eyes solemnly at me.

"I don't remember any of it," I whispered, and it was true. After my vague recollection of leading Hellion through the gate, mounting and riding away, my mind was totally blank, as from a rather long and deep night's sleep.

My father reached out and touched my cheek gently, then brushed a strand of hair from my eyes as Raven stroked my other cheek with a little paw. "Child," he said tenderly. "I think you have the Elfin's answer."

I stared at him. *"What?"*

"Missing memories are a sure sign of human contact with the Elfin. They protect themselves well."

"You think I *found* them!"

"Well, I don't think you knocked yourself senseless half a mile from Albany House and lay there like that for over a month undiscovered, let's put it that way."

I chewed my lip in rapidly increasing agitation. "But...but if I *found* them...I must go back, I must go back at once, see if they will help...!"

Raven gave me a disbelieving look and shook her little head at me, as my father's expression became grave and his hand crept towards me in unconscious, heart-felt appeal. "Child, I would ask you not to try and leave for the next week or so... I would...very much like to have you near me." I stared at him. Clearly he did not intend to *let* me leave, but, what did he mean? And then it hit me. Six weeks. Over a month gone. March was nearly upon us. I was almost out of time. My *father* was almost out of time. It was now no longer physically possible to ride to Elfindale and fetch help, even on post horses—and even assuming help agreed to come straight back.

I swallowed, dry-mouthed, feeling sick with fear. "Pa," I whispered, reaching out to grip his bony hands. "Pa, I won't leave you, I promise."

He leant in to place a kiss on my forehead, then sank back into his armchair. He moved like an old man, and the effort of even that slight exertion was clearly enormous. It was like what had happened to my mother, all over again.

I moistened my lips and frowned in thought as Raven cocked her head at me and cheeped...encouragement? Our direct elfin relatives would not help us. But Siridean had surely helped me on the grounds of my elfin blood alone. There must be a few elfin around, even in London. I'd just have to find one of *them*.

My father clearly trusted my promise not to leave, for when I ordered the grooms to tack up Hellion the following morning, they did so without demur.

"My lady?" Susie came scurrying up just as I was about to ride away, looking very anxious. "I'm so sorry, but you know that odd...uh, I mean, that new dress that had to be washed? Well, it's shrunk so very badly, I don't see how you could possibly wear it now. It wouldn't even reach your ankles! Should I send it down to the home with those other old things that are going this morning? I'm so very sorry, I simply don't know how it could have happened..."

I wasn't sure which garment she meant, but right now I was far too worried about my father to concern myself over a shrunken dress, new or not. "Don't fret about it, Susie. Just send it to the home if it's still useable."

"Thank you, my lady." Looking relieved, she hurried off to finish getting the latest clothes' parcel ready.

I turned my attention to the grooms, still hovering respectfully to see me out of the stable yard. "I'll be back by noon," I told them, just in case my father did ask where I'd gone.

I knew I ought to have someone with me, really, when riding outside the grounds, but Susie was no horsewoman and I didn't want the grooms to spread it over the entire of London that Lady Ravena was showing an uncommon interest in all things elfin. I'd dressed in my plainest and simplest riding habit and pulled a very drab cloak around me. Most people would take me for a minor noblewoman or even a farmer's daughter. Anyway, I had my young age to excuse me.

I rode a little way into London, then turned off onto a major road that ran out into the countryside, past Fynesburie Field. I had a very clear memory of a childhood picnic at a barrow that lay uncommonly close to this main road. So certain was I that I could locate it easily, it seemed the logical place to start my search.

There were slightly more small lanes to be negotiated than I expected, but in a short time and with only one bestowment of a coin in return for directions, I found myself outside a field gate. In the centre of the field rose the barrow, or what was surely an elfin fort. I studied it for a moment. Long and oval-shaped, covered seamlessly by the grass of the pasture. No entrance was visible on the side that faced me, but Raven popped her head out of my bodice and stared avidly.

I dismounted to unfasten the gate and led Hellion through, gripping the bridle firmly when he seemed to decide that a nip would best show his affection for me. Closing the gate again, I had just remounted when I felt

Raven pop back down out of sight—a moment later, a red-faced farmer came puffing up the lane.

"No, no, no!" he gasped, in a tone of some exasperation. "It's private property, miss, now come out of there at once!" I was briefly perplexed. We'd picnicked in this very field when I was a child. He must have made an exception then. Ah. I'd warrant I knew why. I slipped off my cloak, which I didn't really need, leaving the superior cut of my riding habit and the richness of the fabric bare to the early morning sun. And reached into my purse. "It must be a trouble to you, I'm sure," I said, "people traipsing over your field and leaving gates open. I would not wish my visit to leave you out of pocket."

I held out a silver piece. To my surprise he shook his head and made no move to take it, though his tone was now considerably more respectful. "Sorry, my lady. But I really can't make exceptions. The...er...the animals, my lady. They don't like to be disturbed."

I eyed the only visible occupants of the field, four dairy cows that looked laid back enough to chew their cud throughout a bombardment of cannon, and reflected for a moment. The creatures in this field that didn't like to be disturbed must be the sort of creatures that prevented your offspring from dying, your cows from going dry, and your crops from failing. Clearly the farmer could be persuaded to make an exception now and then, but it cost more than a silver piece. Fair enough, really.

I reached into my purse again for a fat gold coin. "I have ridden all the way out from London, and my friends said the place was fascinating. Could I not take a quick look? I will not disturb the animals."

A gold piece was more than a farmer could refuse. With a rather guilty glance towards the barrow, he accepted it. "A quick look, my lady," he said reluctantly. "And if it would please you not to...poke around. It disturbs the animals."

"Of course," I said, and touched my heels to Hellion's sides before he could change his mind.

The cows greeted my approach with absolute bovine apathy. One of them actually raised its head to look at me, blinked its large, liquid eyes, licked its nose and went right on chewing.

I rode slowly around to the back of the fort, eyeing it closely. But it looked like nothing so much as a grass-covered mound. I slid from Hellion's back once out of sight of the farmer and crouched down to run my hands over the grassy sides. Raven was out of my dress in an instant, leaping straight onto the mound and sniffing intently, her tiny head moving from side to side as she inspected everything. Something about the whole place made the back of my neck prickle with slightly heightened awareness, but nothing more.

Raven soon gave up her survey and merely gamboled around on the mound, rolling in the grass with evident enjoyment. She returned often to one central point on the mound's side, sniffing and nosing around it with more serious interest, but though I kept a hopeful eye on her, she never found anything.

Could it be an *abandoned* fort, I wondered, when I'd reached the other end without having felt anything other than grass and slope. But the farmer's anxiety suggested otherwise. Was the entrance on the side facing the gate? No, that was foolishness. The farmer couldn't guard the place night and day, and I'd run all over the entire mound during that childhood visit. An entrance there must be, but it could not be accessible to humans, otherwise half the people who came to this place would stumble into it by accident and leave with gaps in their memories. Which would become more than a little obvious.

I stood for a moment, but I could think of nothing else to do, so slightly discouraged, I persuaded Raven to abandon her thrilling play site, wishing she could tell me what it was that attracted her so much. Seeing her safely hidden again down the front of my dress, I got back up on Hellion. I'd make sure to be home in good time, so my father need not worry.

Perhaps I needed to come back and hide behind a hedge or something. Wait for an elfin to come out... But I had a sneaking suspicion the Elfin would not be as easy to surprise as all that.

Reaching the main road, I would've pressed Hellion to a trot but found myself behind a rumbling ox-drawn wagon. Another rider was approaching in the other direction, so I checked Hellion to an amble and waited for him to pass. He was a tall slender youth on a tall slender horse, with gold-blonde hair and a thin face. Small stud earrings graced his ears, his hair was held back in a clip and he wore spectacles. He stared at me rather harder than was polite.

It would have been logical to assume that his attention was caught by my growing female attributes, since that was where his gaze was fixed. But I felt a strange certainty that he was looking at Raven, curled between them, asleep after her exertions. Which was ridiculous because my dress was in the way. There was something slightly familiar about his face, though.

Hellion frisked a few more impatient steps after the wagon, then my iron grip on the reins drew him to an abrupt halt. I'd just remembered who the man's face reminded me of. I paused in another split-second of indecision. If wrong, I was about to make a complete fool of myself. But my father did not have enough time left for me to worry about my pride.

I swung Hellion around, my mouth opening to speak.

The other rider was gone. The road behind was empty. I drove my heels into Hellion's sides, sending him plunging back the few feet to the lane I'd come from. That also stretched away into the distance, deserted. Heedless, now, of what anyone might think, I climbed carefully up to stand on top of the saddle. Raven popped her head out with a sleepy peep of inquiry as Hellion turned his head around to eye me disapprovingly and sidestepped shiftily, but I kept my balance and ignored him, ignored them both, scanning the surrounding area in all directions. No golden-haired, lanky rider who could have been Siridean's younger cousin was to be seen.

Swearing quite vilely, I slithered back down into a sitting position and kicked Hellion to a gallop down the lane. I did not draw rein until I reached the field, and then I jumped from Hellion's back and led him into the shelter of the hedge, peeping through it, only then murmuring an apology and an explanation to a now thoroughly disgruntled little dragonet. But though I waited until the sun was high in the sky, I saw nothing.

Dejectedly, I remounted. I should have been home by now. My father would be worried. But as I cantered along the main road, my spirits began to lift. All right, so I'd let an elfin ride right past me without realizing it. But I *had* found an elfin. And on my very first search. Things were surely looking up.

CHAPTER 29

Lord Ystevan

"Well, you really mustn't go riding around on your own," my father said rather breathlessly, as we climbed into the carriage after a hasty meal.

"You're going to exhaust yourself," I grumbled, ignoring his admonishment. "What's so important about going to court today, anyway?"

"What's so important," my father replied, once settled in the carriage, "is that you are not of age and must have a guardian. I could scarcely arrange it before, not knowing if...well." He shook his head as though to dismiss the fears and worries of the last month.

"The thing is, child," he went on, "we have no relations close enough to be discovered without lengthy scrutiny of family trees and thus none close enough to act as your guardian. This means upon my death, as a senior noblewoman, you will automatically become a ward of the Queen. Now, I think you are aware that I have great respect and affection for her majesty, but nonetheless, this must not under any circumstance be allowed to come to pass."

"Why not?" I asked, rather puzzled. Raven turned her head to one side as well and blinked inquiringly.

"Because her majesty will arrange your marriage for the good of England, not your own happiness," explained my father. "I wish to secure as your guardian someone with enough power to deflect pressure for you to marry strategically, enough influence to arrange the marriage of your choice when you have made it, and enough honesty not to force you to marry he himself for the sake of your fortune."

"Well, that hardly asks for much in a man," I said, feeling decidedly glum. Though not as glum as I might have felt if I were not more determined than ever that I would get the Elfin to heal my father. "I trust you have a wide circle of upstanding acquaintances from whom to pick?"

Alban looked grim. "I have very few acquaintances altogether and few that I know well, after all these years away. I have in mind an acquaintance that I made much more recently, when dealing with the business of those two assassins, and with whom I have had much contact during the last month, seeking his help in the search for you."

"Who is it?"

"Sir Allen Malster," replied my father and I choked in shock. Raven's little ears shot straight up.

My father looked dismayed, and I wondered just how short his list was. "You do not approve?"

"No, no," I hastened to reassure him, "I just did not expect to know...to have heard of...the man." I had never mentioned who it was that Master Simmons had wanted dead, or just who I had sold that information to. "From what I know," I added, "if you are looking for an honest man, you could do very much worse, and he certainly has the Queen's ear."

"Aye," said Alban, looking relieved. "My only concern is that the Queen made him, and could unmake him just as easily. But as far as that is concerned, there is only so much pressure from her majesty that anyone can withstand. If she truly sought a particular match for you, even I could not necessarily prevent it. And an honest man, as you say. I can think of no one better, anyway. I hope he will agree to it."

I contemplated the Ravena fortune for a moment. "I said honest, not a saint," I said dryly. "I should think he'll agree."

My father gave a soft snort at this and sunk into a weary silence.

~+~

Watching my father making his laborious way along the palace corridors with the aid of a stick, my heart filled afresh with chagrin over the morning's tantalizing failure. I wished I could be out searching for elfin right then, rather than wasting precious time here. But the uncertainty of my future situation was clearly weighing on my father's mind. It would be better for him to get it settled.

Sir Allen Malster had an office here at Whitehall Palace, and this was a time when he should be in. We were crossing the courtyard nearby when we caught sight of the man we had come to see. He leaned against the wall in a corner, in conversation with a tall, lean, bespectacled young man whose black hair was clipped back from his face, showing the small studs in his ears.

I felt my father stiffen in surprise, and inside my bodice, Raven's little body went still as well. "That's the man who brought you home," he said to me, under his breath.

I eyed the stranger more closely. About eighteen or nineteen years of age, he was dressed in a shirt and breeches of fine wool with a sleeveless robe over the top, fastened at the front and made of some sort of dark blue velvety material. It was not an English style. He wore soft black leather boots and held a cane or stick, though he grasped it more as one would hold a sword, like it was a weapon. He and Sir Allen turned to look at us as we approached.

I swayed as a wave of disorientation washed through my mind. *I huddled in a crack in a hillside, agony in my arm despite the deathly drowsiness sucking me down. Rain hammered down outside and my breath misted before me. But there was a stag...and a man...a man with pointed ears...a man who...*stood before me now, in this London courtyard. He looked subtly different, something more than his current dryness and neatness. His ears looked rounded and ordinary from this distance. But I had no doubt whatsoever what he was. My fingers crept to my arm. The break was as gone without a trace as my memories had been, until this moment.

I struggled to contain my excitement. *So they did heal!* They definitely, without a shadow of doubt, could heal! Sorcery was no doubt very different to normal illnesses, but still.

The man returned my gaze, betraying no obvious sign of recognition, but his eyes strayed to where Raven was coiled out of sight, literally trembling with her eagerness to peep out but thankfully staying put.

"Pa," I hissed, "I want to speak to that man whilst you talk to Sir Allen. Thank him. Will you make sure he doesn't slip away?" My father shot me a contemplative look that made me wonder if he suspected the true nature of the foreigner himself. "*Please?*" I appealed, but he gave just the tiniest shake of his head. He still was not prepared to do anything to seek healing. Or perhaps he simply wasn't keen to leave his daughter alone with a stranger, even one who'd helped her.

I sighed. Fine. I'd just have to secure him myself.

"Sir Allen," my father was saying, "I do not wish to interrupt. If it is convenient for us to speak this afternoon, I will wait in your office."

"No need, your grace," said Sir Allen. "Lord Ystevan and myself have about finished." He turned his attention back to the stranger. "I'm sorry I could not be of more help this time, my lord. I will let you know if I hear anything of interest to you."

"Thank you, Sir Allen," said Lord Ystevan. His accent was strong, musical and quite unplaceable. "I will be on my way."

He turned to leave, and my father did nothing. The man hadn't even looked at the Duke once, come to that. Only at me. *Hang propriety*, I thought, and stepped forward quickly. "I'll leave you two to your business," I said. "I'm sure Lord Ystevan will keep me company whilst I wait."

Lord Ystevan looked as though he intended to do nothing of the sort, but his polite pause to hear me out allowed me to attach myself to his arm with the grip of a

186

poor baron's daughter taking the arm of a wealthy unmarried earl. As most wealthy unmarried earls would attest, it was a feminine grip that could give a limpet a run for its money and which was well proven to be virtually inescapable. Lord Ystevan gazed down at me with an expression of bemused frustration on his face, though another, unreadable, emotion also flitted through his eyes.

Sir Allen's obvious amusement made my cheeks burn. The sight of an adolescent Duke's daughter throwing herself at a dark and handsome foreigner was surely worth a few chuckles. My father just looked quietly embarrassed, for all he clearly understood what I was doing. To my relief, though, he simply departed with Sir Allen with an air of faint resignation.

"Lord Ystevan." I turned eagerly to face him as soon as we were alone, one hand going to my bodice to quell Raven's surge upwards. "I would like to thank you for helping me, but there is also something else of vital importance about which I must..."

Lord Ystevan had just removed his spectacles with his free hand and tucked them into a pocket. I broke off as he stared down at me. His eyes, delicate, narrow and almond shaped, had irises like Siridean's, very gold around the pupil, radiating into green around the edge. More of a forest green than the emerald of mine and my father's, but bright, for all that. His free hand reached out and slid around the back of my neck, and his green-gold eyes seemed to expand all around me and swallow me up...

Raven's angry screech was the last thing I heard.

CHAPTER 30

Sir Allen Malster

I swam slowly up towards wakefulness, feeling as though I fought my way through fluffy clouds. My father's face wavered into view.

"Serapia?"

I blinked up at him. "Pa?" I looked around at my bedroom. "Did we see Sir Allen? What happened?"

My father sighed heavily and rolled his eyes towards the ceiling. "I left you in the company of Lord Ystevan. It seems you collapsed shortly afterwards. The poor man was most upset, by the servant's account. I've brought you straight home, anyway."

I frowned. "Lord Ystevan? Who is Lord Ystevan?" Raven sat up on my shoulder and rumbled angrily. Someone she wasn't too happy with right now, that was clear.

But my father just said vaguely, "Someone Sir Allen knows."

I frowned even harder. Things were flitting through my mind, tiny shreds of memory, gone before I could grasp them. I struggled to catch them, to see them, until I thought my head might explode. They just wouldn't quite come into focus.

"It was Lord Ystevan who brought me back here yesterday..." I couldn't remember it, but the knowledge was there in my mind. Raven cheeped excitedly, then looked cross again.

"That too," admitted my father. "I do not know the man, though."

But Sir Allen does. I rubbed the back of my neck reflectively. *And Raven seems remarkably interested in you, Lord Ystevan. I can't remember who you are, but there is something very strange going on. Every time I meet you, I forget all about it.*

"Did you speak to Sir Allen?" I asked, changing the subject.

My father sighed. "I was just about ready to mention it when the servant came knocking at the door. If you're sure you're alright I'll go straight back now. Sir Allen said he would be there for an hour or two more."

I caught his gaunt hand, regarding his pale face with concern. "Right now? Why don't you wait until tomorrow? You'll wear yourself out!"

Alban gently removed my hand from his and placed it back on the bed with a little pat. "I want this settled. I cannot know how long I have. Don't you overexert yourself, now."

I gave a faint snort. I felt absolutely fine. I eyed my father for a moment, wondering whether to accompany him. But it would probably be better for him in the long run if I used the time to lay a plan of campaign.

Against the mysterious Lord Ystevan.

"Sir Allen agreed, as you predicted," my father said once he returned and was slumped in an armchair by the fire, his face grey with exhaustion.

"Good," I said, encouragingly. I didn't intend to need Sir Allen's guardianship, but my father's condition twisted my heart.

"He will be as nominal a guardian as possible," my father went on rather faintly. "He knows about your urchin-hood, so he understood why his position was more of a formality than it would be for most young women of your age."

After a moment's silence, he added, "He will live at Albany House only if you wish it. If you do not want his presence he will stay at his own house and you may live here with Anna and the servants."

I had scarcely stopped to consider what things might be like if my father actually did die. The idea of a stranger

189

moving in in my father's place... I swallowed.

"That's...that's good."

"Yes, he suggested it himself," my father replied. "Good man."

He sounded so tired I greeted his next words with a gentle hand on his lips. "Pa, rest. Please. I'm sure you've arranged everything as well as you can. You can tell me about it another day."

Raven jumped over and curled against his neck, crooning softly. The Duke sighed and closed his eyes. He was asleep in moments.

The following morning I drew Hellion to a halt outside Sir Allen Malster's Fleete Street house slightly earlier than was entirely polite. But I was becoming all too aware that I had no time to waste and besides, having left my chaperone again and been too impatient to wait for the coach to be prepared, there seemed little point pretending to be a model of propriety.

A groom came to take my horse, face showing no trace of what he might think of an unaccompanied girl on horseback arriving at that hour. Sir Allen probably got a lot of odd visitors, come to think of it. I rang the bell and waited, touching Raven gently through the cloth of my dress to remind her to stay out of sight. Sir Allen would never take her for a rare exotic creature. The street was quiet. No one was abroad visiting yet.

"I would like to see Sir Allen Malster, if it please him," I said clearly to the servant who answered it, trying not to yawn. I'd had a horrible nightmare last night, and the sense of urgency that had come with it had kept me awake long afterwards. I *had* to find Lord Ystevan!

Before the servant could say anything in response, there was from above us the sound of a window opening all the way. "Who is that speaking...?" demanded a familiarly harsh voice.

I looked up to see Sir Allen staring down in his shirt

sleeves.

He started as his eyes fell upon me. "Lady Ravena!" His brows drew together in sudden enlightenment. "Ah-*ho*, Lady Ravena the *urchin*. Do come in. I had not realized that we had met before..." He disappeared from the window, fastening his cuffs.

I bit my lip, feeling awkward. He'd failed to recognize my voice yesterday, coupled with so different a figure than he associated with it. But hearing my voice alone... I did not think much slipped past Sir Allen Malster.

I followed the servant inside and was shown to a good-sized drawing room.

In only a very few minutes Sir Allen arrived, now fully dressed. "Lady Ravena..." he paused in what I realized was an awkwardness of his own. "You, ah, are aware of what your father discussed with me yesterday?"

"Oh. Yes, quite aware," I reassured him. "That is not why I have come, though of course in the circumstances I would be happy better to make your acquaintance." I hardly wished to seem unfriendly when I needed his help so badly. Sir Allen could provide me with a very much needed short-cut to the elusive Lord Ystevan, and if my suspicions were correct, the Elfin.

"Ah. I assume you have not come to talk over...old times?"

I blushed slightly. "No. Nothing like that, Sir Allen. Though, I can't help wondering... Why did you not tell me about my father, when I asked you before?" I couldn't help my voice coming out rather cold. I'd been thinking about it ever since we went to court and I'd realized that Sir Allen simply *must* have known *of* my father, even if he'd never actually *met* him.

Sir Allen raised an eyebrow. "You asked me about a Duke of Albany. I had not heard of such a man. I knew of the existence of a Duke of *Elfindale*, but your father has not been much at court since I began to move in...such circles. It was only some months after we spoke that first I heard the jesting title 'Duke of Albany', upon his return to England. And I did spare a regretful thought for the fact that I had learned the information too late to help that strange urchin who'd climbed onto my house roof one night."

"Ah...oh." I could feel my cheeks heating. It was so obvious, I felt a total fool. He hadn't kept anything from me, after all. "Well, um, what I'm *actually* here about... Well, I rather hoped you could tell me where I might find Lord Ystevan."

Sir Allen's eyebrow rose again and his expression hovered between amusement and concern. "Lady Ravena," he said rather delicately, "Lord Ystevan is only a visitor to these parts, and an infrequent one at that. And in the light of my future position with regard to yourself, might I take the liberty to point out that you are still rather young to..."

"Sir Allen!" I interrupted, my cheeks on fire. "You entirely misunderstand me. Despite any impression you may have gained from my behavior yesterday, my interest in Lord Ystevan is of an extremely serious and most urgent nature that has nothing whatsoever to do with girlish infatuations! If you know where I can find him you must... that is, I most strongly request that...you tell me!"

Sir Allen regarded me more seriously, the amusement gone from his face. "Pardon my misinterpretation. However, I do not know where Lord Ystevan is to be found. He has never told me on any of his visits."

My heart sank in disappointment at this, but I could not help one eyebrow rising slightly. "You, ah, have no objection to this?" A man like Sir Allen would surely greet such secrecy with disfavor.

"I can contact him," said Sir Allen evenly.

My heart bounced eagerly up again, whilst my mind raced. "You can contact him..." I said slowly. "Well, would you be prepared to arrange a meeting with him? Here, perhaps?"

"That would be easily enough done," said Sir Allen just as evenly, eyeing me curiously.

"Would you be prepared to do so without any mention of me?"

Sir Allen's eyes narrowed. "You are asking me to do something that will inevitably put the trust that exists between us under significant strain."

"I also wish you to stay in the room whilst I speak to him," I went on firmly, "out of earshot but in the room. And if I should faint or behave in any way oddly, I would like you to keep Lord Ystevan here, tied up if necessary, until I have come to myself."

"Are you trying to get me killed with this peculiarness?" declared Sir Allen. "If a man like Lord Ystevan wishes to leave, he generally leaves. I am not fool enough to try to stop him without excellent good reason."

"Then fill your hall with guards once he arrives," I said in a tone of exaggerated patience. Sir Allen was making excuses.

"Tell me, Lady Ravena, why I should do this for you?" demanded Sir Allen. "I am not your guardian yet and once I am, whilst I may not intend to give over many orders, it will still be for me to give them, not you. Why don't you explain yourself, for a start?"

I shook my head. "You of all men should know that explanations are not always possible."

"Then why should I do this for you?"

I stared up at him for a long moment. "You underpaid me," I said at last. "I was very lucky to escape with my life, and you gave me two little silver pieces. You owe me."

Sir Allen rubbed his chin for a moment, regarding me steadily. "True," he said softly at last. "But I need to know a little more than nothing."

"You know my father's dying," I replied quickly. "Lord Ystevan comes from a country where they have a kind of medicine that will help him. But they don't like to let foreigners have it, so he's avoiding me. That's the truth, my word on it."

"Some of it, perhaps," murmured Sir Allen, still watching me intently. "Very well," he said at last. "I will bait the trap for you. I hope you know what you're doing."

I remembered his remark about men like Lord Ystevan leaving when they wanted to. I bit my lip. Certainly my last two meetings with Lord Ystevan had not exactly gone to plan, even if I could not remember precisely how they had not. "When can you arrange the meeting?"

"Oh, if ever I get information Lord Ystevan wants, he wants it fast. I can get him here by this afternoon."

I brightened at that and felt a soft flick against my skin as Raven's ears pricked up. The less time wasted the better. "This afternoon would be excellent."

"You are going to Sir Allen's this afternoon?" said the Duke, with a faintly surprised smile. "Well, that is a good idea. I should have thought of it myself." He shook his head wearily. "I fear I will be poor company today, anyway."

I suspected he was right. He lay on a couch in the drawing room with several blankets over him, and he looked frail and exhausted. The previous day's exertions had been far too much for him.

"You just lie quietly and rest." I pressed his hand gently. "Things are as good as sorted with Sir Allen so there is nothing for you to worry about."

"Aye," he sighed. "I'll just lie here. I can do naught else, anyway. Off you go to get on with your twisting of Sir Allen around your little finger. I do wish you luck." He chuckled almost inaudibly, clearly finding even that tiring.

I shot him a suitably reproachful look and departed. My father clearly ascribed my sudden interest in Sir Allen to his intended position as my guardian. Which was perhaps a little short-sighted of him, but he was not well at all.

I climbed into the coach that I had ordered for travelling to Sir Allen's at this rather more visible time of day and turned my plan in my mind. Raven leapt around, swinging from the curtains and unashamedly making the most of things before she would have to curl up and hide again.

A man like Sir Allen Malster was almost pathologically curious by nature. It was what made him so good at his job. Hence I'd dumped my tantalizing instructions on him in their entirety at the outset. He couldn't shake the truth out of Lady Serapia Ravena, so as I'd suspected, he'd agreed to cooperate in the hope that he might discover more through the unfolding of events.

Which I could not allow to happen. Not the whole truth. Using Sir Allen Malster to save my father from self-inflicted sorcery was akin to smothering a fire with a keg of gunpowder. If my mother had left my father because of his involvement in sorcery, to expect my father's new-formed friendship with Sir Allen to stand the strain would be foolish in the extreme. Sir Allen saw sorcerers burned at the stake— and he was quite active in pursuing them. But what choice did I have? Save my father's life first, then worry about Sir Allen.

I turned my mind firmly back to my upcoming meeting with Lord Ystevan. My third meeting, I rather suspected. I bludgeoned my brain for a while, but still I could not quite grasp those floating wisps of memory. But they related to Lord Ystevan, that I felt sure about.

CHAPTER 31

The Guardian of the Fort

"All is ready," Sir Allen told me when I arrived. "The drawing room windows are well barred anyway. I have a detachment of soldiers out of the way in the stables, from whence my butler will fetch them as soon as Lord Ystevan is in the drawing room. You said you wished to wait at a distance until Lord Ystevan is safely inside the house, so you will be in the dining room, over here. Is all satisfactory, my lady?" he added sardonically.

"Perfectly satisfactory, thank you," I returned blandly.

Sir Allen gave me a curt nod and gestured for me to precede him to the dining room. His face was amused, but a tinge of frustration peeped from underneath. He had not been forthcoming about the nature of his occasional information exchanges with Lord Ystevan, but he clearly misliked the idea of upsetting the man unnecessarily.

Lord Ystevan was punctual. I heard the bell ring and a short time afterwards, the sound of the drawing room door closing. I waited a few moments more, Raven writhing in excitement, until the muffled tread of numerous boots had passed the door, then I slipped out and made my way to the drawing room. I eased the door open a fraction and briefly applied my ear to the crack.

"I can't apologize enough for inviting you here like this, Lord Ystevan," Sir Allen was saying. "It was not my idea at all, I confess. But really, what a man can do?"

Pushing the door open, I marched in just in time to see him finish the sentence with a suitably helpless gesture in my direction. I shut the door behind me and turned resolutely to face Lord Ystevan, who greeted my appearance with a peculiar expression that seemed to mingle self-

196

deprecation with resignation. And another emotion I couldn't quite determine. Dismay? *Delight?*

I blinked as the memories settled into place in my mind like a flock of birds alighting on a tree. I clutched my healed arm in quite definite delight of my own. Lord Ystevan was an elfin, as I had rather suspected. Not just a link *to* them, but an elfin himself!

And...another memory had just joined the others!

I lay in a cozy bed, under warm fur blankets, waking slowly.

I could hear voices but it was a while before I was awake enough to concentrate on what they were saying.

"I know why he went out to look for it, but why did he bring it back here? Why didn't he take it down to the village and leave it on the doorstep of the inn?"

Another voice replied, as feminine as the first, but gentler, albeit rather firm. "Peace, Alvidra. The human would not have lived if he had not brought her straight back here."

"That's as may be, but why is she still here? Why doesn't he take it away before it wakes up? He's making more work for himself!"

"Since," said the second voice, a trifle dryly, "as you say, it will be his work, I suggest you ask him. If you really need to—surely you can see this human is far too young to simply be abandoned at the inn? Anyway, he asked me to take care of the human when he was summoned to the Queen, and I have done so. It's not as if you have been inconvenienced."

"I'm not complaining about inconvenience, Mother," protested the voice of Alvidra. "I just don't like having a human here..."

She broke off as there were footsteps and the 'Mother' said, "Ah, Ystevan, there you are. Is everything all right?"

"Routine, routine," said a new voice, a male one. "Rat-gnawing, mice-gnawing, demon-gnawing, the usual. How is the little one?"

"Asleep," replied Alvidra, sounding deeply uninterested. "Best if she stays that way and you take her to the village," she added pointedly.

There was a moment of silence, and I sensed a gaze being

197

turned on me.

"Not so asleep, I think," said the male voice after a moment, and the footsteps approached the bed, which then sunk as though someone was sitting on the edge of it.

"Then bespell her, quickly!" urged Alvidra. "We don't want it waking up!"

"Oh, stop flapping, Alvi," responded the male voice. "A single human is not dangerous. Anyway, they're such fascinating creatures, don't you think?"

This was too much.

"I am not a creature," I declared, and opened my eyes.

A male elfin—a he-elf—was sitting on my bed, looking down at me. I struggled quickly into something more of a sitting position, then I regarded the he-elf, and the he-elf regarded me.

I saw a person who at very first glance could have passed for human, but only at the very first glance. Then the attention was drawn to so many things that it was hard to know what to take in first.

He was extremely slender, and looked long-limbed. He was probably tall. He looked about eighteen or nineteen. His hair, no longer wildly tangled by wind and rain, was neatly brushed, and a strange mixture of gold and black, falling to his shoulders at the sides, and a little further at the back. His ears, as I had established previously, were beautifully pointed, and the chin of his rather narrow face was somewhat pointed as well.

His eyes, delicate, narrow and almond shaped, had irises like Siridean's, very gold around the pupil, radiating into green around the edge. It was more of a forest green than the emerald of my eyes and those of my father, but it was bright, for all that. His complexion was extremely light and his fingers were long and graceful. He was dressed in a shirt and breeches of fine wool, with a sleeveless robe over the top, fastened at the front, and made of some sort of velvety material. His boots were soft black leather, and the robe was dark blue...

Raven's excited movements jerked me back to Sir Allen's drawing room. But I'd clearly met this...he-elf...properly, at the fort.

198

Right now the he-elf's hair, neatly brushed and clipped back, appeared plain black all over, as it had when I'd seen him at the palace. He still held that cane of his and I now noticed a rather long leather pouch at his belt, hanging opposite the dagger that lay at his other hip.

"Lord Ystevan, Lady Serapia Ravena; Lady Serapia, Lord Ystevan," Sir Allen was introducing us formally. "Lady Serapia," added Sir Allen apologetically, "seems to think you have been avoiding her."

The corner of the he-elf's mouth turned down slightly, at that.

"To put it mildly," I said rather cuttingly.

"Indeed," said Lord Ystevan dryly. "Well, now that you have me so thoroughly at your disposal, Lady Serapia," he tilted his head towards the door significantly, "might I inquire what it is that you actually want?" The look he threw at Sir Allen was not entirely without recrimination, but did not seem to portend undying enmity.

"Lord Ystevan," I said, drawing a little closer to him but making no move to take his arm. Or to come quite within reach. "If we could step across to the window there and have a little conversation. Sir Allen will remain over here, but he is not going to leave the room, you understand."

"I dare say he isn't," said the he-elf, still in a rather resigned tone. He followed me to the window at the other end of the room readily enough.

"Perhaps we could...admire the view as we talk." I turned so I largely faced the glass but could still just about see Lord Ystevan's face. At my companion's raised eyebrow, I elaborated, "I believe Sir Allen may be able to read lips, as the deaf do."

"Ah." With no further demur, the he-elf turned so that he mirrored my position.

I was silent for a moment. Now that I finally had the man...he-elf...there, I wasn't quite sure how to begin. "I, ah, I did mean it yesterday, when I thanked you for helping me," I said at last.

A faint, slightly strained, smile flitted across his face. "You're welcome."

"Well, I'm sorry to have caused you so much trouble," I persisted. Especially if I'd actually stayed with them longer than I'd hitherto realized. More memories were stirring, even as I spoke...

There was a dragonet curled around the he-elf's shoulders, staring at me. It was much bigger than Raven, about the size of a small cat, but the same grey color, except that its skin gave off iridescent shimmers of vibrant green as the light caught it. Even as I watched, a tiny puff of flame flickered from its mouth...

I felt a little self-conscious at the he-elf's scrutiny, and despite the fire-breathing dragonet, I eventually averted my gaze. Strange as it might seem, I probably looked as odd to him as he did to me. Seeking to break the silence, I looked up again and said, "I'm Serapia. Thank you for, um, rescuing me."

The he-elf regarded me for a moment, one long finger absent-mindedly rubbing the dragonet behind its little ears.

"You are welcome," he replied at last, only now his English was accented.

I couldn't help frowning at him, puzzled. Why was he pretending he couldn't speak perfect English?

"I am Ystevan," added the he-elf. He gestured politely to the two other elfin who were standing in the doorway. I looked at them for the first time. They were both she-elves, one just a little older than Ystevan, the other much older.

"This is my mother, Haliath," he told me, gesturing to the older of the two, who raised a hand in friendly acknowledgement, "and my sister, Alvidra. My mother will find some food for you. Hungry, yes?"

I gave him a frustrated look as he persisted in using that thick, though musical, accent, but couldn't help nodding. Yes, I was very hungry.

The mother, Haliath, exchanged a few words in some incomprehensible language with Ystevan and she and Alvidra disappeared from the doorway. Why the foreign language now I was awake? And why this Ystevan was making an idiot of himself speaking English like a foreigner I could not understand, and I supposed there was only one way to find out.

"Why are you talking like that?" I asked bluntly. "I know you can speak English properly, I heard all of you speaking properly!"

He looked back at me, his brow rucking up in thought. "Yes," he said slowly, "you heard me say 'creature'. Odd. I apologize for my imperfect English. I go among humans now and then but not often enough to pass as a native in my speech."

"What do you mean, odd?" I challenged. "It's not me, it's you, you're talking differently! Why don't you want me to know that you all speak perfect English?"

He regarded the hand I had thrown out towards the doorway—so did the dragonet, rather disapprovingly.

"They do not speak any English," he told me gravely. "None." He was silent for a moment, then, perhaps observing that I was about to break out again in frustration, he held up a silencing hand. "Let's try something. If you will close your eyes..."

Slightly apprehensively, I obeyed, hoping I could resist the temptation to peep at the dragonet.

"Now I will tell you a story about a pair of eagles," said Ystevan. "You simply listen to my voice. The eagles have a nest with three eggs. Soon two eggs open up. The parent eagles have two fine chicks. But still the mother sits on the third egg, keeping it warm..."

I'd quickly found myself drifting as I listened to his deliberately monotonous voice. But I suddenly realized that the trivial tale he was relating had slipped into unaccented English.

"You're speaking properly now," I exclaimed and would have opened my eyes, if his fingertip hadn't touched my lids very gently.

"Keep them shut a little longer," he told me. "We don't want to have to do this again. Soon the third egg hatches and the parent eagles have a full nest, and are ever so busy bringing food for their offspring. Every mouse in the area goes in fear and trembling, and the rabbit population takes a severe dip... All right, you can open your eyes, but keep holding onto my meaning..."

That was a very strange way of putting it, I thought, but I did as I was bid.

"You still understand me?" he asked.

I nodded, mystified.

"Good. Because I am speaking in elfin now, not my poor English... And don't you dare let go of my voice just because I told you that!"

Startled, I listened more closely as he continued with a few more lines of the eagle story. It was true. He spoke in a musical tongue of which I recognized not one word, yet I understood what he was saying. Weird.

"I don't understand," I said, flushing a little as I remembered how angry I had been getting with him before. "How am I understanding you?"

He gave me a thoughtful half smile, then reached out and slipped a hand behind my head, to the nape of my neck. I jerked back slightly, startled by what seemed a liberty, but his touch was clearly clinical, so I stayed still and let him run his fingers up and down the back of my neck, over the three bumpy vertebrae I had there, much as Siridean had once done. In fact, his fingers lingered on these vertebrae and his touch there sent shivers up my spine.

The dragonet made a snorting sound, another flicker of flame coming from its mouth, leapt into the air, startling me with its wingspan—five times that of Raven's in proportion to its body—and soared out of the room. Ystevan simply smiled slightly and continued his investigation. "Don't mind Eraldis. He just doesn't know what to make of you."

Finally he took his hand away, and feeling rather ruffled, I took the offensive and retaliated by slipping my hand behind his neck.

He drew away with a quick, "Careful!"

But I'd already jerked my hand back as I felt a prick of pain—a bead of blood was forming on my fingertip. Confused, I looked at the he-elf. "May I...?"

He nodded and half-turned, arching his neck so as to present his nape for inspection. I carefully parted his black-gold locks, soft under my probing fingers, and discovered three sharp bony ridges along the back of his neck. My eyes widening, I reached out to touch one, although with great care, for the edge was razor sharp.

His shirt had a strip of leather sewn inside it to minimize damage. I ran a finger around the edge, where the bone went into the skin, and he gasped and shrugged me away.

"Little one, please," he said hoarsely, looking caught between surprise and amusement.

I'd realized now why those strange ridges looked so familiar. "It's just like Raven's crest!"

He gave me a slightly odd look, as if something wasn't adding up. "You have a...Raven?"

"No, she's not a Raven, that's simply her name. She's a dragonet, like yours—well, smaller—but she has a crest just like that, only not so sharp yet." I tried to remember if Eraldis had a crest too. Yes, he had...

"You have a dragonet, and a partial crest, and you can speak—and hear—with your mind as the Elfin do," stated the he-elf, giving me a very curious look. "You must have our blood in you; you are kin to us."

I nodded in delight; I'd expected to have to recite my family tree numerous times to gain such an acknowledgement. "Yes, I am. My great, great, er, great, grandfather, he married a she-elf, so she was my great, great, great grandmother."

Ystevan nodded to himself. "That would explain a lot."

Raven wriggling out of my dress snapped my mind back to the present. My little friend was staring avidly at the he-elf as though she could restrain herself no longer. I threw a rapid glance at Sir Allen to check he couldn't see her.

"Well, hello Raven," murmured Lord Ystevan, reaching towards me. He certainly hadn't lost *his* memories of our previous meeting. *Meetings?*

Raven popped into his sleeve, re-emerged at his collar on the side away from Sir Allen and began to fiddle and chew at his stud earring, clearly fascinated. I frowned at his ear myself in sudden concentration, realizing I could see a slight double image of a point. Emboldened by both Raven's acceptance of Lord Ystevan and Lord Ystevan's acceptance of Raven, I reached up, and found that I could touch this point as I had at our very first meeting.

Lord Ystevan gently took my hand and moved it from his ear with a little flick of his eyes towards Sir Allen. His plain green eyes. I stared up at them intently. Remembering Siridean... I would wager those glasses were hiding their true—and oh-so-unusual—coloring.

"Why did you bring me all the way back to London?" I demanded, still rather angry at the loss of so much precious time, and uncomfortably conscious that I couldn't remember everything that had happened between us and he clearly could.

"I had to come to London anyway," he replied, but his green eyes studied me, guarded. "So it made sense to see you safely home. Because of your youth, for one thing, to say nothing of the fact that trying to make humans with elfin blood forget meeting us is always a little hit and miss. It seemed best to place you as far away from the fort as possible, to avoid you seeing anything that would bring the memories back to you. I fully intended to avoid you for the duration of my stay." He smiled ruefully. "So much for that."

"But if I'm your *kin*... That's what you called me! *Why* did you make me forget?"

"There are no exceptions. Well, aside from humans who are *so* closely related to us that we actually *cannot* keep them from remembering an encounter with us."

I edged away from him slightly at this conclusion and he flashed me a smile that came close to a grin, albeit a resigned one. "I will not try to make you forget again, Ser... my lady. You have recovered your memories so rapidly after each of my attempts that even bearing in mind that you have met me again each time, I would not bother. I doubt you would need to even see me to remember a third time."

His eyes were still searching mine. Oh. He was wondering how *much* I remembered. How much was there *to* remember? Every time I thought about it, a little more seemed to unfold...

"A lot of our...what you would call supernatural, abilities are seated in our crests," Ystevan told me a bit later, after I'd eaten a

tasty bowl of rabbit stew. Eraldis was on his shoulders again, staring at me unblinkingly, his tail wrapped around Ystevan's neck like a thin leathery scarf. "It's fairly certain that these crests do in fact linger from the dragons, who certainly, whichever theory you subscribe to, had a large part in our creation."

"And that's why I can understand you?" I questioned, full and comfortable by now but excessively curious about everything. Perhaps falling off Hellion hadn't been quite the disaster it seemed. Which reminded me of something, and I flexed my arm as I listened to his reply.

"Unquestionably," he said. "Although I doubt your skills are very pronounced, I'd have thought you'd have been aware there was something a little...unusual...about you."

I nodded a bit distractedly. "Yes, I was... What happened to my arm? I mean, I'm pretty certain it was broken but there's nothing wrong with it now."

Ystevan smiled at my perplexity. "I wouldn't worry about that, it wasn't serious." He blinked and fixed me with a look. "I nearly forgot, let's see that finger of yours."

"Well, this really isn't serious," said I, but I proffered my cut finger. He took my hand and stroked the fingertip with one of his own, just once. I shivered as a strange tingle ran through me, and when he released my hand the cut was gone. I struggled to contain my excitement. So they did heal! Sorcery was no doubt very different to normal illnesses, but still...

"How did you find me?" I asked suddenly, remembering the darkness and the wildness of the storm. "How did you even know I needed help?"

Ystevan gave a laugh that came close to a snort—the dragonet went right on staring. "Little one, when a human rides across the outer wards at night, it is the business of the duty guardian to see what they are up to. I was the guardian on duty, so I headed for my chambers to dress more suitably, it was not a nice night," he added wryly.

I nodded agreement, quelling a different sort of shiver at the memory, even as I puzzled over all the unknown things he referred to.

"As for knowing you needed help," he went on, looking amused, "I was only halfway to my chambers when you started crying out for it loudly enough for every elfin in the fort to hear. At which point I abandoned the idea of changing and came straight out to find you. Fortunately, considering your condition. And you were curled up in the side of the fort itself, you were not very difficult to find."

I nodded slowly, understanding the essence but mystified by the detail.

"That's why it occurred to me to try and teach you to hear us while fully awake," the he-elf remarked after a moment. "The Lord knows I'd never have bothered trying it on a human I thought completely normal!"

"Hmm," I said, for that had sounded rather slighting towards normal humankind. "But, I have some questions. What's a ward, and a guardian, and a duty guardian..."

He flicked his fingers in the air as if dismissing his lack of explanation. "A ward is... Hmmm, well it's a fixed barrier—not necessarily a physical barrier, you understand—enclosing something, but actively linked to its maintainer or maintainers—the guardians, in the case of a fort. 'Fixed' means that even if the maintainers were all killed it would still be there. 'Actively linked' means that normally they can also feel if anything touches or crosses or damages the ward in any way. There several around the fort. They're spherical, so there's no way around them. Are you following me?"

I nodded, fascinated, but Eraldis yawned—flame-flickeringly—and flew off.

"Now, the fort guardians," Ystevan went on, "well, our title is fairly self-explanatory. Our job is the protection of the fort. As well as taking care of the wards, and some other things, we do this by working hard to ensure the goodwill of our human neighbors— healing livestock, people, even crops, sometimes. Humans are rather...dangerous, to be quite frank."

"That is a somewhat lesser job for a fort this isolated, though. All sheiling-forts have a fort guardian; they're the small forts that may be on human farmland, but a torr-fort guardian is also *responsible for helping them when they need it, and a torr-fort—like this one—needs at least four guardians."*

He broke off and shot a glance at me, as though to check I was following him. Apparently I did not look mystified, for he continued, "Anyway, a duty guardian is simply the guardian on duty any particular night. In daylight hours we're all aware of the wards, and we all have our sections to check daily.

"At night, though, the ward-awareness is all channeled to the duty guardian, so that the others can sleep undisturbed, and more importantly, so that the duty guardian will wake up if anything so much as brushes the wards. Night duty starts at dusk, and we just rotate, so with seven of us at present, we're only doing one day a week. It's not very common to have to actually go outside for any reason."

"Sorry," I muttered, guiltily.

He just laughed. "Don't apologize, child, I'd much rather fetch you in from the rain than have to venture out and drive off a particularly determined demon."

I stared at him. "Demon?"

He just nodded as if it was the most natural thing in the world. "Yes, they chew on the wards sometimes. But enough of this. How are you feeling? We got you warmed up nice and gently, you don't seem too bad to me."

I dutifully considered how I felt. Well fed, rather tired, and despite my raging curiosity, not a little sleepy. "I'm quite all right, thank you."

"Well then, perhaps you should get to sleep." He rose to leave.

Wait! I hadn't yet broached my reason for being here. But...for one thing, it hadn't been mentioned, and for another, I would make my case better after a good night's sleep. So I simply bid the he-elf goodnight, and was bidden it in return.

My mind came back to the present again. I eyed the he-elf, so friendly and engaging in my memory, but now so...wary. Had I already asked him to heal my father? Surely I had! What had his reply been? Well, that was fairly clear.

So I needed to ask him again.

I licked my lips and glanced at Sir Allen. He stood staring at us with narrowed eyes and an expression of such intense frustration on his face that I suspected he had indeed planned to read our lips.

I turned carefully back towards the window before speaking. "If I have your word that I am indeed safe from any further attacks of forgetfulness, might we go somewhere rather more private to continue our discussion?"

Lord Ystevan also glanced at Sir Allen. "I think that would be an extremely good idea." He reached across to me again and Raven ran up my dress and disappeared back down the front of it. He made to turn towards the door...

"Ah, your word, Lord Ystevan?"

He paused and looked down at me. Amusement touched his eyes but also something close to respect. And an odd sadness. "I give you my word," he said and offered me his arm. I took it and we turned and walked back down the long room to our host.

"Sir Allen," I said when we reached him, "I am very grateful to you for arranging this meeting, but now that Lord Ystevan and myself have sorted out our misunderstanding, we would not dream of taking up any more of your time."

He eyed me, clearly trying to determine if I were myself. "Do you plan to take up any old hobbies, my lady?" he asked obliquely.

"No, indeed, Sir Allen," I replied promptly. "I have sworn off drain-pipe climbing. I hope I can visit you again soon, but by the front door."

Sir Allen, clearly as reassured as he could be in the circumstances, nodded and went to the drawing room door. By the time Lord Ystevan and I followed him out there was nothing but the distant tramp of boots along a paved corridor and a certain amount of dirty straw strewn over the hall.

CHAPTER 32

Of Safyr and Sorcery

"Have you a private room?" I asked the innkeeper of The Star and the Ram.

"This way, my lady, my lord," the man said, and ushered us into a private chamber behind the inn common room.

When we were seated, I eyed Lord Ystevan expectantly. I was definitely ready for something to drink. But the he-elf just sat there, looking at me with much the same expectant look I was giving him. I chewed my lip in frustration.

"Ah, can I get you anything, my lord?" prompted the innkeeper, after a few more moments of silence.

Lord Ystevan started slightly. "Ah...yes, of course. Tisane, please. Dandelion, if you have it." He looked inquiringly at me and I nodded my agreement with this choice. He belatedly took out his purse, and I was relieved to see him tip the man enough to justify the use of the private room.

"Sorry," he said distractedly, when the innkeeper was gone. "Amongst the Elfin it is always the she-elves who initiate hospitality, as you kn... Uh, well, sometimes I forget the human ways."

I stared at him, fascinated by this snippet of information and eager to learn more...though his slip of the tongue suggested I knew already. Or *had*. Before...before he *stole* my memories. I couldn't help frowning at him as I thought about it.

Yes, no wonder he was so wary. He was waiting for my fury to break against him. And the more I remembered, and the more I thought about what he'd done, the greater the anger that welled inside me. But...my father's healing was more important. I couldn't rage at him, no matter whether he deserved it or not.

Still, I found it hard to begin again. "What did you mean about dragons and creation?" I asked at last.

He was silent for a moment, clearly trying to link my question with what he'd said, and *when*, then his eyes cleared. "Oh, that's a long story," he said quietly. "I'd better not start on it now." Something about the way he spoke made me suspect he'd told me it before.

I turned my mind to what I *could* remember, hoping more would come back to me. Surely I must have asked about my father very soon? Yes...I had...hadn't I?

The following morning, Haliath brought me a large breakfast, in bed. I wasn't entirely sure what everything was, but it was very tasty. There was an egg of some kind, various cooked roots, equally indeterminable, a piece of venison, and mushrooms, of which I could recognize the family but not the type on my plate.

Slightly embarrassed to be waited on in such a way, I tried to get up afterwards, but Haliath insisted on tucking me back in, 'at least for the forenoon,' as she put it. Having secured my acquiescence, she glided out, bearing my empty plate, and Ystevan took her place in the doorway and knocked on the doorframe.

"Uh. Come in," I said, slightly flustered at this courteous behavior since the door was open—in so much as there was a door; it seemed to be a thick curtain—and it was his home. He entered, tall as I had suspected, and graceful as he came and perched on the edge of the bed.

He was dressed rather differently today. Instead of the fine attire of the day before, he wore plain clothes in browns and greens, with a pair of stout undyed boots. It reminded me of the sort of thing worn by gamekeepers and huntsmen. He still wore a sleeveless over-robe, buttoned at the front, but it was only knee length, and it was green. But he seemed exactly the same, it was just the clothes that were different. No sign of Eraldis, though.

"Good morning, Serapia," he greeted me.

I felt pleased he remembered my name, for all it was not a hard one. "Good morning, Ystevan."

He smiled as if he too, was pleased I had remembered his name, which was a hard one. Although, mine was perhaps as hard to him as his was to me.

"I trust you are well rested and further recovered?" he inquired.

I nodded, uncertain how I could introduce my reason for being there into the conversation.

"When you said you were kin to us," he asked me, "did you mean Torr Elkyn specifically?"

"Torr Elkyn is...here?" He nodded, so I said, "Yes. We call this area Elfindale, and it belongs to my father. I mean," I stumbled, blushing suddenly, "I'm sure he doesn't claim right here, but generally, in human terms, he is the Duke, you see," I managed, feeling that I was tying myself in knots, trying not to give offence.

Ystevan just smiled, looking more amused than anything, but he looked slightly surprised as well. "Your father is a Duke?"

"Yes," I said, chin rising, "I am Lady Serapia Ravena, and he is Alban Serapion Ravena, the Duke of Elfindale. It was his great great grandfather who married the elfin lady."

"Hmm, I wondered. It was before my time, but the match is still remembered here. You are certainly our kin."

"Was the lady a relation of yours?"

"No, not of mine. She was of Clan Elendal. I am of Clan Valunis," he added, with a smile. "Tell me, now that we have been more fully introduced," he looked at me with a sharp, but friendly gaze, "why did you come here?"

I returned his gaze firmly. "I was looking for you. For the Elfin of Elfindale, that is."

He nodded without any sign of surprise. "I thought as much."

I couldn't help remembering his sister's words the previous day. "Is that why you let me wake up here? Instead of at the inn? Though I don't see the point of putting me there. I would have had to come straight back up here."

Ystevan laughed very softly. His gold-green eyes gleamed. "You would have woken up at the inn and you would have remembered nothing."

The hair rose slightly on the back of my neck. I believed that he could do it.

"You still could, of course," he added lightly. "But although

211

you are human not elfin-kind, your age requires that we ensure your safety as well as your silence. And since you are our kin, we have twice the reason to take good care of you."

That made me feel rather warm inside—though I couldn't help wondering just how old—or rather, how young—he took me for. Despite my growing womanly attributes, I was still skinny and under-sized after those years in the gutter. In light of what he'd just said, I didn't feel in any hurry to correct him. "Thank you," I said softly.

"You're welcome. But may I ask why you have sought us out? You have come a long way, have you not; for I believe the Duke lives in London?"

I nodded. "Yes, I've come a long way." My heartbeat accelerated as the time came for me to make my appeal as persuasively as possible. "Well," I said after a deep breath, "I'm here because of my father. He's...he's very ill."

Ystevan regarded me closely. "That should not be a problem," he said simply. "He counts as a neighbor of this fort, and he is kin to us. But what is the nature of his illness?"

I could feel his gaze upon me. "It's...it's sort of a wasting disease."

"A wasting disease?" said Ystevan, "no problem, but a 'sort of' wasting disease? You'd better be more specific."

I wanted to squirm under his eyes, but resisted. "Its cause is...somewhat unusual," I admitted, still shrinking from naming the evil.

Ystevan's eyes hardened somewhat with irritation. "You are not being entirely truthful, little one. There is something important that you are not saying. I cannot possibly say whether or not you are like to find help here if you do not trust me with all the details. The Queen will hardly wish to allow one of her guardians to travel all the way to London only to find that this concealed factor makes any action on their part impossible. There are things that cannot be healed, even by elfin skills. They are not many, but they exist. Perhaps your hesitation stems from your fear that he is afflicted with one of these diseases, but all the same, you must share with me all you know of it."

212

I could not hold his gaze while I told him, and lowered my eyes to the blankets. I started right back at the beginning of the tale, seeking to offer some explanation in advance. When I first mentioned sorcery, I thought I heard Ystevan draw in a sharp breath, but I did not dare look up, simply continuing with as much control as I could manage to the sorry end.

"So you see, soon he will die, and I will lose him. And I can't! And I know you elfin can heal him," I finished. The dream had not been coincidence. I wasn't even sure if there was such a thing.

There was a long silence, until eventually I risked a peep at his face. It was closed, and his eyes had gone hard and dark and almost angry. When time dragged on and on, and still he didn't say anything, I finally ventured a timid, "Well?"

"There can only be one answer to a request such as yours," the he-elf declared, his voice like iron. "And that is No."

My stomach knotted at this, but I wasn't prepared to accept it. "But he's not a bad man," I returned urgently. "He was foolish, many years ago, but he has been truly penitent for such a long time..."

Ystevan cut me off by taking my hand. "Little one, you are bound to be partial, but there is no such thing as a good sorcerer. They are all damned and the sooner they are in hell the better."

I yanked my hand away and waved it angrily in the air. "He is not damned! And he's not actually a sorcerer. Please don't be so quick to jump to conclusions! I've tried to explain, but you're not listening, are you? Let me try again..."

I would have launched into another account of the matter, but he captured my hand again.

"Peace, little one. At any account, there is no point going on at me, it is not my decision. Since you have come so far, you may as well go before the Queen and make your request. The answer will be No, please don't hope for anything else for you will be disappointed. But I suppose if you do ask, it will make you feel better about it."

I regarded him with a mixture of mutiny and relief. Perhaps the elfin Queen would be more sympathetic.

The he-elf patted my hand reassuringly. "You will still be

made welcome here. Your father's evil is not yours."

It was nice to hear that, I had to admit. I'd been a little afraid his manner would change towards me once I had told all. I shot him a look. "I know London's a long way away," I pointed out. "And no doubt what I'm asking isn't even easy. But he is a good man. And any elfin who saved him, it would be worth their while."

He fixed me with a sharp look.

"I brought some jewels with me," I said frankly, "but they're gone with my horse. But I've got many, many more back home, and the elfin who saved my father could take their pick."

He frowned, his expression rather indeterminable. "Don't be so quick with your bribes. You should not be so willing to give your jewels away. They don't like it."

I was confused. "Sorry? Who doesn't like it?"

"The safyrs," he replied, then seemed to notice my bewildered look. "The jewels. Or that is to say, the jewel-spirits, the safyrs."

I stared at him. "The jewels don't like being given away," I repeated, astonished.

"Indeed not. Jewels like to stay in one family, passed down the generations with respect and veneration, if not love. Being bartered like common coin upsets their safyr. Or angers them, depending on their disposition. If they get really, really angry, and they're power-ful by nature...well, I'm sure you've heard of plenty of 'cursed' jewels. They're not really cursed, of course, just angry."

I found this a little hard to take in. Elfin, yes, dragonets, yes, jewels? Why not, really? Then I realized that if the Elfin would not want to take jewels, I didn't have much to offer them. Unless I converted the jewels to money.

"Well, I have money too," I said after a moment, but it seemed that I did not fool him.

"My, you're single-minded. But we are not that enamored of gold, you know. We have enough already. So do not sell your poor jewels. I'm sure they've never done anything to deserve it."

"But you sound as though you like jewels," I persisted. "There might be some that wouldn't mind belonging to you. I've got some very nice ones."

Ystevan laughed at this and unfastened the buttons of his

sleeveless robe with a few flicks of his long fingers and folded it back. *"You seem to think I am short of jewels."*

I gasped and stared, fascinated. He wore a wide collar around his neck, lying flat around his chest. It was made of a sort of metal mesh, flexible like chain mail, and it was set literally all over with jewels. If this was not amazing enough, a broad belt of a similar construction was fastened around his trim waist. He pushed up his sleeves to show wide wristbands studded with semi-precious stones. He was a walking safe!

"I am not short of jewels," he said rather ironically, *"and my jewels are my friends. I certainly would not part with them."*

He brushed a fingertip over one of the jewels on the collar, and something wild and whirling spun up from it and shot around the chamber before disappearing back into the jewel.

I couldn't help starting back. *"What...what's that?"*

"A safyr. A rather excitable one though. Let's see," he mused, looking down at his jewels, *"why don't you come and say hello to Serapia."*

He touched another jewel with his fingertip, and a little shape flew up and landed on his finger. He held it out for my inspection. This one was shaped like a bird, but wispy and insubstantial looking, like mist. It was as blue as the sapphire out of which it had come, and it puffed out its chest, cocked its head on one side, and trilled a proud but soundless song. Could Ystevan hear it? After a few more moments, it leapt up and flew back into its jewel.

"So..." I said after a moment, *"how come my safyr have never come out to say hello?"* Even as I said it, something fell into place. The hematite had never come out, but it had often said hello, after a fashion.

Ystevan was laughing. *"You are human,"* he said simply. *"Safyr require elfin power to manifest themselves. They love to manifest, though, so if they do get displaced from their family their next preference is to end up in elfin hands. Preferably in the hands of an elfin powerful enough to let them manifest frequently."*

Still reeling from all this, I somehow didn't quite feel like pulling out Siridean's dagger to show him. *"So...you're actually a very wealthy elfin?"* I ventured, somewhat chagrined. Wealthier

215

than I was, that was for sure! I'd seen no servants since waking up in his home, and had assumed...

"Each clan has their own ancestral jewels," he explained, smiling. "They are distributed among the clan for keeping according to the power of each elfin in the clan. Obviously I, ah, have quite a few of Clan Valunis's."

"Why do you cover them? And come to it, why do you wear all of them all the time?"

His lip twitched at this miniature barrage of questions. "I cover them so they don't gleam and make me visible for miles," he replied dryly, "and also so they are protected from scratches and other damage. And I do not wear them for the fun of it. Safyr require an elfin's power to manifest, but they also bring power to their keeper; that is why they are distributed according to an elfin's strength. There's no point anyone having more than they can use, and equally, it is a shame for a weaker elfin to lose the extra power jewels will bring them. Fort guardians are expected to wear all their jewels, so they can always be at maximum strength to deal with anything that may arise."

"Do you wear them in bed?" I asked, rather incredulous.

"No, little one," he said gently, "I just put them on the table by it."

"Oh."

I would probably have found some more questions to ask, but there was another tap on the doorframe, and Alvidra stood there, fixing Ystevan with a look.

"Mother says are we to have any food today or nay, little brother?" she said rather cuttingly.

Ystevan cocked his head on one side as if considering something unseen and far away. "Alas, yes, it is a bit late," he said, unruffled. "I had best be off." He stood and looked down at me. "My mother will look after you," he assured me, "but I am a bad he-elf, and have chatted half the morning away."

He strode off and was gone through the doorway. Alvidra followed him hastily, as though I might be able to bite clean across the room...

The arrival of the pot boy with our tisanes jerked my mind back to the little private room, but at least I'd remembered *something*. I'd asked Lord Ystevan and he'd said no. But I'd been going to ask the Queen...

What had the *Queen* said? I tried to make the memory unroll further, by sheer force of will, but it remained blank. A stubborn absence. I would have to ask Lord Ystevan again anyway, all unknowing... Blast him for taking my memories!

I picked up my cup and sipped, glancing at the memory-thief. Raven had just popped out from under his hair, where she'd hidden from the boy, and was climbing across his chest, but the he-elf had clearly been sitting there in silence, the whole time I'd been thinking...or rather, remembering. Because we'd had this conversation already? How *many* conversations had we had?

Curiously, I poked his chest with a finger. Yes, he was wearing his jewels. Their hardness was unmistakable, hidden though they were beneath his outer layers.

His watching eyes noted my little investigation. Ticking it off from some list in his head? *Things the human knows...* A sudden wave of something more like pain than anger closed my throat, tight. For some reason it *hurt* to think that he had done this to me, it really *hurt!* I just had to say *something*, or I was going to...to *cry*.

"So...so if you're a fort guardian," I demanded, "and the protection of the fort is your absolute priority, what are you doing here in London?"

"I am hunting a rogue elfin," Lord Ystevan said, his voice suddenly as cold as midwinter ice. "A dark elfin. And that is all we are going to say about that."

Raven squeaked and ran inside my dress. I drank the rest of my tisane in silence. His tone had quelled any possible questions I might have had about dark elfin.

I *had* to ask him about my father, but it was so hard, not knowing all that had been said between us before.

"Will you tell me about the dragons and creation?" I asked at last, as lightly as possible, hoping to ease the tension.

He gave me a somewhat disquieted look. "No, there is not much po.... Well, I think it best if I do not. I have promised not to bespell you and cannot do so effectively, besides, but I think it best if we go our separate ways again."

I stared at him furiously. "What about my father?"

"What about your father?" he said coolly.

"He's *dying!*"

"By his own hand, if rather slowly," said the he-elf imperturbably.

"You heartless beast!" I exclaimed, stung. How could he be so friendly one moment, and so remote and feelingless the next?

"Ser...Lady Serapia, since I have no fear that you would ever use anything you know of my people to harm us—your own kin—this renewed acquaintance causes me no real concern. However, I think that must be that. As for the rest, I did my duty, and I pray you can one day forgive me for it." He took up his stick, raised it in salute and headed for the door.

"Lord Ystevan, *please!*" I cried. "How can I contact you?"

He paused to look back at me with a much softer expression, and his eyes were very sad. "It is best that you do not," he said quietly and slipped through the door.

I knew better than to hesitate by now and bolted to the doorway as though the room was on fire, but when I reached it, he was already gone. I ran out to the street and looked around, but not entirely to my surprise, he was nowhere in sight.

I went back into the inn and sat down again in the private room with my head in my hands, dizzy with the events of the last few hours. On the one hand, Lord Ystevan had never once said that my father *couldn't* be healed, only that *he* wouldn't *do* it. But on the other hand, after going to extraordinary lengths to find the he-elf, he'd slipped through my fingers yet *again*.

CHAPTER 33

The Clothes' Problem

I was mildly annoyed to find some hours later that I had drifted off again. I had meant to insist that I was fine and get up. Still, I did feel better now. Even better, that was.

I couldn't tell exactly how long I'd slept, for I had yet to see a window in the fort, and I suspected there probably weren't any. The light in the room came from a piece of rough quartz sitting in a little metal ring that was suspended from the ceiling on three chains. It gave a steady, almost wholly unwavering light of a kind that I had never before seen from a man-made lantern. Of course, this 'lantern' wasn't exactly man-made.

My stomach was starting to complain a bit, so I pushed back the covers and got up, finding myself tolerably steady on my feet. I cast around for my clothes, but couldn't find them. I did find something along the general lines of a chamber gown, and a pair of slippers, so I put those on. I emerged into a slightly irregularly shaped chamber that seemed to be a living room and dining room combined, since it had a circle of armchairs around a hearth, and a table and chairs.

Alvidra was there, laying a new fire in the grate. Apparently sensing my presence, the she-elf sprang to her feet, shot a look over her shoulder, and hurried through another doorway. Before I could reach this doorway, Haliath came hurrying out, smiling.

"Are you awake, then, elfling?" She paused and smiled deprecatingly. "Sorry, the word is child, I believe. But are you feeling better?"

I nodded, pushing away the memories evoked by that diminutive. "I really am fine now," I added, in case I was in danger of being put back to bed.

"That's good," said the she-elf, then, as my stomach gave an audible grumble, "We'll be having luncheon as soon as Ystevan gets back. And I must just check on it."

She headed back through the doorway she'd appeared from. I followed and found myself in a kitchen. A very sophisticated looking stove had pride of place, with a pan bubbling away on top of it.

The stove fascinated me. While the fact that they clearly cooked for themselves sat at odds with my human idea of them being well off, I could already see that Ystevan was far from unimportant in the fort, and this stove... I doubted anything like this existed in my world.

A door creaked open somewhere, and after a moment Ystevan came in. He bore a large wickerwork basket on his back, held on with leather shoulder straps. A quiver was woven onto the basket on one side, and on the other a holder for a bow, both of which were occupied. He gave me a smile and went through a doorway in the kitchen wall. Haliath and Alvidra followed, so I did likewise.

We entered no simple larder, but a good-sized room. Shelves and wicker baskets lined the walls, and several rabbits and fowl hung from hooks over a wide stone shelf. A big table stood in the middle of the room, the top a mighty slab of smooth slate.

Ystevan emptied his basket swiftly onto the table and the two she-elves whipped the various foodstuffs away to different baskets and shelves.

"Sorry it's a bit sparse," apologized Ystevan, absently examining the two parts of a broken arrow.

"It's more than adequate," said Haliath without concern, although Alvidra sniffed and remarked,

"Avragrain never gets distracted from his providing."

This seemed decidedly cryptic to me, but Haliath went on with her work and Ystevan went back to examining his arrow as if the remark was of no importance whatsoever.

"Have I got time to fix this?" Ystevan asked after a moment.

"No," said Haliath, "the elfling...the child's hungry."

I felt myself turn pink at this, and was entirely unsure what to say.

"Luncheon, then," returned Ystevan, apparently unconcerned.

~+~

I couldn't resist asking some questions over luncheon since I hadn't the faintest idea about the Elfin way of life. I learned that the day was split into two halves. The first half was for family work. This generally meant that the he-elf of a family would go out and gather food, while the she-elf cooked, cleaned, and cared for the elflings. That did not seem particularly strange to me. What was a little stranger was that if a she-elf preferred to do the gathering, there was no problem; so long as there was a provider and a home-maker in each couple, no one was worried.

So in the morning, generally, he-elflings went out with their fathers, and she-elflings stayed to help their mothers, although most tended to have at least a basic knowledge of the other skills. Luncheon was fairly late, and in the afternoon was communal work, and academic schooling for the elflings.

The very most powerful elfin were the fort guardians—so long as they were brave and virtuous enough, Haliath added proudly, making Ystevan give unwarranted attention to the contents of his plate. Their work was checking the wards, and usually for part of the afternoon, attending on the Queen for more serious discussion. Many who were not fort guardians were also counselors to the Queen, so all these would spend the afternoon in finer clothes, which explained the discrepancy between Ystevan's two sets of garments.

Some of the remaining elfin were teachers or pursued other such specialized occupations. Others saw to the maintenance of the fort, which included the cleaning of communal areas, and the care of the odd bullock, pig or sheep. These were occasionally staked outside a sheiling-fort by a grateful farmer and sent up to the torr-fort for care until the next feast day. Apparently hearing one's gift lowing from inside an elfin fort tended to erode the Elfin's mystical status.

Haliath had charge of the clan laundry in the afternoon, I learned, so she was hardly unimportant herself. And Alvidra, it turned out, was only there for a brief visit, and was actually married, and normally lived at a smaller sheiling-fort with her he-elfen, as a husband was called. It was all a lot to take in. I ate with

222

my ears wide open and several times restrained myself from asking after Ystevan's father.

Having unsuccessfully attempted to help Haliath clear up from luncheon, I followed Ystevan into a little side chamber, where he sat at a table and started mending his arrow with glue and some very thin gut-twine. His slender fingers were nimble, and he worked the repair in an unwarrantedly short space of time.

I hesitated to disturb him and watched in silence, but eventually, when the repair seemed to be essentially complete, I ventured, "I don't want to say something wrong in front of your mother...so, I was wondering if you could tell me..."

"Ah, my missing father," remarked Ystevan. "Thank you for not saying anything, my mother is very sensitive about it. And it's easily explained. He's dead. A long time ago, now. My sister and myself were still fairly young, so mother didn't pine away after him, which is something."

I was a little startled. "Is that, normal?"

Ystevan nodded as if surprised I asked, then cocked his head on one side as he had earlier and rose to his feet. "It is time for me to get ready to go to the Queen. I will be back later."

"Can I come with you to the Queen?" I demanded.

The he-elf covered a smile as he looked at me, and I became belatedly conscious that I stood there drowned in a nightgown and chamber gown that were both far too big for me.

"Tomorrow," he replied gently. "By then you'll be right as blue sky and mother should have found some clothes to fit you!"

I blushed, faintly mortified to have forgotten about the clothes' problem. How quickly might Haliath be able to find me clothes? But Ystevan disappeared through another curtained doorway off the living room, and when I went into the kitchen to find Haliath, she was still washing the last dishes, and I felt I couldn't trouble her. I returned to the sitting room and sat in an armchair feeling decidedly purposeless.

Ystevan smiled when he saw me sitting there, as he reappeared in fine wool and velvet. "When I get back I'll take you on a tour of the fort, if you're dressed," he told me, clearly seeing how I felt. Then he was off down a corridor and out the wooden

223

door that clearly led to the rest of the fort.

I was extremely pleased when Haliath, after a little more time in the kitchen, disappeared briefly to return with an armful of clothes. We withdrew to 'my' room and I tried on garment after garment, trying to find some that fitted. The she-elves seemed to wear just-below-knee-length dresses with elegant leather boots to the knee for general wear—all of which came rather further down my shorter human legs, though they still barely reached my ankles. Haliath had also brought some full-length dresses of much richer fabrics, clearly aware that I would be seeing the Queen.

"You're so curvy," said the she-elf after a while. "The younger she-elves will be mad with envy, but it's making this rather tricky..."

"But I'm terribly skinny," I protested—even though yet another dress had just failed to fit around my hips.

Haliath seemed puzzled by this. "Yes, Ystevan thought so, but you seem pretty curvy to me. Well, try this one."

Finally I was buttoned into a smart little day dress and boots, and Haliath had coaxed Alvidra into letting out a few seams of a much finer formal gown for the next day.

"Thank you," I said awkwardly. "I'm sorry it's taken so long." Haliath said don't mention it, so, a thought striking me, I asked, "What happened to my, er, clothes?" I must have turned up dressed as a groom...

"Oh, they've been to the laundry and are drying," said Haliath, apparently unconcerned by the oddness of the garments. Perhaps she didn't know what a human groom's uniform looked like. "And the laundry is where I must be," the she-elf went on. "I hate to think of the chaos that could be unfolding in my absence. You can come with me, if you like, or stay here and rest. Or if you badly want something to do you could help Alvi with that dress," she added with a humorous glint in her eyes.

"I don't need any help," came a swift, sharp retort from the living room.

"Is Alvidra not used to humans?" I asked, as we headed along the passage. "Since she lives in a sheiling-fort, I mean?"

"Ah," replied Haliath quietly, "that is why she is so nervous of them. She was raised here, where there aren't any, and then moved to a sheiling-fort, where humans are a much greater danger, and something one must be constantly aware of. And she's still not used to it.

"In truth," she added, as she opened the door, "I think that's why she visits us quite frequently. Coming here gives her room to breathe. So if she's a bit grouchy sometimes, please don't mind her."

Haliath glided off through the fort like a ship under full sail, and I had to scurry to keep up, consequently able to take in very little about my surroundings. But Ystevan had promised me a tour that evening, so I did not mind too much.

I rode back into the stable courtyard, tired and discouraged by the day's failure, coming as it did atop yet another night of bad dreams. Leaving Hellion well out of the way at nearby farms, I'd spent all the daylight hours—from the first to the last moment it was light enough to see anything—hidden outside three different elfin forts. No simple hiding behind things, I had wormed into hedges, deep leaf-filled hollows and, most uncomfortably of all, an old badger set.

I'd seen no elfin and tried to make good use of the time chasing those elusive memories. They were coming back, but all too slowly. Sometimes I'd see something that would bring a bit back, all in a rush, but I *still* couldn't remember meeting the Queen or what she had said.

Did it matter? She must have said *No*, or I wouldn't be back here in London trying to shake the memory of it out of my pillaged skull.

Yielding Hellion to the grooms, I for once went straight up to the house without stopping to oversee his care. I ached all over and my clothes were sodden with damp and mud. Ignoring the servants' glances, I hurried on. My father would be waiting to eat dinner. I trudged up the stairs as fast as I could force myself to go and soon Susie was peeling me out of my soggy clothes and ushering me to the hot bath that I'd had the blessed foresight to arrange in advance. Raven dived in with a little plop and swam in lazy circles, crooning contentedly to herself. I quickly joined her in the hot water.

I did not luxuriate for long, though, and was soon downstairs again seeking my father. "Pa," I said gladly, hastening to the couch in the drawing room. The only trouble with all this elfin-hunting was that I saw so little of him. He did not stir, though, so I sat on the edge of the couch and touched one cadaverous cheek gently.

He opened his eyes at last and blinked up at me. "Serapia," he said, his eyes warming with pleasure. "*There you are.*"

I felt a twinge of guilt at leaving him alone so much, after he had made it so clear he wanted me around. But I didn't really have any choice.

"I, ah, I thought we'd eat in here tonight," he said, in a would-be casual tone, and began to lever himself up into a sitting position.

I bit my lip and hastened to assist him. Just last night, he'd greeted that very same suggestion from me with an impatient, 'I'm not dead yet, child,' and requisitioned the assistance of the butler to get into the wheeled chair he was using. He was now so weak that the chair had to be carried up and down stairs at the beginning and end of the day—and it seemed he no longer wanted even to move into that unnecessarily anymore.

His condition was deteriorating *so* fast.

I stabbed my beef fiercely as I ate. No more hiding and waiting. It wasn't working. I *knew* there was an elfin guardian in the city, and I had to find him again, by whatever means possible.

CHAPTER 34

The Audience

I was dreaming. I crouched on the arm of an armchair. My father sat in the chair. His thin face was drawn, and a frown creased his brow as he stared unseeingly into the fire in the hearth. After a moment, he stirred and reached out to pull the bell cord. The butler entered and came to stand beside the chair, while Anna hung about the doorway anxiously.

"Is there any news?" asked my father quietly.

"Not since half an hour ago, my lord," replied the butler just as quietly, and with a suspicion of gentleness in his tone.

The Duke sighed heavily and covered his eyes with a hand in a gesture that spoke all too clearly of his feeling of impotence.

Anna, apparently unable to help herself, hurried forward into the room. "I'm sure she's just fine, my lord," she broke out comfortingly. "She's a good rider, after all, and that's a good horse she's got with her..."

"Yet for all we can tell, they could be anywhere in this world or the next," retorted Alban in a tired voice. He gave a flick of his hand and the servants withdrew, Anna clearly frustrated by the failure of her comforting words. My father went back to staring into the flames.

I woke in my cozy elfin bed with a start and lay for a moment staring at the ceiling. Everything was dark. Someone must have doused the quartz, and from the quality of the silence it was deep night and everyone else was in bed as well. I was really annoyed. With myself, of course, I could hardly blame Ystevan for not waking me when they were still half treating me as an invalid.

With a sigh I lay back down. Tomorrow I was to see the Queen and the dream had only strengthened my resolve. No doubt Ystevan would show me the fort then as well.

~+~

When I woke again I could sense Haliath and Ystevan moving around, so I got out of bed and pulled on the day dress and boots before joining them for breakfast. Eraldis lifted his head from Ystevan's shoulder as I entered, staring at me with particular intentness, and Ystevan also looked at me curiously, rising and coming over to me. Eraldis swooped ahead of him and actually deigned to land on my shoulders for the first time, nosing at my hair. I held very still.

Ystevan turned his head this way and that, not exactly sniffing, or not with his nose anyway, and then he raised his hands and ran them through the air a few inches from me, as if touching something invisible.

"Er, what on earth are you doing?" I asked.

He withdrew his hands, apparently satisfied by his examination. "There is power around you. It is dragonic in nature."

I blinked, surprised, and considered my dream in a new light. "Oh. Then...I think Raven may have sent me a dream. To...let me know how they are, I suppose."

"Aha," said Ystevan, with a satisfied nod, and went back to his breakfast. Haliath hadn't gotten up, though she'd been watching with interest.

I seated myself—carefully, since Eraldis still clung to me—and helped myself to a bowl of heather and nut porridge. So the dream was real. Well, it was nice to see that they were all right, but seeing the anguish I was causing my father made my heart ache. Still, it wasn't like I was going to stay any longer than I had to. As soon as they agreed to help me, I'd go back to him.

Soon enough—and without accidentally setting fire to my hair, not that I really thought he would—Eraldis leapt into the air, landed back on Ystevan's shoulders just long enough to give the he-elf an affectionate rub with his head, then flew away up into a little dragonet-sized tunnel in the roof which I'd learned led—eventually—to outside the mountain.

"Eraldis seems to come and go a lot," I remarked. "Raven almost never leaves my side."

"She won't, yet," said Ystevan. "She needs you to stay warm. When she comes of age, her internal fire will light up and then

228

she'll be able to keep herself warm. And breathe fire. She'll get more independent after that. But if you are her Firstling, she will always come back to you."

"Oh. Good. You know..." I said cautiously, "I do rather have the impression Eraldis...doesn't like me."

Ystevan grimaced slightly. "Umm," he conceded. "He hasn't entirely taken to you." He shook his head. "I'm really not sure why, though. He's usually very friendly with strangers."

I thought Haliath's eyebrows twitched up slightly, at that. Did she know why? But she made no comment, so maybe I was mistaken.

I ran my hands down my dress nervously as I followed a smartly dressed Ystevan along the corridors of the fort. Alvidra had proven very competent with her needle, and the dress fitted as though it'd been made for me, sliding over my hips to flow out around my ankles, the bodice fitting decidedly snugly around my new curviness. I'd never worn a woman's dress before, only the shapeless girl's dresses that mimicked the adult style without coming close. Of course, this was a she-elf's dress, not a woman's... I had to stop myself from smoothing the dress down yet again.

Haliath had told me I looked very beautiful, which I took with a pinch of salt, knowing my skinniness, but Ystevan, who had said nothing, had shot a couple of looks at me since I'd appeared in it. Perhaps I was attractively curvy among the Elfin, or perhaps something else was bothering him.

I was almost glad of the dress's distraction, for my thoughts churned with what I would say to the Queen, how I was going to persuade her that my father deserved healing. I'd gone through it in my mind over and over again that morning, until I felt near distracted.

We reached a large pair of double doors, and Ystevan stopped and looked back at me. A definite spark of sympathy lit his green-gold eyes.

"Don't hope for too much," he told me softly, and he'd made his opinion clear enough that I knew he meant don't hope for anything. But I just raised my chin a few inches and squared my jaw. I'd been as good as sent here by a being I had every reason to trust. I would get my help here. I had to.

We entered a chamber so breathtakingly beautiful that I paused mid stride to take it in. It must once have been a natural cave, for walls and ceiling glittered all over with sharp, white crystal, and interspersed amongst these, jewels and gemstones had been set so cunningly that the sparkling white was overshone here and there by a rainbow multitude of color. It was incredible.

After a moment I recollected myself and hurried after Ystevan, who was approaching the dais at the far end of the vaguely oval chamber, around which the elfin counselors stood or sat on benches carved into the walls. The throne on the dais had clearly been cut from the rock itself, and was gilded here and there with gold and silver and other metals, in which were set more jewels. Considering my new-found knowledge of safyrs, did it act as some kind of huge power focus?

The she-elf sitting on the throne looked around fifty to me. She had the black-gold hair of her kind, with slightly more gold than Ystevan and Haliath. Her eyes were firm, if not hard, and she had the poise and manner of a very strong woman...that was, she-elf. A narrow circlet, set all the way around with jewels, rested upon her head.

Ystevan bowed gracefully, clearly quite at home in these surroundings and this company, as was to be expected. I attempted to curtsey with equal grace.

"Ah," said the Queen, "so here is the little human you had to bring in. Let's have a look at her, then."

I took this to mean I should come closer, and did so, meeting the eyes of the elfin monarch as respectfully as possible.

"This one is many generations on, I suppose," mused the Queen, after taking a close look at my face, "but I can still see something of Aramantha in her. You say you have taught her to speak?" The Queen was still clearly talking to Ystevan, and I could not quite quell a small sound of indignation at this last. Everyone in the room, the Queen included, looked at me. A ghost of a smile crossed the Queen's face.

"So you talk, do you?" she asked me directly.

"Well, I don't actually know your language, Your Majesty, but I can understand you."

"So I see," said the Queen. "Anyway, as kin, we will take good care of you until you can be returned home in safety. But I believe you have not come all this way on a mere search for distant relatives. Ystevan said you should explain it yourself, so tell me, child, what do you seek?"

"I seek healing for my father," I replied resolutely.

The Queen fixed me with a look not unlike the one Ystevan had turned on me. She saw there was more to come. "What is the nature of his ailment?"

I refused to hesitate or swallow or do anything that would suggest I was ashamed of the subject. "Due to the nature of his affliction, Your Majesty, there are certain things that I must explain before I name it, so I beg your indulgence while I narrate how his sickness came about. But before I even do that, I wish you to know that my father, whatever he thinks of himself, is a good man. He is brave and strong and loyal, and he does many great works of charity with humility and modesty."

I shot a look at Ystevan, whose face was a carefully non-committal mask.

"Ystevan has suggested that I am prejudiced in his favor because he is my father, and therefore I wish you to know that I never saw or heard of him in my life until four or five months ago, and have formed my opinion of him on rather better ground than childish worship.

"My father and I are both kin to you, and it is actually with this fact that I must start my story. As a result of his elfin blood, my father experienced the gift of foresight in regard to my mother, whom he had recently married, and with whom he was madly in love. I say madly, and I mean it. He clearly loved beyond all reason."

I could tell I had the attention of everyone in the room, and continued, picking my words with exquisite care. "He foresaw that she would die of some untimely accident and his feelings for her were such that he was prepared to do anything to save her. It was his one great foolishness, and it led him to his one great crime. But I do not believe that one foolish action, least of all when blind with love and half mad with foresight, can outweigh a man's true character and all his good. My father turned to sorcery to save my mother."

A gasp and a physical recoil greeted my words, and I saw faces that had been listening with interest and sympathy close in anger and judgment. I could have screamed with frustration. It was happening again. Despite everything I had said, as soon as the word sorcery came out, they forgot everything!

"My mother prevented him from completing the sorcery," I went on quickly, "and left him as well, which brought him to his senses. Since that day he has been truly penitent. But he pledged himself as security for the sorcery, and since it will never be completed, he has bare weeks left before it kills him. And if you have no pity for him, then show some pity for me. I lost my mother four years ago and was quite alone until I found my father. Please don't let me lose the only person I have left! Please don't leave me to be alone again!"

I felt in danger of becoming overwrought, and fought back tears, struggling to become more collected. "You must believe me when I say he is penitent. What he needs to complete the sorcery has actually come into his...possession, but he does not even think of carrying it out. He would rather die, and he will, if you won't help him! If you won't help me."

I fell silent for a moment, then couldn't help adding, "Please try and see beyond your natural abhorrence of sorcery! I loathe it, but we are not talking about a hardened, evil sorcerer, we are talking about a good man who made one mistake, many years ago." I stopped speaking and waited in breathless silence.

The Queen's lips were compressed, and she did not look very amused. "A rather monumental mistake, dear child," she said at last. "Surely you understand that there are some things from which there is no going back?"

My chin slid out mutinously. "Not so. Your Majesty. All those who truly repent are forgiven. It says so in the Bible. In the English and the Latin." I faltered slightly as something occurred to me. "Although," I went on, slightly embarrassed, "I don't actually know

232

what religion you follow here."

The Queen just smiled slightly. "All are forgiven by God, child. There are some sins where the only thing to be done is hustle the individual off to God as fast as possible, and let him deal with them. One can't let a sorcerer live! It's not safe."

"He is not a sorcerer!" I broke in, but the Queen just shook her head with something that scarcely warranted the title of regret.

"We have only your word for that, child, and the only solid evidence of this case is that your father has had recourse to sorcery. Therefore, he definitely comes into the category of those who are to be helped on their way if necessary. Helped to judgment, most definitely not helped to remain here!"

She was going to refuse, I could see it in her face, hear it in her voice.

"But I asked how to save him!" I cried, halfway between desperation and anger. "I prayed, and the answer was to come here, get your help! You must help me!"

The Queen looked at me for another long moment, her expression inscrutable. "And what precisely is it you seek, child? Would you state your request formally."

An utter silence gripped the hall and I could feel everyone listening for my reply. Why was this important?

"I seek healing for my father," I said after a moment, repeating my earlier words.

The Queen's lips tightened slightly, as if this answer did not please her, but when she spoke again her voice was still firm as rock. "Child, I will not help your father or order any of my guardians to help your father. But regrettably, since you seek healing rather than the removal of sorcery, I cannot forbid anyone to help you.

"When to heal is a personal decision that must be taken by each elfin individually. But I may as well say plainly that there are only two guardians of sufficient power in this fort to do what you ask and I know them both very well, child, and neither of them would ever do such a thing. So accept that the answer is no, and smother your hope as quickly and painlessly as you can."

I thought my heart would burst with relief. It wasn't an

233

absolute 'No'. I'd been so sure that utter, irrevocable refusal was coming that I felt quite dizzy. I still had to persuade one of these grim-faced elfin to help me, but I was free to try!

I curtseyed politely. "Thank you, Your Majesty. May I inquire as to the identity of the two guardians you mentioned?"

Ystevan give a soft sigh from beside me, as though he recognized that I had taken it not in the slightest as a refusal.

The Queen, however, looked rather amused by my question. "Say really, three, but I am the third, and have given you my answer. Lord Alliron, please make yourself known to the child."

A bony he-elf who looked fairly advanced in his middle years stepped forward. His expression of disdainful disgust did not fill me with undue hope. "I am Lord Alliron, human. I would be more than happy to speed your father's passing; do not hope for anything else."

I bristled inside but forced myself to be polite. I curtseyed again to the guardian and smiled at him. "I'm sorry to hear that, Lord Alliron," I said sweetly, "but I'm very pleased to meet you."

Ystevan made a sound halfway between a sighing sob and a laugh. Alliron had already beaten a retreat, so I looked inquiringly at the Queen, who just smiled again.

"The other, need hardly make himself known to you, but still. Lord Ystevan..."

I turned to my host with more familiarity and less sweetness. "You?"

"I fear Alliron and myself must have done something to offend Her Majesty," sighed the he-elf. "Either that, or she does not yet appreciate what she has done."

"Come, come, Ystevan," said the Queen, at that, "I hardly had any choice. If you were worried, you should have advised her to ask for the removal of sorcery instead of standing back so impartially and letting her ask what she would. Anyway, Ystevan, she is just a little girl, and a human at that; no offence, dear," she added to me. "She'll pester you for a few days, and then she'll realize it's no use. So there's hardly much cause for concern on your part."

Ystevan smiled wryly and shook his head to himself.

"I expect she's settled in with your family by now," the Queen went on, "so as long as it's all right with Haliath, she'd best remain with you. Look after her, now, she is our kin, and Aramantha was very dear to me."

Ystevan nodded and bowed. "Of course, Your Majesty," he replied, then added, "I don't think I'm needed now, am I?" The Queen shook her head. "Indeed not, so take our guest away and show her around."

I curtseyed and followed Ystevan from the chamber, my heart singing. I had hope still, real hope. Alliron and Ystevan. One of them had to help me.

CHAPTER 35

Cutridge Lane

"*S'trewth*, now what?" said Sir Allen Malster as he came downstairs the next morning to find me in his hall.

"Is that any way to speak to your future ward?" I asked rather dispiritedly. I really was going to end up his ward, at this rate. Only three elfin in that big fort who even *could* heal my father, and only one of them here in London. Still, at least there was *one*. If I could ever find him again.

He came forward and took my shoulders, looking down at my unhappy face. "Oh, come now, girl, what can I do for you?"

When he'd guided me into the drawing room and seen me settled in an armchair, he took the wooden chair from the desk and sat on it backwards, chin on folded arms, eyes fixed on my face. "So?" he inquired.

I drew a rather shaky breath. My father's condition was terrifying me. "Lord Ystevan can get the medicine that will help my father," I told Sir Allen. "But he refused to do so. He gave me the slip and now I can't find him again."

Sir Allen shook his head without raising it from the chair back. "Don't look at me, girl. I have genuine information for Lord Ystevan but he didn't respond to my summons yesterday. I dare say you are the reason why not. It is not of much account. Normally he knows these things ahead of me, only occasionally not."

I bit my lip. In truth, I had not really expected to trap Lord Ystevan in the same way twice, but Sir Allen was my only link. "What is the information? Might it help me find him?"

Sir Allen just shook his head.

"Please? It's terribly important."

"Serapia," said Sir Allen, giving me a long, searching look. "You seem so desperate to acquire this medicine. But surely your father's condition is such that the best medicine in the world will do little but...ease his passing. Is it worth all this trouble and unhappiness?"

I looked at my hands for a long moment, debating with myself. An honest man, but not a saint. Control of the Ravena fortune... How honest a man was he? I wasn't sure I had anything to lose, though.

"Sir Allen," I said at last. "The medicine I seek would actually save my father's life. That is why I seek it so desperately. Perhaps you will think me a silly girl, but I swear, it exists. Lord Ystevan has it and I simply *have* to find him."

He stared at me for a moment. "I do not think you are a silly girl," he said quietly, "but I do think you perhaps underestimate the seriousness of your father's illness."

"Please, Sir Allen," I said. "The information you have for Lord Ystevan, what is it?"

Sir Allen shook his head and stood, pacing up and down. "It pertains to matters in which I cannot possibly allow you to be involved. It is out of the question. Especially in light of my future responsibility for your safety."

"That information could save my father's life," I said unrelentingly. "I have survived many things indeed, Sir Allen, and you know it. Are you quite certain it is me you are worried about, and not your own purse?"

He swung around, fury on his face. "How dare you..."

"Well, the mistake is easily made," I snapped. "What am I supposed to think? You have information that could save my father and you will not give it to me!"

"If you would be entirely forthcoming with me I would see to the saving of your father's life myself," Sir Allen retorted.

"Are you going to give me the information or not?" I demanded, ignoring that last remark.

Sir Allen jerked his head dismissively. "Of course I am not! However capable you may be, you are a *fourteen-year-old girl!* Tell me what you know so *I* can help your father, or leave with nothing."

I stared at him, my eyes narrowing. Leave with nothing. *That was not happening.* Not...not so long as he had the information *written down.* And *here.* I pictured a piece of paper with writing on, a very secret, important piece of paper, let the question form in my mind. *Where...?*

The right side of Sir Allen's doublet. Some sort of hidden internal pocket. The information *was* here!

I ducked my head, let my lip wobble...imagined my father really dying...pictured Ystevan—*Lord* Ystevan, that was—ruthlessly wiping all memory of himself and his family from my mind... Tears began to leak from my eyes. I sniffed hard, trying to work up to some real sobs. I didn't dare fake any. Sir Allen was too perceptive. Gah, I needed to be more upset!

Oooouch! Raven had just sunk her tiny fangs into the fleshy part of my arm. My eyes watered freely, and fed with more dismal imaginings of my future if I didn't manage to cry convincingly enough, the sobs finally gathered force.

From the slightly frantic *now, now, there, there* noises Sir Allen had been making, he'd put their slowness in developing down to my efforts to hold them *in,* rather than the opposite. Thankfully.

"Oh dear..." he sighed. And finally closed the distance between us in order to put an awkward hand on my back. When my sobs showed no sign of abating, he crouched beside me—at last! I promptly flung my arms around him, burying my damp face in his shoulder.

Unseen...unseen...unseen... My mind slipped into the familiar—though nowadays seldom used—background concentration, as my fingers eased several buttons from their holes and slid inside Sir Allen's doublet, searching for the opening to that flat, concealed pocket inside the inner lining. There... My nape remained fairly quiescent—after all,

I wasn't stealing. I wasn't even *borrowing*, really. A *look* was all I needed. I eased the paper out, concentration unwavering, and angled my head until I could see. A half page of densely written script.

Unseen...unseen...unseen...

I scanned it rapidly. Most of it was useless to me, a report about the ins and outs of what an unnamed person had been doing, but...*there!* The only hard information on the paper. A one-line address:

64 Gutridge Lane

A pleasant part of the city, that. I'd have to take someone with me.

Unseen...unseen...unseen...

I slid the report back into Sir Allen's pocket, re-fastening the buttons neatly, and made sure my arm was wrapped back around him in a convincingly tearful grip before finally relaxing my concentration.

I had the information. But if Lord Ystevan sometimes had such information before Sir Allen...there wasn't a moment to lose!

Managing at long last to get a bit of a grip on myself—or so I hoped it seemed—I quickly rose to leave.

"Are you sure you're all right?" Sir Allen asked, trailing after me to the door—though his hand did brush momentarily against his doublet—just checking. He wasn't a man who'd overlook the possible consequences of getting so close to a former urchin. That I could have not only reached the paper, but *read* it *and* replaced it without him noticing was clearly beyond the stretch of his imagination, not unreasonably.

"I'm fine," I sniffed. "I'm fine. You made it clear you're not going to help!"

"I *did* offer to help!" His frustrated words followed me down the steps, and I sensed the gaze that followed me was not a happy one.

Leaping up into the coach the moment the footman opened the door, I banged on the ceiling but kept my voice too low for Sir Allen to catch. "The Quays, Richard, as fast as you can. Go." The footmen scrambled to get aboard and we were off. I banged on the ceiling at every pause, urging Richard to go faster. If I missed Lord Ystevan, I wasn't sure what I'd do. I refused to dwell on what would happen if Lord Ystevan never came to the place.

Finally, we were approaching the Quays district. At this speed, we were going to pull up in an extremely conspicuous shower of mud and gravel. I banged on the ceiling yet again. "Pull up gently, Richard."

The coachman did so, in a quiet street. I opened the door myself and was on the ground by the time the footmen got down. "William, Stephen, you stay here with me. Put on your oiled capes. William, take the crossbow. Keep it out of sight. Stephen, take a sword. Richard, you can drive the coach home. I will find my own way back. Tell my father not to worry if I do not return till late, or even not until morning."

Richard's expression suggested that if his daughter told him such a thing after dismounting in the Quays she would get a thick ear and short shrift, but he bowed his head reluctantly and clucked to the horses.

I wrapped my own long cloak carefully around me. No rain fell yet, but I wanted my fine dress and the footmen's tell-tale livery hidden from view. These were not the clothes I would have chosen for a safe foray into the Quays, but there simply wasn't time to change. Hence the crossbow. A crossbow could not really be satisfactorily hidden beneath a cloak from those that knew about such things, and would be an excellent deterrent. I hoped.

I turned to William and Stephen, who looked, if anything, even unhappier than Richard. "You two are going to come with me," I told them. "Now, you are not to start anything, do you understand? If someone actually tries to carry me off, you will defend me, but if they simply slap me on the... Well, you ignore it, is that clear?"

Three well-dressed persons such as ourselves didn't want to start anything in this quarter. No one would pile into the fray. Not to help us, anyway. From the footmen's expressions, they were all too aware of this. They nodded glumly and followed as I set off into a warren of dank alleyways. It was still early and the streets were fairly quiet, which meant we were more conspicuous but there were less people to notice us. Very much a mixed blessing. Fortunately Cutridge Lane wasn't far.

I took advantage of several tiny back alleys to approach number sixty-four unseen. A typical black and white building, it comprised a ground floor with a first floor protruding a foot or two over the street with an attic above that. There was no rear access; the row of houses at the back leant full against it. Another tiny alley did run along one side of it, but from the darkness of our own alley, we could see both this and the front of the house well enough.

Sending Stephen to acquire some ragged fabric from somewhere at a discreet distance, I checked we were unobserved and then arranged the abandoned refuse of the alley into a suitably convincing beggar's squat. It had probably been one fairly recently. When Stephen returned, I wrapped a disreputable cloak over my fine one and oversaw Stephen and William camouflaged as well as possible in an assortment of threadbare blankets.

"Now what, my lady?" asked William uncomfortably, when we were settled.

"Now we wait," I said firmly. "And if anyone should *actually* give us money, I'll say 'Thank 'ee, sir, ma'am', and you'll keep your mouths shut."

The footmen shot me startled looks. Knowing their master's daughter had been an urchin and hearing perfect urchin speech dropping from my lips were apparently two quite different things.

~+~

241

We waited. All day. It began to rain. The footmen shivered miserably behind me. I ignored them. The day was mild
and they were wrapped in their oiled capes. I was getting
much wetter myself, but I paid it no heed. Around midday I
took a careful look in my purse, under cover of my cloaks.

William and Stephen stiffened hopefully. But I had no
more coins small enough to bring into the light of day in this
place, and had to put it away again. The grumbling stomachs
of the young men grew steadily louder as the afternoon
wore on. My own, grown accustomed to the regular meals of
my father's house, began to make a few gurgles as well.

By late afternoon I felt more and more frantic. If Lord
Ystevan had heard about this place of potential interest
before Sir Allen, he might have already been here, the day
before. But I couldn't know, so I couldn't leave. I set my
teeth, striving to drive the increasingly panic-stricken
thoughts from my mind, and went on waiting.

Then Raven suddenly uncoiled from the position of
sleepy lethargy in which she had whiled away most of the
long day. I could feel the sudden alertness in her little body
and looked around with close attention.

After a moment, I saw a lean figure swathed in a long
dark cloak strolling casually along the street in the direction
of number sixty-four. I turned immediately to speak to the
footmen. A visit to the Quays would not have alarmed me
normally, but in my current state of dress I regarded the
idea of walking home alone with apprehension. But surely
Lord Ystevan was too much of a gentle...he-elf to abandon
me in this place. But only if I was truly alone.

"You two can go home now," I said quickly to the
footmen and nodded over my shoulder, "I shall be with that
gentleman; he is very capable, do not worry. Tell cook she is
to give you a good dinner though you are late," I added, in a
flash of inspiration.

William and Stephen brightened visibly, and though
they clearly disliked leaving me there, they obeyed their

orders and with that incentive were gone down the alley almost before I had got to my feet myself.

Pausing only to rearrange the ragged cloak around myself, I slid out into the street and up to the dark-swathed figure.

Lord Ystevan started and looked down at me. "Serapia, *what* are you doing here?"

"What do you *think* I'm doing here, Lord Ystevan? My father's still dying."

He made a sound of intense frustration and with a glance at number sixty-four, drew me into the alley beside it. "*How* did you get this address?"

"Sir Allen. He'd have told you yesterday if you'd shown up."

"He let you come anywhere *near* here!" The he-elf sounded horrified. "And I thought he was so intelligent. The man's an *idiot.*"

"He didn't *tell* me. But I found out anyway."

"Well, the answer is still no, so you've wasted your time. The sooner a sorcerer is before God's judgment, the better for everyone, and good riddance!"

"Good riddance?" I echoed, furious. "You know what your problem is? You don't see him as a loving...and loved... father. Can't you just *think*? What if it were *your* father? Either you're not thinking about it that way, or you didn't like your own pa much!"

"*My* father *died* defending my kin against people like *your* father! Quite clearly it is *you* that doesn't understand!" snapped the he-elf. "You're just a spoilt little girl who thinks she can have absolutely anything she wants because she always has before! Well, I am neither of your doting parents and this you cannot have!"

I stepped back as if he had slapped me, for the first time completely lost for words. Spoilt! Anything I wanted? Always? How dare he! It was so ridiculous I choked! I'd wanted a mother who'd look me in the face and still love me, I'd wanted to keep even the mother who would not, I'd

243

wanted to spend the last years of my childhood somewhere warm with food and clothing that I called home...and I'd wanted someone else to love me and care for me, and I'd only found him to be threatened with losing him again. How could I possibly accept that without fighting all the way? That wasn't *spoilt!*

He eyed me, the anger on his face bleaching into a sort of general unhappiness. "*Serapia...*"

"Why do you presume to call me by my first name?" I snapped. "Do you really think we are *friends?* After what you *did?*"

A flicker of pain and sadness crossed Ystevan's face, but then it closed, becoming an unreadable mask.

"Alms, alms, good sir." An old woman was tugging at Lord Ystevan's cloak. To my relief he ignored her entirely, clearly aware that to show coin in this quarter of the city was a very quick method of suicide.

But the interruption helped my mind to move beyond the pain caused by his words. He didn't understand—*of course* he didn't understand, because I hadn't told him everything—at least, I didn't remember ever having done so. My urchinhood hadn't seemed immediately relevant to my father's healing—not to mention that discussion of it would all too easily lead to the revelation that *I* was to have been the sacrifice. Which had never seemed likely to make the he-elf love my father any more...

Surely Lord Ystevan would never have said what he'd just said if he'd known all there was to know about me? Did I seem *spoilt?* Obstinate, maybe, to an infuriating degree, I was honest enough to concede that, but *spoilt?*

Why was I so upset about what he thought, anyway? I barely knew the man...he-elf...did I? Not really. Perhaps I'd thought I did, perhaps I'd even thought we were friends, but if he could simply turn around and take from me all memories of himself, clearly I'd been wrong.

"Alms, good sir?" the woman was persisting, so he simply turned away from her.

I saw the old woman's face as she straightened, set in hard lines and not nearly as old as her hunched position had suggested. I opened my mouth instantly to give warning, but the woman was too fast. She drew a cudgel from her skirts and brought it smashing down on Lord Ystevan's head. The he-elf crumpled to the ground without a sound; apparently even elfin were not proof against such brutal force.

I reached for my dagger beneath my cloak and would have stepped forward to defend the he-elf from any further attentions from the woman, but a sound made me turn.

For just a split second my eyes focused on the fist that was rapidly approaching my face.

CHAPTER 36

The Fort of Torr Elkyn

The Queen's Hall lay at the very heart of the Fort, and there we started our tour. Things communal to the entire fort's population, such as libraries and school chambers for the elflings, surrounded it, going out from it like ripples on a pond.

Encircling this central section ran the 'Ring' passage, and from this radiated seven other main passages, going to the halls of the seven clans of Torr Elkyn. Each hall contained the private chambers of its members, along with those things communal to the clan, such as the laundry, the bath chambers, and the water closets.

"Well, you've seen pretty much everything," Ystevan told me, after showing me around the hall of Clan Elendal, the clan to which the queen belonged—the clan halls were all pretty much identical, apparently. "There are some store rooms, which really aren't all that interesting, and the stables, where we are headed."

I pictured that fine stag standing in a stall letting me stroke its muzzle and stepped out eagerly to keep up with my long-legged guide.

Soon we came from a long passage into a square chamber with wooden-doored stalls going back into the rock, but disappointingly, there wasn't a deer in sight. A number of tall, long-limbed horses looked over the majority of the doors, a bullock over another, and from several more came bleats and grunts respectively.

What did catch my attention was the filthy black horse that had just nickered at me from a nearby stall. The sound seemed one of great relief, as if the horse were saying, "Finally, a real person!"

"Hellion!" I exclaimed, rushing over to him. He nickered at me again, plainly pleased to see me. He wasn't wearing a head collar, though, so I stopped to pick up a lead rope, which I wrapped around his muzzle so I could control his head. Then I stroked his muddy, sweat-stained face in delight, gripping the rope firmly when he seemed to decide that a nip would show his affection best.

"You seem to know that creature," said a dry voice, and I looked over my shoulder to see an elfin groom flexing a hand accusingly at the horse. "He's sent three of us for healing already and we still haven't got him cleaned up."

I was caught between apology and defensiveness. "He's just nervous, but I hope he hasn't hurt anyone too badly."

"Nothing serious," said the groom easily.

"Where did you find him?"

"I didn't," replied the groom. "A provider from Clan Tarabil brought the animal back with him from gathering this morning. Good job he was a Caller, or he'd never have got the nag here. The tack's over there. It's a bit of a mess, but nothing badly broken."

My saddlebags! I gasped and hurried to the jumble of reeking, muddied leather, unfastening the bags quickly. Everything remained in place, including the bundle containing my mother's jewelry. I showed Ystevan the jewels, a necklace of emeralds and some fine rings.

"I'm glad those aren't lost," I remarked, as he took them to look at and I went back to stroking Hellion, "but I'm even happier to have this friend returned." I couldn't help wondering if Ystevan would save his mount or his jewels first of all. He gave me an ironic look, clearly understanding my rather pointed remark, but I was busy looking the horse over.

Hellion was completely filthy and bore some small scratches, as well as his legs being somewhat cracked from cold and mud, but he stood squarely on all four hooves. Relief and thankfulness filled me—a horse galloping blind across a mountainside in a storm could easily break a leg.

I experienced a sudden pang of loneliness for Raven, whose absence was like having a part of me missing, and for my father, whom I'd recently had reason to believe I might also never see again. But I would see them again, and when I did, either Alliron or Ystevan was jolly well going to be with me!

I scratched Hellion behind the ears, pleased by his display of affection. "You're a good boy," I told him. "It's not your fault the lightning scared you. When God gets as angry as that there's only two things to do, run or hide, and between us I think we covered both of them!" Hellion searched my hands for tasty offerings, and I took them away before he could realize that I had nothing.

Several of the elfin grooms had just entered the stall again. They put a headcollar on the recalcitrant horse, and tied his head unceremoniously to the wall. Hellion rolled his eyes balefully, clearly waiting for them to come within range of his hooves.

I bit my lip. "I've very sorry, I would help you if I wasn't wearing this lovely dress. Perhaps I'd better go and change..."

But the grooms poo-pooed this, and Ystevan led me away, laughing. "They'll be fine."

It occurred to me that I still hadn't seen his fine mount. "Where's your stag?"

Ystevan's eyebrows rose. "You don't think I'd keep him in here, do you? He runs free with his herd, when I don't need him. Come here for a moment..." He lifted my hair carefully out of the way to fasten the emerald necklace around my neck. "Rather an erroneous statement of your power," he remarked, giving me the rings to tuck in a pocket, "but still."

The passage we were in presently emerged from the mountainside. Looking back, it appeared to be nothing more than a cave from outside. The mountain towered above us, and I now knew that this was the fort itself. Or that the fort lay within it, which amounted to the same thing. The entrance was well below the snowline but still quite high up. I peered left and right, looking for the crack in which I had sought refuge, but I couldn't see it.

"By the way," I asked Ystevan, who stood staring down into the forest and valley below us, "what's a Caller?"

He smiled. "This," he said softly, as the soft thud of hoofbeats approached and a fine stag came bounding towards us, antlers raised high. It slowed and sniffed suspiciously, clearly smelling me, but Ystevan held out his hand and it continued up to him and touched its nose to it. I caught my breath in awe as the late afternoon sun shone off the gleaming russet coat, and Ystevan's calming presence allowed me to run my hands over the live animal.

"But you eat deer, don't you?" I asked as we made our way back to Ystevan's chambers for dinner.

"Yes," replied Ystevan, "but we never ever Call an animal when we are hunting. That would be a gross misuse of the power, for when we Call them they come to us in perfect trust."

"How did it go, child?" asked Haliath as we sat down to the light evening meal.

"Not bad," I said. "She won't help me herself, but I'm allowed to ask other people to do it."

"Optimist," muttered Ystevan dryly. "It was a great big No, and you know it."

"Which audience were you in?" I asked sweetly.

The he-elf just snorted and speared a piece of cold venison.

Haliath looked from him to me and said no more on the matter. "Alvi is going home tomorrow," she told her son.

Ystevan made a non-committal noise.

"It's a long walk," Alvidra added pointedly.

Ystevan raised his eyebrows. "You'd better set off nice and early, then."

Alvidra seemed to find this statement immensely frustrating and almost threw down her fork on her plate to fix her mother with a look of appeal.

Haliath sighed. "Calm down, Alvi. But, Ystevan, must your tease your sister so?"

Ystevan turned a guileless look to his mother that did not quite conceal the mischief in his eyes. "But she's so teaseable, mother, even you must admit it." Haliath sighed, but her face grew rather firm, so Ystevan smiled at Alvidra. "Would you like me to Call a deer to take you home to Avragrain?"

"That would be nice," said Alvidra rather stiffly.

How much did my presence have to do with the she-elf's bad mood?

"A fine, fiery stag, perhaps," added Ystevan, apparently quite unable to help himself.

"Mother!" wailed Alvidra in protest.

"The calmest, gentlest hind in the herd," Ystevan said, apparently relenting. "Which will carry you all the way there at the gentlest of ambles, without running off once. We certainly don't want *anything* befalling you just *at the moment,"* he added significantly.

Alvidra looked pleased and smug, and Haliath beamed, and I suddenly understood that there was a lot more to Alvidra's moodiness than I'd realized.

CHAPTER 37

Of Curses and Creation

I clawed my way back to full consciousness to find myself lying on wooden floorboards, my hands bound in front of me. Loud voices filled the room with strident argument. I eased my eyes open just a crack.

"I tell you the money's 'ere, right in this 'un." That was a stocky man who brandished a small box at three other men and the woman from the alley. "I saw 'im count it in with me own two eyes and I saw 'im seal it a'fore me two eyes."

"Then let's *see* it!" screeched the woman avidly.

The man placed the box firmly in the centre of the table, pointing to the wax sealing it closed. "I tell ye, 'e sealed it a'fore me eyes so ye'd know it were all there, and most particular 'e was that t'lanky man's throat was to be slit the moment we 'ad 'im out of sight. A'fore all else..."

"I say," said one of the other men, "we see t'money with *our* own two eyes a'fore we do t'throat slitting. I ain't 'anging for money I never seen..."

"Aye!" shouted the others.

The leader's fists clenched in frustration. "It's there, I tell ye, right in there. We dun wanna cross a man like that, I tell ye. We must slit t'throat right quick, at once, then we can count out our coin to our 'eart's content."

I bit my lip and wondered how long the argument would go on for. The leader would scarcely wish his cronies to get their hands on their share before the deed was done, or they'd all be off to spend it and he'd be left to do the hanging job himself.

The corner of the room in which I lay was shadowed and twisting my head cautiously, I could see Ystevan's slumped form beside me. Strands of escaped hair fell across his face, and he was clearly still unconscious. His hands had also been bound in front of him. Our kidnappers were far too busy arguing to be paying any attention, so slowly, carefully, I rolled onto my side and began to pick awkwardly at the knots that bound the he-elf's hands.

Raven chattered soft inquiry from my bodice.

"Stay there, Raven," I murmured, unheard over the din of voices. I could manage the knots myself, and I didn't want Raven to be seen.

"What 'bout t'filly, anyways?" one of the men was demanding. "Worth a pretty penny, doncha think?"

"We'll take 'er to 'im, stupid," said the leader. "Surely 'e'll pay for t'infurmation an we might get 'er back to sell, after."

"Sell!" scoffed the woman. "Ransom, doncha mean. Seen 'er clothes? Tha's a fine filly, that un."

"Ransom, sell," said the leader impatiently, "but we take 'er to 'im first an collect twice, now let's *do* t'lanky fellow."

"Money first..."

The conversation was, to my relief, becoming distinctly circular. The last knot came undone and I tucked the loose ends out of sight. The he-elf would surely discover the looseness of his ropes as soon as he woke up, even if I couldn't indicate it to him in some way.

When he woke up. I stared at him in anxious frustration. The hair fluttered slightly as he breathed, but he wasn't so much as stirring.

"Ystevan," I whispered, as loudly as I dared, tapping the backs of his hands with my fingers. "Ystevan, wake *up!*" *Wake up and get us out of this!* I feared I'd boasted to Sir Allen prematurely. Even if I risked Raven's discovery by getting her to chew through my own bonds, there was no way I could fight off four men and one woman whilst carrying an unconscious he-elf.

"Let's slit 'is g'dame throat!" the leader was yelling.

"Money first!" roared the others.

I trembled in fear lest the leader lose patience and decide to do the deed himself. Then Ystevan's head moved slightly and a moan crept from his lips. Hastily I raised my bound hands and clapped them over his mouth, hoping the movement would go unnoticed.

He froze, instantly silenced. His eyes opened, gleaming through his hair for a long moment as he presumably took stock. I took my hands away and opened my own mouth to whisper that his hands were free.

Before I could get the words out he raised his still rope-wrapped wrists up behind his head and brought them forward, the rope sliced through. *Oh,* I thought, in fleeting chagrin, *and I was lying here wondering how I could free my own hands!*

He reached out more discreetly, hooking a single strand of my own bindings with a finger and yanking. My wrists felt like they almost came off, but the rope snapped like cotton, and I quickly and surreptitiously shook my hands free.

Stealthily I rolled to my feet, mirroring Ystevan, who paused to snatch up his cane from nearby. He leant on it as he weaved into an upright position as though his balance was decidedly off. How badly was he hurt and how well would he be able to fight?

Over by the table the four men were still arguing vehemently, but unobserved by them, the woman was running her fingernail through the wax seal, breaking it. Ystevan's eyes alighted on the same sight and he swung around, grabbing me and folding me to his chest—in one single, frantic leap, he bore us through the open window.

For a split second, over his shoulder, I saw the woman's hand on the box lid, poised to open it, then we were plummeting towards the cobbles below and the scene was whipped from my sight.

Uh-oh, we'd leapt from the ATTIC *window...*

Ystevan landed on his feet, knees bending to take our weight. And somehow, we were safely down.

Then the screaming began. It was the most terrible screaming I had ever heard. It curdled the blood in my veins to ice and drove shards of terror into my heart. Raven shrieked and scrabbled to bury herself yet more deeply in my clothing. I pressed my ear to Ystevan's chest, clinging tightly and covering my other ear with my hand. It didn't do any good. The screaming was ten times worse than the screams of the man I'd once seen burned at the stake, and it seemed to hammer through me. There was no escaping it.

Finally, there was silence. Slowly, trembling, I eased my grip on the he-elf, relinquishing the rapid but reassuring pounding of his heart under my ear and looking up at him. His face was dead white in the gathering twilight.

"What was that?" I whispered.

"A...curse, for want of a better human word," he replied, his voice almost inaudible. "A curse I would not wish to try and counter whilst awake, let alone unconscious."

In other words, if that box had been opened whilst we were in the room, we would have shared the screamers' fate. I shuddered involuntarily. "Are you...going back in?"

He made to shake his head and staggered slightly. "No," he said firmly. "I have no need to see. Let's get out of here."

One arm still around me, he set off, leaning heavily on his stick for once and weaving slightly; I suspected the arm was not there entirely for my own comfort and support. I didn't query his desire to be gone without delay, though, and I let him lean on me as much as necessary, but for all his lofty height he seemed not at all heavy by human standards.

"That was a trap, wasn't it?" I said under my breath as we walked. Or staggered, in his case.

"Yes," he answered, trying not to nod. "Perhaps if I hadn't been distracted I wouldn't have... I don't know. It was only because I do not *expect* that from human women, you understand."

I shot him a look. Most men would have been suffused with embarrassment at having been struck down by a member of the weaker sex; the he-elf seemed worried that carelessly allowing himself to be struck down by a woman might imply that he *did* consider them the weaker sex. Well, they did seem to have a queen by default, rather than by mere...lack of male heirs. Very intriguing.

He didn't pause until we were out of the Quays and up as far as Lombard Street. Though beginning to tremble with gathering shock and the day's cold, I handed my now conspicuous ragged cloak to a delighted urchin.

Ystevan stopped beside a public trough and leant against it. "We'd best get you a hot drink," he said. "But before we do, perhaps we'd better..." He produced a handkerchief and dipped it, then reached out to wipe my face.

The handkerchief came away stained and I touched my swollen nose and lip. "Ah. Make me look a little less as though I've just been punched in the face."

"Quite," said the he-elf. He gave my face another wipe, then put the handkerchief down beside the trough and traced his fingers slowly over the damage. The ache of the bruises and sting of the cuts rapidly eased. "All better," he said after a moment.

"Good," I said, with relief. "If I went home looking like that my father would probably never let me out again."

Ystevan groaned and leant on the trough. "What did I just heal it for? It was hardly serious!" He sighed and sat down properly on the trough instead, fingers going to his own injury. "Obviously high time I dealt with this."

He ran his hands over the back of his head for rather longer than he'd spent on my face, but his pained expression gradually eased. When he'd finished, his hands came away glistening in the evening darkness.

"My brains were still on the inside, leastways," he remarked, rising easily to his feet. Taking the clip from his hair, he plunged his head into the trough, rinsing the blood away. He straightened, flicking his hair back and then shaking it so vigorously it was clear his head was entirely better.

I peered at his hair throughout this exercise, stroking Raven absent-mindedly through my dress. It seemed to almost glimmer, the gold visible again. But it was too dark for the color to be very noticeable and quickly enough he fastened it back again with the clip, and then it just looked as plain black as usual.

Wringing out his damp handkerchief, he tucked it away, led me to the nearest inn—The Pope's Head—secured us a private room and ordered hot wine. I sat in front of the fire and steamed damply for a few minutes in silence. Finally, I looked up to where he sat opposite, rather quiet, his hair steaming as well. "Thank you, Lord Ystevan," I said quietly.

He made a movement as though to brush my thanks aside, and said rather cautiously, "You can call me Ystevan, you know."

"Are you not a Lord?" I inquired lightly, struggling with such conflicting feelings. The pain of his cruel words still lingered, along with my anger *and* the frustration that he wouldn't heal my father, but...the more I remembered, the more he felt like Ystevan, my friend...and he had just saved both our lives.

He shrugged. "For all intents and purposes, yes. It is the closest human equivalent for the elfin title of fort guardian. But even large Torr forts like Torr Elkyn are small, and we are all largely interrelated to some degree or other, so we are most of the time much less formal with one another."

"Yes. Well, I suppose you *can* call me Serapia. Lady is...rather formal between friends. And I suppose we *are* friends, are we not?" Surely there simply were some things two people just could not go through together without becoming friends—no matter what had passed between them previously?

He smiled faintly, as though he knew what I meant. "Yes, we are friends," he sighed, but his eyes were bright. They quickly became more wary. "Don't think that it changes a thing with regard to that parent of yours, mind."

That would be too much to hope, wouldn't it?

The wine arrived then. I cupped the warm flagon in my hands, sipped gratefully, and looked up before the pot boy could leave. "Soup, bread and cheese for me, please," I said, too hungry to wait and see if Ystevan thought to ask if I wanted anything.

Ystevan looked faintly startled, but added quickly, "The same for me."

When the pot boy had departed, Ystevan sat and regarded me with a rather singular look. "You really are a very strange girl," he remarked. "I'm sure I am supposed to be attempting to bring you around from a swoon about now, but you are sitting there ordering a meal. That is to say, I know perfectly well how plucky you are, coming all that way on your own, and...everything. But still, you seem to have taken what just happened without turning a hair. Comparatively, anyway."

I looked down at my hands, which were still shaking as they held the flagon, though I began to feel much better. "Well, I haven't eaten all day," I said defensively.

"You know that's not what I mean," he retorted, taking one of my hands meaningfully in his. "And...I'm sorry for what I said. I didn't mean it."

I looked down into my wine for another moment, my rough, lined, weather-beaten hand still in his. So. He'd never really thought me spoiled. He'd just been hurt and lashing out. "Alright," I said at last. "I'll tell you the story of my... singularness, if you'll tell me the story about the dragons and the Elfin's creation."

He laughed and shook his head slightly in amusement. "Very well," he said, returning my hand to me. But another flicker of wariness went through his eyes.

The pot boy returned with our food so we moved from the hearth to the table. When the pot boy was gone, I began my tale. I told him about my mother's death, my uncle, my long years on the streets, and how I had finally found my father.

"So you see," I added pointedly as I finished, "I do not say he is a good man from any childish bias!"

He held up a quelling hand. "Not now, Serapia, least, not if you want to hear about the Elfin's creation. If I...uh...need to tell you?"

I couldn't help scowling, at that. "Yes, you do," I said grimly. So he *had* told me before...but I couldn't remember.

For a moment it looked as though he would begin, but then he shot a look at the dark windows. "One moment," he said, then added, as though it explained everything, "the sun is gone."

He reached under his coat to the back of his belt, and I realized he had another pouch there, a long thin one that ran along it. From this he took seven fist-sized rocks and, moving around the table, he placed them down in a circle right around it. Then he settled back into his chair. "Now I can give you my full attention."

I raised my eyebrow, for the performance with the rocks was most intriguing. "What are they?" I asked, nodding to them.

Ystevan looked surprised—then wary again. "Oh. Travelling ward stones."

So I'd seen those before too, had I?

"Well, um, here goes," Ystevan said quickly, with a slightly forced smile. "The reason why demons can hurt the Elfin, and no other living thing on this earth, is to be found in our creation. It has been pointed out, I believe, that the British humans are a—how shall I put it?—*mongrel* race, of Picts, Celts, Romans, Saxons, Normans and so forth. I mean no offence by pointing this out," he added, and I nodded to reassure him. The mixed ancestry of my native land was something well known to me. But...*mongrel race*...I had heard that phrase before.

"Wait a minute..." Suddenly it was unfolding in my mind.

Ystevan had joined me by the fire after dinner, and I'd asked him why demons could hurt the Elfin, and he'd begun his reply in almost the same words...

"Well, if the British are a mongrel race, the Elfin are a mongrel species in many ways. God almost seems to have simply allowed us to come into being through various other of his creations—we're not sure how deliberate we were on His part. Of course, you can say that about any number of other things, so he probably did intend us all along.

"But, let's see," he went on. "You know about the fall of Lucifer and the angels, I suppose?" I nodded, so he continued, "There's a lot of confusion about dragons among humans, because most humans rarely encounter them for good reasons, but by and large they are on God's side. Certainly to begin with, when he set them to guard hell, a job they still do. Demons are free to trickle to and fro from the gates, but the dragons prevent a mass exodus. However, the demons fell through free will, and some dragons have done the same; it's only natural, I suppose.

"Anyway, the dragons were set to guard hell, but eventually their numbers multiplied, and some went to live in heaven instead. But while there were too many to live comfortably in hell, there were not quite enough to be comfortably split between the two realms, and they grew lonely. Some of those still in hell sought solace with the fallen angels, and some of those in heaven...did likewise. There were children born of the unions.

"Anyway, God did not much care for this fraternizing, and he banished the dragons from heaven to the earth, with their half-breed offspring. The devil did not care for the situation either, probably because the dragons were, after all, God's servants, and he also drove away the offending dragons and their children. All these arrived on earth, where the dragons, still not a species large enough in number to easily find mates among their own kind, fell for the occasional human, until their numbers rose sufficiently for the temptation to be removed. But again, half-breed children were born.

"For some time it is believed the dragon children, as we call them, lived in two separate groups: the dark children, those of the

demons, and the fair children, those of the angels. The children of the humans were split between the two groups. But their common blood was such that intermarriage soon came about, especially since they were so few in number themselves. The two groups mingled and merged inextricably and formed the Elfin. So when I say we are mongrel, I mean it," he concluded.

I stared at him. "Dragon, human, angel, demon?"

Ystevan nodded. "Hence demons can hurt us. Angels probably could too, but they don't. Humans and the rest of God's creation are on the physical plane with regard to their bodies. But the Elfin have bodies that exist on the physical and spiritual plane at once. Which is in some ways a fearful nuisance, since it makes us vulnerable to the demons and they don't like us at all."

"Why don't they?" I asked curiously.

Ystevan shrugged. "I think they're just plain jealous. We have their blood in us, yet we live on the earth, very civilized and nice to one another, and they are trapped in hell, in eternal suffering. So they'll kill any adult elfin they can lay their claws on. Hence why none other than fort guardians ever go beyond the wards after nightfall."

"They don't come out in the day?"

Ystevan shook his head. "Not in the daylight, anyway. We're not completely sure why not. It's probably because the day is full of angels, and whenever you have a demon and an angel within a mile or two of one another, feathers and scales soon fly. It's a good thing they can't, though, or the majority of elfin would never be able to go out at all."

A shiver ran up my spine at this narration. "A demon couldn't hurt me, could it?"

"No, of course not. You're human. It can whisper at your soul subconsciously to lead you astray, but it can't lay one claw on you physically."

I thought about all this for a moment. "So are there still dragons living in the world? Or have knights killed them all?"

Ystevan smiled. "The knights only get the few that go astray and acquire a taste for human flesh and livestock, so yes, most definitely there are still dragons. There's a pair living at the top of

the mountain, and another pair nearby. They also like wild places."
...Dragons! Had I *seen* one? Would I ever know, or had Ystevan stolen that from me, forever? I stared across at him. He was doing that searching gaze thing again. Ticking off his list? I knew I should forgive wrongs done to me, but every time I wondered just how much I'd lost the anger surged back...

"Did I see a dragon?" I demanded.

His gaze dropped from mine, but he shook his head slightly. "We...didn't run into one when out and about."

I lowered my eyes as well, and stared at my already almost empty plate. The warmth I'd felt towards him so recently had chilled.

"Serapia."

I looked at him again.

He leant forward and placed his elbows on the table, looking me intently in the eye. "Serapia, I am more sorry than I can say about what I had to do. But it was my duty. Can you understand that?"

"Did you even tell me beforehand?"

As far as I could remember, I'd had no idea what was coming. How had he done it? And when?

He let out a little breath, almost a snort. "Of course not! What if you had bolted to try and avoid it? Aside from the fact you could have got hurt, we'd have had to chase you, and in the—admittedly very unlikely—event that you actually got away, well, I'd have betrayed my kin, wouldn't I?"

I looked down at my plate again. The problem was, from everything he had told me so far, I could see why he hadn't hesitated to put duty first. Why he had considered it necessary. His choice just seemed to hurt a lot more than it rationally should.

I ate the last few bites of my meal, trying to settle my surging thoughts—until the first of London's clocks began to strike the hour. I looked up, appalled at myself, sitting there eating and drinking and listening to—or at least remembering listening to—interesting things. "I must get back. My father will be so worried!"

"I will take you home," said Ystevan, as I hoped he would.

"Oh, but...can you?" I said, suddenly looking at those seven ward stones.

"It's all right," he reassured me. "I would not sleep or be inattentive whilst outside of a ward at night, but so long as I am alert the danger is not great. Generally, a guardian is a match for practically any demon they have the misfortune to meet. That's really the power requirement to be a guardian, and it *is* high. But one doesn't meet demons very often. They don't usually bother attacking a guardian.

"Don't think me complacent," he added, rising from his chair. "I have met, which is to say, fought, four demons. At night, that is. I have hunted many in daylight, the foolish ones trapped by the break of dawn, hiding away in some crack until nightfall. But of those night-time four I sent three howling for hell." He reached for the first stone.

I raised my eyebrows. "And the fourth?"

Ystevan smiled rather a twisted smile. "Oh, the fourth sent *me* howling for home. Without laying a claw on me. So trust me, Serapia, when I say that I am not complacent about demons."

With this less than entirely reassuring revelation, he put the rest of the stones away and offered me his arm.

CHAPTER 38

The Pursuit of Lord Alliron

When we finally reached the tall stone gateposts of Albany House, out on the road to Islington, Ystevan glanced around, then drew out the ward stones again, placed them down in a circle on the grass verge and stepped within. We had walked in silence and I had felt his quivering alertness beside me. He might claim that he could walk around outside a ward at night, but it was clearly not the most relaxing of occupations.

I doubted he would leave the stones behind, but I took a prudent grasp of his arm, all the same. It was far too late to attempt to persuade him to come in for some polite refreshment, more was the pity. Surely if I could only bring him together with my father and make him speak to him properly, to exchange even a few words, face-to-face, eye-to-eye, then he would realize he was not a bad man. But there really was no chance of it at this hour. So I said firmly, "Now, where are you staying?"

He smiled and shook his head slightly. "I am staying at a fort near London, but there is no question of me telling you *where.*"

"Then how can I contact you?"

He looked at me for a long moment and finally pursed his lips slightly. "I suppose if I do not give you some means you will carry on twisting information from Sir Allen and throwing yourself into appallingly dangerous situations," he said wearily.

I pointed at the lights of Albany House, glowing in the distance. "Father. Dying. Remember? Quite right I will!"

"All right," he said quietly. "You know that new chocolate house on St Clement's?"

263

I nodded with some enthusiasm. I'd stood outside it once or twice as an urchin when on route to Westminster, breathing in the delicious aroma. My father had since taken me several times, and I'd been once or twice more with Susie.

"Meet me there tomorrow at eleven, if you wish."

I nodded. "I'd better bring Susie if we're meeting *there*," I remarked, "or my reputation will be in ruins."

"Susie?"

"My maid," I explained. "She doubles as my chaperone. I'm rather afraid that sooner or later it will occur to my father to acquire some awful matron for the position, but at the moment Susie and I are as free as the birds. Almost. I haven't been taking her elfin-stalking, I confess."

Ystevan seemed to hide a smile, then his face straightened. "Leave Sir Allen's information alone, all right?"

"So long as you are there at eleven tomorrow," I returned, evenly.

"Demons and dark elfin besides, I'll be there," he said, turning to collect up his stones.

"Be careful," I whispered, as he disappeared into the darkness. Someone certainly wanted him dead.

He was gone, anyway. I set off along the drive, growing chilled again in my damp clothes, and feeling like I'd walked clean from one end of the city to the other. Which I very nearly had. Raven climbed out and cuddled to my neck, still shaken by the events of the evening, as, if I was honest, was I. I stroked her gently until I reached the house.

Anna, the butler, and my father's chamberlain all rushed into the hall to meet me.

"It's all right," I said. "Here I am. Pa isn't too worried, is he?"

Anna looked guilty. "Well, my lady, when Richard came back and said where you were, seeing as you had William and Stephen with you and they've been all over the continent with his grace, we really didn't feel it necessary to say more than that you were out. And when William and

Stephen came back, well, we knew you were still all right, and that you were with a capable man, as you told them. And since you'd already said you might not be back till late... Well, in short, my lady, your father has been asleep since late afternoon, and we haven't troubled to wake him. So, well, he doesn't know you weren't back at a normal hour."

I eyed the three sheepish-looking adults and had to smile. "Anna," I said, clasping the woman's hands, "you have done exactly the right thing. See, here I am, quite all right." *Now*. But I didn't want anything getting back to my father belatedly and worrying him, and I definitely could not risk my father confining me to the house.

"Rather damp," said the housekeeper, touching my sleeve and trying to shepherd me up the stairs. I turned determinedly towards the drawing room, but Anna stopped me. "Lady Serapia," she said, and I noticed that the other two servants had made themselves scarce. "You left so early, so you don't know, but...your father did not come downstairs today. He sat in the armchair in his room for a few hours, but then he had to lie down again. He was just so tired."

I swallowed hard. Anna's expression suggested that there was more.

"Well?" I asked in a strangled voice.

"Well...I think you should know. The physician was here today."

I struggled to remain calm. "What did he say?"

"He...he does not think your father has very long. At all." I bit my lip far too hard and Anna continued hastily, "Could you not...be around more? Your father is constantly asking after you and we always have to tell him that you are out."

I headed for the stairs in silence and made no reply. I couldn't really explain to Anna just why I was never around.

Genuinely fully recovered by now, I got up early the next morning to accompany the family up to the fort entrance to see

Alvidra off. Ystevan had brought his basket out with him, and afterwards left to gather food, and I went back inside with Haliath, asked her what Clan Alliron belonged to, and accordingly set out for the hall of clan Tarabil. When I arrived, I chose a place on a bench that commanded a view of all the wooden doors and settled down to await the emergence of the elfin lord.

I'd decided to try persuading Alliron first, because I couldn't help feeling grateful to Ystevan. As the Queen had so casually pointed out, it would have been the easiest thing in the world for him to sabotage my chances before I even entered the Queen's hall. I might never even have known why the Queen had said no.

I waited right through until evening, but no Lord Alliron emerged. I returned to Haliath's chambers, puzzled and frustrated by the guardian's apparent abandonment of all his duties, only to have Ystevan—clearly torn between sympathy and amusement— break it to me that there were back passages all over the fort. A whole day wasted!

Well, I wouldn't make that mistake again.

The next morning, I helped Haliath as much as I could, since both Ystevan—and no doubt Alliron—had gone out gathering and there was no point scouring the surrounding area for them.

Later in the afternoon, I set off for the Queen's Hall and positioned myself behind a pillar in the antechamber. I hadn't seen another exit from the hall, although there might be one. But I hoped vaguely that the jewel-bestudded crystal walls might mute the elfin lord's ability to sense me until it was too late.

With this end also in view, I called as many dragonets to me as I could—though Eraldis just gave me a look and flew off—until I was so covered in the friendly—but hot!—little creatures that sweat ran down my brow. Ystevan had sensed dragonet power on me before, but Alliron would not associate me with the creatures, so I hoped I wasn't standing there overheating myself for nothing.

After some time, the doors opened, and counselors began to drift out in groups, talking. Alliron eventually appeared, so deep in conversation with a middle-aged she-elf that I wondered if I'd needed to bother with my fiery little friends, whom I now shooed quickly away, stepping around the pillar and striding towards my prey.

Alliron's eyes flicked to me almost at once, and he threw a look over his shoulder at Ystevan, who followed not far behind. "This one's yours," he said caustically.

"Actually, Lord Alliron, I was hoping to speak to you," I said as sweetly as possible.

"Shame. I'm too busy." The he-elf turned away from me.

I planted myself firmly in his way, struggling not to get angry at his brusque manner. "I'm sure you can spare a few minutes." The words came out rather more grimly than I'd intended.

Ystevan snorted with laughter as the older he-elf eyed the human obstruction with great dissatisfaction. "If you wanted her to show consideration to your plans you shouldn't have left her sitting there all day," he remarked in passing.

"I have no idea what this little exhibition is in aid of," the older guardian told me scathingly, as the other counselors drifted away and I continued to obstruct him. "I have already given you my answer, and I don't for a moment suppose that you have forgotten it."

"Indeed," I said, "I am aware that we have already spoken ever so briefly on this subject, but considering that a man's life is at stake, I'm sure you'll be happy to discuss it more fully, rather than make the wrong decision..."

My reasonable words seemed to have no effect whatsoever.

"You think wrongly," said the he-elf coldly. "I don't doubt that you presented your case as fully and persuasively as you possibly could to the Queen, hence I have given you a more than fair hearing already. And considering the undeniable facts of the affair, there is clearly nothing to discuss. Your father is a sorcerer. He will die of it. The sooner the better. Now excuse me. I have more important things to do with my time..."

This time his effort was so determined that he made it past me, and since I could not hope to catch up with his long-legged stride, I was left standing there, caught halfway between anger and disappointment.

267

Finally, I set off back to the clan hall of Valunis, struggling to think what argument I could possibly bring to bear to penetrate such stubborn obstinacy.

He wouldn't even listen to me! How could I possibly persuade him if he wouldn't even hear what I had to say? I didn't have time for this! I'd been here for days already! I had to get one of them to come back with me right away!

CHAPTER 39

A Guardian's Duty

I was dreaming again... The Duke sat in his armchair by the fire, head resting against the wing of the chair, clearly asleep. Or dozing, at any rate. A heavy old book lay on his knee. I peered unconsciously with my borrowed eyes and determined that it was an Arthurian romance from the library.

Raven felt...frayed, and my father looked terrible. The skin was drawn over the bones of his face, cheeks and eyes growing sunken, fingers skeletal. He looked desperately ill, and when the butler appeared beside the chair and woke him with a respectful, "My lord?" he raised his head wearily, as if even that were a great effort.

"Yes?" he inquired, stroking under Raven's chin with one gentle finger. I ached to be able to give him better comfort than the company of even that faithful little companion.

"It is late, my lord," pointed out the butler matter-of-factly. "I thought you might wish to retire."

The Duke glanced at the clock on the mantelpiece, yawning. "Indeed," he said simply, and allowed the Butler to lever him from the chair, keeping a more than supportive hand under his arm as they made their way slowly from the room. Raven leapt from the chairback and ran after them, cutting off the dream with an abruptness that spoke almost of irritation.

I let Hellion amble across the steep hillside at his own pace, lost in thought and wrapped in a lingering sense of urgency after that dream. Another day had been sufficient to convince me that Alliron was a waste of time. Even were he not much older than Ystevan, and correspondingly more rigid in his ideas, I just could not corner him often enough, let alone get far enough into a conversation with him, to hold out any serious hope of changing his mind at any time in the next decade. Which was rather longer than

I had available to me.

I simply had to get home! I had to get back in time to at least... say goodbye...

No, I wasn't thinking like that! I pulled Hellion up with a gentle twitch of the reins as we approached a cliff edge with a stunning vista back towards the mountain of Torr Elkyn. My shoulders squared, though I couldn't help sighing, but Raven's impatience could not be ignored. I had no time left. I would simply have to turn my attentions to my kind host.

Not, of course, that he was strictly my host, for I had learned that among the Elfin she-elves owned chambers, and a he-elf would only ever hold a set of chambers in trust until he should marry, at which point ownership of the chambers would revert to his she-elfen. It was a system that I found it quite hard to get my head around, but which I regarded as being far from unpleasant. Ystevan didn't seem to mind that his mother owned their chambers. He clearly viewed the idea of a man inheriting property by default with just as much surprise as I viewed their system.

But that was beside the point. I turned Hellion and let him amble on his way back towards the fort. The point was, that I was not so blind as to think that Ystevan, whose view on sorcery could hardly be called flexible, could be persuaded to help my father without long debate, that was, argument, and in short, many ructions to our domestic peace. If only I could have persuaded Alliron!

I allowed Hellion to break into a canter across a flat area of slope. I would have to go on somewhat carefully with Ystevan. If I upset things too much, it was not beyond the bounds of possibility that he would send me to live with some other family, and then he would become almost as inaccessible as Alliron. I must avoid that at all cost.

Anyway, I didn't want to go and stay somewhere else.

Even at that hour in the morning there were already several gentlemen in the chocolate house and a couple of ladies, their maids standing behind their chairs inhaling as deeply and surreptitiously as possible.

"I want to be your maid forever and ever, Lady Serapia," sighed Susie, sipping her chocolate with an expression of bliss on her face.

"You are an excellent maid," I said absently, sipping my own chocolate with rather less appreciation than usual, eyes on the door. "I do not see why you should not have a cup of chocolate."

Susie clearly considered it impolitic to reply, "Well, the price!" and went on sipping away happily.

My mind strayed back to my stay at the fort, and my previous attempt—attempts?—to persuade the recalcitrant guardian...

I returned Hellion to his stall after his much-needed exercise and headed back up the entrance tunnel to the open air, directing my steps along the mountainside to where I thought I'd spotted a certain he-elf.

Sure enough, there was Ystevan, standing, running his hands, finger-spread, over something invisible. His eyes were half-closed, and occasionally his fingers twitched as if smoothing or manipulating something. His faithful little—or not so little—dragonet was curled around his shoulders, but as I approached Eraldis gave his customary affectionate head rub to Ystevan, and flew off with his—equally customary—disapproving snort in my direction.

I hovered uncertainly, afraid of disturbing Ystevan, and indeed, after a moment, he said, without opening his eyes fully, "Perhaps you could stand outside the ward..."

I assumed that outside was on the other side of him from the mountain, and complied, but he had not sounded annoyed. I watched him for a while, but there was not a lot to see, and I wasn't sorry when he took his hands away, raised his head and turned to look at me.

"That will hold for another night," he remarked, clearly satisfied with his work.

"Did I distract you?" I asked, and then, as I absorbed his words, "Only one night?"

He smiled. "Having you so close inside the ward...well, I was picking up a human presence so strongly that it was rather hard to feel anything else. But outside was fine. And the ward...this bit probably won't need touching again for days, but that's just because the demon will almost certainly have a go at a different bit next time."

More questions about wards blossomed in my mind, but I resisted the temptation to ask. I must not get distracted. I had time only to discuss my father, nothing else. Racking my brains as to how I should bring up the matter, I followed, keeping outside the wards, as Ystevan walked on around the mountain, trailing one hand along the invisible ward beside him.

But when I finally drew in a breath to speak, he turned his head to me with a very sharp look, and spoke instead. "I will not heal a sorcerer, little one, so do not think me an easier target than Alliron."

"We are having a conversation," I said sourly. "That automatically makes you an easier target than Alliron."

The he-elf barked a short laugh, half his attention clearly still on the ward under his left hand.

"If you're saying no, you could at least enlarge your reason for doing so."

"So you can start thinking up counter arguments, you mean?" queried the guardian, arching a brow at me. "Still, I suppose I should explain myself. I might convince you." He did not sound very hopeful, though.

He took his hand away from the ward and stopped walking. Apparently, we had come to the end of his section. He turned to face me, and for all he was still refusing me, it was so nice to have someone taking me seriously about all this...

"Ooh, that's a tall, lean fellow." Susie's remark jerked me from the memory and I looked up in time to see Ystevan entering the room.

I watched as patiently as I could whilst the he-elf got himself a cup of chocolate and had a quick word with the proprietor. Coins changed hands. Finally, he approached. "We may have the garden for our private use," he told me and nodded towards the back door.

Susie giggled and shot me an apologetic look, no doubt for her previous comment.

"Come along, Susie," I said briskly.

Susie sprang up and gave her cup an anguished look.

"Bring your chocolate," I urged her, so she seized it and followed us.

The garden was fairly small, overhung all around with creeper. There were seats here and there, so I indicated the one by the door. "If you wait there, Susie, that will be best."

Walking with Ystevan to the farthest end of the garden, I looked around for a seat. But he drew me towards a wooden gate in the wall, largely overhung by the foliage, and pulled it open. "There is a park behind here. Far more private than this place with so many walls, behind which one knows not who listens."

I shot a look back down the garden, found that we were well hidden from Susie and followed him through.

"Have you reconsidered about healing my father?" I demanded urgently, as soon as we had settled ourselves on a grassy knoll under some tall shady trees—the sun was shining ever so brightly today—and well away from any eavesdropping walls. If the physician was right, I was almost out of time entirely.

Ystevan gave me a rather frustrated look. "There is nothing to reconsider. Sorcerer, remember?"

"Father, remember?" I said. "And he's *not* a sorcerer. He just did one bad, foolish thing many, many years ago. If he were *really* a sorcerer, he could have saved his own life by now. He has what he needs. But he will not do it. *Nothing* will make him touch sorcery again, do you understand? *Nothing.*"

"No," said Ystevan quietly. "The answer is no." He placed his cup beside my empty one, staring off across the park. There was no one else in sight at all, right now. Raven was sitting happily on my shoulder, hidden from any distant gaze by my hair.

"Won't you explain? Please?"

"I've explained, Serapia," he said tiredly. "I explained until I was *hoarse.*"

"Are you looking for *sympathy?* Because I'm afraid you'll just have to explain again, since *for some reason,* I can't remember your poor throat's torment!"

Ystevan sighed heavily. Looked at me intently and—recited? From memory? "The threat posed to the Elfin by sorcery is actually very similar to that posed by dark elfin..."

It was enough...

"The actions of the former put us in danger unintentionally," Ystevan told me, his hand straying, absent-mindedly, back to the invisible ward beside him, *"not that a sorcerer would care, while the second endanger us deliberately, but apart from that the scenario is similar. Supernatural events occur among the humans, and someone is usually seized, although often not the sorcerer and usually not the dark elfin responsible. Sometimes it is just a scapegoat. This sends tales and rumors all over the country, sparking countless other alarms and/or scapegoat-seizures, which in turn fuel more rumors.*

"In some places, if the panic and suspicion whipped up is sufficient, then the humans will attack anything supernatural, whether it has any connection to sorcery or the devil whatsoever. Such mobs are mindless and vicious, sometimes so much so that they will forget all the good the Elfin have done in a certain area in the face of the sole fact of our 'supernaturalness'. It doesn't happen very often," he conceded, *"but when it does it is usually very nasty. Especially for sheiling-forts. Torr-forts are much safer due to size and isolation."*

I opened my mouth to protest that all this was irrelevant since my father was not a practicing sorcerer, but Ystevan cut me off. "I know what you will say, you will say that your father is a good man, and so forth, and will never do sorcery again. That is not good enough. He has had recourse to sorcery.

"Think, little one. If I should heal your father, how would I feel if he went away, and prompted, perhaps, by some Foreseeing of danger to you, he reverted to sorcery again, caused panic to sweep

the country, and a sheiling-fort, say Torr Shyvalere—my sister's home—to be destroyed, all its elfin slaughtered.

"No, I will not heal your father, and that is why. *Or rather, that is merely the primary* practical *reason why I will not. It is morally out of the question, of course." His tone was icy...*

I looked back up into Ystevan's watchful face and tried not to bite my lip.

"You remember?"

I nodded and thought it best to drop the subject for a while. Give myself time to think how to respond. What *had* I said? *Then?* Clearly it hadn't worked. Not an encouraging thought.

"So...so why *do* demons chew on the wards?" I asked. "You did say they chew on the wards, didn't you? Are they that desperate to kill elfin?"

Ystevan shrugged. "I think when they chew on the wards they are thinking not so much of wholesale slaughter but of getting to our elflings. You probably remember that I told you that they would kill any adult elfin, but elflings are a different matter. Their chances of taking an adult are extremely low, but elflings are far, far more vulnerable. You can be sure we guard them very closely indeed. Young elflings must not go beyond the wards without an adult, even in daytime. Older elflings must always be in a group until they come of age."

I frowned to myself. "You are very careful then," I could not help remarking, "since you say demons cannot even come out in the daylight."

"Indeed they cannot, but they can be hiding in shade," replied the guardian, "*and* accidents can happen that can prevent any elfin or elfling from getting within the wards before nightfall. And can you imagine, Serapia, what it is like to lose one of one's young ones like that?"

Uneasily, I queried, "Lose...?"

Ystevan looked grim. "If they are lost to a demon. Think, Serapia. One dark elfin in among the humans, engaged in acts of spite, malice or sheer evil, and what are the repercussions for us? Humans are so dangerous—and so *many*—and our safety lies in their goodwill. A lost child can rarely be recovered, and they are far too dangerous to be left alive."

I swallowed, understanding. A decision like that must touch everyone in the fort if the population, by human standards, was so small. There could be no impartial executioner among the Elfin.

"That's why you're here," I said softly.

Ystevan looked away for a moment, then back at me, his eyes dark. "Yes. It is a guardian's duty. We are the ones who are responsible for seeing that they are not lost in the first place. It's a matter of fort security, after all."

Now *that* must be a good incentive for the guardians to perform their duties fastidiously... Oh. No wonder he was so willing to steal my memories.

I pushed that thought away for now, and started racking my brains as to how I could bring up the matter of my father again, trying to keep my mind on that rather than Siridean, to whom it kept turning.

But when I finally drew in a breath, he turned his head to me with a very sharp look and spoke instead. "I think I have made it plain, Serapia, that it is a similar reason why I will not heal a sorcerer."

"But..." I began.

He cut me off. "I have a much-loved nephew. Well, what you humans would call a fourth cousin, but we elfin are very close to our extended family and we have a lot of it. I dandled little Arathain on my knees when I was an elfling, played with him as he grew. I was there the first time he rode a deer. I helped teach him as he grew strong in his elfin abilities. He was sweet-natured and brave; we all thought he would grow up to be a guardian.

"Then one day he went out with his decade group, and he got separated from them. Failed to make it back within the wards before nightfall. We have searched for him for many years and found nothing. But now we know that my little nephew is here in London. And so I have come to find him. And when I find him, I will kill him. Do you understand?"

His face was hard as granite, but his nostrils were pinched with pain. "My people's security is my duty and *nothing* can come before that. Do you really think there are any circumstances in which I would agree to heal your father?"

I stared at him in silence, temporarily rendered speechless. Well before I could form any reply, he suddenly craned his neck in that odd way that was not exactly sniffing. Or perhaps it was, but sniffing with his *crest*.

A split second later he dived forward as though to escape something rushing at him from behind—Raven shrieked and recoiled so violently she fell from my shoulder—as Ystevan went, he twisted onto his back, both his hands shooting out, palms thrusting with considerable force, and a cloud of...of *safyrs*... rose from his body to hurtle in the direction of whatever he was fleeing... For just a second, they seemed to strike against an unseen shape, momentarily outlining—impeding—*something*...

As they began to fade, Ystevan rolled up into a crouch, his stick in one hand, the other darting to that long pouch he wore at his belt—and coming out with a...an *arrow!*

By the time he'd raised the shaft, his other hand held not a stick, but his *bow*, on which he notched and released the arrow in one smooth movement. It flicked across my vision and...*disappeared*, about where the safyrs had betrayed the presence of that unseen *thing*. Raven hung from my hair, wings thrashing as she tried to climb up again and I reached back to help her.

Ystevan was already notching and releasing another arrow, rising seamlessly to his feet even as he did so—I knew he was a skilled hunter, but for the first time, Sir Allen's comment about Ystevan's martial prowess came back into my mind. He made my dueling father look as graceless and harmless as a toothless old sow.

277

Ystevan was moving forward now, eyes bright and fierce, as though driving something before him. He loosed another arrow, and followed his unseen aggressor a little further—tables firmly turned by now, it seemed fairly clear.

Raven safely back on my shoulder—in fact, plastered to my neck, shaking—I trailed after him at a distance as he closed in on one of the thickest trees, getting within about ten feet of it before suddenly whipping out his dagger and darting around to place the trunk between himself and the hollow knoll that lay between two wizened roots.

As he reached around the trunk to drive the dagger into this hole, hard, several times, I edged close enough to get a good look—though keeping something of a distance. The knoll was large enough that I myself could have squeezed in, at a pinch, but I still couldn't spot anything.

After a few more blows, Ystevan finally stepped back, still with the trunk between himself and the opening, wiped his (clean) dagger in the grass and returned it to his sheath. He glanced around the park—still deserted—then gave the bow a quick shake and suddenly he held his stick again.

Now I understood why he carried the silly thing everywhere!

He brushed a hand over the quiver that hung at his side, and it was once more that strangely long pouch. "Let's find some sunshine, shall we?" he suggested airily.

But he was frowning as we headed out from under the trees. "A demon should *not* have ventured out into that level of light," he muttered to himself. "Unless..." He scowled even harder.

"Unless what?" I asked.

"Uh...no matter."

"I'm not a fainting violet!"

"Very well, someone must have put the word out to kill me. And put it out pretty wide. Someone powerful, if they're ordering demons around. That thing would *never* have come out otherwise, let alone attacked a guardian. Still," he gave a satisfied nod, and spoke much more lightly, "That's one demon that will be too busy crawling home tonight to get up to anything else."

"You didn't kill it?"

Ystevan gave a slight laugh. His black mood seemed to have eased somewhat. "Could one kill an angel? I'm afraid demons can't be killed. I always think it's rather unfair, but that's how it is. That one, however, will not feel like troubling anyone for some time to come."

"I couldn't see anything," I pointed out.

"Did you really expect to?" Ystevan asked with rather a teasing smile, sitting down on the grass—in full sunshine.

Biting my lip, I sat beside him, suddenly feeling foolish. Of course I couldn't see anything! I concentrated on stroking Raven, who still seemed so terrified she'd surely seen all there was to see.

"Oh, my poor little friend," Ystevan said, reaching out to Raven himself. "Never had a demon rush at you before, hmm? Come here, eh?" Quivering, she crept onto his palm, her head and body held low, peeping up at him rather hopefully. His gentle fingertip found all the right places, running up under her chin and rubbing in between her ears. He crooned softly to her as he stroked, and before long she was curled up in his palm, her tiny forepaws wrapped around the base of his thumb, calm and happy.

Thinking about what Ystevan had told me about the creation of the Elfin, it was only then that a most horrible thought struck me. "Could...that demon have hurt *Raven*?"

Ystevan smiled slightly. "Theoretically, but since the Good Lord designed dragons to guard hell, it's probably not surprising that on a spiritual level their hide is fairly demon-proof, and dragonets are no different. A demon might harm one if they really put their mind to it, but even a little dragonet like Raven would be such a tough nut to crack, a demon would need to be really motivated. But I think this poor little one is far too young and inexperienced to know that." He directed a tender gaze at Raven.

"I remember when Eraldis met his first demon!" He shook his head. "You'd have thought he'd been laid in the wrong hearth, you really would! But he's a proper guardian's dragonet now. Minor things like demons don't concern him at all!"

Yes, Eraldis, suspicious Eraldis...where was he? When I peered closely at Ystevan's willowy form, from top to bottom, he laughed. "Oh, he's back at Torr Elkyn, safe with my mother. He's getting too big to hide, now. He'll be glad when I'm back. So will I, for that matter. I don't like leaving him, but I don't have much choice."

"So, dragonets aren't...wild?" Had I asked this before?

Apparently not—at any rate Ystevan shrugged and replied. "There are *some* wild dragonets, but not many. The dragonets have been living with the Elfin for so long most of them have forgotten how to live on their own. They're terribly cuckooish with their eggs, as well, which has helped their, er, domestication, if I can call it that. Sometimes a newly mated couple will raise a chick, but usually they just choose an elfin's hearth, lay their egg there, and go away and forget about it. The chick becomes the elfin's problem, or treasure, as the case may be, hence it's small wonder if it never occurs to them to go off and live wild in the hills with their big cousins."

He smiled down at Raven again. "Goodness knows I was desperate for a dragonet of my own when I was little. When Eraldis's egg was finally laid in our hearth, you should have seen me hovering over it, day and night! I was so worried I'd miss the hatching and the chick would choose Alvidra instead!"

"Didn't she hover too?"

"Alvidra, hover over a dragonet egg? No, she wasn't bothered. Thankfully, or things would have been much more fraught."

"But why did Raven's mother lay her egg in a *human's* hearth?" I asked. "Raven was nearly killed at birth!"

Ystevan sighed. "Well, their maternal and paternal

instincts have been very much eroded by generations and generations of fostering their chicks on the Elfin. They are far less concerned about their eggs than dragons are. Anyway, her mother could have been hurt and had to lay the egg in the nearest suitable place, or something like that. For I must say, a human's hearth seems careless even for a dragonet!"

He glanced at Raven again—she was fast asleep. "Well, this little one's calm enough, now. She'll feel better after a nice nap." He tipped Raven carefully into my waiting hand, and I tucked her down my bodice. She turned drowsily, making herself comfortable in the new space, and went back to sleep.

Ystevan unfastened his cuff and only then did I notice the bloody gashes on his arm. Suddenly dragonets and hearths and eggs were wiped from my mind...

"Don't look so worried." He started to run a finger over the wounds in a tracing, stroking motion, and the bleeding ceased.

"That was the *demon?*" I demanded, my pulse accelerating.

He nodded. "It got me just at the end there. Even if it can't be killed, you can hardly expect *anything* to sit still and be stabbed without fighting back. Least of all a demon. But it was worth it to ensure it's thoroughly incapacitated for a while."

"That's *it!*" I declared. Finally, *finally* I knew.

"That's what?"

"It was a demon! A demon cut him to pieces. That's why I couldn't see it!"

"Cut who to pieces?" said the guardian, thoroughly baffled.

"Siridean," I replied distractedly, running through my memories again. Yes, I was quite certain. The mystery was finally solved.

"Siri..." Ystevan broke off as though he couldn't believe what he had just heard. "Are you talking about an elfin?" he demanded harshly.

I blinked and gave him my attention again. "Well, yes, I'm pretty sure he was."

Ystevan's lips drew into a grim line. "The only elfin I know of with that name is a dark elfin!"

I bristled at his tone but was somehow not particularly surprised by his words. "Well, he's dead."

"Good," retorted the guardian. "Good riddance."

"He wasn't all bad," I snapped, unable to hold my tongue. "He was kind."

"Don't be ridiculous. He was a dark elfin—evil through and through."

"He was not!" I cried, stung by his tone, manner, words and all. "He saved my life! He fought a demon rather than hurt me, and it killed him! How can you make such a presumption? Did you even know him?" My voice broke and I felt perilously close to tears. It was no surprise to learn that Siridean had not exactly been on the side of the angels, but to hear him condemned as irredeemably evil was unbearable. And, I felt quite sure, untrue.

Ystevan blinked and touched my shoulder gently. My distress and my fervent certainty seemed to have made an impression on him. "I did not know him, little one, you're right," he said levelly. "Why don't you tell me how you came to do so?"

So I stumbled through the sad tale for the first time in my life. The guardian listened intently and allowed me to reach the tragic conclusion without interrupting. When I'd finished, he remained silent for a moment, clearly lost in thought.

"Siridean of Clan Varannis," he said at last, "was from a fort in the south of England. He was taken by a demon at the unusually advanced age of twelve *hadavin*, or sixty by human reckoning. He and the demon were pursued, of course, but never caught..." He fell silent again for a moment and I waited patiently, hungry for more information, though a whole raft of elfin age-related questions were blossoming in my mind.

"From what you say," Ystevan went on, "it sounds as though the demon never really managed to make Siridean his own. The process of corruption is as follows, you see. The demon succeeds in taking an elfling in thrall; you might call it possession, for want of a better word. Once the elfling is in thrall the demon can control them and make them do all manner of wickedness, calculated to exploit that elfling's natural weaknesses. Small things, to start with, hence why the sooner they can be caught the better; the less harm they will have done. But also why they are much harder to find and, if not caught the moment they are taken, often go undiscovered for quite some time.

"Gradually the evil deeds grow in scale and the impressionable elfling becomes truly corrupt. Once the demon is sure of them, they will release them and seek a new victim, leaving them to their evil-doing. At this point, Serapia, there really will be no good left in them. I'm not exaggerating. Don't you ever, *ever* trust a dark elfin, or...or think you can get them to repent.

"But it sounds as though the demon never corrupted Siridean quite enough to feel sure of him and had to keep him in thrall far longer than was practical. Like skin, bones and virtually everything, an elfin's will toughens as they get older and the permeability that leaves them vulnerable to demons is lost. So eventually, I surmise, Siridean managed to break free of his demon and there was still enough good in him that he was not prepared to let it take him again, even though he must have known that to resist was certain death."

I swallowed, remembering. I felt pretty sure that Ystevan was exactly right. "I told you he was good really," I whispered.

Ystevan gave me a rather pitying look. "Serapia," he said gently, "he clearly meant well by you, but the state he must have been in, I think you were safer without him."

I swallowed again and said nothing. A tiny practical voice said that he might be right, but four years of intense longing for the kindness and security that had been briefly offered and so cruelly snatched away were not easily silenced.

I rubbed the hilt of my dagger through the slit in my skirts, feeling that slight, comforting presence. Ystevan eyed the place where the dagger was hidden as though he could sense it through the cloth, but with surprisingly endearing tact, did not inquire about it. Was the hematite's safyr still loyal to Siridean? Was that why it looked out at me with his eyes? Maybe it was the power of the safyr combined with my tiny talents, that made the dagger fly true... But... questions for another day, perhaps...

Eventually I looked again at his bloody arm and my thoughts returned to his chilling declaration concerning the duty that had brought him to London. His own nephew...

"Why did they send you?" I asked at last. "Was it...was it your...fault?"

He shook his head, his expression subdued. "It was nobody's fault, as such. Other than that of Arathain and his friends, for letting themselves become separated. Most of the other guardians are related to him as well, at some distance or other. I was sent because I am the youngest. Always the oldest and most experienced guardians stay at the fort whenever possible. The youngest are sent to deal with such things. You do not, after all, become a guardian until you are trusted to be steady-headed enough not to show your skills in front of humans, under any inducement whatsoever. Even at the cost of the dark elfin getting away. You let them go, and you catch them another day."

"It's such a long way," I said, remembering my long ride to Yorkshire. "Why don't the London guardians...take care of it?"

Ystevan shook his head sadly. "That would hardly be fair. Though it is no one's fault, it is surely more our fault than that of the guardians of the London forts. This is not to say," he added, "that *any* guardian would spare a dark elfin they happened across. That any *elfin* would. But it is only guardians who venture among humans. Anyway, as far as hunting down dark elfin is concerned, each fort deals with their own as far as possible." He turned his attention back to his arm.

I watched as he put the finishing touches to his healing, then rolled his sleeve down and gave me a real smile.

"All better," he said, then smiled ruefully as he explored the rips in his sleeve. "My mother will get in a state when she sees these, though. Not that she'll let on, as I'm sure you can imagine." He added, in a mock confidential tone, "I would try to hide the evidence, but then she'll just have words with me for making a mess of the repair! Needlework isn't really my, er, forte, y'know."

I couldn't help laughing at the way he made this confession, despite my thronging thoughts. For a moment, humor glinting in his eyes, he looked more his age, more like the cheerful young guardian I remembered from Torr Elkyn, as though momentarily freed from the weight of the crushing responsibility he'd carried to London with him.

Looked his age... There was one thing I had to know. "How old are you?"

Ystevan smiled. "How old do I look?" he teased.

"Eighteen, nineteen years old?"

The he-elf chuckled. "My, aren't I precocious, then. How old are you?"

"Fourteen," I admitted, since he'd clearly figured out by now that I was not quite so young as he'd originally supposed when he'd brought me into the fort. "But you haven't answered *my* question yet."

"I've just turned nineteen *hadavin*—a *hadavin* is a half-decade in English," Ystevan told me. "So not so precocious."

"You're joking!" I exclaimed, for I really had thought I must have misheard what he said about Siridean. I began to remember those tales of the Elfin...but they seemed so human...well, comparatively, anyway.

Ystevan raised his eyebrows. "Of course not, although I suppose it must seem quite old to you."

I frowned as I absorbed this new and surprising information. *Wait a minute...* Something that had been vaguely niggling at my mind for a while suddenly crystallized. "The Queen! Your queen, that is... She spoke as if she knew my great, great, great grandmother personally."

"Well, it was only a little over twenty *hadavin* ago," said Ystevan mildly. "I only just missed knowing your esteemed ancestor, of course the Queen knew her. She was the Queen's cousin, I believe, of some degree."

While this news was certainly flattering, I scarcely paid it any heed. It must have all happened over a hundred years ago. "How old is *she*, then? The Queen, I mean?"

"Hmmm," said Ystevan, clearly trying to remember. "It would be...seventy-three *hadavin*, I believe."

I performed a quick calculation. Over three hundred and sixty-five years old. "So how long do elfin live?"

"Oh, somewhere around one hundred *hadavin* is normal—or five hundred years in human reckoning," replied the guardian. "You can translate human-elfin development to one year for a human equals one *hadavin* for an elfin, so that's the equivalent of about a hundred years."

"Long-lived all round, then," I responded dryly. "How do you live so long?"

The he-elf pursed his lips. "It seems to be our natural span. Although there is a certain phenomena whereby elfin who go away from the fort age more quickly while they are away. But it's only just perceptible. What is *much* more perceptible is that any human who comes into a fort will age at near elfin speed for the duration of their residence. When they go back outside their ageing will gradually return to what is normal for them."

286

I could feel my eyes widening. So there was more to the stories of people disappearing into elfin forts and emerging decades later unchanged than met the eye. "So...when I left the fort I wasn't any older than when I *arrived?*"

"You *were* older," Ystevan told me, "but scarcely older than any of us elfin were."

That was quite something! But I couldn't help performing another little calculation. "So...you *are* about nineteen?" I hazarded, "um, comparatively?"

He nodded. "We grow and learn at a rather more relaxed pace than humans, so yes, I am merely a rather worldly-wise just-nineteen-year-old, comparatively."

I shook my head. Now that really was strange.

"Well, this has been most charming," said Ystevan, glancing up at the position of the sun. "Some of it, anyway," he added dryly. "But I really do have other things to be getting on with, you know."

We walked quickly back to pick up our cups. I paused him before we could go through the gate, though. "My father?" I asked desperately.

"Dragonsbreath, *no*," said the guardian. "No, no, *no*." He tried to move forward but I still stopped him.

"How can I contact you, then?"

He glowered down at me, rather. "In the interests of keeping you from anything suicidal rather than from any possible intention of changing my mind," he said sarcastically, "here again, tomorrow, same time. Satisfied?"

I nodded reluctantly. But there didn't seem to be much else I could do.

We crept back into the garden, where Susie was still stretching into the depths of her cup with a finger, trying to capture the very last streaks of chocolate, and walking together through the chocolate house, we went our separate ways.

CHAPTER 40

Nightmares

I found that working on persuading Ystevan to save my father was remarkably like trying to persuade my father to seek the Elfin. I could only push so far at one time before I had to stop, although the he-elf tended to show irritation, rather than outright anger. But when sufficiently irritated he got extremely sarcastic, and nigh-impossible to talk with. He seemed to have a hundred reasons to say no and he trotted them out with firm eloquence.

If it weren't for my failure in this most important area I would have enjoyed the next few days immensely. After trying to help Haliath around the chambers, I quickly perceived that it was taking the she-elf longer to show me how to do things than to do it herself. So although I had no experience with the elfin bows—and could not hope to draw one, besides!—I asked Ystevan if I could help him with his gathering. It would give me extra time to work on him, and he could at least point out greenery for me to collect.

But when he saw that I could move quietly enough to stalk game, he lent me a rather antiquated crossbow that had clearly seen little use. A semi-precious stone was set into each of the fat bolts in the quiver, and they worked much like Siridean's dagger—not that I'd ventured to show that to Ystevan yet—so soon enough I'd contributed a couple of rabbits and a wild fowl to the table.

"Alban Serapion Ravena, Duke of Elfindale, you hereby stand accused of black sorcery and accompanying heresies for which the appointed punishment is the cleansing fire of the stake. How do you plead?"

The Duke stood before the thronged court room, one hand gripping the edge of a table in a white-knuckled grip; clearly only this kept him upright. Gaunt beyond belief, he raised a skeletal hand and laid it on the Bible that was presented to him. He raised his hollow face, and a strange, brief, pale smile flickered on his lips. "It is with great regret," he said, voice weak but firm, "that I must plead guilty." The roar of sound that followed a stunned silence drowned him out as he added tiredly to those nearest to him, "and I'm afraid I really must ask for a chair..."

I jerked awake with a cry of protest for those dark robed judges—it pierced the night quiet of the fort, and I stifled it hastily—then sat up to try and regain my equilibrium. It was just a dream. A nightmare, like the others, not a true dream such as Raven sent. I could feel the difference. My father was in grave danger of his life, but from my continued failure, not from a court of law. But there was a sense of urgency to the dream, much the same degree of urgency that I felt from Raven, but far more compelling. There was not much time left.

I picked up a leather-bound chunk of quartz that lit up as I touched it; a gift from Ystevan. I slipped out of bed and found the notebook Haliath had given me when I asked her for some paper, in which I had been keeping a strict diary about my time at the probably-only-once-in-a-lifetime-to-be-seen elfin fort. I flicked backwards, counting the days with growing dismay. I'd been here almost two weeks, and that was excluding the days on the road! But it wasn't as if I weren't trying! But...

I couldn't help biting my lip. I would bring up my father at regular intervals throughout the day, and Ystevan would simply refuse...until I felt I should leave it for another hour.

Blast! He was no fool, no wonder he wasn't looking very harried, he'd clearly learned exactly how to behave to make me drop the subject. And I'd been so happy here that despite all my best efforts, I hadn't noticed that I was getting absolutely nowhere. Well, that was it with the velvet gloves. I didn't have enough time left. Attrition had failed, so bombardment was left. Every other word out of my mouth was going to be to the point, from now on.

By midday, Ystevan was certainly looking harried but was by no means more compliant. What I now suspected was feigned irritation—designed to make me back off—had long since given way to genuine irritation. He strode ahead of me down the corridors as though beginning to think that Alliron had the right idea after all. He escaped to the throne room straight after luncheon, leaving me frustrated—and more frightened than ever—by my continued failure.

By wordless agreement we had long since made the dining table a battle-free zone, out of consideration for Haliath. But after dinner, when I'd finished helping Haliath with the dishes, I returned to the living room and began to steel myself to tackle Ystevan again. This time, he had to listen! Or I really would have to set off home, if I was to be sure of seeing my father before...before...

Oh, Ystevan, please listen to me!

Ystevan was moving towards his favorite armchair as though determined that he should at least be comfortable...

But then he stopped. A frown crossed his face. And suddenly he was heading for the door instead.

"Where are you going?" I asked, dismayed.

"The Queen summons me," he said, but despite this unexpected reprieve he didn't look happy. The wooden door thudded softly to behind him.

I sat down in an armchair with a bump, staring disconsolately into the flames.

The faggots were piled high around the foot of the stake, and the crowd pressed close, as eager as wolves at a kill. The condemned man was led out in his sackcloth, his bald scalp oozing blood where the jailers had been careless with their knife. He was so frail the two guards supported rather than led him, and those on the opposite side of the stake could hardly see him at all. They chained his hands to the post and tied an extra rope under his arms to ensure that he could stand upright.

The magistrate read out the sentence of sorcery and heresy, but the crowd drowned him out. An old priest stood by the stake, holding his crucifix before the condemned's eyes as well as he could. Some of the crowd taunted and mocked his diligence, but he paid them no heed.

The executioner thrust a flaming torch in among the faggots, *here and there around the circumference, conscientiously setting all alight. The crowd howled, but the man at the stake held his head up and looked steadily at the cross until the smoke and flames obscured it from view.*

...I jerked upright in the armchair, breathing in harsh sobs and struggling to get hold of myself. It was just a nightmare. Just a nightmare. But the sense of urgency it brought was overpowering, worse than ever before.

What should I do?

I'd run out of time, and I knew it.

Well, for starters I would not go to bed tonight until Ystevan returned. But tomorrow...if he still refused...

Tomorrow I had to choose. Stay here longer in the hope I might still return in the nick of time with a guardian in tow. Or leave and be sure of...of being able to say goodbye...

I swallowed hard, tears pricking at my eyes. My intentions had been so good. But I'd only succeeded in wasting the time I would have had left with my father.

Almost more importantly, I'd wasted the brief time he had left with me. I'd deprived him of the company that might have made his long illness bearable, left him alone in miserable worry, for weeks, and for what...? To trickle home and mumble a shame-faced 'sorry' as he drew his last breath? I was a stupid, stupid little girl, trying to re-form the world to my wishes, and I had the awful feeling that I might never forgive myself. Would he...?

No, I thought, brushing hair and tears from my eyes, some part of me stirred to anger by my agonized self-reproach. It wasn't for nothing. The cure is here. It is *possible*. I just can't...get it.

He told you that from the start, the resigned half of me said sadly.

He wasn't prepared to even try, *the angry part of me shot back,* but at least *I* tried.

And I wasn't leaving that instant, I still had this evening. But I sighed and swallowed. Why would Ystevan yield now, and not before? He must realize I could not stay indefinitely. All he had ever needed to do was play a waiting game—my position had never been strong.

Thinking about Ystevan made me feel even worse. I was sure I would miss him terribly. Yet still he said no, still he condemned my father to death so...so pitilessly...

I was actually able to have luncheon with my father for once in his room. I ate a good meal, still hungry from my chilly and underfed exploits the day before, but my father seemed to have no appetite at all. He tried his best, clearly aware of my anxious gaze on him, but he still put his plate aside largely untouched.

"It's not as if I need much food, sitting around all day like this," he joked from the depths of his armchair.

I was neither amused nor comforted, but there wasn't much I could say. I knew he'd made an effort.

"I suppose you'll want to be off out again," my father said quietly, when the butler had taken our plates away.

The quiet sadness in his voice wrung my heart. "I'm staying right here with you this afternoon," I said, squeezing myself into the armchair and wrapping my arms around him. A few strands of grey now streaked his hair at the temples, I noted unhappily.

He sighed contentedly into my hair, though. "Ah, child, I have missed you so much," he murmured. "And I love you even more."

This unusually blunt declaration of affection told me more clearly than anything how close he felt himself to be to the end. I nestled to him for a few short hours until exhaustion forced him back to bed and sleep rapidly claimed him. I sat with him for a while longer, staring at his pale, emaciated face in mingled love and terror.

Eventually, I could stand it no longer and departed for the stables. As soon as Hellion was saddled, I set off for the first fort, the one where I'd seen the golden-haired elfin youth. Or near which I'd seen him; presumably that was where he'd been heading.

I struggled to stay awake, afraid of another nightmare and even more afraid of missing Ystevan, but I was dozing when the sound of the door and soft footsteps along the passage brought me fully awake.

Looking around as Ystevan entered the living room, I saw Haliath pop her head from her own chamber and give her son an inquiring—and rather anxious—look. His eyes travelled from her to me, and he stopped about halfway between us.

"I must to London," he announced. "I leave at safe light tomorrow. I am to take you with me, Serapia, and see you home."

My mouth fell open in shock. He was going to London? We were going to London. My thoughts skidded around in confusion...was this good, or bad? Well, there were three guardians here who could heal my father, and only one would be accompanying me...but considering I'd given up all hope as far as the other two were concerned.

This would get me back to my father in time whilst simultaneously giving me extra days to persuade Ystevan—all while getting the guardian to exactly where I so desperately need him to be.

This wasn't good, this was...perfect!

Packing in the morning was a quick enough task. I chose two elfin dresses that I thought likely to pass without over-much comment among humankind, one to wear and one for a change of clothes along the way. No need for groom's garb and that excruciating corset when travelling with my very own elfin guardian, though I slipped the uniform into my saddlebags. Just in case I ever needed it again.

Most of my time was spent carefully wrapping the notebook Haliath had given me to protect it from rain, and placing Ystevan's prized gift—my hand-quartz—securely in the bottom of the bag.

That done, I went out for an early, goodbye-breakfast. Even fort guardians did not—if they had a choice—travel at first light, but rather at safe light, which was not until the sun's demon-scattering rays actually peeped over the horizon.

293

There was a terrible lump in my throat afterwards, when it was time to say goodbye to the motherly she-elf. She'd made me so welcome. "Thank you for everything," I told her, as she hugged me tight and I hugged her back. "I'll never forget you."

"Be safe, child," she said softly, kissing the top of my head. "Be safe." Turning, she held Ystevan close in turn. "Be careful," she whispered, "please be careful..."

"I will, I promise," Ystevan whispered back—but he hugged her long and hard.

Clearly dark elfin hunting was not the safest of tasks. How had his father died? I'd never quite liked to ask, but I knew he'd been a guardian too. For the first time I found myself viewing Ystevan's journey to London with something other than selfish delight. Almost wishing, in fact, that he didn't have to go at all.

When they finally broke apart, Haliath placed a hand on his shoulder and gave him a long, penetrating, look, her anxiety changed to deepest sorrow and sympathy. Ystevan just ducked his head, bending to pick up both sets of saddlebags, and hurried towards the door.

No, killing someone was never a pleasant thing to have to do—especially in cold blood. Let alone a relative. No wonder Haliath felt for him.

Another damp and uncomfortable afternoon in a prickly hedge gained me nothing but a slobbery lick from a curious cow.

Concluding that if the cow could find me so easily the Elfin surely could too, I departed and spent a couple of hours behind the hedge that ran alongside the main road, near the turning, since that was where I'd had my previous success. But nothing elfin-like happened by. In fact, nothing of any note happened whatsoever, apart from Hellion succeeding in sidling up to me and decorating my elbow with tooth-shaped bruises. So I turned Hellion towards home in reasonable time, eager to spend more time with my father.

When I hastened to my father's room, I found him propped up against the pillows but not alone. Father Francis sat beside the bed, his face such a shade of white that I immediately knew that my father had finally made a *completely* full confession. The old priest held my father's hands clasped in his, though, and both seemed deep in prayer.

Something seemed to snap inside me. "What are *you* doing here?" I screamed at the old priest. "We don't need you, we *don't*, go *away*, get *out!*"

They looked up at me with compassionate, pitying looks, and I turned and fled. I slammed my room door behind me and my wardrobe door too, curling up in the darkness with dresses and cloaks brushing my head.

I thought I'd understood before, thought I'd been afraid before, but it was nothing compared to the terror and absolute certainty that had gripped me as I looked at my father and the priest together. Finally, after holding it back for all these years from even that dearest and most trusted confidante, my father had confessed his gravest and most terrible sin...

At some point, probably in the next day or two, he truly was going to die.

CHAPTER 41

Lord Vandalis

I thrust my own barely tasted cup of chocolate into Susie's hand the moment Ystevan arrived and dragged him into the garden without giving him time to get a cup of his own. I hustled him through the gate and with scant ceremony, appealed, *"Please* heal my father, *please!* He's so ill!"

"We've been through this," he retorted irritably and strode off through the park.

After a night of sleepless anguish, having to talk to his back simply infuriated me. I put a spurt on and caught up with him, seizing his arm and swinging him around to face me. *"Don't* just walk away from me!" I snapped furiously. "What happened to explaining your reasons!"

"I have explained them. Thoroughly," he retorted, his voice low and beginning to approach a snarl. "I have a higher regard for your intelligence than to suppose that you have not understood me! I have been patient, but this is growing ridiculous. There is nothing left to explain!"

"Nothing left!" I cried. "No, it is *I* that will have nothing left! Explain to me why you would leave me without a father? *If he dies, it will be your fault!"*

"It will be his own cursed fault," snapped the guardian, clearly beyond restraint. "He is a sorcerer, and the sooner he dies, the better!"

I choked, and half blind with gathering tears, lashed out at him with my palm. His spectacles went flying but my wrist slammed into the circle of his fingers before my hand could strike his face, and they closed like a vice. His eyes had bled to pure gold. I'd finally made him truly angry.

"*Don't* do that," he told me in a near-whisper. "It is considered very bad manners for a she-elf to hit a he-elf." And he gave my arm a little shake as if to drive the point home.

I wrenched slightly, but to no avail. I could feel that he could crush every bone in my wrist without exerting himself. But I did not fear him. That choking lump in my throat seemed to be growing bigger, pure panic; what if he wouldn't, what if he really *wouldn't* do it? I tried to push it down, but just then, it was no good, and it rose up, and the tears overflowed my eyes, and I buried my face against his chest and wept.

He released my wrist and put his arms around me comfortingly, holding me close, stroking back and hair. "It's all right, little one, it's all right," he soothed me, but I just sobbed, "It's *not*, it's *not!*" and hit his chest with my feeble fist, but he made no effort to stop me and I hurt my hand on his jeweled collar. So I put it around his neck instead, retaining just enough sense to avoid further injury on his crest. But his concern brought another memory rushing back to me.

"Serapia? Serapia? Are you alright? Wake up!" Someone was knocking on the door...

I opened my eyes, breathing hard, my nightgown clinging to my sweaty body, and stared around in the dim moonlight coming through the inn's grubby window. Not another nightmare! I was on my way back! And for an unexpected bonus, time-wise, Ystevan's own mission turned out to be of an urgent nature. With my heavier human self mounted on post horses, and the elfin-light guardian riding Hellion—who hardly seemed to notice he was up there—we were making speedy progress. But we still had to stop to sleep occasionally.

"Serapia? Are you alright?"

Oh, I hadn't answered yet. "I'm fine. Just a nightmare." Though I'd wager he knew the latter, or he wouldn't merely be tapping politely on my door. Then my eyes went back to the moonlight streaming through the window. "Thank you for waking* me, but you get back inside your...your room!" I couldn't shout about wards in the night-quiet.

It hadn't really occurred to me until we set off that an elfin away from the fort gained not the slightest protection simply from being within a human dwelling. Although we stopped at inns at nightfall, he sat alertly as we ate our meal, his eyes shifting warily, and only relaxed when he was in his allotted room and had set out his seven egg-sized rocks in a circle and gone within it.

These stones clearly provided a temporary ward powerful enough to withstand demonic assault for an entire night without maintenance—necessary, or guardians would never have been able to get any sleep when away from the fort. Normally he dragged the bed into the centre of the room to get it within the circle. If the bed happened to be built into the wall, he would sleep on the floor instead.

"As you wish, my lady..." His voice came teasingly through the door, but I couldn't hear his light footsteps as he padded away. Barefoot, no doubt.

I settled down in my bed again and watched the clouds disturbing the play of the moonlight on the floor. In two more days, we would be in London. Ystevan was still refusing to aid me, but I had a plan. What I needed to do, what I really needed to do, to break this impasse, to change his mind, was to actually bring him face to face with my father. Surely, once he actually met him properly, he would sense what I had sensed the first time I met my father—that he was a good man. And the guardian's stony, duty-bound heart would be softened.

I knew how to achieve it, as well. This journey provided the perfect opportunity. When we reached Albany House, I would invite him in for refreshments. If he resisted the idea—which he probably would—I would make much of human propriety. I would explain that to refuse hospitality after so long a journey was offensive in the extreme, tantamount to a declaration of hostility, that such behavior was unthinkable...

If all my eloquence failed, I would cry. Surely that would work.

And if it didn't? Well, I would jolly well swoon right there on *the verge. Then he could either leave me lying there in the grass—not likely—or he'd have to pick me up and take me to the house. Yes, if I could just bring this off, all might still be well.*

My mind returned to the park. Ystevan went on shushing me soothingly until my tears died down, but I was still suffering from a minor case of the disconsolate sniffs when I felt his body tense. "Serapia," he murmured in my ear. "Friends of yours?"

I opened my eyes and peeped over his shoulder. Quite a few people were now loitering in what had been a quiet park. I stiffened as I focused on the closest one.

The feral youth, the late Master Simmons' bodyguard... and that one, that was the older man with the cruel eyes, who'd also worked for Master Simmons.

"I'm guessing they're after me?" added Ystevan, very softly.

"Actually, two of them...*could* just possibly be after me..." I muttered back. "If they know my urchin identity, that is..." But then my eyes travelled on to a third man, and I tried not to frown. Ralph Fletcher, surely? All right, so ratting on your boss to save your neck might be looked upon with somewhat more sympathy than simply ratting on your boss for coin, but there was still no way these two would have left him alive unless...unless...*unless* they were all working for the same new employer, and a powerful one. "No, if this lot are working together, I think they're after you."

"What a surprise," breathed Ystevan. "All right, stick close to me. They won't care if you get hurt."

Quickly, I touched Raven through my bodice. "Stay in there, Raven," I whispered. "Understand?" I felt her little head nod against me as I slipped my hand through the slit in my skirt to ease out my dagger. The hilt was warm in my palm.

"Are you *sure* that safyr is reliable?" asked Ystevan, as I released him. He scooped up his spectacles, and we turned to stroll on along the path, back towards the chocolate house, still pretending we saw nothing suspicious about the men who...yes, there were four or five loiterers in this direction as well. Someone had amassed quite a force.

"I've no idea what it would make of *you*," I retorted. "But I'd trust it with my life. Frequently have."

To my surprise a faint smile flicked across Ystevan's face. "Fair enough," he conceded. "All right, watch out..." The men were converging on us, would-be casually, and he sounded tense.

I glanced at him... Oh no, he couldn't use his bow, could he? He wasn't allowed to reveal his elfin powers in front of humans under any circumstance, that's what he'd said. So he'd a dagger and his stick...would it be enough?

I'd like to have thought that he had me too, but since I wouldn't actually be much use at close quarters, I knew in reality he was going to have to protect me as well as himself.

The men suddenly abandoned their pretence and rushed us in a surprisingly disciplined silence. Ystevan moved so fast I could hardly follow him. His first three encounters left one man bent double, clutching a broken wrist, a second unconscious on the ground, and a third on his knees, hugging his rib cage. Ystevan wasn't even *using* his blade, he was just using his hands and his feet, and it was clear he could've left all three men dead if he'd chosen to.

It was plain from the way the other men's advance checked momentarily, that they could see it too... But they pressed on, closing in around us. Someone had put the fear into them all right. And they all held knives.

I tried to stay close to Ystevan, as he'd said, but he had to keep springing from side to side, like a whirlwind, tackling one assailant after another.

Ralph Fletcher made a dash for Ystevan's back, so I concentrated hard and hurled my dagger, sprinting after it to yank it out of his shoulder even as he slumped down to his knees, mouth open in shock. As he crawled away, I tried to return to Ystevan, but the feral youth was there, eyeing me with a disturbingly intent look, and a moment later the

300

cruel-eyed man was beside him. I saw the glance that passed between them.

"Fancy bladework for a lil'lady like yourself..." said the man. "Do we know yer, eh?"

I backed away as they advanced, horribly conscious that I had only one blade and two targets—and much shorter legs than either of them, so running wasn't a good plan... Which one to go for? The older one would be slower, so...the feral one it was. Unless... I'd never tried something this big before.

They rushed me, knives raised. I gripped the dagger as tightly as I could.

Unseen...unseen...unseen...

They blinked, rapidly, as though they were struggling to focus on me...not good enough.

UNSEEN!

The dagger pulsed in my hand, burning hot. The older man slowed down, looking confused, but the feral youth gave a berserk howl and charged at the spot where he'd last seen me. I almost dodged but he clipped my shoulder, carrying me to the ground. I was trying to roll clear when he grabbed hold of me, raising his knife.

I drove my dagger up into his chest, whacking his blade away with my other hand. He gasped, snarled like a wounded dog...then collapsed on top of me. Frantically I tried to wriggle out from underneath and yank my dagger free, all at once. Too late, the cruel-eyed man was looming overhead.

"You little witch!" He kicked me in the side, hard, jerking a cry of pain from me, then kicked me again, before bending over me—I could feel Raven scrabbling to get out of my dress and attack him, but his knife was almost at my throat... "This'll teach you, *you!*" A look of pained shock crossed his face, then all expression left it and he toppled across the feral youth... *Ouf!*

Ystevan stood there, his dagger in his hand. "Will that teach *you* not to attack females?" he demanded of the dead man. Bending, he seized a collar with each hand, dragging the corpses off me. "Serapia, are you hurt?" Kneeling, he gathered me up with gentle arms, carrying me quickly away from the scene of the fight.

Raven had missed being squashed by the falling man, thankfully, but I pushed her back gently so no one would see her. "Good girl," I whispered. "Everything's all right now."

Over Ystevan's shoulder, I could see that most of the men were writhing or kneeling on the grass in positions of varying discomfort. A few seemed to be missing all together, they must have fled. He'd dealt with *all* the others whilst I was scuffling with just two of them... As I watched, some of the men started grabbing one another for support and stumbling away.

"Aren't you going to...turn them over to Sir Allen, or something?" I wheezed, clutching my own ribcage in serious discomfort of my own.

Ystevan made a dismissive noise. "Far better to leave them alive, and loose. One or another will surely lead me to someone of importance, maybe even Arathain himself."

He must have made sure he could track them in some way. But being so close to him, his face near mine, a memory was stirring, one it almost felt like I'd been unconsciously trying to hold back, to keep forgotten...

"Well, here we are," said Ystevan, as we drew rein outside the massive gateposts of Albany House. "We've made good time."

"Yes," I agreed, my heart pounding now that the moment had arrived—with fear, but mostly with intense hope. If I could only get him inside.

I'd just drawn breath to speak when his hand came to rest gently on my shoulder—he'd pressed Hellion close alongside my mount. I looked up at him, meeting his green-gold eyes—he'd removed his spectacles and tucked them in a pocket. The look of naked sorrow on his face startled me.

"Serapia...I really am more sorry than...than I can ever express...about this."

This? Since when had he cared... "About my father?"

He gave a tiny, sad, smile. "That, too."

The corners of his eyes were full of water. Tears? What...?
His hand slid along my shoulder, his fingertips touched the
nape of my neck, and his wonderful eyes expanded and swallowed
me up...
I toppled from my saddle, and the last thing I felt was his
strong arms catching me...

Ystevan was carrying me...yes, we were in the park...the
men had attacked us...attacked him. I felt disorientated by
this last memory, far more so than by any of the others. My
chest...ached. Not just from my assailant's violent kicks.
Even the memory of Ystevan's tears couldn't relieve the
pain. Because he'd still *done* it.

It was his *duty*...

It was a total betrayal...

My mind and my heart did not agree at all on this one.
But I'd *known* how it ended. Ever since meeting him again in
London, I'd known. Why was I so upset?

But come to think of it, where were the two gifts he and
Haliath had given me whilst I stayed with them? He'd stolen
those too, hadn't he?

Ystevan set me down on the grass at last, just outside
the chocolate house's gate, and placed his hands on my
sides. Mercifully, the physical pain eased and breathing
became much more pleasant again. The other ache didn't go
away, though.

All the same... "Thank you!" I said, with feeling. "I'm
sorry I wasn't much use."

He gave me an incredulous look. "You dealt with three
of them, I could hardly ask for more!"

"Uh...technically you dealt with the third one..."

He waved this away. "You kept him occupied, which was
what mattered. With those three on me as well, I could have
been overwhelmed. But I strongly suggest you don't experi-
ment with your modest abilities in that way. In public like
that. It's very dangerous—and I don't just mean for my
people, but for you too. First of all, *for you.*"

I bit my lip as I thought of what I'd done. He was right, it had been horribly indiscreet. *Witch,* the man had called me. At least the only two who'd been paying attention to me were dead. Was that...the real reason why Ystevan had slain the last man or had his protective instincts simply been roused? I wasn't sure I wanted to know. On the other hand...

"I'd have been dead a whole lot sooner if I hadn't done it," I pointed out. "But I certainly won't do it again unless I have to. I feel like...like a kitten now, for one thing." My whole body did feel appallingly weak, as though I'd just had that near-fatal cold all over again.

But he just placed a hand each side of my face and stared at me. "*I'd have died otherwise* is not a good enough reason, Serapia. In these situations you simply *have* to find another way. Humans are not good at telling the difference between natural elfin abilities and the devilish magic of a witch. You need to think, what would you have done if you had no such abilities?"

I knew he was right about the danger, and that I had perhaps been too easily tempted into experimenting, but he was still making me angry acting as though I'd done something totally stupid—especially coming on top of that excruciating memory. "Run, and probably died!" I retorted.

"You would not have died, I would have reached you in time."

"You hope!"

He flushed slightly, sounding every bit an offended nineteen-year-old as he protested, "I would! Fighting evil is what I'm trained for!"

Evil? Like my *father?* The thought popped into my head and my temper rose even more. I pushed away from him and got to my feet, only slightly shaky.

"You can't talk about evil!" I snapped. "*Thief!*"

"Technically elfin do not *steal* memories, we only *cloak* them."

"I'm not just talking about that! Where is my hand-quartz? My diary?"

His flush deepened. "By the time it became clear you actually believed that we would deliver you back to your father with your memories intact, we'd already given you those things...but just to use while you were with us, was how we saw it."

"Among humans, a gift is a gift, and once given it belongs to the person it's given to. And taking it back is *stealing*."

"I know," he said quietly. "I'm sorry. You were never supposed to...miss them. I didn't mean to...to upset you."

His gentle words just made me feel even worse. Because what did they mean, coming from him? He'd still do his duty, come rack or ruin. For all I knew, he was planning to steal my memories all over again before leaving London, promise or no.

"Why do you even bother acting as if you care a ha'penny about me?" I demanded.

"I do care, Serapia. Very much."

"No, you don't! You won't even heal my father!"

"A sorcerer is a sorcerer," he snapped. "*Why* can't you see that?"

I stared at him. I hated it when he trotted out his absolutes. "You act as though a sorcerer—which my father isn't, anyway—is the same as a dark elfin. But they're not, are they? A dark elfin can't help themselves, at least, not at the beginning. A human would have to be possessed to be the same. And a human who's not possessed can choose not to be bad. Again and again, even if just once they chose poorly. Humans always have to choose. You could heal a good human and they could choose to do evil tomorrow."

"What's your point?" ground out the guardian.

"My point," I said emphatically, "is that you're judging sorcerers by exactly the same criteria as dark elfin and it just doesn't work! It's not like there aren't exceptions even with dark elfin! Even you admit Siridean wasn't evil."

"Probably wasn't," corrected Ystevan. "And I still don't see your point. Sorcerers only become sorcerers by consistently choosing evil. The fact that they *could* choose other scarcely matters."

"It matters because my father is *not* a sorcerer," I persisted. "He chose sorcery *once*, and ever since then he has always chosen good, though it will mean his death. So why won't you save him?"

"One choice of that nature is more than enough," said Ystevan coldly.

My frustration boiled over. It was like talking to a brick wall. "You just don't want to admit that a person can go that far into evil and come back!" I cried. The words tumbled from my mouth one after another and I couldn't seem to stop them. "You'd have killed Siridean yourself, wouldn't you? The virtuous elfin or the evil demon, it was just a question of which of you found him first! You've decided Arathain can't be saved, and it's easier for you if you think that no one can be!"

Ystevan's face whitened to the shade of chalk, and my hand flew to my mouth.

"No circumstance. *Ever*," he bit off, then turned and strode towards the gate.

"Ystevan?" I gasped after a moment, but he did not look back. "Ystevan? I didn't *mean that...*"

I hurried after him as fast as my tired legs would go, but I could not catch his long-legged form. I pursued him through the chocolate house and into the street beyond.

"*Ystevan!*"

But he was gone.

I sank down on a nearby bench, fighting back tears. He'd probably never even want to speak to me again, and I could deny the truth no longer. He was never going to agree to heal my father.

Susie hurried up to me, but I dug a coin blindly from my purse, belatedly checking myself for bloodstains, but thankfully my dress was a dark color and nothing had stained the lace of my ruff. "Go back inside, Susie," I told her in a choked voice. "Have another cup of chocolate. I will be just out here."

Casting anxious looks behind her, Susie obeyed. I sat there for some long moments in miserable silence and solitude, until finally I realized that someone had sat beside me.

"Pardon me for coming up to you like this..."

I stared at him blankly, not really seeing him.

"Forgive me if I am mistaken, but it looked as though you and Lord Ystevan had had a bit of a row."

Startled, I focused properly on the person beside me and my eyes widened. "I saw you on the road the other day!"

The golden-haired youth smiled and nodded. "So you did. You gave me quite a turn. I had to hide ever so fast. But I know it is all right to speak to you now. You are the Rare Exception," he finished humorously.

"You know Lord Ystevan, then?"

"Of course," said the young he-elf. "We are colleagues, as you would express it."

Of course, he was a guardian. What had Ystevan said? That only guardians ventured among humans.

"Lady Serapia Ravena," I said formally, holding out my hand. "Delighted to meet you."

"Lord Vandalis of...well," he smiled apologetically, shaking my hand with his own gloved one, "forgive me if I do not actually name my fort and clan."

"Have you been a guardian long?" I could not help asking. He seemed closer to my own age than Ystevan. He could be sixty years old, though, small wonder if he was already trained and trusted. I didn't get so much of a...feel of him...as I got from most people. He felt strangely...blank. Maybe he was nervous and closed in, speaking to a human.

"Not very," he was replying, with a slightly embarrassed smile. "This is my first er...task...in the human world. You must forgive me if I was curious to meet you. It is a rare thing to meet a human with whom one may actually be oneself."

"Oh, you're welcome," I said. "I really am delighted to meet you."

"You looked so upset, too," Vandalis added a little shyly. "I don't know what Ystevan said. He can be rather...hard." He shrugged as though apologizing for his fellow guardian's insensitivity.

"Yes, he *can*," I agreed ruefully, frantically marshalling what I hoped would be the most polished and persuasive version of my father's tale yet.

"What did you two, ah...?" Vandalis was inquiring delicately.

"I've been asking him to heal my father," I replied.

Vandalis fixed me with a look not wholly unlike the one Ystevan and the elfin Queen had turned on me. He knew there was more to come. "I cannot imagine why he would refuse you. What is the nature of his ailment?"

"I will tell you all about it, but I should mention first that, due to complicated circumstances, I never met my father—or knew of him at all—until this very year, so nothing I say is prejudiced in his favor in the way it might otherwise have been."

I shot a look at Vandalis, but his face still showed nothing but polite interest.

Quickly, but calmly, I began at the beginning, explaining about my father's love for my mother, about the onset of his foresight, how it had driven him near-mad with fear and grief.

I could tell I had Vandalis's complete attention and continued, picking my words with exquisite care. But as I spoke the word "sorcery", Vandalis's face closed into an unreadable mask. I could have *howled* with frustration. Was it happening *again*?

I hurried on, desperately, desperately seeking the words to break through his preconceptions and make him listen.

"He truly is penitent. He has been penitent for years. Nothing will make him turn back to sorcery. If he were prepared to do so, he could actually have saved *himself* by now. But he chooses to die, instead. That is how penitent he is. How resolved to choose goodness at any cost to himself. Please, I beg you, won't you help him?"

And I waited, trying not to bite my lip, for his reply.

Vandalis's expression was still decidedly indeterminable. "Sorcery is not some venial little sin," he remarked at last. "Indeed, it is not considered to be something from which one can come back."

"God's forgiveness covers everyone! Even a penitent sorcerer. And he's *not* even a..."

"It isn't *safe* to allow a sorcerer to live," interrupted Vandalis. "It simply *isn't.*"

"But he is *not a sorcerer!*"

Vandalis looked thoughtful. "You say not, but I have only your word for that. Certainly the only solid evidence of this case is that your father has had recourse to sorcery. As such he definitely comes into the category of those who are to be helped on their way to judgment if necessary. Still, let me have all the facts. How is it that he could now complete the sorcery if he chose?"

I thought my heart would burst with relief. I had been sure that utter, irrevocable refusal was coming. Perhaps he might yet be persuaded to help me.

Carefully, I explained what the sacrifice was to have been, how my father doubted whether he could actually have done it anyway, and my certainty that he could not have done. I told him about the sorcerers' attempt, how my father had rescued me, sent them packing and destroyed the temple.

"Hmm," he said, when I'd finished, frowning in thought. "What can I make with all this... These sorcerers," he went on, after a moment, "who were they? They *were* human?"

"Well, the leader was this horrible staring man. I'm as sure as I can be that they were human, yes."

Vandalis nodded to himself. "I don't know," he said at last. "Ystevan would tan my hide for helping your father.

But the man is clearly no sorcerer. Ystevan is so very in-flexible about these things."

"Would you come and look at my father?" I asked, struggling to contain my eagerness. "I mean, you could just come and *look* at him, see what you thought. Decide then..."

Vandalis shot a glance at the sun, apologetic again. "I really cannot, not right now," he said. He'd been looking up and down the street as we'd been speaking, so not wholly to my surprise he went on, "I have my business to attend to; I'm going to be ever so busy this afternoon. But..."

He paused again, then shrugged. "I am not in Ystevan's league, you understand, but... Well, I will be staying tonight at a well-warded house in London; I will not have time to go home. I really would rather not wander around at night without very good cause; did Ystevan explain about that?"

I nodded, breathless with hope.

"Anyway, if you bring your father to me at sixty-six Hounsdiche at say, eleven o'clock in the evening, I should have finished up everything to do with my business by then and be free to see him. And I will heal him if it lies within my power. I wouldn't like to *promise*, you understand," he added. "Though it is most likely that I can do it."

I nodded, my heart pounding with joy. He was prepared to try to heal my father, and he thought he probably could do it!

"I truly cannot thank you enough, Lord Vandalis," I said. "I'm delighted to find that not all elfin are so uncompromising."

Vandalis smiled ruefully. "Perhaps I will be so as well, after a few decades in the job. But just now, I hope I retain my sense of proportion." He stood and bowed to me, so I rose hastily to curtsey back. "I will see you tonight, then," he said, then added, "I, ah, really wouldn't mention this to Lord Ystevan, by the way," and was gone down the street.

Mention it to Ystevan! Not likely. I gathered my cloak around myself so that Raven could climb out of my dress for a hug. "Did you hear, Raven," I hissed. "He's agreed to help!"

Raven chattered her delight, but after a moment pawed at my thumb and shot a look in the direction Ystevan had gone.

"I know," I sighed, for sweet-tempered and helpful as young Lord Vandalis seemed, I had to admit that I wasn't entirely sure I didn't like the stubborn and irritable Ystevan better. But he probably never wanted to set eyes on me ever again.

"Pa will be healed, please God," I whispered to Raven, "and that's what really matters."

CHAPTER 42

Hounsdiche

There was just one more obstacle to my father's healing, I realized as I strolled home with Susie, and that was my father himself. He was far too unwell to be lured from the house by any pretence of entertainment or visiting, yet even now I felt quite sure he would refuse to accompany me if I told him the truth. I didn't want to deceive him, but I really didn't think that honesty would work.

Perhaps it would be best to say nothing at all. A small dose of sleeping draught in the wine he drank with his evening meal would do the trick. I could have him carried into the coach as though for an urgent trip to the physician. I bit my lip, considering. I hated the idea of treating him in such a way but...I really rather thought it was the only way I would get him out of the house.

My father was asleep when I got home, so I ate a lonely luncheon and then sat around for a while, wondering if I would ever see Ystevan again. Even if he *wished* to see me again, he hunted someone who was hunting him back. Someone so evil they could hand a person their payment in a box cursed with such a curse... I shuddered just to think about it.

Once activity in the house reached its lowest, mid-afternoon ebb, I paid a visit to the medicine chest in my father's room and got what I needed. The suspense was torturous and eventually I went for a walk, or stride, around the grounds. I was tempted to take Hellion out and ride long and hard, but today was not the time to have a fall.

Father Francis was in the graveyard as I passed the church, and after a moment's hesitation, I went up to the wall. "I'm sorry I spoke to you like that yesterday, Father. I didn't mean it."

But he just replied, "It's quite all right, child, I know how you must feel." He shot a look at my face, clearly reading tension as anxiety. "I can be a bit of a harbinger, alas." He held out his black robes and flapped, crow-like, and succeeded in drawing a laugh from me.

When I got back to the house my father was awake, so I cuddled to him in silence until it was time for the evening meal. He was too tired to talk much, and I feared my manner might give something away. Slipping the sleeping draught into his goblet unseen was ridiculously easy. I swallowed a painful lump in my throat as I remembered how fast and strong my father had been when he dueled my uncle.

He will be fast and strong again, providing you do not falter, I told myself.

I sat beside him, my head resting on his shoulder, and kept watch as he slept the long evening away. Raven curled up between my head and his neck, occasionally sharing hope-filled glances with me.

When the clocks finally began to strike ten, I knew that it was time to act. I went to the room door. "My father must see a physician at once," I told the waiting footman. "Order the coach."

He went off at a run, and I occupied myself wrapping my father in warm layers against the night air. "Carry him gently," I urged them, when two footmen came to say that the coach was ready. My father was borne carefully downstairs and placed in the coach without a flicker of suspicion from anyone, and I scrambled in after him.

"Sixty-six Hounsdiche, quickly," I called to Richard. I did not want to be late, and it seemed best to keep up the pretence of urgency.

By the time we reached our destination my father was stirring sleepily. "Serapia?" he murmured, as I braced him against the swaying of the coach. "Wherever are we going?"

313

"There is a physician I have found," I told him. "A physician who will be able to make you much more comfortable."

"Oh, child," he said with a breath of gentle exasperation. "You know my *eternal* comfort or discomfort will be decided very soon now. What point is there?"

"Pa," I said, in a suitably upset tone. "I hate to see you suffering."

He snorted. "As far as these things go, Serapia, I am drifting away in the utmost comfort. Or I am when I am not being shaken around needlessly in a coach. Do tell Richard to take us home."

Fortunately, the coach drew to a halt before I had to reply. "We're here now, Pa," I said. "We may as well at least go in and see what he recommends. *Please?*" I added with the utmost appeal, when he began to shake his head tiredly. To my relief my tone succeeded in stopping the head shake in mid swing.

"Oh, very well," he sighed. "If it will really make you feel better."

William and Stephen lifted him carefully from the coach, placing him in his wheeled chair.

"Wait here," I instructed Richard and the footmen, and wheeled my father towards the door as fast as I could. Hounsdiche ran just around the outside of the city wall, a long single row of houses backing onto open countryside. Sixty-six was about a far from the Bishop's Gate as it could be, almost at the Olde Gate.

"Is this a physician's, child?" he asked, looking perplexed as we drew closer. "It looks like a private house."

His mind was still quick enough, I was glad to see. "I arranged a special visit," I replied as though it were nothing to remark upon, and knocked at the door.

My father twisted to look around at the street and the moon in the sky. "Just how late is it, Serapia?" he demanded, eyeing me far more closely, and not without suspicion.

"Don't worry, we're on time," I said blithely, keeping my face turned towards the door.

"Serapia, look at me," he said, his voice growing still firmer. I ignored him, and fortunately the door opened then and Lord Vandalis looked out at us, smiling.

"Lady Serapia, welcome. This must be your father. Do come in."

Alban frowned at Lord Vandalis, though it was rather dark for his spectral ear points to be visible. He turned one of the chair's wheels as though he wished to return to the coach.

"Come on, pa," I urged, wheeling him forward.

"Serapia," said my father in a warning tone, as he was pushed inside. "If you have somehow arranged something above the order of normal medicine, you know quite well I will have no part of it."

"Fear not, your grace, you cannot object to this," said Lord Vandalis cheerfully, closing the door behind us. The elfin led us along the hall and to a flight of stairs. "I'm sure we can manage these," he said. "I do my best work down here."

"Serapia," growled the Duke, "I shall beat you, I swear. I shall beat you and marry you to Sir Allen so you can get up to no more mischief!"

"Now, pa," I said gently, "I am too young to marry and you are too weak to beat me. We'll have you down the steps in no time."

My father glowered at me as Lord Vandalis took the back of the chair, bumping it down the steps as carefully as possible, and I walked ahead, steadying it and preventing my father from falling forwards. There was nothing he could do about it. His impotence wrung my heart so much that if anything other than his healing had lain below, I could never have forced him in such a way.

"Here we are, then," said Lord Vandalis when we reached the bottom.

I went through the doorway just before my father and stopped dead, feeling Raven freeze against me. "Run!" I gasped, turning towards him, but there was no possibility of him so much as standing.

"If there is danger, *you* run," he said all in one breath. But I grabbed for the back of the chair regardless. Lord Vandalis took my arm and pushed me firmly into the room, wheeling my father in behind.

Five men stood within, dressed in long, hooded red robes. All five were painfully familiar. A pentagram covered the stone floor and an altar of crudely carved wood stood behind it, rimmed with lumpy candles and heaped with the dead and rotting corpses of animals. My neck burned with the evil of the place and I wondered if I'd passed through some sort of ward at the doorway.

I looked again at the so-youthful guardian, who no longer felt *blank*, oh *no, no, no...* Instead...the choking feeling that had enveloped Siridean...only a hundred times worse. A penny the size of the Queen's golden coach dropped sickeningly in my mind. *Too late.* How could I not have felt it before? I'd shaken his *hand! Oh.* His *gloved* hand. Gloved *and* warded?

The elfin stopped beside a bench, and my father stared pale-faced at the scene before us. "Serapia, child, what have you *done?*" he whispered.

I threw myself down on the bench, arms wrapping around him protectively. "*Nothing*, pa," I said, anguished. "They're not meant to *be* here, *nothing* like this! Lord Vandalis tricked me and I took him for that which he is not! I'm so sorry. I'm so sorry, please forgive me!"

"I forgive you, child, it is not me I am worried about," he murmured, his own arm snaking protectively around me.

The golden-haired he-elf put his hands on his hips and looked down at us, chuckling. "Are you so sure, Lady Serapia, that I cannot do what the oh-so-virtuous Lord Ystevan will not?"

"I know, *Arathain*, that I would have nothing to do with anything *you* can do," I retorted.

"I see my dear uncle has been telling you tales about me. Unkind ones, no doubt." He smiled at us, still a sweet-natured smile but with a much less pleasant light in his eye. "You asked me to help save your father's life, Lady Serapia, so I intend to do so."

My father's grasp on me tightened convulsively, and his face paled even more.

Help us, oh help us! The burning heat at the back of my neck cooled slightly, soothingly, and I gripped my father's hand, staring at the he-elf with all the contempt I could muster. "Fine, kill me," I snapped. "But it will be entirely your doing, not that of my father!"

Arathain laughed merrily. "Oh, my dear girl. You asked me to save your father's life, not his soul. And I would much, much rather smite his soul. See what I have acquired specially?" He waved a hand and one of the sorcerers brought forward a small, cloth-wrapped bundle that squalled slightly at being moved.

"Now, my dear duke," went on the dark elfin, eyes now on my father. "Here is a small sickly babe that will be dead in a few days quite naturally. I have uncovered what these incompetent oafs could not," he jerked a dismissive thumb at the sorcerers. "It is a sorcery that allows one living thing to be substituted for another of a similar kind. So here we have a baby girl and a half-grown girl, one of your blood, one not. But close enough.

"So here is how it is. All you need to do is kneel down at our so-powerful altar and perform the sorcery that makes this sickly baby the acceptable substitute for your own child. Nothing too arduous, just a prayer to our dark master and a few drops of your blood. Then, if you would rather these gentlemen see to the completion of the sorcery that threatens your life, you need do nothing more. You will live and nothing will die but a babe that will not survive anyway. What have you to lose?"

"My soul," replied Alban, looking at the he-elf in disgust.

"Ah yes," said Arathain, and there was nothing sweet-natured about his smile now. "But did I forget to say?" He reached out and tore me from my father's side. Raven shot from my bodice and headed for his hand, tiny fangs bared. I snatched her hastily and stuffed her back out of harm's way even as I myself struggled, twisting and striking at Arathain.

But Arathain's fingers dug into each side of my neck and all the strength went out of me. I hung from his grasp helpless, like a limp doll. He shook me effortlessly, just hard enough to make my head whip from side to side and to prove that he could snap my neck like a twig if he chose. "I believe I did forget to say. If you do not do it, Serapia will die." He flung me down in a heap at my father's feet.

Alban dropped his face to his hands with a tortured groan. "Is this my punishment?" he whispered hoarsely. "Am I thus punished? Mercy, *mercy...*"

"Mercy is no fun," said Arathain happily, spinning on his heel and going to tickle the chin of the squalling baby.

I managed to climb back up onto the bench to my father's side. I pulled his head up and met his eyes. "You are not punished!" I told him fiercely. "This is entirely his sick doing, it is nothing to do with you. You must not go along with it, that is all. You must not!"

"Are you so eager to die?" smiled Arathain, from across the room.

I eyed him in a moment of wild calculation, then bolted for the doorway. I was his leverage. Without me, he had no hope of forcing my father to do *anything*. Arathain made no move to stop me, though, and my suspicion about a ward was confirmed, painfully, when my headlong dive for the doorway struck thin air that was much the consistency of a brick wall. I stumbled back and fell to my knees, clutching my broken nose, Arathain's laughter ringing in my ears as a red haze of pain momentarily obscured my vision.

"Enough of this," said Arathain. He walked back to my father and crouched briefly, running his hands down the sick man's legs. "You will stand for our dark master. Consider it a...gift." He gripped the Duke's collar and jerked him to his feet, dragging him into the pentagram.

My hand flew to my dagger, under cover of my cloak, then paused. Arathain was the one that really mattered but an assault on him was almost certainly futile and I didn't dare waste my only weapon too precipitously. Reluctantly, I eased my hand away again.

"Tell him what to do," Arathain ordered one of the waiting sorcerers, letting go of Alban, who wobbled slightly but stayed upright.

The sorcerer he'd spoken to shot a look at his fellows. The staring man who was their leader ignored him, moving to one tip of the pentagram, but the other sorcerers pointedly raised their eyebrows.

"Look, sir," the sorcerer ventured, clearly emboldened by this. "Why are we doing this? What's in it for us? We work for pay, you know."

Arathain reached out a hand, seized the man's head and turned it through one hundred and eighty degrees with a hideous crunch. He let the corpse fall and addressed the other sorcerers. "*You* will get your lives."

The leader prudently gave a deep bow before speaking. "I assume your honor will fill in, come the ceremony?"

"I will fill in for you *all* if necessary, so get on with it," said Arathain dangerously.

The remaining sorcerers hurried into their positions. One stood on the left of the altar holding the baby ready, another stood on the right with a large book, from which the Duke was clearly expected to read. Alban just stood there, legs shaking with the effort of remaining upright despite whatever the dark elfin had done to them.

"Don't do it!" I cried, running forward, but the staring man blocked my path. "You *will not* do this for me! You will not!"

319

Alban still stood there, staring at the altar in a frozen silence.

"Your dear daughter," cajoled Arathain. "Your dear dead daughter, if you do not do this. You shall *watch* me kill her!"

Alban shuffled an unsteady step forwards.

I stepped clear of the staring man, watching my father. Every ounce of my attention seemed to narrow in on him. Slowly, unwillingly, my hand crept under my cloak again and closed around the hilt of Siridean's dagger.

"Your poor, poor Serapia, all dead," Arathain all but sang.

Alban took another step towards the altar.

I gripped my dagger, agonized. I could not let him do it. I could not even let him take a final decision to do it, for that would surely damn him just the same. My clenched fingers shook around the hilt as I fought for the strength to save him from himself.

Alban took one final step so that he stood before the altar. He stared at the mass of rotting lifeless things that provided its powerful consecration to evil, his shoulders rigid.

The dagger pulsed under my shaking hand in a way that was not physical, an encouraging warmth that matched the beat of my pounding heart. My hand steadied and my eyes found the spot between my father's shoulder blades. Concentrate. Concentrate... I eased the dagger from its sheath.

A final muscle-cracking moment of tension and Alban's shoulders relaxed.

My hand relaxed as well and the dagger slipped back into its sheath. *I did not lie to Ystevan. He will not do it.* My heart sang, though my mind advised me to compose my own soul.

My father reached out and touched the gory altar cloth contemplatively with both hands. I stiffened in irrational but inescapable delight. *Do it!* I thought gleefully.

320

Alban did it. His fingers twisted swiftly into the cloth and he flung himself backwards, using his own body weight to provide the force he could not. The altar cloth and all its consecrating contents went tumbling to the floor, candles hissing and smoking as the fall snuffed them out. The sorcerers stared, frozen in shock and dismay.

Alban took advantage of the moment's inaction to scramble up over the pile, yank his cross from about his neck and place it squarely down on the altar. He grinned savagely up at the sorcerers through a tangle of dark hair. He looked slightly mad. "Oh, I'm sorry," he panted, "but I do believe your altar needs re-consecrating."

That was all he had time for because the sorcerers were on him like a pack of mad dogs. They struck him to the ground and their booted feet began to slam into his frail body.

I ran forward desperately, but Arathain was on me in a flash. "Stop," he ordered coldly, and the death of their associate must still have been fresh in the sorcerers' minds, because they did so. With evident reluctance.

"Let the dear Duke recover himself," said Arathain silkily, and despite his would-be calm I could feel his anger. "There is something very particular that he must watch."

My father lay there, gasping, for so long that I began to fear that the blows might prove fatal. But eventually his breathing eased and he looked around him. Arathain smiled at me in terrible anticipation. Recklessly, I drew my dagger and stabbed at him in one quick movement, but it struck him much as I had struck the open doorway and skidded to one side.

He caught my wrist and squeezed viciously until the blade dropped from my hand. He kicked it away with a disdainful smirk. "Such a bold little girl, aren't you?" he said, shifting his grip to my neck, so that I once more hung there helplessly.

Raven shot out again and I couldn't stop her. The dragonet sunk her teeth into the dark elfin's finger, but with

321

a flick of his other hand, Arathain sent her flying across the room. She smacked into the wall with a squeak of pain and fell to the ground.

My father rolled halfway to his knees, struggling to rise, to reach us.

"I'm sorry, my dear Duke," said Arathain. "But I believe I made your choices plain. You have refused the life I offered you. Now you will watch her die."

"I think not," said a soft voice from the doorway.

Arathain spun around, with me swinging from his grasp.

Ystevan stood there, his bow in his hand and an arrow drawn upon it. For one shocked second, Arathain remained motionless. Ystevan did not. The arrow slammed squarely into Arathain's heart with a nasty thunk.

For a long moment Arathain stared back at the guardian, and there was nothing on his face but sweet-natured confusion. "Uncle Ystevan?" he whispered.

Then he crumpled to the ground, taking me with him, and did not move.

From my position with my cheek flat against the floor, I saw the last sorcerer dump the baby on the altar and dart for a door on the opposite side of the room, following his fellows. Ystevan finally seemed to notice their escape—he notched another arrow with breath-taking speed and almost casually dropped the man in mid-step.

Breathlessly, I flung off the lifeless hand and started crawling towards my father—until Raven's warning screech drew my attention. She raced across the cellar full-tilt, her tiny, undeveloped wings spread for extra lift and speed. *What had she seen?*

With a soft 'poof' the fallen altar hangings caught fire, the flames licking up the wax-soaked wood with tremendous speed. Raven hurtled up the pile of rotting dead things and leapt onto the altar, flinging herself on top of the small, wriggling bundle that had been abandoned there...

I gasped in horror and struggled to rise, staggering dizzily. "Ystevan! The baby!"

Raven wrapped her wings protectively around the helpless infant, then the flames roared up over the altar-top, hiding them both. *"Raven!"*

Ystevan was already moving, but before he could reach them, my father launched himself up the pile and stretched into the flames. He pulled the dragonet-baby bundle out and rolled it to the bottom of the soft, damp, decaying heap, then slumped against the altar, too weak to get clear himself.

"Pa!" I was on my feet, now, but I'd never get there in time.

Ystevan leapt over the baby and grabbed my father, using his momentum to propel them sideways and out of the flames. Another age-long moment as I hurried forward, finally shaking off the last lingering effects of Arathain's nasty neck-hold, and I'd reached them, gathering my father in my arms.

"Serapia..." he murmured in a tone of overwhelming relief as he slipped from consciousness.

"It's all right, pa," I whispered, hugging him to me, then craning to look at Raven and the baby, to whom Ystevan had immediately returned. *"Are they all right?"*

Ystevan detached Raven with gentle fingers and set her on the stone floor. "This little one is as flame-proof as they come. Not a mark on her. This precious mite..." he gathered the baby in his arms, "...needs a little more attention. Though she is almost unharmed by the fire. Raven protected her well. But her health is very poor indeed." He fell silent, his fingers tracing the baby's limbs and torso.

Raven was already climbing dizzily up to my shoulder. "Raven, you were wonderful," I told her. "You saved that poor baby's life!" Raven just rubbed her little face against my cheek, as though more worried about me than her own heroics. "It's alright. I'm fine," I told her, then I pressed my face to my father's hair in turn and held him close.

Wait... Raven had climbed down and was licking the Duke's hands... Oh no, they were burned. Though it scarcely

323

mattered now, did it? He was unconscious, and could not feel it. Would he even wake up again?

Ystevan had crossed the room and now knelt beside the dead elfin, his face a ghastly, expressionless mask. After several long moments, he reached out and slid the blank eyes closed.

"How can you still care about *him*?" I demanded, my voice ragged.

"He was a lost youngling," said the he-elf softly. He stretched his hand over that dead face for a few moments, moving it from eyes, to ears, to hair, and I wondered if he was doing something that would camouflage the odd appearance of the body after the inevitable looting of spectacles, hairclip and ear studs.

Soon, he rose, gathered up the baby, and walked over to me, picking up my dagger as he came. He handed it to me, then reached out his free hand to my nose, but I brushed it away.

"I've got to get pa home," I said, choking back tears.

He just reached out again and took my broken nose between finger and thumb. It tingled violently, and then he was handing me his handkerchief to once more mop blood from my face. "I'll help you," he said. He gave the bow an absent-minded shake, turning it back into his stick.

Ignoring him, I got my arms around my father and tried to lift him myself. But even in his emaciated condition he was far too heavy for me.

Ystevan eased him away from me, slipping the baby into my grasp instead. "I'll take him; you bring this little one," he said gently, and rose, lifting the Duke without apparent effort.

I trudged after him as he strode from the room, too numb for thanks, or protests, or anything. My marvelous hopes of earlier had been cruelly smashed to pieces, but at least my father had avoided a fate worse than death and I had been spared the most terrible of choices.

But as far as his imminent death was concerned, that now seemed inevitable.

CHAPTER 43

Mercy

My father lay in his big bed, barely making a lump in the blankets. He looked helplessly fragile against the expanse of white sheets, and bruises were already visible on his hollow face.

Ystevan had absent-mindedly healed the burns on the journey home but had shown, *how* my father had just acquired them notwithstanding, no inclination to do anything more—*no circumstance, ever*, he'd said, and clearly he meant it. He must've acted on pure reflex when he pulled the Duke out of the fire.

Now my father's chest barely moved as he breathed, and he was unconscious still. I took one bony hand. His fingers were cold. He wasn't even going to wake up, was he?

The thought was too much. I folded forward silently over the bed and clung to him, tears pouring down my face as sobs shook me. I cried so hard I could barely breathe. Raven quivered against my neck, pawing at me in helpless comfort.

A hand touched my shoulder gently. "Serapia..."

Ystevan. I ignored him.

"Serapia, don't cry."

"Don't cry!" I sobbed. "There's nothing else I can do, don't you understand? I'm out of ideas. *Lord Vandalis* was my last hope and look what came of that! There's nothing else I can *do!*" My last words came close to a wail of despair.

I dimly heard the sound of the room door being closed and the key turning in the lock. A slender hand entered my field of vision, placing three things on the bedside table: a pair of spectacles, a pair of stud earrings, and a hair clip.

Blinking, I sat up, wiping tears from my eyes as I looked around. Ystevan's ears rose to graceful points, his hair fell around his face, that strange shimmering mixture of gold and black, and his gold-green eyes stared solemnly down at me. He looked quite gloriously eldritch.

"I will take the sorcery off," he informed me. "But you must understand, Serapia, he has virtually no strength left. He is drained. He may not survive the removal, and there is nothing I can do but my best."

I stared at him in shock, too afraid to hope again. Eventually I bit my lip and nodded gingerly. I watched as he stepped forward and began to run his hands through the air a fraction away from my father's body, fingers spread and twitching in a gathering movement like a peasant woman carding wool. His eyes bled almost to pure gold.

Although I could see nothing, I could easily imagine him clawing and collecting the sorcery from around my father's helpless form. It took some time, and he worked steadily, a strange feeling building in the air and especially in my father's thin hand, which I still held. Eventually I had to lay it gently back on the bed, and yet I could not define what made me unable to go on holding it.

Ystevan's hands moved away from the Duke now, working together in the air on something that made me think of a cord... He took a good grip and started to pull, and pull, like drawing a bow, and to my shock my father's body began to bow up from the bed, arching, as if under some great strain.

My heart pounded faster and faster as I watched. It was brutally physical yet so much of it was unseen... Like *every* battle between good and evil? Strange thought. My skin was crawling with the dread and the strangeness of it...

Ystevan pulled and pulled grimly, apparently no way to soften it, until finally he staggered backwards a couple of steps, quickly regaining his balance, and my father's body fell back onto the bed and lay still, hair fanning over the pillows. Too still; he was not breathing.

I hunched in on myself, hands clenched, staring at him, willing him to breathe, willing it not to be true... "No, no, *no*," I whispered to myself, as if the very force of my words could make it not so.

Ystevan had finished disposing of whatever unholy, invisible thing he had removed from the Duke and now strode quickly to the bedside. He leant over and touched an investigative hand to the Duke's quiet, still face, laid another over his heart.

Then he flung back the blankets and with equal haste tore the night-shirt open to expose his chest. Unfastening his own coat swiftly, enough to reach his collar, he touched something—a hidden spring?—and one of the largest jewels swung up, allowing him to take a ring from a concealed cavity. It bore a diamond, faceted to a razor-sharp point, and he slid it onto his left forefinger, fitting it in between the knuckles. After a pause to collect himself, he drove the diamond, quick and hard, into the Duke's chest above the heart.

My trusting stillness broke as my father jerked, drawing in a long breath. But his breathing steadied, and my father and I both settled back onto the bed. Ystevan calmly withdrew the diamond, healing the tiny wound it left with a touch of his finger. He cleaned the ring carefully on a sleeve, making sure no trace of blood remained to stain its purity, then replaced it in its hidden home.

At first, I could only sit and watch my father's chest moving, up and down, up and down. He lived! He *lived*.

Oh thank you, thank you, thank you... I felt weak, drained with joy and relief.

After a while I noticed Ystevan, clip, spectacles and earrings back in place, heading for the door. I leapt up and hurried to him. "You're not leaving?" I questioned anxiously.

"I...I'm sorry, but really, I just want to go home now," he said softly. He looked tired, but I doubted it was primarily physical.

"Wh...why did you?" I faltered. "Thank you, thank you more than I can ever...but why?"

Ystevan stared at the man asleep in the bed for a long moment.

"I confess, I was standing outside that cellar room for some time before I showed myself," he said quietly. "And, well, when I said in no circumstances... I have to admit I hadn't ever conceived of anything like that. When you said before that he wouldn't do it again...well, of course I didn't believe you..."

"But you called it *immoral* before," I said, wonderingly.

Ystevan looked back at me, his eyes too bright. "Well, perhaps tonight there had been enough death," he whispered. And after a moment he added, as though he couldn't help himself, "It could have been me."

"What do you mean?"

"It could just as easily have been me. Me who wandered away from my friends. Me who..." He shook his head as though to shake his words away. "You are a good, brave girl." He touched my cheek gently.

I stared at him. He must've been referring to what had happened this evening, but really... "I couldn't possibly let him do it!" I exclaimed. "No matter what happened to me! How could I possibly?"

Ystevan just smiled. "Exactly," he murmured.

I frowned at him. I couldn't see that I had done anything exceptional, myself. And as for the terrible thing, unbeknown to him, I had *almost* done, it had seemed my only option at the time, but... Now I wasn't so sure. What had my father said? *There was never any excuse for sin...*

Ystevan's eyes strayed to the door again and the matter slipped from my mind. "Won't you stay just a little?"

He shook his head. "I will not. But since there is not the slightest point *any* elfin attempting to cloak your memories again—every time a memory cloak is applied, it is less effective, you see—you are welcome to visit us again. Since you really are one of the exceptions. As a guardian I have the authority to issue such an invitation."

My heart leapt—then sank again. My eyes went to my father and I began to shake my head.

Ystevan held up a long-fingered hand. "When your father is quite well, naturally. I do not mean at once." He drew several little cards from inside his coat and flicked through them. They looked blank, but he seemed to be reading them. Finding the one he wanted, he put the others away and ran his hand over the remaining one. He held it out to me, and several lines of writing appeared upon it. "You may write to me at this address to arrange your visit, when you are free to come. We have an...arrangement with a local farmer."

I nodded, accepting the card. "When my father is better I would love to come and visit properly." I could feel my eyes shining at the thought. "I would love to see Haliath again! And you never did show me a dragon!"

He smiled, at that. "I will look forward to it." He raised his stick in salute, then tilted his head meaningfully towards the bed.

I glanced that way as well, saw that my father was stirring and ran to his side. A few minutes later, I heard the sound of hooves receding down the drive and knew that the he-elf was gone.

Epilogue

FIVE MONTHS LATER

The steady clop of dinner plate-sized hooves ceased as Velvet reached the mounting block, but I had already slid lightly from Hellion's back, Raven flapping her wings for balance—rather gleefully—as she clung to my shoulder. I looked up at my father and my chest tightened in delight, as it always had this last month, to see him riding again.

Despite his use of the mounting block, he slid from Velvet's back energetically enough. Noticing my beaming face, he chuckled and patted the great black horse beside him. "It's like riding on a sofa," he told me. Velvet lipped at his hat placidly.

"Cannon proof," I agreed, tightening my grip on Hellion's bridle as his teeth strayed towards my elbow and handing him over to the hovering groom.

My father offered me his arm to walk back to the house, and I took it happily. It had taken him a long time to regain his strength, but he was *so* much better now. He hadn't exactly been pleased with me when he woke to find himself alive and recovering. To put it mildly. But life was sweet, even if you did not believe you deserved it.

"Post, my lord," said the butler as we headed for the dining room.

"Thank you."

"Post, my lady."

"Oh, good." Something from the urchin home, no doubt. Maybe an update on baby Felicity, as Father Francis had baptized her. All efforts to trace her mother having failed, I'd employed a wet nurse to care for her and she was not just alive, but thanks to Ystevan, flourishing, and the darling of the home.

As Raven raced down my arm in surely excessive excitement, I accepted an envelope of thick parchment and turned it over. It was addressed in a peculiar, flowing script that I'd only seen once before, on a small card.

"Oh, *good!*" I gasped, with considerably more feeling. No wonder Raven was excited. I had to admit, the previous elusive behavior of the card-giver had made me wonder if he truly would reply.

"Who's that from?" asked my father absently, sorting through his own letters, as Raven pawed impatiently at the envelope I held.

"A friend," I replied, hugging the letter gleefully to my chest.

The End

If you enjoyed this book, would you consider leaving a review on Amazon, Goodreads or your favorite retailer?

Reviews really help readers choose books, so a big thank you!

Corinna Turner

1

DRIVE!

Carol's scream assaults my ears, even as I'm bringing the gun round... I fire, hitting the raptor in the tail as it darts away... No time to check on Carol, I turn again...the pack matriarch is busy ripping the grille back from Harry's window...

One gun's enough, is it, Dad? Really? We have so had it...

IN DARRYL'S WORLD, THE WILDLIFE IS RATHER...

...WILD!

When Darryl's Dad suddenly remarries, she and her brother Harry are taken completely by surprise. Their new step-mom is a glamorous fashion designer who's never been outside the city fence in her life.

How will she cope with a life of dinosaur farming?
Still, they try to make up their minds to be welcoming.

But first, Darryl's Dad needs to get his new bride safely to the farm. And things don't go quite to plan...

"A cross between Jurassic World *and* Mad Max! *I read it 3 times in 2 days!" - Steven R. McEvoy, Blogger*

Turn over for a SNEAK PEEK!

Or turn to p.340 for the 1st chapter of I AM MARGARET!

DARRYL

I knock back my last swig of coffee, slip on my denim jacket, and pause on my way to the gun locker to check my reflection in the hall mirror. Shoulder-length brown hair brushed—and loose, for once—face clean, blue eyes...glum. But this has happened, whether I like it or not, so I might as well make a good first impression.

"Harry, get down here, we're going to be late!"

The volume of Dad's latest bellow up the stairs shows that he means business. Well, *I'm* ready, at least.

I thought my younger brother had come around to the 'might as well make a good impression' viewpoint as well, but there's still no noise from upstairs. The fact is, when your dad comes back from a routine weekend market and supply trip to the city and announces that he's got honest-to-God *married*, and that the woman—sorry, step-mom—will be coming to live with you, three weeks really isn't enough time to deal with it.

Harry totally lost it. Screamed Lord knows what at Dad, then ran off to the nearest barn. I managed not to do any screaming, but I had to go up and shut myself in the turret for almost an hour, and talk to myself *a lot*. You know: *Dad's been alone a long time, Darryl; if he's fallen in love that's wonderful, isn't it, Darryl; you want your father to be happy, don't you, Darryl?*

He totally sprung it on us, though. I guess he was so scared Potential Step-Mom—sorry, Carol—would come to her senses and decide that no handsome, propertied man of her own age was worth going and living OutSPARK on some farm. Carol's a city girl, all right. When I finally managed to go back down and say something about being happy for Dad and try to show some interest in his new bride, he showed me a photo on his phone, and my heart didn't lift. Just sank even further. Manicured Carol looked like she'd never got within a mile of the city fence in her life, let alone stepped outside it. A less likely farmer's wife I had never seen.

334

Dad could tell what I was thinking, of course. Brain not completely scrambled by love. "I know Carol's no farmer, Darryl my girl," he told me, "but really, it doesn't matter, does it? We've run the farm by ourselves all this time. She can run her fashion consultancy business from the house—I'm getting a faster Net connection put in. And *we'll* run the farm, just as before. And you and Harry will inherit it, Darryl, no question. Carol has her own money."

I reach the gun locker and place my hand on the scanner. Much as I hated to hear Dad talking about *his will*, it's a relief to know the farm is safe. I could put up with a harem of step-moms if I had to, but if someone took the farm from me...

As I take my rifle from the rack I can't help smiling at the thought of Dad with a *harem* of Carols. No, not Dad. We're Catholic, you know. One spouse at a time. Carol's 'not religious', apparently. I hope that won't matter. Dad did say he thinks she's 'open to it' so that's something.

I throw my ammunition sash on and check the pouches. Three hold full mags, but since we'll be travelling unSPARKed... I'll add the fourth pouch. I put my hand on the scanner to open the ammo box and take a handful of HiPiRs, or Hide Piercing Rounds. Penetrate any hide up to T. rex, these will. Though for T. rex, I really would prefer a bigger gun. *Much* bigger.

"HARRY!" roars Dad, then heads over to me. "Whoa girl, wait up. Come on, put the rifle away."

"What?" I turn an incredulous look on him. "We're going OutSPARK, Dad."

"Carol's nervous enough about the trip as it is, let alone living out here. If we turn up looking like Rambo-family, she's going to freak out. I'll have my rifle. Leave yours here. Just this once."

"But why have one rifle when you can have three?" I demand.

"Most people don't take *any* weapons when they travel, Darryl."

"*City* people. And sometimes when they break down or crash, they get eaten."

"Come on, Darryl, just this once. It will make Carol feel so much better."

His pleading tone is too much. I unsling my rifle from my shoulder and put it back in its place. "All right. But we'd better not end up Raptor Food."

"Of course we won't." He sounds downright cheerful with relief.

Footsteps on the stairs. I glance at Harry as I finish slipping the HiPiRs into the mag. No point leaving it half full. Harry's changed out of the clothes he was wearing for early morning chores. Was he really dragging his feet, or was he agonizing over what to wear? He's thirteen, three years younger than me, but very fair-minded, and I thought he was finally trying to get into a welcoming frame of mind, this last week. He helped clean the whole house from top to bottom without a word of complaint, anyway.

"You've missed breakfast," says Dad. "Grab something to eat in the truck."

"I'm not hungry," mutters Harry. Yeah, definitely freaking out about meeting her, not sulking. He joins me by the locker and takes his rifle from the rack. "How many mags are you taking, Rell?"

"None," I sigh, putting the now fully loaded mag back in and adding my ammo-sash.

"Huh?"

"Apparently Carol's nervy and Dad reckons three guns will scare her. So he's just taking his."

"What? But why take one gun when you could..."

"You don't want to traumatize your new step-mom, *do you?*" says Dad, taking Harry's rifle firmly from his hands and replacing it, taking his own out, then sealing the locker again. "Come on, in the truck, chop-chop!" He moves to the House Control and taps the usual commands. The light level in the hall plummets as the stainless steel shutters slide over all the windows and lock into place with a reassuring snick.

Heading for the front door, I check the ScreamerBand around my wrist, but the light glows green. Our fence has suffered no power loss; no alarms have been tripped since I came in for breakfast. All secure. I still scan the screens before opening the door—the yard is empty.

Pausing to listen as soon as I've stepped outside is second nature, I don't even think about it. But the Hum is there, the soothing sound of our twin fences, of safety. The quiet noises of the livestock in their barns, behind their own steel shutters. Our mammal-stock gets some time out at grass each day, but never while we're away from home.

I feel naked, though, as I walk around to the pick-up, parked where it won't cause dead-space in the door cameras. I haven't been OutSPARK without my own gun since I was old enough to have one. And living what most city-types would erroneously term 'OutSPARK' (I mean, what do they think that humming thing is if not an electric fence?) that's quite a long time, now.

Still, what Carol is doing is a big deal, and there's no getting away from that. Leaving her nice safe city cocoon to come and live out here. She must be equally in love with Dad. Unless she hasn't as much money as she's clearly made out. I hope that's not it. The thought of Dad giving himself for life to a gold digger. Ugh.

Our farm's not worth that much, anyway. Who wants to farm, nowadays? It used to be called 'the good life', according to my history TuteApp, and loads of people craved it. But that was before the scientists failed to grasp that just because you *can* do something doesn't mean it's a good idea to actually *do* it. Dad says mankind got too big for their breeches and the Almighty allowed us to take ourselves down a peg or two.

It's pretty boring when the older folk start going on about 'how things used to be', to be honest. We're not at the top of the food chain any more, and that's that. I've never known anything different. Even Dad hasn't.

I get in the front seat—this'll be Carol's seat from now on, no doubt—and touch the statue of St Desmond on the dash, murmuring the travelling prayer myself to save time. Dad circles the vehicle, gripping each window grille with both hands and shaking violently, checking the wheel shields, suddenly unhurried. *Checks in haste are blank checks for raptors,* as the saying goes.

Harry's piled in, and Dad finally gets in too. He reaches for the ignition and stops. His hands goes towards St Des...

"I've said it, Dad."

"Good girl." He gives St Des a quick pat anyway, and starts the engine. We barrel off between the barns and out through the empty mammal-stock pastures. Soon the fence looms up ahead. I reach for my ScreamerBand...

"Can I do it?" Harry's not quite too old to take pleasure in things like that. To be honest, I quite like opening the gates as well. Very dramatic. But...

"Sure. Go ahead."

Harry presses his button and the inner gate swooshes open. No posturing slowness for modern gates—what use is that if something is chasing you?

Dad drives straight through, then slows to a crawl while Harry shuts the inner gate—swoosh!—and opens the outer one—swoosh! I press the 'record' button on our WhatHap Box and say clearly, "William, Darryl, and Harold Franklyn, travelling to Exception City to pick up Carol Franklyn, to return same day. Now officially unSPARKed."

Although I speak calmly, I feel a shiver of nervous excitement in my gut as I say the word. The knowledge that there's no longer high voltage steel between you and the nearest pack of hungry raptors will do that to anyone.

Get DRIVE! from Amazon or your favorite retailer today!
Paperback ISBN: 978-1-910806-83-8
ePub ISBN: 978-1-910806-62-3
Kindle ASIN: B07791NWVY

I AM MARGARET

CHAPTER 1

The dragon roared, its jaws so close to Thane's head that

I waggled the page gently in the air, waiting for my writing to dry. One final, blank double spread remained. Good. I'd made the little book myself.

The ink was dry. I turned to that last page and found the place on the computer printout I was copying from...

he felt his eardrums burst. But the sword had done its work and, eviscerated, the beast began to topple.

Thane rolled frantically to his feet and ran. The huge body obliterated where he'd been lying, but Thane wasn't interested in that. He kept right on running to where Marigold was struggling to free herself.

"That's the last time I go riding without my spurs!" she told him. "I could've cut my way out of here by now..."

Thane ignored her grumbles. He couldn't hear properly anyway. He whipped out a dagger and freed her. "Marigold?" He could hardly hear himself. "Are you all right?"

"Oh, I'm fine. At least I had my rosary."

Thane thought of all the things he wanted to

say to her. The way he felt about her, he wanted to do everything just right. Could he get down on one knee without losing his balance and would he be able to hear what she said in reply...?

Then Marigold's arms wrapped around him like vines around their supporting tree. And when she kissed him, he knew the answer to all his questions was a heartfelt,

'Yes.'

I wrote the last word with great care and put the lid on the pen. All done. I smiled as I pictured Bane reading the tale. *Where are the slain dragons? Where are the rescued maidens?* he would complain after reading my stories. Just this once, in this tale just for him, there were all the dragons he could desire. But only one maiden.

A funny way to declare your love, but I couldn't leave it unsaid. And if I *did* pass my Sorting...well, we were both eighteen, we'd be leaving school at the end of the year and would be free to register, so perhaps it was time we were finally honest with each other.

Picking up the printout of the story, I ripped it into small pieces and threw it in the bin, then closed the handwritten book, slipping it into the waterproof pouch I'd made for it. On my aged—but no less loved for that—laptop, I called up the file and pressed 'delete'. Bane's story was his alone.

The pouch went into my bag as I checked its contents again. Clothes, underwear, sewing things, my precious bookReader—filled to capacity—and what little else was permitted. No laptop, alas, and no rosary beads for Margaret in this all too real world. I touched the waterproof pouch— must warn Bane not to show the story around. A dangerous word had slipped in there, near the end. A little bit of myself.

The contents of the bag were all present and correct, as

they'd been since last night. Zipping it up, I stood for a moment, looking around. This had been my room since I was born and how I wanted to believe I'd be back here this evening, unpacking my bag again. But I'd never been very good at fairy tales. Happy Ever After didn't happen in real life. Not while you were alive.

I kicked at my long purple skirt for a moment, then picked up my jacket and slipped it on. Sorting day was a home clothes day. No need for school uniform at the Facility. I was packed and ready—packed, anyway—and couldn't delay any longer. I put my bag over my shoulder and headed downstairs.

My parents were waiting in the hall. I almost wished they weren't. That they were off with Kyle—*gone*.

Mum's face was so pale. "Margo, you can't seriously intend to go today." Her voice was hoarse with desperation. "You know the chances of...of..."

"I know the chances of me passing are very small." With great effort I kept my voice from shaking. "But you know why I have to go."

"It's not too late..." Bleak hopelessness in Dad's voice. "The Underground would hide you..."

I had to get out of there. I had to get out before they wore down my resolve.

"It's too late to teach me to be selfish now," I snapped, switching automatically from Latin to English as I opened the front door and stepped out onto the step.

"Margo..."

I turned to meet Mum's embrace and I wanted to cling to her like a little girl, except that was how she was clinging to me. I stroked her hair and tried to comfort her. "It'll be all right, Mum, really," I whispered. "I might even pass, you know."

She released me at last, stepped back, mopping her eyes—trying to be strong for me. "Of course. You may pass. Keep the faith, darling." Her voice shook; right here, right now, she could hardly get the familiar words out.

"Keep the faith," said Dad, and his voice shook too. I cupped my hand and made the Fish with finger and thumb, behind my bag so the neighbors couldn't see. "Keep the faith." It came out like an order. I blushed, smiled apologetically, took one last look at their faces and hurried down the steps.

The EuroBloc Genetics Department inspectors were waiting at the school gates to check off our names. I joined the line, looking into the boys' schoolyard for Bane. A hotel car pulled up and a white-faced woman helped a tall boy from the back seat—who was *he*? His hair was like autumn leaves... Oh. He held a long thin white cane with a soft ball on one end. Blind. My insides clenched in sympathy. What must it be like to have no hope at all?

"Name?" demanded the inspector on the boys' gate.

"Jonathan Revan," said the boy in a very cold, collected voice. "And wouldn't it be an awful lot simpler if my parents just dropped me at the Facility?"

The inspector looked furious as everyone sniggered their appreciation at this show of courage.

"Name?" It was my turn. The blind boy was passing through the gates, his shoulders hunched now, as though to block the sound of the woman's weeping. A man was shepherding her back to the car.

"Margaret Verrall."

The woman marked off my name and jerked the pen towards the girls' yard. "In."

Inside, I headed straight for the wall between the schoolyards. Bane was there, his matte black hair waving slightly in the breeze. His mother used to keep it short, to hide its strangeness, but that'd only lasted 'til he was fast enough to outrun her. The inspector on the boys' gate was shooting a suspicious glance at him.

"Looking forward to being an adult?" Bane asked savagely, watching Jonathan Revan picking his way across the schoolyard, his stick waving sinuously in front of him. Something clicked.

343

"That's your friend from out at Little Hazleton, isn't it? The preKnown, who's never had to come to school?"

"Yeah." Bane's face was grim.

"Did you hear what he said to the inspector? He's got some nerve."

"He's got that, all right. Shame he can't see a thing."

"He'd have to see considerably *more* than a thing to pass."

"Yeah." Bane kicked the wall, scuffing his boots. "Yeah, well, I always knew there was nothing doing."

"It was nice of you to be friends with him."

Bane looked embarrassed and kicked the wall even harder. "Well, he's got a brain the size of the EuroBloc main server. He'd have been bored out of his mind with only the other preKnowns to talk to."

Oh no, perhaps I flattered myself, but...if Bane was preoccupied with Jonathan Revan...he really hadn't realized I was in danger! Although I'd always tried so hard not to let him figure it out part of me had assumed he knew by now. I mean, how could he not have *realized*? We'd known each other since, well, forever. He'd always been there, along with Mum and Dad, Kyle, Uncle Peter...

"Bane, I need to talk to you."

He looked around, his brown eyes surprised. He sat on the wall and rested his elbows on the railings. "Now? Not... after our Sorting?"

Were his thoughts running along the same lines as mine earlier? I sat down as well, which brought our faces very close. "Bane...it may not be very easy to talk...after."

His eyes narrowed. "What d'you mean?"

"Bane..." There was no easy way to say this. "Bane, I probably won't pass."

His face froze into incredulous disbelief—he really hadn't realized. He'd thought me Safe. *Bane, I'm so sorry.*

"You...of course you'll pass! You're as smart as Jon, you can keep the whole class spellbound, hanging on your every word..."

"But I can't do math to save my life."

There was a long, sick silence.

"Probably literally," I added, quite unnecessarily.

Bane remained silent. He saw the danger now. You only had to fail one single test. He looked at me at last and there was something strange in his eyes, something it took me a moment to recognize. Fear.

"Is it really *that* bad, your math?"

"It's almost non-existent," I said as gently as I could. "I have severe numerical dyslexia, you know that."

"I didn't realize. I just never..." There was guilt in his eyes, now; guilt that he'd gone through life so happy and confident in his physical and mental perfection that he'd never noticed the shadow hanging over me. "Didn't Fa... your Uncle Peter...teach you enough?"

"Uncle Peter managed to teach me more than anyone else ever has, but I'm actually not sure it's possible to teach me *enough*."

"I just never thought..."

"Of course you didn't think about it. Who thinks about Sorting unnecessarily? Anyway, this is for you." I put the pouch into his hand. "Don't let anyone see it until you've read it; I don't think you'll want to flash it around."

His knuckles whitened around it. "Margo, what are you *doing* here? If you think you're going to fail! Go, go now, I'll climb over and distract the inspector; the Underground will hide you..."

"Bane, stop, stop! I can't miss my Sorting, don't you understand? There was never any way I was going to get out of it—no one's allowed to leave the department with preSort age children and after today I'll show up as a SortEvader on every system in the EuroBloc..."

"So go underground!" He dropped his voice to a whisper. "You of all people could do that in an instant!"

"Yes, Bane, I could. And never mind spending the rest of my life running, can't you see why I, *of all people*, cannot run?"

345

He slammed his fist into the wall and blood sprung up on his knuckles. "This is because of the Underground stuff, isn't it? Your family are in too deep."

"Bane..." I captured his hand before he could injure it any more. "You know the only way the sanctuary will stay hidden is if the house *isn't* searched and if I run, what's the first thing they'll do?"

"Search your house."

"Search my house. Arrest my parents. Lay a trap for the next Underground members who come calling. Catch the priests when they come. You know what they do to the priests?"

"I know." His voice was so quiet I could hardly hear him.

"And you want that to happen to *Uncle* Peter? *Cousin* Mark? How can you suggest I *run*?"

He said nothing. Finally he muttered, "I wish you'd given this stuff up years ago..."

Bane had never understood my faith; he knew it would probably get me killed one day. He'd tried his hardest to talk me out of it before my sixteenth birthday, oh, how he'd tried. But he accepted it. He might not understand the faith angle, but getting killed doing something to wind up the EuroGov was right up his street.

The school bell began to ring and he looked up again, capturing my eyes. "I suppose then you wouldn't have been you," he murmured. "Look, if you don't pass..." his voice grew firmer, "if you don't pass, I'll have to see what I can do about it. Because...well...I've been counting on marrying you for a very long time, now, and I've no intention of letting anything stop me!"

My heart pounded—joy, but no surprise. How we felt about each other had been an unspoken secret for years. "Anything, such as the entire EuroBloc Genetics Department? Don't bite off more than you can chew, Bane."

He didn't answer. He just slipped an arm through the railings and snagged me, his lips coming down on mine. My arms slid through the railings, around his strong back, my

346

lips melted against his and suddenly the world was a beautiful, beautiful place and this was the best day of my life.

We didn't break apart until the bell stopped ringing.

"Well," I whispered, looking into his brown eyes, "now I can be dismantled happily, anyway."

His face twisted in anguish. "Don't say that!" He kissed me again, fiercely. "Don't worry..." His hands cupped my face and his eyes glinted. "Whatever happens, *don't worry.* I love you and I *will not* leave you there, you understand?"

Planting one last kiss on my forehead, he swung his bag onto his shoulder and sprinted across the schoolyard, the pouch still clasped in his hand. I watched him go, then picked up my own bag and followed the last stragglers through the girls' door.

The classroom was unusually quiet, bags and small cases cluttering the aisles. Taking my place quickly, I glanced around. There were only two preKnowns in the class. Harriet looked sick and resigned, but Sarah didn't understand about her Sorting or the Facility or anything as complex as that. The known Borderlines were every shade of pale. The Safe looked sober but a little excited. The pre-Sorting ban on copulation would be gone tomorrow. No doubt the usual orgy would ensue.

Bane's last words stuck in my mind. I knew that glint in his eye. I should've urged him much more strenuously not to do anything rash. Not to put himself in danger. Now it was too late.

"I saw you and Bane," giggled Sue, beside me. "Jumping the gun a little, aren't you?"

"As if you haven't done any gun jumping yourself," I murmured. Sue just giggled even harder.

"Margy...? Margy...?"

"Hi, Sarah. Have you got your bag?"

Sarah nodded and patted the shabby bag beside her.

"They explained to you, right? That you'll be going on a sleep-over?"

347

Sarah nodded, beaming, and pointed at me. "Margy come too?"

"Perhaps. Only the most special children will be going, you know."

Sarah laughed happily. I swallowed bile and tried not to curse the stupid driver who'd knocked her down all those years ago and left her like this. Tried not to curse her parents, who'd put her into care, sued the driver for his Child Permittance so they could replace her, and promptly moved away.

"Children..." The deputy headmistress. She waited for quiet. "This is the last time I will address you as such. This is a very special day for you all. After your Sorting, you will be legally adults."

Except those of us who would scarcely any longer count as human. She didn't mention that bit.

"Now, do your best, all of you. Doctor Vidran is here from the EGD to oversee your Sorting. Over to you, Doctor Vidran..."

Doctor Vidran gave a long and horrible speech about the numerous benefits Sorting brought to the human race. By the time he'd finished I was battling a powerful urge to go up and shove his laser pointer down his throat. I managed to stay in my seat and concentrated on trying to love this misguided specimen of humanity, to forgive him his part in what was probably going to happen to me. It was very difficult.

"...A few of you will of course have to be reAssigned, and it is important that we always remember the immense contribution the reAssigned make, in their own way..."

Finally he shut up and bade us turn our attention to our flickery desk screens for the Intellectual Tests. My happiness at his silence took me through Esperanto, English, Geography, History, ComputerScience, Biology, Chemistry and Physics without hitch, but then came Math.

I tried. I really, really tried. I tried until I thought my brain would explode and then I thought about Bane and my parents and I tried some more. But it was no good. No motivation on earth could enable me to do most of those sums without a calculator. I'd failed.

The knowledge was a cold, hard certainty in the pit of my stomach all the way through the Physical Tests after a silent, supervised lunch. I passed all those, of course. Sight, Hearing, Physiognomy and so on, all well within the acceptable levels. What about Jonathan Revan, a preKnown if ever there was one? Smart, Bane said, really smart, and Bane was pretty bright himself. Much good it'd do Jonathan. Much good it'd do me.

We filed into the gym when it was all over, sitting on benches along the wall. Bane guided Jonathan Revan to a free spot over on the boys' side. In the hall through the double doors the rest of the school fidgeted and chatted. Once the end of semester assembly was over, they were free for four whole weeks.

Free. Would I ever be free again?

I'd soon know. One of the inspectors was wedging the doors open as the headmaster took his place on the stage. His voice echoed into the gym. "And now we must congratulate our New Adults! Put your hands together, everyone!"

Dutiful clapping from the hall. Doctor Vidran stood by the door, clipboard in hand, and began to read names. A boy. A girl. A boy. A girl. Sorry, a young man, a young woman. Each New Adult got up and went through to take their seat in the hall. Was there a pattern...? No, randomized. Impossible to know if they'd passed your name or not.

My stomach churned wildly now. Swallowing hard, I stared across the gym at Bane. Jonathan sat beside him, looking cool as a cucumber, if a little determinedly so. *He* wasn't in any suspense. Bane stared back at me, his face grim and his eyes fierce. I drank in the harsh lines of his face, trying to carve every beloved detail into my mind.

"They might call my name," Caroline was whispering to Harriet. "They might. It's still possible. Still possible..."

Over half the class had gone through.

Still possible, still possible, they might, they might call my name... My mind took up Caroline's litany, and my desperate longing came close to an *ache.*

"Blake Marsden."

A knot of anxiety inside me loosened abruptly—immediately replaced by a more selfish pain. Bane glared at Doctor Vidran and didn't move from his seat. Red-faced, the deputy headmistress murmured in Doctor Vidran's ear.

Doctor Vidran looked exasperated. "Blake Marsden, known as Bane Marsden."

Clearly the best Bane was going to get. He gripped Jonathan's shoulder and muttered something, probably *bye.* Jonathan found Bane's hand and squeezed and said something back. Something like *thanks for everything.*

Bane shrugged this off and got up as the impatient inspectors approached him. *No...don't go, please...* Yes! He was heading straight for me—but the inspectors cut him off.

"Come on...Bane, is it? *Congratulations,* through you go..." Bane resisted being herded and the inspector's voice took on a definite warning note. "Now, you're an adult, it's your big day, don't spoil it."

"I just want to speak to..."

They caught his arms. He wrenched, trying to pull free, but they were strong men and there were two of them.

"You *know* no contact is allowed at this point. I'm sure your girlfriend will be through in a moment."

"Fiancée," snarled Bane, and warmth exploded in my stomach, chasing a little of the chill fear from my body. He'd read my story already.

"*If,* of course, your *fiancée,*" Doctor Vidran sneered the un-PC word from over by the door, "is a perfect specimen. If not, you're better off without her, *aren't* you?"

Bane's nostrils flared, his jaw went rigid and his knuckles clenched until I thought his bones would pop from his skin. Shoulders shaking, he allowed the inspectors to bundle him across the gym towards Doctor Vidran. *Uh oh...*

But by the time they reached the doors he'd got sufficient hold of himself he just stopped and looked back at me instead of driving his fist into Doctor Vidran's smug face. He seemed a long way away. But he'd never been going to reach me, had he?

"Love you..." he mouthed.

"Love you..." I mouthed back, my throat too tight for actual words.

Then a third inspector joined the other two and they shoved him through into the hall. And he was gone.

Gone. I might never see him again. I swallowed hard and clenched my fists, fighting a foolish frantic urge to rush across the gym after him.

"*Really,*" one inspector was tutting, "we don't usually have to drag them *that* way!"

"Going to end up on a gurney, that one," apologized the deputy headmistress, "So sorry about that..."

Doctor Vidran dismissed Bane with a wave of his pen and went on with the list.

"They might..." whispered Caroline, "they might..."

They might...they might...I might be joining Bane. I might... Please...

But they didn't. Doctor Vidran stopped reading, straightened the pages on his clipboard and glanced at the other inspectors. "Take them away," he ordered.

He and the deputy headmistress swung round and went into the hall as though those of us left had ceased to exist. As we kind of had. The only decent thing to do about reAssignees was to forget them. Everyone knew that.

One of the inspectors took the wedges from under the doors and closed them. Turned the key, locking us apart.

My head rang. I'd thought I'd known, I'd thought I'd been quite certain, but still the knowledge hit me like a bucket of ice-cold water, echoing in my head. Margaret Verrall. My name. They'd not called it. The last tiny flame of hope died inside me and it was more painful than I'd expected.

351

One of the boys on the bench opposite—Andrew Plateley—started crying in big, shuddering gasps, like he couldn't quite believe it. Harriet was hugging Caroline and Sarah was tugging her sleeve and asking what was wrong. My limbs felt heavy and numb, like they weren't part of me.

Doctor Vidran's voice came to us from the hall, just audible. "Congratulations, adults! What a day for you all! You are now free to apply for breeding registration, providing your gene scans are found to be compatible. I imagine your head teacher would prefer you to wait until after your exams next semester, though!"

The school laughed half-heartedly, busy sneaking involuntary glances to see who was left in the gym—until an Inspector yanked the blinds down over the door windows. Everyone would be glad to have us out of sight so they could start celebrating.

"After successful registration," the Doctor's cheerful voice went on, "you may have your contraceptive implants temporarily removed. The current child permittance is one child per person, so each couple may have two. Additional child permittances can be bought; the price set by the EGD is currently three hundred thousand Eurons, so I don't imagine any of you need to worry about that."

More nervous laughter from the hall. Normal life was through there. Exams, jobs, registering, having children, growing old with Bane...but I wasn't in there with him. I was out here. My stomach fluttered sickly.

"ReAssignees, up you get, pick up your bags," ordered one of the inspectors.

I got to my feet slowly and picked up my bag with shaking hands. Why did I feel so shocked? Had some deluded part of me believed this couldn't really happen? Around me everyone moved as though in a daze, except Andrew Plateley who just sat, rocking to and fro, sobbing. Jonathan said something quietly to him but he didn't seem to hear.

The inspector shook Andrew's shoulder, saying loudly, "Up." He pointed to the external doors at the other end of the gym but Andrew leapt to his feet and bolted for the hall. He yanked at the doors with all his strength, sobbing, but they just rattled slightly under his assault and remained solidly closed. The inspectors grabbed him and began to drag him away, kicking and screaming. There was a sudden, suffocating silence from beyond those doors, as everyone tried not to hear his terror.

Doctor Vidran's voice rushed on, falsely light-hearted, "And I'm *sure* I don't need to remind you that you can only register with a person of your own ethnicity. Genetic mixes are, *of course*, not tolerated and all such offspring will be destroyed. And as you know, all unregistered children automatically count as reAssignees from birth, but I'm sure you're all going to register correctly so none of you need to worry about anything like that."

They'd got Andrew outside and the inspectors were urging the rest of us after him. It seemed a terribly long way, my bag seemed to weigh a very great deal and I still felt sick. I swallowed again, my hand curving briefly, unseen, into the Fish. Be strong.

"And that's all from me, though your headmaster has kindly invited me to stay for your end of semester presentations. Once again, congratulations! Let's hear it for Salperton's New Adults!"

The school whooped and cheered heartily behind us. A wave of crazy, reality-defying desperation swept over me— this must be how Andrew had felt. As though, if I could just get into that hall, *I'd* have the rest of my life ahead of me too...

Reality waited outside in the form of a little EGD minibus. Imagine a police riot van that mated with a tank. Reinforced metal all over, with grilles over the windows. Reaching the hall would achieve precisely *nothing*. So *get a grip, Margo.*

I steadied Sarah as she scrambled into the minibus and passed my bag up to her. She busied herself lifting my bag and hers onto the overhead luggage racks, beaming with

353

pride at her initiative.

"Thanks, Sarah." A soft white ball wandered into my vision—there was Jonathan Revan, the last left to get in after me. I almost offered help, then thought better of it. "Jonathan, isn't it? Just give a shout if you want a hand."

"Thanks, Margaret." His eyes stared rather eerily into the minibus. Or rather, through the minibus, for they focused not at all. "I'm fine."

His stick came to rest against the bus's bumper and his other hand reached out, tracing the shape of the seats on each side, then checking for obstructions at head height. Just as the EGD inspectors moved to shove him in, he stepped up into the bus with surprising grace. I climbed in after him just as the school fire alarms went off, the sound immediately muffled by the inspectors slamming the doors behind me.

"Bag?" Sarah was saying to Jonathan, holding out her hand.

"Sorry?"

"Bag," I told him. "Would you like her to put your bag up?"

"Oh. Yes, thank you. What's your name?"

"Sarah."

"Sarah. Thanks."

Bet he wouldn't have let me put his bag up for him! Sarah sat down beside Harriet, so I took a seat next to Jonathan. The first pupils were spilling out into the school-yards and I craned my neck to try and catch a glimpse of Bane. A last glimpse.

"Any guesses who set that off?" said Jonathan dryly.

"Don't know how he'd have done it, but yeah, I bet he did."

The minibus began to move, heading for the gates, and I twisted to look out the rear window, through the bars. Nothing...

We pulled onto the road and finally there he was, streaking across the schoolyard to skid to a halt in front of the gates just as they slid closed. Bane gripped them as though he wanted to shake them, rip them off their hinges or throw them open...

The minibus went around a corner and he was gone

Get I AM MARGARET from Amazon or your favorite bookshop today!

Paperback ISBN: 978-1-903858-04-2
ePub ISBN: 978-1-903858-05-9
Kindle ASIN: B00ZMCBTHY

ACKNOWLEDGMENTS

There are lots of people I would like to thank for their help with this book, so here goes. Firstly I'd like to thank my parents for all their support, and my mum for her ruthlessly honest critiques!

I'd like to thank Victoria S., Theresa Linden and my agent Amanda Preston for all their excellent editorial input.

And I'd like to thank the incredibly talented Katy Jones for painting the most gorgeous cover artwork!

Thanks to all who supported the Kindle Scout campaign!

I'd also like to thank all the old Authonomy crowd who gave so much help, support and feedback, back in the day.

And not forgetting the patrons of the book, St Alban and St Serapion!

ABOUT THE AUTHOR

Corinna Turner has been writing since she was fourteen and likes strong protagonists with plenty of integrity. She has an MA in English from Oxford University, but has foolishly gone on to work with both children and animals! Juggling work with the disabled and being a midwife to sheep, she spends as much time as she can in a little hut at the bottom of the garden, writing.

She is a Catholic Christian with roots in the Methodist and Anglican churches. A keen cinema-goer, she lives in the UK. She used to have a Giant Snail called Peter with a 6½" long shell, but now makes do with a cactus and a campervan!

Get in touch with Corinna...

Facebook/Google+: Corinna Turner

Twitter: @CorinnaTAuthor

or sign up for **news** and **free short stories** at:
www.UnSeenBooks.com

DOWNLOAD YOUR EBOOK

If you own a paperback of *Elfling* you can download a free copy of the eBook.

1. Go to *www.UnSeenBooks.com*
   or scan the QR code:

2. Enter this code on the book's page:
   SREA73FF

3. Enjoy your download!

CPSIA information can be obtained
at www.ICGtesting.com
Printed in the USA
LVHW051452110521
687112LV00001B/104